JONATHAN STROUD

The Creeping Shadow

Lockwood & Co.

BOOK FOUR

Disney • HYPERION
LOS ANGELES   NEW YORK

First Edition, September 2016

Printed in the United States of America

1 3 5 7 9 10 8 6 4 2

FAC-020093-16211

Library of Congress Cataloging-in-Publication Data
Names: Stroud, Jonathan.
Title: The creeping shadow / Jonathan Stroud.
Description: First edition. | Los Angeles New York : Disney-Hyperion, 2016. |
Series: Lockwood & Co. ; book 4 | Summary: "A terrible crime forces Lockwood
to turn to Lucy for help, setting them on the trail of dark secrets at the heart of
London society. Both professionally and personally, their investigation stirs up
forces they may not be able to control . . . "—Provided by publisher.
Identifiers: LCCN 2016014383 | ISBN 9781484709672 (hardback)
Subjects: | CYAC: Ghosts—Fiction. | Supernatural—Fiction. | Psychic ability—
Fiction. | London (England)—Fiction. | England—Fiction. | Mystery and
detective stories. | BISAC: JUVENILE FICTION / Mysteries & Detective
Stories. | JUVENILE FICTION / Fantasy & Magic. | JUVENILE FICTION /
Horror & Ghost Stories.
Classification: LCC PZ7.S92475 Cr 2016 | DDC [Fic]—dc23
LC record available at https://lccn.loc.gov/2016014383

Reinforced binding
Visit www.DisneyBooks.com

For Louis, with love

Contents

I
Two Heads

Chapter 1

I knew at once, when I slipped into the moonlit office and eased the door shut behind me, that I was in the presence of the dead. I could feel it in the prickling of my scalp, in the way the hairs stirred on my arms, in the coldness of the air I breathed. I could tell it from the clots of spiderwebs that hung against the window, thick and dusty and glittering with frost. There were the *sounds*, too, centuries old; the ones I'd traced up the empty stairs and hallways of the house. The rustling linen, the crack of broken glass, the weeping of the dying woman: all were louder now. And there was the sudden intuition, felt deep in the pit of my gut, that something wicked had fixed its gaze on me.

Mind you, if none of *that* had worked, the shrill voice coming from my backpack might also have given me a clue.

"*Eek!*" it cried. "*Help! Ghost!*"

I glared over my shoulder. "Cut it out. So we've found the phantom. There's no need for you to get hysterical."

"She's just over there! Staring, staring with her hollow sockets! Ooh, now I see her grinning teeth!"

I snorted. "Why would any of that bother you? You're a skull. Calm down."

I shrugged the backpack off onto the floor and flipped up the canvas top. Inside, radiating a smoky greenish light, was a large glass jar with a human skull clamped in its depths. A hideous translucent face pressed against the glass, nose bent sideways, poached-egg eyes flicking to and fro.

"You asked me to raise the alarm, didn't you?" the skull said. *"Well, this is me raising it. Eep! There she is! Ghost! Bones! Hair! Ugh!"*

"Would you please shut up?" In spite of myself, I could feel its words having an effect on me. I was staring into the room, unpicking its shadows, hunting for an undead shape. True, I saw nothing, but that brought little comfort. *This* particular ghost worked by special rules. With feverish speed I began rummaging through the backpack, pushing the jar aside, sifting through salt-bombs, lavender grenades, and iron chains.

The skull's voice echoed in my mind. *"If you're looking for the mirror, Lucy, you tied it to the back of the rucksack with a piece of string."*

"Oh . . . yes. So I did."

"So you wouldn't forget where it was."

"Oh, yeah . . . Right."

Its eyes gleamed up at me as I fumbled for the string. *"Are you panicking?"*

"Nope."

"Just a little bit?"

"Certainly not."

"If you say so. She's creeping closer, by the way."

That was it. No more small talk for me. Two seconds later I had the mirror in my hand.

It was a peculiarity of this Visitor that it could not be seen directly, even by agents with decent psychic Sight. It was said to be the spirit of the murderous Emma Marchment, a lady who had lived in the building in the early eighteenth century, when it was a private house and not the offices of an insurance company. After dabbling in witchcraft, and allegedly being responsible for the deaths of several relatives, she had been stabbed by her husband with a spear of glass from her own smashed dressing table mirror. Now she appeared only in reflections—in mirrors, windows, and polished metal surfaces—and several employees of the company had recently lost their lives to her surreptitious touch. Hunting her was a ticklish business. Our team tonight had brought hand mirrors, and there'd been a lot of slow shuffling backward, and much wide-eyed peering over shoulders into dark corners. Me, I hadn't bothered with any of that. I'd trusted my senses, and followed the sounds, and not reached for my mirror until now.

I held it up and angled it so that I could see the reflection of the room.

"Nice piece of equipment," the skull said. *"Real quality plastic. Lo-o-ve the pink ponies and rainbows on the rim."*

"So I got it from a toy store. It was all I could find in the time available."

Moonlight flashed confusingly on the glass surface. I took a deep breath and steadied my hand. Immediately the image stabilized, becoming the bright grid of the window, with cheap curtains hanging either side. Beneath the sill was a desk and chair. I panned up, around, and down, seeing only a moonlit floor, another desk, filing cabinets, a hanging plant suspended from the darkly paneled wall.

The room was just a boring office now, but once it would have been a bedroom. A place where tempers snapped, old jealousies flared, and intimacy contorted into hatred. More ghosts have been created in bedrooms than anywhere else. It didn't surprise me to find that Emma Marchment's death might have happened here.

"I don't see her," I said. "Skull, where is she?"

"*Far right corner, half in and half out of that bureau thing. Got her arms stretched wide like she wants to hug you. Eek, but her nails are long. . . .*"

"What are you tonight, a Yorkshire fishwife? Stop trying to freak me out. If she moves in my direction again, I want to know about it. Otherwise, quit warbling."

I spoke decisively, projecting confidence. Show no fear, show no anxiety; give the restless spirit nothing to feed on. Even so, I wasn't taking anything for granted. My left hand hung at my belt, midway between my rapier and the magnesium flares.

I snatched a glance away from the mirror. Yes, there was the corner with the bureau. It was very dark; hardly any moonlight reached it. Strain as I might, I picked out nothing standing there.

So, let's see . . . I returned to the mirror and panned it slowly around, over the desks, past the hanging plant, following the paneled walls, until it reached the bureau.

And there it was. The ghost, swinging shockingly into view.

I'd been expecting her, yet I almost dropped the mirror.

A bone-thin figure, white drapes falling from it like a shroud. A livid face hanging in a cradle of smoke-plume hair. Black eyes staring, white skin clinging to the skull like melting wax. You could see the skeletal neck, the stains on the dress, the jaw unnaturally agape. Her hands were raised, the fingers bent toward me.

The nails *were* very long.

I swallowed. Without the mirror or the skull to guide me, I might have wandered unaware into those clutching arms.

"Got her," I said.

"*Have you, Lucy? Good. Now, do you want to live or die?*"

"Live, please."

"*Call the others.*"

"Not yet." My hand was shaking again, the mirror wobbling. I kept losing sight of the pale form. I cleared my mind. I needed a moment's peace for what I had to do.

"*I know you're annoyed with them,*" the skull went on, "*but this isn't something to tackle on your own. You need to get over your little tiff.*"

"I have gotten over it."

"*Just because Lockwood—*"

"I'm not worrying about Lockwood. Now, will you shut up? You know I need absolute silence for this." I took a deep breath, and double-checked the mirror. Yes, there was the face: a ragged smear haloed by a cotton-candy swirl of hair.

Had it stolen closer to me? Maybe. It seemed a tad bigger. I shook the notion away.

The skull stirred again. *"Tell me you're not going to do your silly thing? She was an evil old biddy whose spirit only wishes you harm. There's no need to reach out to her."*

"I am doing my thing, and it's not at all silly." I raised my voice. "Emma?" I called. "Emma Marchment? I see you. I hear you. What do you want? Tell me. I can help you."

That was how I always did it. Everything boiled down to basics. The Lucy Carlyle Formula™—tried and tested many times over the long dark nights of the Black Winter. Use their name. Ask the question. Keep it simple. It was the best strategy I'd devised so far for getting the dead to speak.

Didn't mean it always worked, though. Or worked the way you wanted it to.

I watched the white face in the center of the mirror. I listened with my inner ear, blocking out the skeptical snorting of the skull.

Soft sounds drifted across the bedroom, through an abyss of time and space.

Were they words?

No. Just the flap of a bloodied nightgown and some shallow, rasping death sighs.

Same old, same old.

I opened my mouth to try once more. Then—

"I STILL HAVE IT. . . ."

"Skull, did you hear that?"

"Only just. Sounded a bit husky. Still, I have to give her credit. It's amazing she can say anything at all with her throat torn open. What does she still have? That's the question. . . . Blisters? Bad breath? Who can tell?"

"*Shh!*" I made a grand and welcoming gesture. "Emma Marchment—I hear you! If you desire to take your rest, you must first trust me! *What is it that you have?*"

A voice spoke close behind me. "Lucy?"

I cried out, ripping my rapier clear of its Velcro clasp. I spun around, sword held ready, heart throbbing against my chest. The door to the bedroom had opened. A tall, slim figure stood there, silhouetted by swirling flashlight beams and clouds of magnesium smoke. One hand was on his hip; the other rested on his sword hilt, his long coat rippling around him.

"Lucy, what *are* you doing?"

I snatched a glance back, stabilizing the mirror just in time to see the faint, pale shape, like a breath-smudge in the air, pass through the paneling behind the bureau and disappear.

So the ghost had retreated into the wall. . . . *That* was interesting.

"Lucy?"

"All right, all right, you can come in." I sheathed my sword and beckoned—and into the room strode Ted Daley, team leader (second class) at the Rotwell Agency.

Don't get me wrong. I'm not complaining. There were many advantages to my new life as a freelance psychic operative. I could choose my jobs. I worked whenever I wanted. I could build up a little reputation of my own. But one definite drawback was that I could never pick my fellow agents. Each case I took on, I had to fit in with whoever worked for the company that had hired me. Of course, some were okay—decent, professional, and competent. Others . . . well, they were more like Ted.

Seen at a distance, in a soft light, with his back turned, Ted was tolerable; closer inspection was invariably disappointing. He was a gangly, sad-eyed youth, long in all the wrong places, with a permanently semi-open mouth hanging above a scrawny neck. Somehow he always gave the impression of having just swallowed his chin. He had a reedy voice, and a tight and nitpicking manner. As team leader, he had nominal authority over me that evening, but since he ran with his arms flapping like a goose, had the personality of a limp stick of celery, and, crucially, didn't seem particularly psychic, I more or less ignored him.

"Mr. Farnaby wants a word," he said.

"Again?"

"Wants an update on how we're doing."

"Not a chance. I've cornered the ghost; we deal with it now. Bring the others in."

"No, Mr. Farnaby says—" But it was too late for Ted; I knew they'd be loitering at the door. Sure enough, in an instant two nervous shapes had slipped into the room, and presto, our team was complete in all its glory.

It wasn't exactly a breathtaking line-up. Tina Lane, Rotwell field agent (third class), was a wan girl, peculiarly colorless in a way that suggested all her warmth and vibrancy had drained out through a hole in one of her toes. She had hair like bleached straw, bone-white skin, and a slow, faint way of talking that made you lean ever closer to her in an effort to catch what she said. When you realized it wasn't worth listening to, you leaned slowly back again and, if possible, continued in the same direction until you'd left the room.

Next up: Dave Eason, Rotwell field agent (third class). Dave had slightly more to him, in a damaged-goods sort of way. He was a dark-skinned kid, squat, burly, and belligerent, like an angry tree stump. I guessed he had strong natural abilities, but his experiences with Visitors had left him skittish and too free with his rapier. Tina had a scar where Dave had struck her on a previous occasion; and twice that very evening *I'd* almost been skewered when he'd caught sight of me in his mirror out of the corner of his eye.

Wan Tina, mediocre Ted, and jumpy Dave. Yeah, that was my team; that's what I had to work with. It's a wonder the ghost didn't just evaporate in fear.

Dave was pumped up, tensed. A nerve twitched in his neck. "Where've you been, Carlyle? It's a dangerous Type Two we're dealing with here, and Mr. Farnaby—"

"Says we have to stick together," Ted interrupted. "Yes, we've got to keep in strict formation. It's no good you arguing with me and waltzing off. You have to listen to me now, Lucy. We've got to report back to him straightaway or—"

"Or," I said, "we could just get on with the job." I'd been kneeling, closing up my backpack; the others didn't know about the skull, and I wanted it to stay that way. Now I got to my feet, put my hand on my rapier hilt, and addressed them. "Listen, there's no use wasting time with the supervisor. He's an adult. He can't help us, can he? So we use our own initiative. I've found the probable location of the Source. The ghost disappeared into the wall just over there on the far side. Didn't the old story say that after she was stabbed Emma Marchment fled from her husband into a secret room? Then they broke in and found her lying dead among all her pots and poisons? So my guess is we'll find her room behind that wall somewhere. Join me, and we'll put an end to this. Okay?"

"You're not our leader," Dave said.

"No, but I know what I'm doing, which is a nice alternative."

There was a silence. Tina looked blank. Ted raised a bent finger. "Mr. Farnaby says—"

It was hard to keep my temper under control, but I'd gotten better at it these last few months. So many agents were like this: lazy, ineffectual, or just plain scared. And always so concerned about their supervisors that they never acted like proper teams. "Here's how I see it," I said. "The secret door's by that bureau. One of us finds it and breaks through; the others stand guard with mirrors. Any funny business from the ghost, it's salt-bombs and rapiers all the way. We get the Source, we shut it down, and we're out of here before Farnaby gets halfway through his hip flask. Who's with me?"

Tina blinked around at the silent room. Ted's long white hands worried at the pommel of his sword. Dave just stared at the floor.

"You can do this," I persisted. "You're a good team."

"*They so aren't.*" That was the skull, in whispers only I could hear. "*They're a bunch of knock-kneed losers. You know that, right? Ghost-touch is too good for them.*"

I didn't acknowledge the voice. My smile didn't falter, nor did my purpose. They may not have answered, but they weren't arguing with me anymore, so I knew I'd won.

After five minutes' further hustling, I'd gotten us all set up. We'd pushed some desks and tables to the side, to give us a good free space. A protective arc of iron chains lay on the floor, closing off the corner with the bureau. Within this, we had three lanterns glowing by the wall. I was there, too, my mirror hanging at my belt and my rapier in my hand, ready to hunt for secret doors. My three companions stood safely beyond the barrier with their mirrors in position, angled so that they had coverage of the whole area where I'd seen the ghost. I only had to look back at them to check that I was safe. Right now the only thing that was reflected in the mirrors was me, just me three times and nothing else.

"Okay," I said, keeping the encouragement going, "that's perfect. Well done, everyone. I'll start looking. Keep those mirrors steady."

"*I admire your confidence,*" the skull said from my backpack. "*These idiots can barely walk and breathe at the same time, yet you're relying on them to keep you safe. I'd say that's risky.*"

"They'll do just fine." I spoke so low that no one else could hear, meanwhile shining my flashlight on the old dark paneling. What would it be? A lever? A button? Most likely a simple pressure-release board that, when pushed, allowed a weighted door to open. It had been closed a long time; maybe it had all been sealed up, in which case we'd need to smash it in. I changed the angle of the beam of light. Now one section of the wood seemed slightly shinier than the rest. I pushed at it experimentally. Nothing stirred.

Or at least, nothing *natural* did. But my inner ear caught a gentle cracking noise close by, like glass shards being trodden underfoot.

The woman had been stabbed to death with broken glass. My stomach twisted, but I kept my voice upbeat. "Anything in those mirrors?" I said. I shoved at the panel again.

"No, you're good. All's clear." That was Dave, his tone flat with tension.

"It's getting colder," Ted said. "Getting colder *really* fast."

"Okay." Yes, I could feel the temperature draining away; the wood was freezing to the touch. I struck the panel with cold and sweaty fingers, and this time felt it move.

Glass crunched.

"She's coming back, pulling herself out of the past," the skull said. *"She doesn't like you being here."*

"Someone's weeping," Tina said.

I'd heard it, too: a desolate, angry sound, echoing in a lonely place. And with it came the rustling of approaching linen—sodden fabric, wet with blood. . . .

"Watch those mirrors, everyone," I ordered. "Keep talking to me. . . ."

"All's clear."

"Getting colder . . ."

"She's very near."

I shoved again, harder—and this time it was enough. The piece of wood swung in—and out seesawed a narrow door: a section of paneling cracking free of the wall, wreathed in cobwebs and trailing dust.

Beyond it? Only darkness.

I wiped the sweat from my face; both hand and brow were freezing. "There we are," I said. "As promised—one secret room! Now all we need to do is go inside."

I turned back to the others, gave them all a beaming smile—

—And looked into their mirrors.

There was my pale face, reflected three times. And close behind it, *another* face, its skin melting off the bone. I saw pale hair like clouds; I saw bared teeth as small and red as pomegranate seeds. I saw the black and glinting eyes; and last, in the split second I had left, the five clawed fingers reaching for my throat.

Chapter 2

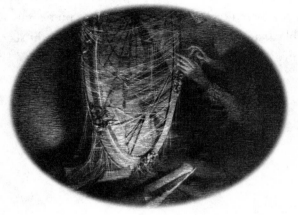

We all reacted, in our different, self-defining ways. Tina screamed and dropped her mirror; Ted leaped back like a scalded cat. Only Dave held his mirror firm—or firm*ish*—while he scrabbled for something at his belt. Me? Before Tina's mirror had shattered on the floor, I'd reversed my rapier and driven it behind me. Wheeling around, I stared into emptiness. But smoke rose from the middle of my sword, and a worm of ectoplasm writhed and fizzed on the iron blade.

I slashed the rapier frantically to and fro. Then I did it some more.

"*Waste of time*," the skull said, after a pause. "*She's gone back inside the wall.*"

"Why didn't you tell me that right away? I hit her. How badly did I hit her?"

"It was hard to see, what with your immense display of raw skill blocking my view."

"Well, where—?" But at that point I was blown sideways by a blast of salt, iron, and white magnesium fire that erupted from the wall a few feet to the left. For a second the room shone bright as day; it was like we'd been dropped into the sun. Then the flames drew back, and darkness closed in, and I was lying in a bed of ash and glowing cinders, with my ears ringing and my hair over my eyes.

I got stiffly to my feet, tapping at my ear, supporting myself with my sword. Through the smoke I could see Ted and Tina goggling at me from a far corner of the room. Close by, Dave was crouched like a small, squat panther, a second magnesium flare ready in his hand.

"Did I get it?"

I patted down a small white flame licking from my sleeve. "No, Dave. No, you didn't. But it was a very good try. And you don't need to chuck another one. She's gone into the secret room." I coughed out a glob of ash. "We have to follow her and finish this. We— Yes, Ted?" From his corner, Ted had raised a hand.

"You've got a trickle of blood coming from your nose."

"I know." I dabbed at it with a sleeve. "But thanks for pointing it out. Right, we need to go in. Who's coming with me?"

The three of them might have been carved from stone. Their fear was so solid it was like a fifth person in the room. They stared at the opening in the wall. I waited while wreaths of smoke spread and mingled, filling the office, blocking them from my sight.

"Mr. Farnaby says—" Ted's voice began.

"Like I *care* what Farnaby says!" I cried. "He's not in here! He's not risking his life with us! Think for yourselves for once!"

I waited. No answer came. Rage and impatience filled me. I turned alone to the secret door.

I could still feel the wave of cold following the ghost like a bridal train, running away into the dark. The side of the bureau shone with nets of ice crystals, as delicate as lacework. The paneling was frosted over, too. I flicked on my flashlight.

It was a narrow passage, wooled with cobwebs, bending almost immediately to the left and out of sight. Darkness hung there, and also a faint tart tang, the smell of dust and death.

Somewhere inside was the Source of the haunting, the place or object to which the ghost was tied. Suppress that by covering it with silver or iron and you trapped the Visitor, too. Simple. I took my mirror in one hand, my flashlight and rapier in the other, and squeezed into the hole.

It wasn't something I *wanted* to do, exactly. I could have waited for the others; I could have spent ten minutes cajoling them to follow me. But then *I* might have lost my nerve as well. Once in a while you have to be a little reckless; that's a skill I learned somewhere.

The passage was so narrow I brushed against brick on either side, the cobwebs tearing off as I passed through. I went slowly, steeling myself for an ambush.

"Do you see her?" I whispered.

"No. She's tricky; flicks in and out of this world. Makes her hard to pin down."

"I wonder what the Source is, what she's guarding."

"*Some bit of her, more than likely. Maybe the husband got over-enthusiastic, hacked her into pieces. A toe rolled off, say, went under a chair, and got lost. Easily done.*"

"Why do I ever listen to you? That's so disgusting."

"*Hey, there's nothing disgusting about random body parts,*" the skull said. "*I'm one myself. It's an honest profession. Steady here— blind turn.*"

Darkness bled around the corner. I took a salt-bomb from my belt and chucked it ahead of me, out of sight. I heard it burst, but there was no psychic impact—I hadn't hit anything.

I raised my flashlight and peered around. "Maybe she *wants* us to find it," I muttered. "That's a possibility, isn't it? It's almost like she's showing us where to look."

"*Maybe. Or luring you to a miserable death. I reckon that's an option, too.*"

Either way, we didn't have far to go. The concentration of spiders—always a sign of Visitors—told me that. Ahead was a little room, choked with a thousand cobwebs; they were strung from wall to wall, fireplace to ceiling. Over and through each other they passed, forming a maze of soft gray hammocks and lumpy, dust-encrusted intersections. My flashlight beam was fractured, split, and inexplicably absorbed. I was inside a bird's nest of maddening distortions. Tiny black-bellied bodies moved on the fringes, scuttling to find shelter from the light.

I hesitated, letting my eyes make sense of the confusion. The place was a former dressing room, I guessed, sealed behind the fake panel; remnants of tattered wallpaper backed this up. One wall had rows of empty shelves, another a small brick fireplace, with a skeleton of a bird lying amid the sooty rubble. There was no window. Black dust washed in dead, dry waves against the sides of my boots. The room had been shut up for a long time.

I listened; somewhere close I heard a woman weeping.

A tall, gold-rimmed dressing table mirror stood against one wall. Its pane of glass was smashed; dust caked the few remaining shards.

When I'd first looked around the corner, I'd sensed—just for an instant—a faint gray shape standing before the mirror, bent slightly, as if looking in. But the apparition, if such it was, had instantly vanished, and I was left to cut my way through the cobwebs with my rapier, scowling as they stuck to hand and blade. The mirror was cocooned like some giant fly.

In the story, Emma Marchment had been stabbed with glass from her mirror. The looking glass might be the Source. I opened one of the pouches at my belt, shook free its silver chain net, and draped it over the top of the mirror. I listened again. The weeping noise continued; the feeling of wrongness in the room remained.

"No . . ." I said. "Pity . . ." I was turning my gaze slowly around the room. The mirror . . . the fireplace . . . the empty shelves. The cobwebs were a nightmare; in places, visibility was down to nothing. I cursed the Rotwell group softly. "It's so hard," I muttered, "doing this on my own."

"*What?*" A shrill voice of protest echoed from my backpack. "*Who are you talking to, if you're 'on your own'? Let's have some accuracy here.*"

I rolled my eyes. "Sorry. Scratch that. Aside from an evil talking skull imprisoned in a dirty old jar and carried around out of a perverse sense of pity, I'm on my own. That makes a world of difference."

"*How can you say that? We're pals, you and me.*"

"We are so *not* pals. You've tried to get me killed dozens of times."

"*I'm dead, too, remember. Maybe I'm lonely. Ever think of that?*"

"Well, keep a close watch now," I ordered. "I don't want her leaping out at me."

"*Yeah, a kiss from old jawless* would *be a bit messy,*" the skull said. "*Mind you, she's not the worst we've come across. That must've been that Raw-bones in Dulwich. Remember its moaning?* 'I want my skin! I want my skin!' *Yeah, yeah, so you've lost it! Tough! Get over it!*" The skull chuckled to itself, then stopped abruptly. "*Oh, wait, hold on a second—you're not trying that, are you? Lucy, Lucy . . . it never ends well.*"

Which was only partly true. One of my Talents, along with Sight (fair) and Listening (better than anyone I'd worked with), was Touch—a variable and frustrating gift, which often gave me nothing (or too little), and sometimes far too much. In recent months, its accuracy had noticeably improved, and it was worth a try here. I stretched out my hand to the mirror and touched a fragment of remaining glass. Closing my mind to the present, I opened it to the past, inviting the object to loop me back to long ago.

As so often these days, the sounds came swiftly, and with them, dim images. . . . The weeping noise faded, to be replaced by the pop and crackle of burning logs. I shut my eyes, saw the same room, but now it was filled with color and variety—as different from its modern incarnation as a living body is from bones. A fire flickered in the hearth; the shelves gleamed with jars and pots and leather-bound books. On a table, piles of herbs lay scattered, together with other, bloodier things.

A lady with long dark hair stood by the hearth, her dress stained red by firelight, the lace fringes of her sleeves rippling in the currents of warm air. She was doing something to the chimney, adjusting the position of a broad, thin stone. As my gaze alighted on her, she froze. Her head turned, and she glared across at me; it was a look of such malignant possessiveness that I recoiled. My shoulder bumped against the wall behind me, and I was back in the present, in the dark, cold empty shell of the little room.

"*You took your sweet time,*" the skull said.

I rubbed my eyes. To me it had been a fleeting instant. "How long was I gone?"

"*I hankered for a newspaper and slippers, I was that bored. Find anything?*"

"Maybe." I flicked my flashlight beam onto the black hole of the fireplace. A little higher up, scarcely visible under its patina of dirt, was that broad, thin stone.

I still have it. That's what the ghost of Emma Marchment had said.

Still in there. Her special thing.

I took my crowbar from my belt. In two steps I was at the stone, prying and scraping at its edge. It wasn't the nicest thing in the world, turning my back on that cobwebby room, but there was no alternative. Years of black soot had filled the gaps around it, and the stone was hard to move. I wished I was stronger. I wished I was part of a *proper* team. Then I'd have had someone to stand behind me, guard my back, and watch the shadows. But I didn't have that luxury.

"*Speed it up. A mouse could pull that pebble out.*"

"I'm trying."

"*I could do better, and I don't have hands. Put some beef into it, woman.*"

My only answer was a muttered curse. I had the crowbar wedged in, and the stone was moving, but the weeping noise was getting louder, and once again I could hear the soft tread of footsteps on broken glass. I looked around. Ice was spreading along the cobwebs in the room.

"She's coming," I said. "I'd prefer insights to insults at this stage."

"*Oh, with me you get the full package. This is a tight spot, Lucy. Why don't you set me free? I'd put you out of your misery then.*"

"I bet you would. I've almost got it. . . . Just keep watch."

"*You want me to tell you when she's creeping close?*"

"No! Before that!"

"*When her fingers are closing around your neck?*"

"Just tell me when she's in the room."

"*Too late for that. She's here.*"

The hairs on the back of my neck did that thing they always do when I'm no longer alone. I took one hand off the crowbar, picked up the mirror dangling at my belt, and angled it over my shoulder. The chamber was black, but a faint gleam shone in the center of the glass. It was the chilly blue glint of other-light, cast by a stick-thin figure, drifting toward me through the dark.

It was at this point I remembered I'd left the silver net draped over the looking glass on the far side of the room.

Desperation gave me strength. I dropped the mirror, plucked a salt-bomb from my belt, and threw. It burst and scattered. There was a smell of burned ectoplasm. The falling granules of salt picked out a woman's form in tumbling, burning green. The shape became two snake-like strands that split and darted away. The salt burned out, and darkness fell again. I launched myself onto the crowbar and heaved; the stone came free. I danced aside as it dropped to the ground. Where was my flashlight? There, lying in the fireplace. I snatched it up, angled it into the shallow recess left behind the stone.

Inside: a large dark object, like an irregular-shaped soccer ball, heavily spun with cobwebs, and with spiders crawling on its surface. It was furry with dust and age.

"Oh," I said. "A head."

"*Yep. Old. Mummified. Nice.*"

"But not *her* head."

"*Nope. Or if it is, there's another good reason her husband killed her: she had a beard.*"

Even under the cobwebs you could see the wiry black tufts sprouting from the chin.

I picked up the head. Yeah, yeah, I know. It's the sort of thing we have to do.

"Where is she, skull?"

"*The apparition has re-formed. Now she's standing by the mirror. Ooh, there are cobwebs running through her wounds. That's weird. Now she's moving forward. She's not happy you've got her Source— she has her hands stretched out. . . .*"

I could have thrown a flare, I guess, but there was nowhere for me to hide from the concussion. I could have used the rapier, but

I couldn't have held that *and* the mirror *and* the Source all at the same time. So I did what I'd learned to do, back when I'd worked with proper agents. I improvised.

I threw the head away from me across the room. I felt the wave of cold shift sideways, saw cobwebs ice over as the ghost moved instinctively after it. At the same moment I sprang the other way, over to the looking glass, where I seized the silver net, and spun around. I snatched up my hand mirror just in time to see the ghost turn back to me. There was a whole host of horrid details on show right then—you could take your pick of which was worse, the ravaged, bloody body or the deranged wickedness in the face—but I took no notice of any of them. I was doing the matador routine that Lockwood had taught me long ago, feinting with the silver net, darting in and out, keeping the Specter at bay. All at once I let my guard down, stood unprotected. The ghost surged forward, fingers raking; as it did so, I twisted aside and, with a flick of the arm, tossed the net directly into the face of the apparition.

Silver did what it always does: the ghost shimmered and went out.

I picked up the net again, bent down to the head, lying on its side against the wall, and covered it with the silver. Something popped in my ears; the feeling of immanent evil in the room burst and was gone.

I spoke in the general direction of my backpack. "How's that?"

"*Not bad, I grant you.*"

I sank to the floor, and regarded the bundle at my feet. "This is some Source. Whose head do you think it is? And why did she want it?"

"She'll have picked it up at a gallows, most likely. That was the usual way witches did it, back in the old days—to aid them in whatever useless spells they were attempting."

"Ugh. That is so foul."

"Yeah . . ." The skull left a significant pause. "Hanging out with a severed head . . . What kind of sick person would do something like that?"

"I know." I sat there in the dark of the secret room until my breathing returned to normal and my heart stilled. Then I got stiffly to my feet, swaddled the head securely in the silver net, and went to find the others. I didn't exactly hurry. The dangerous part of the night was over, but the worst bit was just beginning.

Chapter 3

LUCY CARLYLE
Consultant Psychic Investigation Agent
Flat 4, 15 Tooting Mews, London
Psychic Surveys and Visitor Removal
Aural phenomena a speciality

Y ou might think that finding the head was the end of the matter. Ghost gone, Source suppressed, another building made safe—everything done and dusted. But no. Because we now come to the main drawback of being a freelance psychic detection agent: reporting to the adults at the end.

This was the central paradox of the agencies. Only children and teenagers had decent psychic Talent, so operatives were young. We were the ones who dealt with ghosts; we were the ones who risked our lives. Yet it was the grown-ups who ran the show. They called the shots, they paid the salaries; they were in charge of all the teams. The adult supervisors had zero psychic sensitivity and, since they were mortally afraid of going anywhere near an actual Visitor, never ventured far into a haunted zone. Instead, they hung around on the sidelines, being old and useless, and shouting orders that were utterly out of sync with whatever was going on.

Every agency worked like this. Every agency in London, except one.

Mr. Toby Farnaby, my supervisor from the Rotwell Agency that evening, was typical of his breed. He was a man well into rotund middle age, and thus hadn't seen anything remotely supernatural for more than twenty years. Nevertheless, he considered himself indispensable. He had parked himself in the marble foyer of the house, close to the exits, and safe within a triple circle of iron chains. When I slowly emerged, limping, onto the second floor balcony, I could see him squatting below me like an enormous potbellied toad. His ample backside rested in a folding canvas chair; a hip flask and a stack of sandwiches sat on a trestle table beside him.

At his shoulder stood another man, slight, willowy, a plastic clipboard in his hand. His name was Johnson, and I'd never seen him before that night. He had a soft, forgettable face and nondescript brown hair. He also worked for Rotwell's, and as far as I could make out, was supervising our supervisor. It was that kind of company.

Right now Mr. Farnaby was busy lecturing the other members of the team, who had evidently slinked down to report to him when I disappeared into the wall. Tina and Dave were standing slumped in attitudes of bored dejection. Ted, conversely, stood at attention, an expression of fatuous concentration on his face.

"And it is paramount," Farnaby was saying, "that when you go back up, you proceed with the utmost caution. If Miss Carlyle is dead, which is more than possible, she will only have herself to blame. Keep close, and watch each other's backs. Remember, Emma Marchment poisoned her stepson and attempted to kill her husband! If she was so cruel and vengeful in life, her restless spirit will be worse by far."

"I think we should hurry, sir," Dave Eason said. "Lucy has been gone for ages. We ought—"

"To follow regulations, Eason, which are there for your protection. You have earned two demerits for interrupting." Mr. Farnaby put soft, plump hands together and cracked a knuckle; he reached for a sandwich. "The girl chose to rush off on her own instead of reporting back to me. This is the problem with freelancers. They haven't been properly trained, have they, Johnson?"

"No, indeed," said Johnson.

I called down from the balcony. "Hello, Mr. Farnaby." I took a bleak satisfaction from seeing them all jump.

Farnaby dropped his sandwich in his lap; his little eyes glinted as he gazed up at me. "Ah, Miss Carlyle has elected to join us. I heard about your reckless behavior! At Rotwell's, we work in teams! You cannot be a maverick here."

I tapped my fingers slowly on the parapet. Below me, Farnaby's lank black hair glistened in the lantern light; his stomach cast a shadow like a lunar eclipse. Sacks of iron and salt littered the floor at his feet. Officially he was guarding our supplies; unofficially, they were guarding *him*. "I'm all for teamwork," I said, "provided it's the right kind. Field agents need to be left alone to use our psychic Talents."

Farnaby pursed his lips. "I hired you this evening for your admirable Listening skills, Miss Carlyle, not because I need your shrill opinions. Now, you will do what I asked for an hour ago, and that is to give me a proper report on your actions, which—"

There was a stirring in my backpack. *"This guy's a drag."*

I spoke under my breath. "He sure is."

"Know what I suggest?"

"Yep. And the answer's no. I'm not going to kill him."

"Oh, you're no fun. There's a plant pot over there—you could drop it on his head."

"Hush."

Farnaby looked up at me. "Sorry, Miss Carlyle—did you speak?"

I nodded. "Yeah, I was just saying that I've got the Source. I'll bring it down to you now. Save me a sandwich; I'll be with you shortly."

I limped off, found the stairs, and descended to the foyer. Ignoring my fellow agents, who were all gazing at me blankly, I strolled across the lobby, the silver bundle under my arm. When I got to Farnaby, I dumped it on the table with a flourish. It made a satisfying *thud.*

The supervisor drew back. "This is the Source? What is it?"

"Take a look, sir. You might want to move your snacks back a little."

Farnaby lifted a corner of the net. He gave a cry and sprang away, bowling over his chair. "Fetch a silver-glass box, quickly! And put that thing on the floor! Don't bring it anywhere near me!"

A box was found, and the head placed inside. Sweating, dabbing at his pate, Farnaby returned to his seat. He inspected the box from a distance. "What a hideous thing! You think this was Emma Marchment?"

"It's not *her* head," I said. "But it most definitely belonged to her. I got a flash of what the secret room was like, back in her day. Lots of pots and herbs, weird books and charms. She was into some kind of nonsense sorcery, that's for certain. This old head was one of her prized possessions, which is why her ghost is so attached to it."

"Fascinating." Bland-faced Mr. Johnson made a note on his clipboard. "Well done, Carlyle."

"Thank you, sir. It was a joint effort. Everyone played their part."

Farnaby grunted sourly. "It's certainly an unusual specimen. The sort of thing your boys at the institute would like, eh, Johnson? Want to take it home?"

Mr. Johnson smiled thinly. "Sadly, that's no longer possible under the new DEPRAC regulations. It will have to be destroyed. I'll make a report that the premises are now clear. A notable success for your team, Farnaby, despite your lack of personal control." He patted the supervisor on the shoulder, stepped out of the circle, and drifted off toward the doors.

Mr. Farnaby sat in silence for a moment, brooding. When he spoke, it was to Ted, who was nervously standing near. "I blame you for this, Daley," he said. "You were in charge of the team. You should have kept Miss Carlyle on a tighter leash. It'll be five demerits for you."

Annoyance flared within me. I could sense Ted shrinking away. "Excuse me, sir," I said. "The team achieved its objectives. Our actions were entirely correct."

"Not according to me," Farnaby said. "And that's all there is to it. We will begin packing up now." He waved me away and made to take up his hip flask, but I stood my ground.

"There was no time for me to consult you," I went on. "I had to pinpoint the exact location of the Source before the Specter disappeared. It was the most efficient thing to do. And the team worked very effectively in the initial confrontation. They helped me locate the secret room, and Dave helped drive away the Specter. You were an agent once, sir; you remember how you have to make certain decisions on the ground. It's good practice to trust your fellow operatives. Isn't that right, Ted?"

I looked around to find Ted some ways off, busily lugging a sack of iron toward the door in preparation for departure. I blinked at him. "Tina?" I asked. "Dave . . . ?"

But Tina was packing away some unused salt-bombs, Dave folding away the iron chains. They were silent, disconnected, intent on their work. They paid me no attention.

I found myself suddenly cast into shadow. Farnaby's stomach blocked the lantern light; with ponderous finality he was rising from his chair. His eyes were burned raisins at the best of times; now they had shrunk even more to become fragments of glass, black, malevolent, and glittering. I stepped back, my hand instinctively moving to my rapier.

"I know where you worked before, Miss Carlyle," Farnaby said. "I know *why* you act the way you do. It is a mystery to me why DEPRAC has never moved to shut down that ramshackle, disreputable little outfit. An agency run by children? The idea is absurd! It will end in disaster soon enough, mark my words. But, Miss Carlyle, you are not at Lockwood and Company anymore. Whenever you work at Rotwell, you will find it a *real* agency, where child agents know their place. And if you wish to be hired again, you will keep silent and in future do as you're told. Do I make myself clear?"

My lips were a tight white line. "Yes, sir."

"In the meantime, since you're so keen to improve our efficiency, you can finish tonight's job for me. As Mr. Johnson said, new DEPRAC rules demand that all Type Two Sources be destroyed immediately. There is a black market for precisely this kind of vile object, and we cannot take any chances." He nudged the silver-glass box with his boot. "Here is the mummified head. Take it to Fittes furnaces and see that it is burned."

I gazed at him. "You want me to go to Clerkenwell? Now? It's four o'clock in the morning."

"All the better—the furnaces will be roaring. When you send me their stamped certificate tomorrow, I will pay you for tonight's work, and not a moment before. You others"—he glanced at the industrious trio—"I was going to give you the rest of the night off. But since Miss Carlyle has such a high opinion of your energies, we will see whether we can't fit in a second job. I believe there is a Changer in Highgate Cemetery that needs tackling. I shall drive you there. So, hop to it and finish your tidying!"

He turned away from me and began packing up his sandwiches. My fellow agents, with evil glances in my direction, wearily did as they were told. I was otherwise ignored. I picked up the silver-glass box.

"Skull," I said.

"*What?*"

"You had a point about that plant pot."

"*There you are, see? Didn't I say?*"

Without further words, I tucked the mummified head under my arm and left the house. I was tired, I was angry, but I didn't choose to show it. Arguments with supervisors were nothing new; I had them almost nightly. It was just how things were, part of the deal of my new freelance life.

From the start I'd done things properly. I'd gotten myself a card, nicely laminated, with a classy silver-gray border. Here's what I handed out to all my employers, and why they all wanted me, even if I *did* annoy them.

LUCY CARLYLE

Consultant Psychic Investigation Agent

Flat 4, 15 Tooting Mews, London

Psychic Surveys and Visitor Removal

Aural phenomena a speciality

I could have gone for a swanky logo, with crossed rapiers or skewered ghosts or something, but I preferred to keep it simple. Just being a consultant was enough to get me noticed, because that meant I was independent. There weren't many psychic investigation agents working solo in London, on account of most of us ending up dead.

As a freelancer, I could hire myself out to any agency that wanted my services, and let me tell you, during the course of the Black Winter, a lot of them had wanted those services *bad*. My special sensitivity—Listening was my particular Talent (and between you and me, I was better at it than any agent I'd ever heard of, except perhaps one)—gave almost any group an additional edge. An extra bonus for them was that I knew how to survive. I knew when to Listen and look, I knew when to use my rapier, and I knew when to get out. That's what it always boiled down to, in the end. Three options, and simple common sense. It's how you stayed alive.

In short, I was very good at what I did. Of course I was. I'd learned my trade with the best.

And I wasn't with them anymore.

The Black Winter had been a decent time to start a business. Right now, in late March, there were signs of seasonal respite. The weather was improving, the days were lengthening, pretty spring flowers were showing their heads beside crusted flecks of ancient snow, and you were marginally less likely to be fatally ghost-touched when venturing out for an evening pint of milk. We hoped the ordeal was easing for a time.

Over the previous few months of seemingly endless nights, however, the Problem—the epidemic of ghosts that had long beset our country—had intensified considerably. No single cluster of hauntings as bad as the infamous Chelsea Outbreak had taken place, but the winter had been unrelenting. Every agency had been sorely stretched, and many agents, young and younger, had fallen in the line of duty and been buried in the iron tombs behind Horse Guards Parade.

Nevertheless, the difficulties of the season *had* enabled some companies to thrive. One of these was Lockwood & Co., the smallest psychic detection agency in London. Up until the beginning of the winter, I'd worked for them. It had just been me; Anthony Lockwood, who ran the show; and George Cubbins, who researched stuff. We'd lived in a house in Portland Row, Marylebone. Oh, there'd been another employee as well. Her name was Holly Munro; she was new, a kind of assistant to the rest of us. She sort of counted, too, I guess, but it was George and Lockwood who had meant the most to me. Meant so much, in fact, that in the end I'd been forced to turn my back on them, and go a different way.

Four months earlier, you see, a ghost had shown me a glimpse of one possible future. It was a future in which my actions would lead directly to Lockwood's death. The ghost itself was malignant, and I had no reason to trust it, except for one thing: it echoed my own intuitions. Time and again, Lockwood had risked his life to save mine, the line between success and disaster growing finer and less definite on each occasion. Coupled with that, even as my psychic Talents had grown strong, my ability to *master* those Talents had become frayed. Several times during cases I had lost control of my emotions—and this had dangerously strengthened the ghosts that we were fighting. A series of near catastrophes had ended with me unleashing the power of a Poltergeist; in the ensuing battle, Lockwood (and others) had nearly died. I knew in my heart that it would take only one more mistake and the ghost's prediction would become a reality. Since that was something I could never bear, it stood to reason that I had to avoid it. Hence I'd left the company. That had been my decision, and I knew I was right.

I knew it.

And now, assuming you didn't count a talking skull, it was just me.

As far as I could judge from reading the papers, my departure from Lockwood & Co. had coincided with a period of great activity for my former colleagues. In particular, their success in locating the Source of the Chelsea Outbreak—a room of skeletons buried deep beneath the Aickmere Brothers department store—had earned them the publicity that their leader had long desired. They were rarely off the front page, with photos of Lockwood particularly in evidence. There he was, with George, standing among the broken masonry of the Mortlake Tomb; there he was, alone, posing beneath the blackened outline that was the only remnant of the St. Albans Ghoul. And there he was, finally, in perhaps my least favorite image of the sequence, receiving the coveted Agency of the Month award at the *Times* offices in London, with the slim and elegant figure of Holly Munro standing picturesquely beside him.

So they'd done well, and I was happy for them. But *I'd* thrived, too. My part in the Aickmere's department store case had not gone unnoticed, and no sooner had I rented a room and placed a small ad in the Agencies page in the *Times* than I began to acquire customers of my own. To my surprise, from the first, most were other companies. I worked with the Grimble Agency on the Melrose Place Murders, and with Atkins and Armstrong on the Phantom Cat of Cromwell Square. Even the mighty Rotwell Agency had used me several times; and whatever Farnaby might say, I knew that they'd turn to me again.

Yes, I was flourishing.

I was succeeding on my own.

And did I *mind* being on my own? Not really. For the most part, I got along fine.

I kept busy. No one could say I didn't get out much, or didn't meet all corners of the community; it was just a pity that most of them were dead. In the past week, for instance, I'd seen a ghost child on a swing; a skeleton bride sitting in a church; a bus conductor floating past without his bus; two squashed workmen; a phantom dog being led up Putney High Street by a vast black shadow; a headless librarian; a suitcase containing three nimbuses, two Glimmers, and a Wisp; a wandering severed hand; and a semi-naked neighbor.

That last one had been alive, by the way. I kind of wish he hadn't been.

Yeah, the nights were always frantic, packed with incident. It was the days that sometimes felt a little hollow. Particularly at dawn, after just finishing a case, when I walked back through the empty streets, bruised and weary, with the weight of the solitary hours ahead pulling at my insides. I couldn't even rely on the skull in the jar for a chat; he often dematerialized during the day. *That* was when I really missed the company of others, those moments when I was quietly heading home.

Not that, on this particular night, I *was* going home. Not yet. Thanks to Mr. Farnaby's sour vindictiveness, I had another place to visit first. I was taking a Source in a silver-glass box to one of the most terrible locations in London, and it wasn't even a haunted house.

Quite the opposite.

It was the place where ghosts were destroyed.

Chapter 4

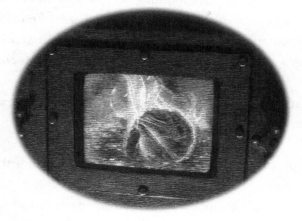

The Greater London Metropolitan Furnaces for the Disposal of Psychic Artifacts—the Fittes furnaces, as they were generally known—were located in the eastern industrial district of Clerkenwell. They had been created by Marissa Fittes, legendary founder of the Fittes Agency, more than forty years previously, when the need for the safe destruction of psychic Sources was becoming clear. In those early days, the furnaces had occupied the site of an old boot factory, sandwiched between a printer's studio and a hat warehouse. Now they filled two full city blocks in which the furnace halls rose like great brick temples, and a forest of tall, thin chimneys blew ash toward the river and the sea. That, at any rate, was the idea; as often as not, the wind dropped it on the surrounding districts, peppering people's coats and hats with gray-black powder. "Clerkenwell snow," as it was called, was mostly tolerated for being harmless.

High walls, topped with iron spikes, bordered the yards where agency vans pulled in each morning with fresh deliveries of Sources gathered during the night. Originally intended for Fittes operatives alone, the complex had for decades been open to all agencies. It was neutral ground. The fierce rivalry that existed between companies, which on the street could end in shrill disputes and sometimes violence, had no place within these walls. Rapiers were left with aged doormen, and agents' behavior was closely monitored by grim-faced attendants who threw out anyone creating a disturbance.

If you came on foot, as I did, you passed through the pedestrian entrance on Farringdon Road, depositing your rapier on the way, then crossed a cobbled courtyard where runnels of freshwater provided extra defense against all undead things. After climbing some steps, you pushed aside a silver-glass door, and entered a wide reception chamber decked with lavender and iron. Seven attendants sat here in separate booths, processing each new object brought for destruction. This was the vetting room.

As I walked through the empty waiting area, between the lines of frayed guide ropes, I heard someone calling my name.

"Hey, Lucy! What have you got for me today?"

The attendant in booth four was a thin young man with pale skin, hooded eyes, and large, rather knobbly hands. His name was Harold Mailer. At eighteen, he knew the furnaces as well as anybody, since he had worked there since the age of eight. He had a horse's laugh and a skittish, nervous manner. He'd taken Sources off my hands several times over the winter. We got along well enough.

I entered the booth and, with some relief, set the silver-glass box on the counter. It was surprising how heavy a mummified head could be. Harold watched me, scratching an ear.

"Looks like you've had a busy night." He turned the box from side to side. "Who's this fellow?"

"No idea. Eighteenth-century criminal, most likely. Haunted—would you believe—by a witch's ghost. Think we could toast him fast? I'm bushed."

Harold Mailer pulled a wad of forms across the desk and selected a pen with an impressively chewed end. "Anything for you, Lucy, anything for you. I'll need the usual details."

I gave the time, place, and circumstances of the capture, and handed over the authorization form, signed on behalf of the Rotwell Agency.

Harold had cropped fair hair, freckles, and protruding ears. His eyebrows were remarkably faint; I could only just see him raising them sky-high. "Rotwell's again? Not old Farnaby's bunch?"

"Yeah. This really *is* the last time. They're useless."

"You should spread your net wider, Lucy."

"I will."

"Why don't you partner with Anthony Lockwood again? I had him in here last week with that Holly girl. They'd just finished that epic job at Camden Lock. I expect you read about it in *True Hauntings*."

"No. No . . . didn't catch that one."

"A Screaming Spirit, manifesting from a skeleton at the bottom of the lock gate. No one had thought to look there, it being water—but canals aren't *running* water, are they? They're stagnant. It was Lockwood who figured it out, of course."

I pushed hair out of my face. "Yeah, he generally does."

"He and that girl were still on a high when they came in. Quite exhilarated. Laughing, giggling together . . ." Harold scratched his nose. He took a rubber stamp, pressed it in red ink, and put the furnaces' acceptance mark on the paper. "So, all I need now's a rating for this Visitor, Lucy. . . . Lucy? Are you concentrating? A rating. Number from one to ten."

"I remember your system. Eight."

"Where one is weakest, about the level of a Wisp; and ten is strongest, about the level of that Poltergeist you fell afoul of in November. The one that trashed the store." He grinned at me and did his horse-laugh thing. "An eight? That's pretty powerful."

"Yeah."

"Mm-hm. Oka-a-y. Want to leave it with me?"

"Farnaby wants me to witness the burning."

"Or you won't get paid. I know. All right, come around."

He took the box and flipped up a hatch in the counter. I passed through the back of the booth and went out a swinging door into the concrete and steel corridor that ran around the perimeter of the furnace house. The corridor was busy, as it always was near dawn. Orange-coated attendants pushed cartloads of empty ghost-jars and silver-glass boxes toward the storage depots. Others accompanied brightly jacketed agents to and from the viewing areas. Carts squeaked, people talked; the fabric of Harold Mailer's jumpsuit crackled softly as he walked. The boom of the fire-gates echoed in my ears and reverberated under my feet. Even so, it was still possible to feel the underlying psychic terror of the place, the frisson that came from the destruction of dozens of Sources every hour.

A giant board at the end of the corridor indicated, by way of green and amber lights, the furnaces that were presently in operation. Harold glanced up and, without breaking stride, halted at Door 13.

"This is me," he said. He patted the silver-glass box under his arm. "Say good-bye to your little friend, Lucy."

"Good-bye, head. How long will it take you to get ready?"

"About ten minutes. Make yourself comfortable in the meantime. Toodle-oo."

He disappeared into the blast room, and I went up to the viewing area. It was basically a big metal box hanging from the roof of the furnace house, like the gondola of an airship. It had a faded green carpet and lots of chairs and sofas scattered around tables, as if it were the kind of place you'd stop to chat with friends. Sometimes it was opened to the public, so they could see how well the authorities were dealing with the Problem. Mostly it was used by agents; we didn't socialize, but stood in silence at the long bank of windows, looking down into the infernos below.

As always, I glanced along the rows of chairs to see who was there. A few agents, one or two adult supervisors . . . And, halfway along, who was that silhouetted at the window? Tall, thin . . . He turned, and I caught a flash of a yellow jacket. Some rangy Tamworth operative. No one I knew.

My stomach cramped. It was probably hunger; it had been a long time since I'd eaten. I approached the window and stood there, arms folded, waiting for Harold to appear.

The furnace house was a vast brick shell filled with blast ovens, each separated by a metal walkway that ran above a network of pipes and flues. There were twenty separate furnaces, in two rows of ten: great silver cylinders with big black numbers painted on the side. Their tops were clear, so you could look down from above and see the raging fires within. Each also had a supply chute, fitted with blast doors at the end, where the Sources were tipped into the chamber. Attendants stood close by, adjusting heat wheels on the furnace sides. As far as the eye could see, blast doors clanged, flames roared high; Sources were shoved in and vanished in a twinkling.

They said that if you stood there on the viewing platform after dark, you could spot a dozen ghosts at once, writhing briefly, blue and green, as the flames engulfed their objects and their ties to this earth were finally snuffed out. Right now it was getting light outside and the ghosts were not visible, but even from a distance I could feel occasional psychic aftershocks. Each was like the moment of silence after a scream.

"This place," the skull's voice said in my head, *"is hell on earth."*

I looked around me; no one was close by. I took off my backpack, placed it on a chair, and loosened the top. There was the faint face looking up at me in its swirling cloud of green. "I thought you were asleep," I said.

"Asleep? Me? I'm dead, remember."

"Or departed back to the Other Side, or whatever it is you do."

"Nope, still in my jar, through no fault of my own. I haven't been sleeping. I never sleep. It's one of many things I never do. Like pick my nose, or sigh when I'm dreaming, or break wind while doing my morning jumping jacks, Lucy. The list is long."

I frowned down at my backpack. "I don't do any of those things, either."

"You say that. It's a small room we live in."

"How many times do I have to remind you?" I growled. "We're *not* living in some weird girl-skull roommate situation! I just don't have enough space to store you anywhere better—like in a moldy tomb, which is all that you deserve."

"Ooh, cutting," the skull said. *"Something's put you in a bad mood today. I wonder what. Anyway, we were talking about the furnaces. I don't like them."*

I didn't either, but I didn't answer. I'd just seen Harold Mailer far below me, walking out onto the metal walkway beside furnace thirteen. He had on protective headgear and massive gloves, and he was carrying the silver-glass box. He looked up, raised a cheery thumb, and signaled to the attendant at the blast doors. Wheels swiveled; the doors opened. In the center of the furnace, the flames roared up in welcome. Harold placed the box on the blast tray and fiddled with its silver clasp. The lid opened; Harold tipped. Something dark and round rolled out, straight down the chute and into the center of the fire. At once it began to burn in a shower of green-blue sparks.

The doors swung closed. Harold gave me another thumbs-up. I raised my hand and looked away.

"Another spirit disposed of, then," the skull said. *"How terribly nice and tidy. Makes you feel better, I suppose?"*

I sat down heavily on the seat next to it. My limbs were suddenly leaden; I was very tired. "Not really. I don't feel anything."

"It's a pointless exercise. Cruel, too."

"Sending ghosts back where they belong? How can that be pointless? Or cruel?" I glanced down at the vile face, at the curving yellow bone of the skull beneath; at the swirling poison-green ectoplasm, all trapped beneath the dusty rind of silver-glass that protected me from its foul embrace. "Really I should chuck you in as well."

"Oh, you wouldn't do that," the skull said. *"Not me. I'm your best and only bud. It is pointless, though. Not that I expect you to ever listen to me. When I first spoke to you, I gave you a warning. Remember what I said?"*

I closed my eyes. It was warm in the viewing area. In a minute I could head off, but it was nice to rest for a moment. "Some drivel about death. Your usual threats."

The skull gave a hoot of derision. *"See what I'm working with? Useless! The brain of a flea! No, 'Death's in Life,' I said, 'and Life's in Death.' And I've been waiting for a half-decent response from you ever since. Good thing I didn't hold my breath."* It paused to consider a moment. *"Not that I have any."*

"I didn't respond," I murmured, "because it made no sense then, and it makes even less sense now." I folded my arms, stretched back in the chair . . .

"Lucy?"

With a sudden start, I realized someone was at my side. I sat up, blinking. Harold Mailer stood there, slightly too close to me. His jumpsuit was peppered with black dust; a faint smell of burning hung about him. He grinned down, rubbing the bumpy knuckles of his hands.

"Bit sleepy? That's okay. It's all finished. Time to get home."

"Sure. I was just resting." But I hadn't heard him come over— maybe I *had* nodded off, just for a moment. I got to my feet, all aches and awkwardness, moving slightly away. When I reached out for the backpack, I realized that its top was half open. Most of the jar was hidden; just one corner was showing. The ghost had gone quiet, but a faint greenish glow still emanated from within. I pulled the drawstrings tight, flipped shut the top. When I glanced at Harold Mailer, he was smiling hard at me.

"Interesting gear you carry around with you," he said. "Looks bulky."

I shrugged. "It is. Some kind of new lamp I was trying out. New Rotwell one. Wasn't very good. Too bulky, as you say. . . . So, everything's done, then?"

"Everything's done. If you're ready, I'll escort you to the gate."

It was eight thirty when I finally got back to the little apartment where (whatever the skull might claim to the contrary) I most definitely lived alone. It was a studio on the third floor of a high-rise in Tooting, south London, not far from the Balham ironworks. My room was square, and not very large. There was space for a single rumpled bed beneath the window, a sink next to it, and, beyond that, a dresser for my clothes. On the opposite side of the room the carpet stopped abruptly and a yellowed strip of linoleum marked out a "kitchen" area—a battered stove, a fridge, a pull-down table, and a little wooden chair, all squeezed into a corner. And that was about it. For showers and stuff, I used a communal bathroom on the other side of the landing.

The place wasn't perfect. It hadn't been painted in a long while, and there was a permanent smell of baked beans in the kitchen area, no matter what I cooked. The edge of the linoleum was curling up, and I was always tripping over it. The mattress on my bed had seen better days. But the room was warm and safe and dry, and most of my agency stuff (including the skull's jar) could be stacked neatly between the door and the bed. To be honest, when I was home, I spent most of my time sleeping, so I didn't care about the décor. I'd been there four months, all told. It was okay.

That morning, as I usually did when I got back from a job, I made brief notes in my personal casebook, drafted my invoice for Rotwell's, then went across the landing for a shower. After that I went out and got myself some take-out food. I should have cooked something, but I didn't have the energy. I sat on the bed in my pajamas, dunking fries in ketchup, eating a burger, listening to the traffic pass on Tooting High Street.

A voice spoke from the ghost-jar. *"So, here we are again. Just you and me. Two jolly roommates. What shall we talk about?"*

I dipped my burger into the ketchup. "Nothing. I'm going to sleep in a minute."

There was a moment's pause. *"Mmm, maybe that's for the best,"* the voice said. *"Look at you. Damp-haired, puffy face, eating fast food alone in bed . . . If I had tear ducts, I'd weep for you. You haven't even straightened your bedspread."*

"Yeah, well. It's my dinnertime and I'm hungry."

"Yes—hungry, isolated, and friendless. Aside from me, of course."

"Thanks. I've loads of friends."

"'Course you have. I've seen bag ladies with more active social lives."

Suddenly I realized how very weary I was. I got up to put the tea kettle on.

"*Ooh, careful when you cross the room you don't collide with any of your pals,*" the skull called. "*I can barely see the far wall, there are so many close chums lining up to chat with you. . . .*" When I didn't answer, it gave a chuckle. "*Lucy, I'm a malevolent skull, without an ounce of compassion. You've got to be worried if I'm feeling sorry for you.*"

I'd picked up the french fry packet and paper bag to put into the trash, but when I got there I found it was full, so I set them carefully on the floor. Then I took a detour back to the jar and twisted the lever on its lid closed, shutting off the continuing jibes from the ghost within. Even with the traffic blaring below my window, a sudden sense of peace enfolded me. I decided not to make tea after all, but go to sleep. I drew the curtains, lay back on the bed, and closed my eyes.

I was still in the same position five hours later. Afternoon sunlight streamed past the ironworks and through a gap in the curtains and lay like a shining counterpane across the wasteland of my bed. I had a crick in my neck and an ache in my jaw, and my muscles were stiff with weariness. Consciousness was a struggle; moving was harder. I wouldn't have woken in the first place except someone was knocking on my door.

I shuffled the few necessary paces across the room. It was a puzzled sort of shuffling, since no one ever called on me. Clients didn't come here; I spoke to them on the phone. So who could it be? There was the girl from the floor below who took my clothes on the weekends and delivered them back, washed and pressed, on

Monday mornings. She was due today. But she always just left them outside the door, a neat little package of ironed skirts and under-wear. She never knocked. It wouldn't be her.

There was my neighbor across the landing, a nervous gentleman of late middle age who wore iron ghost-wards in his hat and whose apartment stank of lavender. He seldom spoke to me, and jumped whenever I went by. I think he was unnerved by my profession.

It wasn't going to be him, either.

There was my landlady, a ferocious matriarch who resided like a spider in the basement flat, sensitive to every creak of door and stair, particularly if you hadn't paid your rent. But I'd shelled out three months in advance, and she never bothered me. So it was unlikely to be her.

I didn't know who it was. I went to the door, yawning, blinking, my hand busy scratching at an itchy spot down the back of my paja-mas. I undid the lock and swung it open.

Mid-yawn, mid-scratch, I opened that door.

And it was Lockwood.

Lockwood.

It was Lockwood standing there.

Chapter 5

L ockwood.

After four months, his proximity was shocking; it was shocking, too, how familiar and unfamiliar he was all at the same time. He was standing on the dowdy little landing in his long dark coat, his right hand still hovering by the bell. His hair, as ever, flopped to one side over his brow; his eyes sparkled at me between the fronds. As I met his gaze, he smiled—and that smile was a world away from the hundred-gigawatt version you saw in the papers. It was warm but somehow hesitant, as if it hadn't been used recently. It was the smile I'd hazily imagined a hundred times; only now it was real, solid, meant just for me. He wore the same old coat with the same old claw marks, from the night we opened Mrs. Barrett's tomb. The suit was new, though, charcoal-gray with the thinnest purple stripe; as always, it was elegant, stylish, and slightly too tight for him. I even recognized the tie—it was one I'd given him a year ago, after the case of the Christmas Corpse. So he still had that, still liked to wear it. . . .

I blinked, and stopped thinking about his clothes.

Lockwood was standing at my door.

All this ran through my mind in the first split second. "Hello, Lucy," he said.

I just managed to avoid the worst-case scenario, in which my mouth would simply have stayed wide open while emitting a gassy whining sound. But I didn't get close to the cool, calm reaction I'd dreamed about during those four long months apart.

"Hi," I said. I withdrew my hand from my pajamas. I rubbed hair out of my eyes. "Hi."

"Sorry it's a bit early," Lockwood said. "I see you haven't been up long."

Funny, when I'd lived with him at Portland Row, I'd puttered around in nightclothes all the time. Now that we worked apart, I was suddenly wildly embarrassed. I looked down. No, they weren't even my best pajamas. They were an old gray pair I was using while my laundry was being done.

My laundry . . . My blood went cold. The laundry package! If it was outside the door . . .

I craned my head out, surveyed the landing to either side. No. No sign of it. Good.

"Are you all right?" Lockwood asked. "Something wrong?"

"No, no. Everything's fine." I took a deep breath. *Be calm.* The pajamas weren't a biggie. I could deal with this. It was all going to be great. I put one hand nonchalantly on my hip, tried for an expression of airy unconcern. "Yes. Everything's fine."

"Good. Oh, there was this package on your step," Lockwood said. He produced a see-through plastic bag from behind his back. "Looks like it's got a *lot* of . . . nicely ironed items in it. Don't know if they're . . ."

I gazed at it. "Yeah, those are . . . those are my neighbor's. I'll look after it for him. For *her*." I snatched the bag and tossed it out of sight behind my door.

"You look after your neighbor's underwear?" Lockwood glanced back across the landing. "What kind of an apartment building *is* this?"

"It's— Well, actually I—" I ran harassed fingers through my uncombed hair. "Lockwood," I said, "what are you *doing* here?"

His smile broadened, carrying me with it. It became a sunnier place, that little landing; the smell of my neighbor's lavender plantation receded; I no longer noticed the peeling wallpaper in the stairwell. How I *wished* I was properly dressed. "I wanted to check in, see that you were doing okay," Lockwood said. "And," he added, before I could challenge him, "I've got something to ask you, too." His gaze flicked past me for an instant, into the room. "If you've got the time, that is."

"Oh. Yes. Yes, of course I have. Um, why don't you come in?"

"Thanks."

He stepped inside, and I closed the door. Lockwood looked around.

"So this is your place," he said.

My place. Oh, God. With the shock of seeing him, I hadn't stopped to think about the condition of my room. I glanced around, and with an instant awful clarity I saw everything: the sorry hump of bedspread in the center of the mattress; my pillow, laced with ancient stains; the various mugs and chips bags and plates with toast crusts stacked to the left of the sink; the dirty bags of iron and salt, the rusty chains, the ghost-jar with its horrid skull (now mercifully quiet); the colorful scraps of clothing scattered on the floor. Then there was the carpet. I hadn't vacuumed the place in months. *Why hadn't I? Why hadn't I actually bought a vacuum cleaner? Oh, God.*

"It's . . . nice," Lockwood said.

His voice, so calm and measured, had an immediate effect on me. I took hold of my thoughts and quieted them. Yes. Actually it *was* nice. It was mine, after all. I was paying for it; I was making it work. It was my place. It was fine.

"Thanks," I said. "Look, do you want to sit down? No—! Not there!" Lockwood had made a move toward the hideous tangle of my bed. "There's this chair here. . . . No, wait!" I'd spotted the pink towel draped over the chair back, still damp from this morning's shower. "Let me move that for you."

I whipped it away, revealing a snake pit of tangled gray under-garments I'd tossed there a few days before.

Oh, God.

Lockwood didn't seem to register my squeal of discomfort. He was looking out the window. "I'm actually quite happy to stand. So . . . this is Tooting, is it? It's not an area I know well, but it's a pretty nice view you've got here. . . ."

I threw some clothes under the bed, nudged a crumb-strewn plate under the chair. "Which part? The industrial boiler company or the ironworks?" I gave a light, slightly hysterical laugh. "It's not exactly Portland Row."

"No. Well." He turned back to me. We looked at each other.

"So," I said, "do you want some tea? I could do with some."

"That would be nice. Thanks."

Making tea is a ritual that stops the world from falling in on you. Everything pauses while you do familiar things with taps and kettles; it allows you to catch your breath and become calm. I've made tea on camping stoves while Specters paced beyond my protective iron chains; I've brewed some while watching a Revenant claw itself free of its grave. I'm not normally a shaky tea-maker, but somehow in Lockwood's presence it took me twice as long as usual. Even tossing a tea bag into a mug was a task fraught with difficulty; I kept sending it spinning across the counter. My thoughts were racing; my body scarcely seemed my own.

He was here! *Why* was he here? Excitement and incredulity kept smashing together, like waves colliding at a jetty. There was so much noise going on in my mind that the first priority—making small talk—was a bit of a problem.

"How's business with Lockwood and Co.?" I asked over my shoulder. "I mean, I see you in the papers all the time. Not that I'm *looking* for you, obviously. I just see stuff. But you seem to be doing okay, as far as I can gather. When I think about it. Which is rare. Do you take sugar now?"

He was staring at the clutter on my floor, blank-eyed, as if lost in thought. "It's only been a few months, Luce. I haven't suddenly started taking sugar in my tea. . . ." Then he brightened, nudging the ghost-jar with the side of his shoe. "Hey, how's our friend here doing?"

"The skull? Oh, it helps me out from time to time. Hardly talk to it, really. . . ." To my annoyance, I noticed a stirring in the substance that filled the jar, implying a sudden awakening of the ghost. That was the *last* thing I wanted right now. At least the lever was closed; I wouldn't have to listen if it chose to speak.

I bent down to get milk out of the little fridge. "Did you get someone else, then, to help you?" I asked. "Another agent?"

"I thought about it. Never got around to it, somehow." Lockwood scratched his nose. "George wasn't keen. So it's just the three of us still, muddling along without you."

Still the three of them. For some reason the idea both pleased and pained me. "And how *is* George?" I said.

"You know old George. The same."

"More experiments?"

"Experiments, theories, weird notions. He's still trying to solve the Problem. His latest hobby is buying every new invention the Rotwell Institute churns out. He tests them to see if they work as well as good old-fashioned salt and iron. They don't, of course, but that doesn't stop him from filling the house with all manner of ghost-detectors, divining spindles, hex-wands, and things that look like teacups that are supposed to tinkle when a ghost draws near. All claptrap, basically."

"Sounds like George hasn't changed at all." I poured the milk and put the bottle cap back on. "And how's Holly?"

"Hmm?"

"Holly."

"Oh, good. She's good."

"Great." I stirred the tea. "Can you flip the trash can open, please?"

"Of course." He put a polished shoe on the pedal; I lobbed the tea bag in. Lockwood removed his foot and the lid clanged shut. "Little bit of teamwork there," he said.

"Yeah. We still haven't lost it." I handed him his mug. "So . . ."

He was watching my face. "You know, I think I *will* sit down, if you don't mind. Anywhere will do."

He took the chair; I took the bed. There was a pause. Lockwood nursed his tea; he seemed unsure how to begin.

"It's nice to see you," I said.

"You, too, Luce." He smiled at me. "You're looking well, anyway; and I hear fine things about you from some of the other agencies. Sounds like you're going great guns, doing the freelance stuff. I'm not surprised, obviously—I know all about your Talents—but I *am* happy for you." He scratched behind an ear and fell silent again. It was an odd thing, seeing Lockwood so unsure of himself. I could still feel my pulse beating in my chest, so I wasn't much better off, but at least I didn't have to do the talking now.

As I waited, I saw a greenish light at the end of the bed and realized that the ghost in the jar had fully formed. It was staring at Lockwood with an expression of extravagant disgust and derision, while mouthing soundlessly against the glass. I couldn't lip-read, but whatever it was saying was clearly uncomplimentary.

I scowled at it, then caught Lockwood's eye.

"Sorry," I said. "Just the skull. You know what it's like."

Lockwood set his tea down. For a moment he looked around the room. "I'm not sure this is really the place for you, Lucy."

"Surely that's my business."

"Yes, yes, of course it is. And I'm not here to try to talk you out of it. I tried and failed at that months ago. You made your decision, and I respect it."

I cleared something in my throat. "It was the right thing to do."

"Well, we've been down that road." Lockwood brushed his hair back from his eyes. "Anyway, the thing is, Luce . . . I'll get straight to the point. I'm in need of your help. I'd like to hire your freelance services for a case."

It was one of those moments when a single strand of time looped off from the rest, carrying me on it, and everything else seemed to freeze. I sat there, thinking back across that long, hard winter, to the awful day I'd left the company. To walking with Lockwood through the park as he tried to talk me out of it; to our final dreadful conversation in a café while three successive cups of tea grew cold; to how—growing angry with me at the end—he'd left me there. I recalled my last night in the house, with everyone so distant and polite; and my departure when all the others were asleep in the blue light of the dawn, dragging my duffel bag and the ghost-jar softy down the stairs. Ever since then I'd rehearsed our eventual meeting, running through different scenarios in my head. I'd imagined Lockwood asking me to rejoin the company. Asking, or begging, even—going down on bended knee. I'd thought of how I would have to refuse him, and how the warm pain of it would pierce my heart. I'd also conjured visions of meeting him unexpectedly, while out on moonlit cases, and of us having bittersweet conversations before going our separate ways. Yes, I'd imagined plenty of situations, all sorts of variables.

But never quite this one.

"Run that past me again, slowly," I said, frowning. "You want to *hire* me?"

"I don't ask it lightly. It's just a one-off. A single case. One night's work; two, max."

"Lockwood," I said, "you know my reasons for leaving. . . ."

He shrugged; the smile lessened. "Do I? To be honest, Luce, I don't think I've ever fully understood them. You were frightened of unleashing your Talents on us, was that it? Well, you seem to have them sufficiently under control now that you're doing great things with most of the other agencies in London." He shook his head. "Anyway, hear me out. I'm not asking you to join us again, obviously. I'd never do that. It's just a temporary arrangement. It would be no different from you teaming up with Bunchurch, or Tendy, or whoever else you've been with these last few weeks. Just business, that's all."

"But you don't need my help," I said. My tone was a little flat; something in what he'd said pressed on my spirits. I could feel doors slamming in my mind.

"Well, here's the thing. We do." Lockwood leaned forward, and I noticed a scar on the side of his neck—not large, but white and raised—one I'd never seen before. "You're right, Lockwood and Co.'s been doing pretty nicely these last few months, well enough to be selective about our clients. We've had some interesting ones, like the blind dressmaker who saw ghosts imprinted on her own private darkness, but our latest is in a category of her own. You know her. It's Penelope Fittes."

Hold up. *That* took me by surprise as well. Penelope Fittes was chairperson of the oldest, largest, and most celebrated of all psychic detection organizations, the great Fittes Agency. Along with the head of Rotwell's, and several of the iron and salt magnates, she was one of the most powerful people in the country. I blinked at him. "Er, doesn't she have an agency of her own? Rather a big one, in fact."

"Yes, but she's taken a shine to us," Lockwood said. "She's liked us ever since the Screaming Staircase affair. And after we saved her from assassination at the carnival last autumn, she's made it her business to monitor our progress and send the odd job our way. Well, she's got a new case for us, quite a big one, and the thing is, by all accounts it needs a good Listener."

I looked at him.

"A *very* good Listener."

I said nothing.

Lockwood shifted in his seat. "So . . . I wondered if you could help us out, just this once, in a freelance capacity. . . . You *are* the best, after all."

Time snapped back into one piece; I was wholly in the present, alert and questioning.

"What's the case?"

"I don't know."

I frowned. "Don't you think you ought to find out before dragging me into it?"

"It's difficult and dangerous, that's all I've been told. But Penelope Fittes is intending to brief us—by 'us' I obviously mean me, George, and Holly, but you could join, too, if you were up for it—tomorrow morning at Fittes House. You know how much of a recluse Ms. Fittes is, particularly after that carnival thing. It must be something special if she's personally involved."

"I still don't get it. Why does she want *you* to do this job? She's got a million agents of her own."

"Again . . . I don't know, Luce. But if we do it well, it'll stand us in good stead for further commissions."

"I'm sure it will, and that's great for you, but I'm no longer part of Lockwood and Co., am I?"

"No. I'm well aware of that. But you happily work with other agencies, don't you?"

"Yes, you know I do, but—"

"What's the difference?"

"Don't pressure me, Lockwood. You know it's not the same."

I got up abruptly, grabbed the damp towel, and tossed it over the ghost-jar, blocking the face from view. Its contortions had been growing ever more frantic; they'd disturbed me even out of the corner of my eye, and I couldn't put up with it any longer.

I threw myself back onto the bed, glowering. "What were we saying?"

"I'm not trying to pressure you, Luce," Lockwood said. "I realize it's odd, me just showing up, but if you're worried about risk, the chances of anything going wrong are very small. Almost nonexistent. Maybe you had a wobble a few months ago, but personally I believe you've always had your Talent under excellent control. I don't think there's the slightest chance of you endangering us. You always were too strong for that. Sure, for whatever reason, you no longer want to be a full part of our team. It became a burden for you, one that could no longer be borne. That meant you had to leave us in a hurry, which was difficult for you, I know, just as it was for us. We all had to pick up the pieces. I'm not going to pretend that Lockwood and Co. found it easy after you left. . . . George was pretty upset about it." He looked down at his hands. "Anyway, I've no doubt those feelings of yours still remain. Teaming up for a night would be weird for all of us, but most of all for you. But I *do* think you could be strong enough to ignore the weirdness, Luce, if you thought it was the right thing to do. One night's work, Luce . . . it's almost nothing. Just helping us out. Who knows, it might make us *all* feel a bit better about things, I don't know."

He flicked a glance up at me—it was sad and hopeful all at once, a glance that presumed nothing—then gently lowered his gaze and went back to contemplating his hands. He'd made his pitch; there wasn't much else he could say. I was looking at my own hands, frowning at the scrapes on the knuckles, the faint magnesium staining on the fingers, the dirty flecks of iron and salt crusted under the nails. . . . What was all that about? Flo Bones probably had a better manicure, and she made her living scraping holes in river-ooze. The skull was right: I wasn't in good shape. Sometime over the winter, I'd stopped taking care of myself; I'd let myself go.

But in the meantime, I *had* been focusing on something else, and that was my Talent. Could I control it better now? I thought so, yes—working with adult supervisors was an endless test of the emotions, and I'd never come close to losing control. So perhaps, for one time only, it would be safe enough. . . .

It *would* be good to help them out, redress the balance after the way I'd left them.

I looked over at Lockwood as he sat shoulders-forward, head

slightly bowed. He seemed more diffident than I'd ever seen him: not vulnerable, exactly, but certainly exposed. After what I'd done, it must have been so difficult for him to come here.

"There are other Listeners out there," I said. "Good ones, too."

"Like who?"

"Kate Godwin's okay."

"Oh, come *on*. She's not half the Listener you are."

"There's Leora Jones of Grimble, Melita Cavendish at Rotwell . . ."

"As good as you? You don't believe that! How many of them can buddy up to a talking skull?"

"I *don't* buddy up to it."

Lockwood made a face. "Whatever. Besides, they're not freelance, are they?"

This was true. And he was quite right, incidentally. The rest paled in comparison to me. Only one other person had ever spoken with ghosts the way I did, and she'd died long ago. I was silent for a while.

Lockwood started to get to his feet. "It's okay, Lucy. I understand your reluctance, and I don't blame you in the slightest. I'll go back and tell the others."

"I suppose doing a job for Penelope Fittes might get me noticed," I said.

He hesitated. "It very well might, yes."

"And it would really help out Lockwood and Co., you say?"

"It really would, Luce."

"So if it's just a one-off . . ."

"Yes."

"And you really think my Talent would make a difference . . ."

"There's no one else I would want at my side."

Strange, sometimes, how you make a particular choice. When it's not a specific thought or line of argument that decides you, but more a set of jumbled sensations that changes your mind. I'd been ready to say no to him the entire time; even at the very end I was opening my mouth to apologize and say good-bye. But then images passed across my vision, like a pack of cards being flicked in front of my eyes. I saw Lockwood, George, and Portland Row, the house and life I'd left behind. I saw the Fittes furnaces, and moments from my solitary walks through London. I saw the hapless Rotwell team; most of all I saw Mr. Farnaby himself, in all his swollen pomposity and heartlessness, turning his back on me.

For once, just for once, it would be nice to work with true companions again.

"Okay," I said offhandedly. "You should know that my fees have gone up. There's a going rate for freelancers, but I charge ten percent more. And I don't take orders from anybody. I come in as an independent consultant, and that includes strategy and risk evaluation. Everything we do has to be agreed upon beforehand. If you're happy with those terms, and if you think George and Holly will be, too, then I don't see a problem with your proposal." I held out my hand. "For one or two nights only. I'm in."

Lockwood's eyes sparkled. "Lucy," he said, "thank you. I *knew* you wouldn't let us down."

For the first time, the old grin extended its way fully across his face. Its radiance bathed me; that was something else that hadn't changed at all.

II

The Ealing Cannibal

Chapter 6

"*So . . . Lockwood.*"

"What?"

"*Don't try to deny it. I saw you with him. What was all that about?*"

It was morning the following day, and I was up early, getting ready in front of the mirror. I'd been awake half the night thinking about Lockwood—about his request, and the answer I'd given him. It was a bit annoying not being able to sleep, but it was a change being kept up by moral conundrums rather than Wraiths and Specters. Doubts, like ghosts, gain strength in darkness; even with the dawn I wasn't sure I'd done the right thing. To suppress my misgivings, I busied myself trying on dressier clothes than I normally wore. Fittes House, where I was headed, was a prestigious location. It would be best to look the part.

"*I can see you've agreed to something stupid,*" the skull said.

"You've been standing there for hours. Normally you spend about thirty seconds getting dressed, and that includes your token 'wash.'" The voice grew thoughtful. *"What could it be? Not a date, surely—the boy's got eyes."*

I glared over my shoulder. Ever since I'd retrieved my towel, the ghost had been mouthing urgently at me through the glass. At first I'd ignored it. The skull had no love for Lockwood; its contributions wouldn't have been helpful. But in the end, I'd gotten bored with the silence of my room. Some people had a radio to listen to; me, I had a phantom in a jar.

"Of course it's not a date!" I snapped. "Don't be ridiculous." I glared at my outfit. It had been a while since I'd worn it; I felt unsure. "This is a business meeting."

The skull gave a long, slow whoop of derision. *"Ugh! I don't believe it! You've rejoined them, haven't you? You're back with those fools again!"*

"I'm not 'back' with them," I said. "I'm helping them out. It's one time only."

"One time? Ha! Give it five minutes, and you'll be back sleeping in your cramped little attic at Lockwood's, snuggling up with that Holly Munro. I bet she uses your room now."

"Ack! That's never going to happen."

"Five minutes. Take it from me."

"Holly Munro has her own place. She doesn't sleep there, anyway."

"What do you care whether she does or not?"

"I don't."

"You've got a good thing going here," the skull said. *"It's called*

independence. Don't throw it away. And, speaking of throwing things away—your dress. Too tight."

"You think so? It looks all right to me."

"You're only looking at the front, love."

An altercation ensued here. I won't go into it. I was distracted, out of sorts; I was in a kind of heightened state, swept up by excitement, uncertainty, and irritation. Ever since I'd seen the hollow boy, the ghost that had worn Lockwood's dead and bloodied face, I'd kept my vow to stay away from Lockwood. I didn't want that future; I'd plotted a different trajectory for myself. Yet now, one single visit from him had pulled me—temporarily—off course. I was cross with myself; but the prospect of what I was doing also quickened my heart. One thing was for sure: I wasn't in the mood for fashion advice from a stupid skull.

Even so, the end result was that I changed back into my usual skirt and leggings.

"You're taking me along, of course," the skull said, when I was putting on my rapier.

"No way."

"If it's a tough case, you'll need me. You know you will."

"It's just an initial conversation. If we—if Lockwood and Co. is given this case, I'll come back and get you. Maybe."

There was a pause. *"Whatever."* The skull spoke dismissively. *"Doesn't bother me. See if I care."*

"Fine."

"I don't need you, anyway. I can talk to other people."

I snorted; I was still fed up with it. "Like who?"

"People."

"You *so* don't. Who else have you ever talked to? As a skull, I mean. There . . . see?" I said. "There's nobody."

"*Actually, you're wrong,*" the skull said. "*I spoke with Marissa Fittes once. So you're not the only one, Miss Clever-Clogs.*"

"Really?" I pulled up short. "I didn't know that. When was this?"

"*What, do I have a pocket watch in here? It was ages back. When I was first found, they fished me out of Lambeth sewers, cleaned me up, and took me to her. She asked me a few questions, then shut me in this bottle.*"

"How did you get into the Lambeth sewers?"

The face screwed up in distaste. "*Don't ask. I came to a bad end.*"

"Sounds like it." I stared at the ghost. In many months of irritating, self-aggrandizing conversation, it had never revealed this information about its past. And Marissa Fittes had been the founder of the first psychic detection agency, the only agent that I'd heard of with a Talent similar to mine. She had been the grandmother of the current leader of the company—the woman I was meeting today—and was still a national heroine. It was actually no small deal. I finished with the mirror, looked for my jacket. "So what was she like, Marissa?"

A grimace from the jar. "*Formidable. A powerful, ironhearted psychic who'd have swallowed your precious Lockwood and Company for breakfast, like a shark gulping a minnow. No offense to you idiots, I'm sure.*"

"So she really *could* talk with spirits."

"*Oh, yeah. She did lots of stuff. You're a babe in arms, honey, compared to her. What a lot of questions you have today,*" the skull went on. *"Tell you what, I might answer some more if you hang around a bit and don't go scuttling after Lockwood."*

"Tempting," I said, "and you put it so nicely. But you'll have to talk to yourself this morning. I've got to go."

As it turned out, I wasn't on time, anyway. There'd been a Specter on the Northern Line the night before, and salting parties were working in the tunnels. The Tube was delayed. I arrived at Charing Cross five minutes late. Cursing, perspiring, I ran up the Strand to Fittes House, where my way was blocked by the usual crowds of the desperate and ghost-haunted, all come to petition the company for help. A further five minutes was lost as I pushed my way to the front of the line. Once there, I had to talk my way past the surly doorman. It was like a set of obstacles in a fairy tale; by now I was fifteen minutes late. Even then I somehow caught my coat in the revolving doors and had to go around twice before I fought myself free.

I stumbled at last into the foyer. A row of neat receptionists, each one more bright-eyed and bushy-tailed than the next, regarded me with identical bland smiles.

I closed my mouth, adjusted my skirt, pushed back my hair, and dabbed ineffectually at a sweaty temple with a sleeve. "Good morning. I'm—"

The nearest receptionist spoke. "Good morning, Ms. Carlyle. If you would like to go through, your associates are already waiting in the main hall. Ms. Fittes will meet you presently."

I took a deep breath. "Thank you. I know the way."

Across the foyer I went, past the iron bust of the skull's old confidante, Marissa Fittes. Past the oak doors, the gilded paintings, my boots tapping on cold marble. Then into the conference hall, where tall windows looked out over the snarled traffic of the Strand, and daylight glinted on the glass pillars of the Fittes collection. There they were, safe behind silver-glass: nine legendary psychic objects from the first days of the agency. The tiny Frank Street coffin; Gödel's metal arm; the bones of Long Hugh Hennratty; the Clapham Butcher Boy's terrible serrated knife. . . . At night, trapped ghosts moved colorfully within the pillars; now everything was monochrome and still.

Three people stood beside the column dedicated to the Cumberland Place haunting, studying the bloody nightgown it contained. And now my heart *really* began to hammer, and my nerves started to fail me. I felt far worse than I had during the pursuit of Emma Marchment's ghost two nights before.

Whatever dangerous assignment Penelope Fittes was proposing, *this* was the part I dreaded. My first meeting with my ex-colleagues: Lockwood, George, and Holly Munro.

I confected what I hoped was a relaxed and confident smile. I walked toward them as they turned.

Lockwood, of course, I'd seen already. But this was different. The previous day, he'd been a guest in my house, asking for my help; he'd been at least as uncomfortable as me. Now *I* was the outsider, and he was back in his accustomed position as leader of the company. The awkwardness was suddenly all on my side. Still, he looked relaxed as I approached; and I was grateful for it. He gave me a welcoming grin. "And here she is! Lucy—it's good to see you."

He wore his slim, dark suit; his hair was swept back and, I

thought, subtly gelled. He was making more of an effort than usual. I hadn't seen that attention to detail before.

For me? No. Penelope Fittes was far more likely.

"Hi, Lockwood," I said. With that, I turned to George.

Four months had passed since I'd set eyes on him: George Cubbins, Lockwood's second in command—amateur scientist, researcher extraordinaire, and committed casual dresser. That morning, like most mornings that I remembered, he was doing things with a stained T-shirt and saggy pair of faded jeans that defied both taste and gravity. As I could have predicted, he hadn't made the slightest effort to scrub up. In the elegant confines of Fittes House he stood out like a wart on a wedding day, a thistle in a salad bowl. Some things hadn't changed.

But others had, which startled me. George seemed thinner and, I thought, more careworn. He looked older, too, with harder lines around the eyes. How had this happened in only four months? It was true that agents saw a lot of things, and saw them often. We used up our youth pretty fast sometimes. But I'd never thought George would be prey to that. Seeing it gave me a sharp pang.

"Hello, George," I said.

"Hello, Lucy." As he said it, I watched his face. I wasn't waiting for a grin. You didn't get those with George. His face was similar in shape, color, and texture to a cold milk pudding; and it had the same range of expressions, too. But if you looked closely, you'd see clues to his mood—a twitch of the mouth, perhaps; or his eyes, deep beneath the surface of his spectacles, shining when he was happy or excited. If he pushed his glasses up his nose in a jaunty manner, that was a good sign, too.

But did we have any of that today? No.

He was pretty upset about it, Lockwood had said.

"Nice to see you," I said. "It's been a while."

"Hasn't it?" said George.

"Funnily enough, we were just saying how nice it would be to see *you*, Luce," Lockwood said, clapping George on the shoulder. "Weren't we, George?"

"Yes," said George. "We were."

"Yes, and Holly was looking forward to hearing all about your freelance work," Lockwood went on. "Who you've been working with, how you got along with them. You even did something with the Rotwell group, didn't you, Luce? I hope you'll tell us about it later."

With that he did a kind of wave of the arm that led my gaze to Holly.

And there she was. Charming Holly, as pretty and perfect as ever. *She* hadn't changed much during these last few months; she hadn't suddenly become saggy or bedraggled or noticeably flawed or anything. In fact, because of the importance of the meeting, she'd dolled herself up even more than usual. She wore the kind of dress you need to be poured into; the sort I would have ripped as soon as I tried wriggling it over my shoulders. It was a dress that would have gotten stuck halfway down my midriff, with my arms trapped and my head covered, and left me bouncing blindly off the walls for hours, half naked, trying to struggle free. *That* sort of dress. For completists, who want the details, it was blue.

Unlike with George and Lockwood, where the four months seemed to have lasted a lifetime, it didn't feel as if I'd been away from Holly very long at all. Partly this was because I saw her photos in the papers so much. Also because throughout the winter there'd been a sort of Holly-shaped hole in my brain, into which I used to throw dark thoughts. I probably spent too much time there, like a moody Inuk fishing at an ice hole, sitting on the edge, staring in.

"Hello, Holly," I said. "How's it going?"

"It's going *so* well, Lucy. It's lovely to see you again."

"Yeah. You, too. You look good."

"So do you. Freelancing obviously suits you. I'd love to hear all about how you've been getting on. I've heard great things. I think you're doing *so* well."

Once upon a time it would have annoyed me, the record number of fibs crammed into that single scrap of dialogue. I was sure Holly had about the same amount of interest in my freelance work as she had in my choice of toothpaste (less, actually—given the way her perfect teeth gleamed so brightly every time she smiled). And everything else was a lie, too, since I clearly *didn't* look good at all. As always happens when I'm running for a meeting, I only started properly sweating once I'd arrived and was with others. Right now I felt hot, flushed, and disordered, both inside and out.

But, to be honest, it wasn't my place to get cross with Holly anymore, so I decided to take her niceties at face value.

"Great," I said. "Thanks. I wish I'd gotten more dolled up, though. I didn't think to wear a dress."

"You could try wearing that one," George said, tapping the pillar, where the gory nightgown worn by the Cumberland Place heiress on the night of her brutal murder dangled on its metal frame.

Lockwood laughed. Holly laughed. Taking my cue, I laughed,

too. George didn't utter so much as a titter. I searched his face for clues. Nothing.

Our laughter ended rather raggedly. We stood in silence. "You'd think someone would hurry up and see us," Lockwood said.

"So there's no word yet on what Ms. Fittes wants?" I asked after a pause.

"Not yet."

"Have you done any work for her before?"

"Well, we're not really working *for* her now," Lockwood explained. "As I said, it's more she's looking out for us, sending occasional jobs our way."

"Right."

"How much are you charging?" George asked suddenly. "With this freelance lark?" He was staring blankly down the hall between the columns.

"Me?" I hesitated, remembering that I still hadn't sent my invoice to Farnaby for the last job. If I didn't, I wouldn't get paid. "Does it matter?"

"No. Except I'm not sure I could survive on my own with what Lockwood gives me, so I guess you've had to raise your fees."

"A bit, I guess. I do okay."

"So what do you charge?"

I opened my mouth, and closed it. I could see Lockwood frowning; it was hard to know what to say. Fortunately, George's line of questioning was interrupted that moment by an attendant who reported that Penelope Fittes was ready to receive us.

Two great psychic detection agencies dominated the war against the Problem. If the Rotwell Agency was the brashest and most innovative, the Fittes Agency was the biggest, oldest, and most prestigious. Its chairperson, Penelope Fittes, wielded great influence; even so, she was seldom seen—following an attempt on her life the previous autumn, she had become reclusive and rarely left Fittes House. Industrialists and public figures sought audiences with her; to ordinary people she was less an actual living woman than a name, a symbol, a climate of opinion. To be summoned to her presence was an important accolade.

Her private apartment was on the top floor of the building, but to meet us she had descended to a reception room that was just a short flight of stairs up from the lobby. It was a room of brown and gold. At one end, a large desk overlooking the Strand gave it the feel of a study; the rest was filled with pleasant chairs and sofas, and ornate, rather old-fashioned furniture. There were photographs on the walls and tables, and displays of antique rapiers; the air smelled of sunlight, polish, and expensive furnishings. And of coffee—a pot sat on a central table, with cups arranged around it. Penelope Fittes herself was waiting there; and, with her, as crumpled and hangdog as ever, Inspector Montagu Barnes of DEPRAC, the Department of Psychic Research and Control.

Ms. Fittes greeted us gravely, shaking our hands and indicating our chairs. As always (I had met her on two previous occasions), she was plush and well upholstered, a perfect match for the studied elegance of the room. A strikingly attractive woman, with long dark hair as lushly textured as her dark-mauve velvet dress, she had the kind of beauty that was unsettling because it was so out of the ordinary. It paid no lip service to the commonplace: her skin was lovely, the curves of her cheekbones exquisitely well-defined; her big black eyes were both beguiling and formidable.

She and Lockwood exchanged the usual round of pleasantries. Then she bestowed a smile upon each of us. "Thank you for coming in today," she said. "Mr. Barnes and I have another meeting shortly, so I will get straight to the matter. As I mentioned on the phone, Anthony, I have a juicy little case that Lockwood and Company may be able to attend to on my behalf. DEPRAC has alerted me to it, and I think it is perfect for you."

Lockwood nodded. "Thank you, ma'am. We'd be honored."

I glanced at him; he was all smiles and keen attention. Ordinarily, Lockwood let no one call him by his first name. His dead parents had done so; they, and no one else. But Penelope Fittes, stretched back all languorous and catlike in her chair, had used it, and Lockwood hadn't blinked an eye.

"Solomon Guppy," she said. "Have any of you heard of him?"

We looked at one another. The name rang a faint bell.

"He was a killer, wasn't he?" Lockwood said slowly. "Thirty years back? Wasn't he hanged?"

Ms. Fittes's lips parted in delight. "A killer, yes, and, yes, he *was* hanged. One of the last in England to pay that penalty before the Ghost Prevention Laws put a stop to capital punishment. It's said they held back the passing of the laws for a month just so they could see him twitch and dangle. Because he wasn't only a killer, but a *cannibal*, too."

"Ick," I said.

Lockwood clicked his fingers. "Yes, *that's* right. . . . He ate a neighbor, didn't he? Or was it two?"

"Can you enlighten us about that, Mr. Barnes?" The lady nodded at the inspector. With his weatherworn raincoat, battered face, and graying shoe-brush mustache, he looked even more out of place in the elegant surroundings than I did.

"Just one, as far as is known," Barnes said. "It's thought he invited the victim over for tea one afternoon. The fellow came around, bringing a fruitcake with him. They found the cake on the sideboard a week later, still in its wrapper. It was the only thing that hadn't been eaten."

George shook his head. "That's just wrong. Wrong on so many different levels."

Penelope Fittes laughed lightly. "Yes, little did the neighbor know he *was* the tea. Tea *and* dinner, as it happened, for several days afterward."

"I remember the case well," Barnes said, "though I was just an apprentice on the force at the time. Two of the arresting officers took early retirement after the trial, as a result of what they found when they broke in. Many of the worst details were never disclosed. Anyway, in his confession, Solomon Guppy explained that he'd used a number of recipes—roasted dishes, fricassees, curries, even salads. He was quite experimental."

"Crackers," I said.

"I'm not sure about those, but he might have tried them."

"No, I mean he *was* crackers. He was clearly bonkers. Barking mad."

"Certainly. Mad *and* bad," Ms. Fittes said. "It took six policemen to subdue him when he was finally arrested, owing to his size and ferocity. But arrested he was, and hanged and cremated, and salt was strewn over the prison yard where the ashes were interred. In other words, all precautions were taken. But now it seems that his spirit—or that of his victim—has somehow returned to the scene of the crime." She sat back and engineered one elegant leg over the other. "Mr. Barnes?"

The inspector nodded. "It is a small suburban house in Ealing, west London. The street is called 'The Leas.' Guppy's place was number seven. It's been left empty since the crime, of course, but people live nearby. It's been quiet up till now, but recently we've had reports of certain disturbances in the vicinity, a terror spreading through the street. Sensitives have traced it back to number seven."

"The phenomena are very subtle," Ms. Fittes added, "No apparitions. Mostly—by all accounts—just *sounds*."

She glanced across at me with her dark and serious eyes. From the tone of her voice, you'd have thought Listening was a trivial psychic Talent. But the flash of her gaze implied it was the most important thing in the world.

Her grandmother had been supreme at it. You only had to read Marissa Fittes's *Memoirs* to know that. Long ago she had spoken with ghosts, and they'd answered her. Clearly Penelope Fittes knew I had a reputation, too.

"What kinds of sounds?" Lockwood asked.

"Sounds to do with the previous occupant of the house," Barnes said.

"Mr. Barnes asked me to investigate," Penelope Fittes said, "and I agreed. However, my agency has many challenges left over from the winter, and most of my best teams are still busy. It struck me that I knew another organization with the necessary skills to take this on." She smiled. "What do you think? If you manage it—well, I'm sure I'll have other cases to pass your way."

"We'll be glad to do it," Lockwood said.

"I'm pleased to hear that, Anthony. Yours is a company that I much admire, and I believe we can do great things together in future. I think of this as a joint venture between us, and I will send a representative of the Fittes Agency to accompany you."

"It's the Source that we're after," Barnes said. "That goes without saying. The place was cleaned out very thoroughly back when it all happened, but they must have missed something. We want to know what."

"If that's all," Ms. Fittes said, "I'll introduce you to my secretary, to make arrangements. The house is empty; you can visit tonight, if you'd like."

She stood, a languid flowing movement. That was our cue; we also stood, as one.

While farewells were being said, I waited by a side table. Photographs of past agents studded its surface like gravestones. There were famous operatives, and famous teams posing below a unicorn banner in some swanky hall. The agents themselves were young, smiling confidently in pressed gray jackets. Adult supervisors stood alongside, hemming them in. In some an old, sharp-faced woman in black, hair scraped sternly up, was also present: Marissa Fittes, the founder of the agency.

But one of the photos was different, and it caught my eye. Black and white and faded, it showed a slight, dark-haired woman sitting in a high-backed chair. The room was filled with shadows. She was looking away from the camera, off toward the light. An air of melancholy hung about her; she seemed both thin and ill.

"That was my mother, who died young."

I turned with a start. The others were filing out, but Penelope Fittes was at my shoulder, smiling. Strong perfume garlanded her like flowers.

"I'm sorry to hear that," I said.

"Oh, please don't be. I barely remember her. It was Grandmama Marissa who ran the household, who built the business, who taught me everything." She nodded at the woman in the black dress. "Dear Grandmama made me what I am. Everything you see around you is hers." She touched my arm. "You know I asked for you specifically, Lucy."

I blinked. "No, I didn't know that, Ms. Fittes."

"Yes. When I first mentioned this case to Anthony, he told me you were no longer working with him. That disappointed me, for— between you and me, Lucy—it was because of you and Anthony that I became interested in Lockwood and Company." Ms. Fittes laughed prettily, her black eyes sparkling. "He is a fine agent, but I have long been an admirer of yours, too. I told him that if he wanted the commission, he would have to get you back."

"Oh. Did you? It was your idea? That's . . . very kind of you."

"He said he would try. I'm so glad he did, Lucy. I'm so pleased you agreed to rejoin the agency."

"Well, as it happens I haven't actually—"

"See how you get on with this case," Penelope Fittes said. "I have every confidence in your abilities, but I believe that success will depend mainly on you. A skillful Listener will be essential at the Guppy house. Anthony knows that if it goes well, Lockwood and Company will greatly benefit. Now, you had better catch up with your friends." She waved me on; as I left the room, her scent spiraled around me like twisting arms.

Chapter 7

In some ways, what happened after that was just like the old days. We'd seen the client and had the briefing; next we'd prepare our equipment and research the case. If we were to visit Ealing that evening, there was no time to lose, so Lockwood set the wheels in motion as soon as we left Fittes House. Standing on the crowded sidewalk, he promptly divided forces; he and Holly would buy extra supplies of salt and iron, while George would scour the National Newspaper Archives to find out all he could about the Guppy murder. And I—

What would *I* do? Where did *I* fit in?

"We'll meet you at the Café Royale in Piccadilly Circus, Luce," Lockwood said. "We can all get a taxi from there. Four o'clock okay? That'll give you time to sort out your own stuff, won't it?"

"Sure," I said.

I was still thinking about what Penelope Fittes had said to me a moment before. That it had been *her* idea to involve me. At my apartment the previous day, Lockwood had somehow skirted around that particular detail. Unless I'd missed something, he'd very much made it seem as if the impulse had come from him.

"Great, then we look forward to seeing you later. Isn't it an excellent case? I'm glad you're with us on this one."

"Sure . . ." Obviously, it didn't *really* matter whose idea it had been to bring me along. And I didn't have any right to feel annoyed about it, either. I was the one who'd left Lockwood & Co., after all.

Business, that's all it was; just business. "Actually," I said, "there's just one thing. Four o'clock's too late—it won't give us enough daylight when we get to Ealing. Better to arrive well before dark, so we can get the lay of the land and plan the layout of our circles. It's best to take preliminary readings before sunset anyway. And it'll give us the chance to look in all the nooks and crannies that would be invisible to us after dark. For all those reasons, I'd suggest we meet at two." I smiled coolly at him. "Agreed?"

Lockwood nodded; if he was perhaps slightly taken aback, he hid it well. "I see what you're saying, but would that give George enough time—?"

"I think it's a very good point that Lucy makes," Holly Munro said, unexpectedly. "George?"

George made some minor adjustment to his glasses. "Getting gobbled by a big bloke has never been my idea of fun," he said, "even if said bloke *is* a ghost. I'm all for taking extra care. Yes, I'll be finished at the Archives by two. Let's go with that and get there early."

Lockwood's expression had become one of studious unconcern.

"You're all probably right. Fine. Two o'clock it is, Lucy. We'll see you there."

"Do you want anything from Mullet's supply store?" Holly Munro asked me.

"No, it's okay, thanks," I said. "I've got everything I need. I'll see you later."

I turned before they did and made off into the crowd. I was going against the flow, having to force my way a little, but that suited my mood just then. When I was sure I was out of sight, I took a side road down to the Thames Embankment, where a lot of the cheaper merchants plied their trade under the brick arches of Hungerford Bridge. It had been a fib, what I'd said just then. I was almost out of supplies.

I didn't feel bad about the fib, though. I'd been lied to as well.

The tide was low, and wet gravel glinted steeply at the base of the Embankment wall. Seagulls wheeled high above. The road was busy with traffic; I crossed over and walked upriver toward the bridge. Above my head, spotlighted billboards advertised the latest products of the giant Rotwell Agency. In one poster, their mascot, Roger, a roguish cartoon lion, gave a mighty thumbs-up while trampling a cartoon ghost. In another, Roger held some of the exciting new home defense equipment that had been dreamed up by the scientists of the Rotwell Institute and was now, thanks to their partners in the Sunrise Corporation, available to customers everywhere. In a third, he appeared with his paw draped over the bulky shoulder of Steve Rotwell, the agency's chairman, whose personal pledge— WE FIGHT TO MAKE SAFE YOUR NIGHT—was printed in a speech bubble emerging from his mouth. Steve Rotwell's teeth sparkled, his green eyes twinkled, his chin protruded like the prow of a gun-ship; he radiated more machismo than the cartoon lion. He was the epitome of reassurance in the age of the Problem and—thanks to all this advertising—the most popular figure in London.

I scowled and hurried past. I'd once seen Rotwell kill a man by sticking a sword straight through his chest. The ads didn't have quite the desired effect on me.

I visited the salt merchants, bought my supplies, and came out onto the Embankment again. Beyond the billboards, stone steps led down to the gravel, and here an unsavory figure crouched, a mud-stained burlap bag beside her. She was scraping dirt off a variety of pronged instruments that had been laid out on the Embankment wall. From the sun-blistered puffer jacket, straw hat, slime-caked boots, and the seabirds lying unconscious nearby, I recognized Flo Bones, a relic-girl of my acquaintance. Flo trawled the Thames shoreline for psychic jetsam washed up by the river, and sold it on the black market. She'd helped Lockwood & Co. on several occasions and was prickly, but decent enough, provided you stepped carefully and always breathed through your mouth.

As I approached, Flo was scooping gunk off a strange wide spatula-headed implement. She glanced up, saw me, and flicked a glob of muck over the wall.

"Well, look what the tide's brought in," she said.

"All right, Flo." By her standards, this had been a pleasant greet-ing. She hadn't flicked the muck at me, either, which was a first. "See you've been busy," I said. "Any joy?"

"Found lots of rubbish. Two drowned rats, a pig's head, and now you."

I grinned and sat on the wall beside her. "Sorry to hear that."

"Well, I was at a relic-man's meeting half the night. Only managed a few hours' work. Found me a couple of bones with faint auras, and a rusty whistle that carries some kind of psychic charge. That's all."

"Doesn't sound too bad. You'll sell them, then?"

Flo pushed her hat back and scratched at her hairline, the one clean part of her face. "Dunno. Got to raise my game these days. There's a lot of strong items on the market, and the best of 'em are selling well. They say there's a new collector in town, and the dealers are buying up everything decent." She glanced at me with her shrewd blue eyes. "Guess who was at the meeting last night, snaffled all the good stuff? Winkman."

"Julius Winkman?" He was a black marketeer whom Lockwood & Co. had helped put in prison the year before.

"No. *He's* still inside. It was his wife. Well, his son was there, too, but it's Adelaide who calls the shots. She bought up all sorts of weird and wonderful Sources at the show last night. A haunted painting, a bloodstained glove, a mummified head, a Roman helmet . . ." Flo spat over the wall. "Me, I thought half were fakes, but the kid vetted them and said they were kosher. Old Ma Winkman bought the lot. All going straight to this new collector. Anything good we find, we're to bring it to the next night-market too. I'll polish up the whistle, as best I can, but I'm not sure it'll cut it." She tapped her instrument on the wall. "So, where've you been hiding, Carlyle? Been ages. Barely been able to contain myself, not seeing you."

"I've been working."

"Not for Lockwood."

"No. . . ." I eyed the instrument. "What *is* that thing?"

"Slime flange."

"Oh . . . Yeah, I've been working for myself. But I've just been with Lockwood, as it happens. Going to do a job with him. Only a one-off. I'm not rejoining."

"No, well, of course you aren't." Flo picked up a sharper tool, thick with blue-black river clay. "That Holly Munro's still there, isn't she?"

I paused. "Actually, it wasn't because of Holly that I left."

She scraped muck off her prong. "Uh-huh."

"I had other reasons."

"Uh-huh."

"You don't believe me?"

"Can you hold this muck-prong a tick?" Flo said. "I'm getting dirt everywhere."

"Yeah. . . . Now I'm getting it all over *me.*"

"Just need to wipe my hands." She did so, on her puffer jacket. "There. That's that done. Well, been nice seeing you, Carlyle. I've got to go. There's a lukewarm kebab waiting for me in Wapping."

"Lovely . . . Flo," I said, as she gathered up her tools and shoved them in the belt beneath her coat, "this mummified head you mentioned. What was it like?"

"I dunno. Eyes, ears, nose, and mouth, the usual. Why?"

"Anything else? Just that I came into contact with one myself a couple of nights ago."

Flo gathered up her burlap sack. She leaned over the wall, surveying the line of mud that ran east along the north shore of the Thames. "'S'not high tide for another hour. . . . Think I'll go that way. The head? Hard to tell the details, what with all the cobwebs on it. Man's. Bit of a pointy black beard going on. I wasn't paying much attention. It was in a silver-glass case; and, like I say, it was already spoken for. They said there was a powerful Specter attached to it. Winkman bought it for a lot of cash, I'm sure."

I was frowning at her. "Do you know who brought it in?"

But with a wave and a waft of unwashed air, Flo Bones was gone. In moments she had skipped down the tidal steps and was crunching away from me along the Strand.

The Café Royale showed its broad glass front on the western side of Piccadilly Circus, where double rows of coffee-colored tables stretched beneath its brown-and-white striped awnings. An arc of brick-lined channels, cut into the sidewalk and filled with running water, gave it protection from restless spirits during the night; toward dusk, lavender fires would be lit beside the doors. It was a popular spot even after dark; in early afternoon on this late winter day, the place was almost full, the windows wet and steamy. When I arrived, weighed down with equipment bags and a ghost-jar in my backpack, I found Holly Munro waiting at a table just inside the door. She was reading a copy of the *Times*.

"Have you heard the latest?" she said, as I sank gratefully into the seat opposite. "Says here there are street kids following adults around in London. Late afternoons, on cloudy sorts of days, you know. They make money by alerting the grown-ups to ghosts. They tell them they're being followed, that something in a white sheet is trailing after them, or that there's a Tom O'Shadows dancing at their heels. The kids carry iron railings stolen from outside houses. Cash is handed over, then they wave the sticks around and send the 'ghosts' packing. It's a complete scam, but they put on a real show. Hair-raising to watch, apparently, and impossible for the adults to disprove."

I shrugged off my coat. It was warm in the café, and I was already hot. "Those kids have to make a living somehow. There's a lot of poverty nowadays. We can't all be agents, can we?"

"I know. We *are* lucky, aren't we, Lucy? I'll order some tea. The boys won't be long. Lockwood's fetching the bags from Portland Row, and George will be here soon."

She busied herself making eyes at the waiters, and I sat back and considered her. It was her skin that always got to me. It was darkly buttery, with not a pimple to be seen. And her features, too—everything was in the right place. There'd been a time when her easy perfection drove me mad, and I knew that in my disheveled, wildly imperfect way, I'd done the same to her. To be fair, since meeting her that morning she'd treated me with careful attention and respect; but since the same could also be said of a gloved scientist holding a blob of plague bacillus on a glass slide, I didn't read too much into it.

"How are you finding it, going solo?" she asked once the tea was ordered.

"It's all right," I said. "I get to pick my hours and jobs. I work with many different agencies. I make a bit of money."

"You're so brave," she said. "To leave and strike out on your own. It's very risky."

"Well, it has its compensations. I've learned a lot about my Talents and gotten better at managing other people, even the irritating ones."

She gave a laugh. Oh, joy—it was the special tinkling one that set my teeth on edge.

"Someone at Portland Row really missed you, you know," she said.

I kept my voice light. "Well, I missed everyone, too, of course. . . . Er, who *was* that?"

"Who missed you most particularly?" Her laugh again; her big dark eyes smiled at me sidelong. "Can't you guess?"

It was hot in that café. I did something with the sleeves of my sweater. "No."

"Me."

"Oh. What—? *Did* you?"

"I know we had our issues, Lucy, but it's been odd being the only girl. Lockwood and George are lovely, of course, but they're both off in their own worlds. George with his experiments, and Lockwood . . ." Her brow formed shapely furrows. "He's so restless and remote. He never sits still long enough for me to reach him. I was going to ask you about that, whether you found . . . Oh good, and here are the boys, too."

In a few minutes we were all crammed in together, our bags wedged between us and the steamed-up window. I was bunched close to George, who acknowledged me with the barest nod. Lockwood radiated excitement. His face glowed in anticipation of the night to come. "The team's all here," he said. "Excellent! Right, I've arranged a taxi ride to Ealing in half an hour. The Fittes representative will meet us at the house. He'll have the keys."

George frowned. "I don't like this representative coming along. We're Lockwood and Co.! We don't have supervisors."

"It's to be more an observer than anything," Lockwood said. "Fittes is taking our measure. If she likes what she sees, we'll get more commissions. I think it's okay."

"Okay for Lucy, maybe. She's a sword for hire." George's face was blank behind his glasses. "But we should be independent, surely."

"We are," Lockwood said briskly. "Anyway, time's marching on. George—you've been to the Archives. Did you get all the grisly details about number seven, The Leas?"

"Up to a point." George was pulling a disordered manila file from his bag. "This being a modern case, there was plenty about it in the papers, but I don't have *all* the details. Like Barnes said, it seems they had to suppress a fair amount; the facts were just too nasty. But don't worry, I've found more than enough grimness for us to enjoy." He peered around for a waiter. "Have we ordered yet? I'm famished here."

"Got a pot of tea coming," Holly said. "And cakes. Given the subject of our discussion, I thought savories should wait."

"Mmm." George adjusted his spectacles and opened the file in front of him. "You may be right, though personally I could murder a sausage roll. Okay, the trial of the Ealing Cannibal dates back thirty years. The accused, as we know, was a man named Solomon Guppy, who lived alone in a house in an ordinary street. He was fifty-two years old, and had once earned a living as an electronics engineer. Having lost his job some years before, he now repaired clocks and radios; it was a mail-order business. The items were sent to him by post; he worked at home and rarely, except for trips to the shops on Ealing High Street, left the house. When the police broke in, the place was full of pieces of machinery lying open, with their wires and cogs exposed." George looked up and grinned at us. "Turned out these weren't the *only* internal parts he was interested in."

Holly made a slight noise in her throat. "*George* . . ."

"Sorry, sorry." He leafed unconcernedly through the file. "This is the pitch-black story of a giant maniac cannibal. Somebody's got to supply the jokes."

Lockwood tapped his fingers on the table. "Hold it there. When you say 'giant,' what does that mean? Penelope Fittes said it took six policemen to subdue Guppy when they came to arrest him. So he was obviously big and strong."

George nodded. "Yep. Very big, very strong, and very tall. Six-foot-six in his socks, and bulky. They reckon he weighed three hundred and fifty pounds, and though he had a huge belly, a lot of it was muscle, too. All the sources emphasize what an unnerving figure he was. He barely spoke during the trial, and spent his time glaring around the courtroom from under a mane of unkempt hair. He'd pick someone and fix his eyes on them like he was preparing them for supper. More than one lady felt obliged to leave the room. When they took him to be hung, they had double the usual number of guards escorting him, and the blokes doing it were so frightened, they all got double pay."

"Doesn't sound likely to me," Lockwood said. "All the prison guards I've met have been pretty tough customers. Well, let's see the pictures of this charmer."

George drew out a single glossy piece of paper. "I actually only have one. Oddly, the police never released their line-up shots of Guppy; they kept them secret 'for the public good,' whatever *that* means. But this was snapped by a freelance photographer as Guppy was being led into the courthouse on the day of sentencing. It's not great quality, but it gives you an idea."

He swiveled the photo around on the table. Lockwood, Holly, and I bent close. It was a black-and-white shot, photocopied and enlarged from the original. As George had said, it wasn't good at all—the image was both blurry and grainy. You could see a police officer in the foreground, and another at the back, half out of view. And in between them was a vast, bulky shape, slope-shouldered and indistinct of feature. One great arm extended awkwardly; you could tell it was handcuffed to the officer in front. The other, presumably also cuffed, was out of sight behind. The head was bowed, also awkwardly; maybe it had just ducked out of the police van, but the impression was of a swollen, shambling thing, horribly out of proportion with the men on either side. Most of the face was in shadow. A few dark smears suggested a heavy brow, a wide-lipped mouth. For some reason, I was glad the picture showed no better detail.

We all regarded it. "Yes . . ." Lockwood said at last. "That gives us an idea."

"He *was* a big lad, wasn't he?" I said.

"They had to build a special gallows," George said. "One strong enough to take his weight. And here's another thing. On the morning of the execution, a priest was present. He was officiating in case the condemned had a last confession. Well, when Guppy stood on the platform, just before the trapdoor opened, he beckoned the priest over and whispered something to him. Know what happened?

Whatever he said was so terrifying, so horrible, the priest simply fainted clean away. And they say Guppy was smiling as the hangman pulled the lever."

No one at our table spoke. "Could do with a stupid joke now," I said. "Got any more, George?"

"Not at the moment. I'll save them for when we're creeping around Guppy's house, trying to avoid his ghost."

Lockwood snorted. "There's a fair number of urban legends getting mixed up with your facts today, George. No one's *that* scary, not even a giant cannibal. We all need to relax."

And obviously he was right about this. We all sat back, giving each other broad, reassuring smiles. It was at that point that our tea and cakes arrived, delivered by a waitress with lavender garlands in her hair.

"Right, George," Lockwood said, when we were fortified. "We don't have long before the taxi. Tell us about what happened at the house. What do you know?"

"Found out a little bit about the victim," George said. "Fellow called Mr. Dunn, lived a few doors up the street. Single fellow, amiable, socially conscious. He used to call on housebound neighbors—the elderly and infirm—do odd jobs for them, help with the shopping. Seems he noticed that Mr. Guppy at number seven seldom went out, and made it his business to stop in on him every once in a while. On the night in question, someone saw him heading over with the famous cake. After that, he wasn't seen for days. When he was finally reported missing, the police went over. Guppy answered the door, told them that Dunn had indeed visited, but had left for another appointment. He didn't know what his appointment was, or with whom. It was quite early, but Guppy was already up and making breakfast; the cops could smell bacon cooking in the kitchen."

"Oh, ick," I said. Holly Munro wrinkled her nose.

"Yeah," George said. "Anyhow, the police went away, but they returned a few days later, following reports of smoke coming from Guppy's house. His chimney was blocked; he'd been trying to burn something in the fireplace. That something turned out to be Dunn's clothes. Most of the other things they found weren't made public at the trial."

Holly brushed a length of hair behind her ear. "How utterly horrid. Do we know where the murder actually took place?"

George pulled out a pale blue sheet of paper, unfolded it, and set it before us. It showed the layout of the house, which had two main floors, plus a basement. To the side was a garage. At the front and back were yards or gardens. The identity of each room was labeled neatly in red pencil.

"No one's sure," he said. "There was evidence of the crime in most of the rooms."

I looked at him. "'Evidence of the crime'? Meaning . . ."

"Bits of Mr. Dunn."

"Right. I thought you meant that. Just wanted to check."

"The good news is that it's a small enough place," Lockwood said. "With the four of us, it should be easy to keep tabs on it tonight. Just a thought, though. We don't actually know which spirit is informing the house, do we? Isn't it more likely to be Dunn's ghost, rather than Guppy's? He's the one who died there."

"Could be," George said. "Until we find the Source, we won't know."

"I *hope* it's Dunn," Holly said, and I nodded. It's not often I actively *want* to meet the angry ghost of a murder victim, but after seeing the photograph in George's file, I really didn't want to meet the owner of that blurry shape, even in death. The others were nodding, too.

Lockwood took out his wallet and put some money on the table. "Time to find out," he said.

Chapter 8

Despite our best intentions, the afternoon was far advanced by the time we arrived at the house of the Ealing Cannibal. We'd forgotten that everyone liked to get out of central London well before curfew; the traffic on the arterial roads was sluggish, and repair work at the Chiswick roundabout delayed us even more. As the cab moved slowly through the suburban streets of Ealing, the last commuters were already in force on the sidewalks, hurrying home beneath the flickering ghost-lights. The sun had swung low, and a layer of black clouds lay over us like a broken slab of chocolate, with streaks of blue-and-yellow sky showing through the cracks. The air held the threat of rain.

Whether or not our driver knew the reputation of The Leas, he knew the business we were in and didn't care to get too close to our final destination. He dropped us, and our swords, workbags, and lengths of chain, at the far end of the street, and we walked the final hundred yards to the house where horrors stirred.

It's a common misconception that places that have suffered psychic trauma must *look* sinister, too, with gaping windows, creaking doors, and walls twisted subtly out of shape. As with people, so with houses—a smiling, innocuous exterior can conceal the blackest heart, and number 7, The Leas, didn't look like anything much at all.

It stood halfway along the east side of a crescent of modest detached buildings, each with its own garage, each with its own neat scrap of lawn beside its thin concrete drive. They were fairly modern homes, the windows broad and generous, the roofs made of pleasant reddish tiles. The front doors were paneled with glass and protected by simple, flat-topped porches. It was neither a poor district, nor a rich one. Dark laurel hedges separated the plots, and cypress trees rose up in the backyards, black and sharp as knives.

Number 7 looked in no worse repair than any of the other houses; in fact, in many ways, it seemed in better shape. The nearby buildings were noticeably shabby, with cars rusting under tarps on weedy drives; small signs, perhaps, that what had happened here so long before still worked its poison on the neighborhood. But the house once inhabited by Mr. Solomon Guppy was white and painted; its lawn mowed, its hedges trimmed. The local council, conscious of civic pride, had not allowed it to fall into disrepair.

The street was quiet; the only signs of life were small ones: lights coming on in downstairs windows, curtains being drawn. We hadn't set eyes on anyone until, nearing number 7, a thin figure detached itself from the shadows of the hedge. Arms folded, it waited gloomily as we drew near.

George let out a groan. "Penelope Fittes must have *hundreds* of supervisors. Why did she have to choose *him?*"

The young man wore the silver-gray jacket of the Fittes Agency and had an ornately handled rapier hanging at his belt. His narrow, freckled face was twisted in an expression of sour disapproval, but we'd had enough experience with Quill Kipps to know that this meant little. He was quite possibly in a good mood.

"Looking on the bright side," Lockwood whispered, "Kipps has worked with us before. He already knows we won't listen to a word he says. That's going to save a lot of time. Nice to see you, Quill!" he called. "How's tricks?"

"Before you say anything," Kipps said, "I didn't *ask* to be given this job. I dislike the idea just as much as you do. Let's just be clear about that."

Lockwood grinned. "I'm sure it's a match made in heaven."

"Yeah," Kipps said feelingly. "I'm sure."

Once one of Lockwood & Co.'s bitterest rivals, Quill Kipps had reached his early twenties, and thus seen his psychic Talents leach away. No longer able to detect ghosts effectively, he had consequently been put in charge of others who could. Personal losses had since mellowed him, and he had fought alongside us in the recent past. Despite being as congenial as a mustard sandwich, he was, we knew, both tough and bloody-minded. As Lockwood had said, we could have had a worse companion.

George was regarding him skeptically. "So you're here to spy on us, I take it?"

Kipps shrugged. "I'm an observer. It's company policy to supply one when there's a joint venture with other agencies. Also, Ms. Fittes has asked me to provide you with any assistance you might require. Not that I'll be much use," he added, "since, psychically speaking, I'm practically deaf and blind. The most warning I get of something coming nowadays is a sort of squeezing sensation in my stomach, and as often as not that's gas."

"Remind me to station you in a different room than me," Lockwood said. "Seriously, we're glad to have your help. So: number seven. Have you been inside?"

Kipps looked over at the neat, blank house. The descending sun had reached it; the front windows sparkled with reflected light. "On my own? You must be joking. This is a team effort. Hopefully, one of you will get ghost-touched instead of me." He lifted his hand; a house key hung dangling from a leather fob. "But I *do* have what you need."

Lockwood glanced toward the western sky. "And we've still got a bit of time before things get tasty. Let's go."

We took our bags and walked in silence up the drive. Somewhere in the hedge, a blackbird was singing its lovely, piercing song. There was a fresh smell on the air that afternoon, the faint warmth of coming spring. The house waited at the end of the drive.

We reached the porch without incident; here Lockwood insisted on rigging up a small circle with a lantern inside, as an outer line of defense. With luck, the lantern would remain burning all night, unaffected by whatever happened in the building. It was a place to rendezvous if anything went wrong.

While this was being done, I stepped onto the grass and peered through the big front window. Inside was a bare room, bisected by yellow sunlight. The walls had brown-striped paper on them; there was a yellowish carpet, but no furniture. You could see faint out-lines where pictures had hung; on one wall was an old-fashioned fireplace, swept clean.

George was at my shoulder. "Looks like the living room," I said.

He nodded cheerily. "Yeah. It's where they found the victim's feet. In a fruit bowl on the coffee table, apparently."

"Lovely." I put my fingers on the surface of the glass. Some-times, even outside, even with the sun still in the sky, you get stuff. I listened. Anything? No. Only the blackbird singing. The house was just a house.

Given that the place had been abandoned for so many years, the key turned with surprising, almost ominous ease. Lockwood was the first to enter, then the others filed in slowly. I stayed behind to tend to my backpack. Holly knew about the existence of the skull, but Kipps didn't. I wanted a quiet word with it.

I flicked the valve at the top of the jar. "Heads up, skull, we're here. I'm bringing you inside."

"For what? Get your living *friends to help you. I'm having none of it."*

I rolled my eyes; the ghost had been sulking all day, ever since I'd come back from my meeting at Fittes House. His outrage at my agreement with Lockwood knew no bounds. I hefted the backpack in my arms. "Just tell me if you sense anything."

"No. Why am I always stuck in this bag? I'm sick of it. Let me out."

"I can't right now. If I get a chance, I will."

"You're embarrassed about me, that's what it is."

"Embarrassed? About an evil, moldy skull?" I glared into the jar; sure enough, the face in the glass wore a hurt and haughty look.

"Oh, for heaven's sake. You're a Type Three ghost," I said, "and that makes you rare. If it got out that I could talk to you, neither of us would hear the end of it. I don't want Kipps to know. Keep watch, and I'll check in with you later. We're going in, so stop moaning."

"What kind of way is that to talk to a valued partner? I ought to—" The voice broke off; I had stepped through into the quiet house. *"Ooh . . ."*

I stared down at the ghost. The face had frozen the moment it crossed the threshold. A single translucent muscle in its cheek twitched. Its eyes were saucers of dismay.

"Ooh, what?"

The eyes blinked twice; the face was animated once again. It glared at me. *"Nothing. For a moment, I thought I felt . . . But hey, I was wrong, as us evil, moldy skulls so often are. Forget about it."*

The tone of the voice was unconvincing. I would have questioned the ghost further, but I saw Kipps coming back along the hall. I closed the backpack and swung it over my shoulder. Then I took a deep breath, and absorbed my first impressions of the house.

I was in a narrow hallway, with a staircase running up its left-hand side. As in the living room, the carpet was a worn and faded yellow color, the walls decorated with an old-fashioned and revolting pattern of cream-and-brown squares. At the end of the hall, a door of plate-glass panels opened onto the kitchen, where Lockwood and Holly were laying out a second circle of iron chains. There were two other doors; one which (as I knew from George's floor plans) led to the basement, and one to the living room. The place had a smell of dust and dampness, but nothing worse. Whatever the skull may have noticed, my inner senses detected nothing.

"Grim old hall," I said. George was going past with a heavy bag.

"Yeah. They found the thigh bones here, propped in an umbrella stand. We're getting everything set up. Feel like helping out, or is that not in your freelance contract?"

I opened my mouth to answer, then snapped it shut. It was a fair point. I went to get my bags, and set to work.

It had to be said, we did everything by the book. Within minutes of our arrival, all our defenses were in position. We had an iron circle in the kitchen, and another on the landing, both amply supplied with salt and iron. We had candles burning in every room, and snuff-lights on the stairs. We did it efficiently and well. Kipps didn't gripe too much, and Holly Munro seemed more comfortable with fieldwork than when last I'd seen her. For my part, I discovered that working alongside the others was easier than talking with them, and I soon fell back into the old routines. Lockwood and I didn't say a great deal. That was fine. He wanted me for my Talent, not my conversation.

When all was ready, and with the daylight shrinking, we made our separate ways around the building, quietly taking readings and letting the atmosphere of the house sink in. The one exception was Kipps, who sat cross-legged in the kitchen, drinking hot chocolate and reading a newspaper. He didn't have sufficient Talents to do any psychic exploration.

The first thing to be said is that the Guppy house was small. The ground floor had four rooms—the hall and living room, the dining room and kitchen—while upstairs there was a long, thin landing, with two bedrooms at opposite ends and a bathroom in between. Under the stairs, a steep flight of brick steps led down to a concrete-floored basement. The attic, unfinished, contained nothing. The house was of relatively modern construction, with paper-thin walls and double-glazed windows. All of the furniture had been taken away, the walls stripped of decoration. It held no obvious secrets, and psychically was very quiet. George popped up in every room like a sinister real estate agent, giving macabre tidbits of information about what body parts had been found there, but even with such details, the place was curiously blank.

Despite the history of the place, it was hard not to feel confident as we imposed ourselves upon it. There were five of us, fully armed, in a building of nine rooms. We kept bumping into each other as we went up and down the stairs. None of us was ever more than a few seconds' scamper from anyone else, or from one of the two circles. It was all fairly reassuring.

But the daylight had not yet left us.

The kitchen interested me. It seemed a likely focus for super-natural energies, given what had happened there. I stood in it for a long while, listening, looking at the old-style décor, at the stained Formica countertops with their mustard-colored cabinets below. A metal sink, dark and stained, sat on narrow legs beneath the wide window. The walls were papered with brown-and-orange flowers, the floor laid with brown linoleum. You could see where it had been pried up, when investigators looked for evidence long ago. A pantry closet in one corner had been emptied, its shelves stained with rings from cans and jars.

Three doors led out: to the hall, to the garden, and to the dining room, a small square space connected only to the kitchen.

I concentrated. So many little sounds. Kipps rustling his news-paper; Holly going down into the basement; Lockwood moving around upstairs. And I also sensed other, furtive noises, not tied to anything physical, time-locked, out of place.

"You hear that?" I asked.

Kipps was in the iron circle, sitting back against a sack of salt. He shook his head.

That was the thing about Listening. So often, even when in the company of others, you were on your own. I was used to that. I was a solo operator now. I closed my eyes and focused on the sounds that shouldn't have been there.

"See you're back again," Kipps said suddenly. "Couldn't keep away."

I opened my eyes and glared at him. "I'm not 'back,' as you call it. I'm just helping Lockwood out today."

"And the difference is . . . ?"

"She's getting paid more." A shadow at the hall door. George looked in. "If you've finished your survey, Lockwood wants us to meet in the living room."

"Okay," I said. George disappeared; I could hear him in the hall, calling for Holly. "Yes, I'm freelance now," I went on. "Thing is, Kipps, I prefer the freedom it gives me—working wherever I want, *with* whomever I want. Not being tied down. It's a better life somehow—nobler, simpler. . . ." I gave him a noble, simple smile.

"Is that what it is?" Kipps shrugged. "I thought you'd basically just hoofed it when Holly Munro showed up. Still, what do I know? Think this circle's secure enough? Do we need an extra chain?"

"Yes, it is, and no, we don't. I'm going to the living room." I made for the door. I'd given up on the survey: it was too early, and I suddenly wasn't in the mood.

Outside the big front window the light was almost gone; the laurel hedge by the street was a jet-black bar, a formless mass rearing up to surround us. The brown stripes in the wallpaper had deepened, too. In the flickering light of our candles, they seemed solid, as if we were standing inside a cage. Lockwood and George were there, speaking in soft undertones. They nodded at Kipps and me as we came in.

"Good," Lockwood said. "Time to get everyone's thoughts. Where's Holly?"

"Down in the basement, I think," I said.

"I called for her loud enough," George said. He went out.

"How are *you* doing, Kipps?" Lockwood asked. "Can't be easy for you, being here."

Quill Kipps shrugged his bony shoulders. "I'll just stick close to the chains. It's not normally what a supervisor has to put up with, but I'm used to it. I don't think Penelope Fittes likes me much; ever since we teamed up on that Aickmere's job, I've been given low-quality assignments, like the Rotherhithe sewage works, the Dagenham slaughterhouse case, and now hanging out with you."

"I thought you got a promotion after Aickmere's," Lockwood said.

"They *had* to give me that, because it was such a public success, but they don't trust me now. I showed a little too much independence. Anyway, what do you care?"

The door opened; Holly and George came in. "Sorry," Holly said. "Have you been calling?"

"It's not a problem." Lockwood produced a packet of biscuits; he handed them around. "Well, we've done our first tour. What are your thoughts?"

To my surprise, Holly had taken a biscuit. "A horrible place."

I nodded. "It's as we expected. No room is entirely free of psychic repercussions. Very faint so far, but everything makes me feel queasy."

"That could be the decor as much as anything," Lockwood said. "It's like all the brown paint in London's been used up here. Any sounds yet, Lucy? That's what it's famous for."

"Stirrings, but nothing clear. Wait till it gets dark, then I'll tell you."

"Meantime, I took temp readings throughout," George said. "The coldest places are the basement—particularly one spot near the bottom of the stairs—and the kitchen. Again, that's what you'd expect—those rooms are where forensics found most of the bloodstains, plus a few tasty scraps our friend Guppy didn't get around to sampling."

"Don't," Holly said.

"Otherwise," George went on, "no spectral stuff yet. I thought I saw a skeleton in the kitchen, but it turned out to be Kipps."

Kipps rolled his eyes. "Oh, stop it, George. Has anyone got any bandages? I've just split my sides laughing."

"Sorry, are observers *allowed* to talk?" George said. "Don't you have to save it for when you go scurrying back to Fittes?"

"Okay, okay," Lockwood said. "That's enough of that. Kipps?"

"It's a bad place. But we knew that already."

"What about you, Holly? Anything?"

She looked uncomfortable. "I keep *thinking* I'm being watched. Like there's something behind me."

"I get that feeling, too," I said. "When's it worst for you?"

"I don't like having my back to the center of the room. Any room."

"Well, the death-glow's in the basement," Lockwood said. "That's where the killing happened. Guppy must have lured the guy downstairs. Some of us should probably concentrate our efforts there. I'm thinking that we need to station ourselves in several rooms, and rotate the watch occasionally. Lucy, what would work for you?"

"I'll need to keep moving, follow anything I hear."

"Okay, that's fine. First, though, I've something to show you all. Come with me."

He led us out into the hall. Now that dusk was here, the lantern on the porch was properly visible through the glass panels in the door. The snuff-lights glimmered on the stairs.

Lockwood stepped to the middle of the hallway. He pointed to the wallpaper, at waist height, on the right-hand side. "What do you think this is?"

There was a black scuff on the design, where the sheen of the paper had been worn away in a narrow line. It ran along the corridor, stopping and starting; a faint, thin furrow.

"Belly mark," Lockwood said. "He was so wide, his sides rubbed against the wall as he went along. You've got it on the other side, too, here. The carpet shows the same worn pattern. His flat-footed weight wore a pale track down the middle."

We looked at the lines on the walls. It was a narrow hall, but not *that* narrow. I imagined the size of the stomach that reached from side to side.

"And there's something else." Lockwood took his flashlight from his belt, switched it on, and moved soundlessly down to the kitchen door. The soft, pale light shone on the panes of dirty glass that made up most of the door. The marks on the panes were hard to decipher at first, being so old, and so large. But then your brain made sense of the pattern, and you realized what they were.

"Handprints," Lockwood said. "Greasy handprints, where he used to push the door open. And look at the size of them." We did so, in silence. He held up his own hand, narrow and long-fingered; the ghostly mark below was twice the width, and longer still.

Dusk turned to darkness; out in The Leas, a solitary streetlight came on. Inside number 7, each room had its candle or lantern burning. We ate sandwiches, drank tea, and divided up the watch. For the first quarter of the night, Lockwood would take the basement, George the ground floor, and Kipps upstairs. Holly would move between them periodically, checking that each was okay. I would stay mobile, too, following any sounds that might occur. It seemed a good strategy. It was a small house, and we would keep talking to each other. No one would ever get too far away.

I began in the basement, a cold and hateful place, little more than a square of uneven concrete surrounded by bare brick walls. You could see where investigators had excavated sections of the floor,

‡

thirty years ago. Lockwood had taken up position here, wrapped in his long coat and encircled by candles, leaning against the wall. He grinned at me as I left him, and I grinned back. We were both caught up in the thrill of the investigation. It felt easier between us now than at any time that day.

George was in the dining room, fiddling with some small device that looked like a silver bell suspended from a wire frame. He nodded at me as I joined him but didn't speak. Both of us just got on with the tasks in hand.

Curiously enough, Holly Munro had been the most animated of all of us, the least affected by the strained dynamics of the team. She passed me in the hallway later, as I stood there listening. She smiled, offered me a piece of chewing gum, and went on.

Upstairs, the long landing echoed the hall below. Near the top of the stairs, Kipps stood in the circle of chains, gaunt as a vulture, picked out by a ring of candles. The bedroom behind him was hollowed out pinkly by the gleam of streetlights.

I listened . . . from somewhere there came a faint clicking noise that I could not identify.

Click, click, click . . . It faded.

On the way along the landing, I pointed my flashlight into the bathroom. The sink, the bathtub, and the toilet were soft with dust. You could see scuff marks on the floor where agents, including us, had walked in recent days. The toilet bowl was dry and empty, crusted with lime rings. I moved to the bedroom at the end, looked down into the matte-black garden.

From elsewhere in the house came a thudding noise that made

the floorboards jump. It was not repeated. It might have been one of the others; equally it might not. I checked my watch. It was just approaching nine.

I finished my tour of the bedrooms and came back onto the landing. Kipps was still there, his hand held ready on his rapier, and it occurred to me again how hard it must be for him, waiting there unsighted, deaf, and helpless, his Talent having long ago abandoned him.

"Nothing yet," I said.

"Good. Let's keep it that way."

I started down the stairs. Light came from the lantern left burning on the porch; it shone through the glass of the front door and smudged along the hall. I could see the glow of the living room candles showing under the closed door. Snuff-lights flickered on the stairs, but they projected no strong radiance. Halfway down, standing in blackness, I listened, fingers trailing on the paper. I heard the creak of the wooden step as my weight paused on it; I heard Kipps coughing on the landing, a door slamming up the street, George whistling softly in the kitchen.

All innocuous enough. So why had the hairs on the back of my arms prickled?

An uneasy thought occurred to me. "Kipps," I called, "where are you?"

"Just above you, where you left me."

"Lockwood?"

"On the cellar steps. Is everything okay?"

"Where's Holly? Is she there, too?"

"She's here, behind me."

I looked toward the kitchen, where the gentle whistling still sounded. "George," I called, "tell me where you are."

The living room door opened just below me; a shape poked its head out. "Right here. Taking readings. Why?"

I didn't answer, but craned my head over the banister and stared at the kitchen door. It occurred to me that I should have been able to see the lights of the kitchen candles showing through the glass. But the panes were completely black. The whistling noise continued, soft and husky. And now there came a rhythmic chopping, a knife impacting a wooden surface, which told me someone was working in the kitchen.

Chapter 9

None of the others heard anything, neither the tuneless whistling nor the sound of the industrious knife. The skull in my backpack must have sensed the presence, too, of course, but it was still huffy with me. I tried rousing it, but it refused to answer my whispered questions.

We gathered silently in the hall. Lockwood stood at the door with his ear to a glass pane and his rapier held ready. Even up close, the glass was jet-black: whatever was in there sucked all light into itself and let nothing out again.

"I can still hear it," I said. Every now and then the chopping paused, as if the knife were forcing its way through something particularly hard, but it always resumed.

Lockwood's eyes met mine. "Then let's see who it is who's joined us."

He reached for the handle, turned it, sprang forward into the room. As he did so, the sounds cut out. I was at his side, a salt-bomb in my fist; George and Kipps were pressing at our backs. We came to a halt, surveying the empty kitchen, where the sharp shadows of the cypress trees hung in moonlight on the countertops, and the candles flickered gently around our circle on the cracked linoleum floor.

"Nothing?" Kipps breathed.

My own breath had been pent up; I forced it out hard. "It stopped, the sound, as soon as we came in."

Lockwood touched my arm. "It's playing tricks, which is to be expected."

"Nothing," Kipps said heavily. He looked at me.

"I *did* hear it," I snapped. The sudden deflation we'd all felt on entering the room had made us edgy. George was swearing color-fully under his breath, Holly was visibly shaking.

"No one's saying you didn't, Luce." Of all of us, only Lockwood seemed unaffected. He remained quite still, eyes narrowed, gaz-ing around the kitchen. Then he clipped his rapier to his belt and glanced at his thermometer. "Temp's normal," he said. "There's no visual phenomena that I can see."

"You're forgetting the glass door," I said. "No light shone through it a moment ago."

"True." He rummaged in a pocket of his coat, produced a paper bag of chocolates. "Everyone take two, and let's get the thermoses out. High time for a cup of tea."

We stood there, drinking, calming down. It's never good to let your emotions get the better of you in a haunted house. Ghosts feed off them and grow strong.

"So, it's nine-o-three p.m., and that's our first proper phenomenon," Lockwood said. "Looks as if Fittes and Barnes were right—this thing mainly manifests via sounds. That means Lucy's going to bear the brunt of it. You're okay with that, Luce?"

I nodded. "That's why you brought me in."

"I know, but you need to be happy with it."

My heart was still pounding, but I kept my voice cool and professional. "It's not a problem."

Lockwood nodded slowly. "Okay . . . so we go on much as before. We'll meet again at eleven thirty, see if anyone has a clue to the Source. Those of us on stationary posts can swap rooms then. Meanwhile, we call to each other whenever we have the slightest doubt about anything."

One after the other, everyone slipped away—everyone except George and me. We remained standing in the kitchen. It seemed the obvious place for me to concentrate my efforts, and George had clearly had a similar idea. From a bag he brought out the odd little contrivance I'd seen before—a silver bell suspended from a wooden frame on a lattice of thin wires. With extreme care, elbows out wide, fingers clinically spread, he placed it on a butcher-block table in a shaft of moonlight, and stood back to consider it.

I could contain myself no longer. "George, what *is* that?"

He ran a hand distractedly through his mop of sandy hair. "PEWS. Psychic Early Warning System. New item from the Rotwell Institute. Half of these zinc wires are standard, and half have been coated with spider's silk, which reacts with special sensitivity to ghostly emanations. The movement differential between them disturbs the balance of the central bar, which . . ." He glanced at me and shrugged. "It's supposed to ring *before* the ghost appears, basically."

"And does it work?"

"Can't say. First time I've tried it."

"You think it's more sensitive than our own Talents?"

"I don't know. Better than mine, maybe. Maybe not as good as yours." His voice was flat. He turned away to survey the circle in the center of the room. "I think we should reinforce the defenses here. I don't know why, I just do. Can you fetch me those chains over there?"

"Sure." I did so. "George," I said, "you know I'm very happy to be working alongside you all again."

There was a silence. "Are you?" he said. "That surprises me."

I set the chains down with a clatter. I didn't look up. I could feel him gazing at me. "And why wouldn't I be?"

He didn't answer for a time, but knelt to adjust the chains, pulling them around to envelop the existing circle. He did so methodically, carefully, in that way he tackled every important task, creating a wall of double thickness. "Well," he said at last, "there's Holly."

"Not you as well!" I let out an angry oath. "I keep telling everyone. *I didn't leave because of her.* Didn't you see us earlier? Didn't you see us chatting at the café? We smiled and laughed and everything."

"Just because you managed a fleeting conversation without strangling each other with your bare hands doesn't make you bosom buddies," George said. He took off his glasses and rubbed them thoughtfully on his sweater. "I think we'll add some snuff-lights, too—got any handy?"

"In the plastic Mullet's bag." I found it, took some, threw the bag over to him. "We get along fine now, actually," I said. "Holly and I get on like a house on fire."

George nodded. "*Sure* you do. As in savage destruction and widespread loss of life." He tossed me a box of matches.

"*That*," I said stiffly, "was *before* the Poltergeist. Afterward, we sorted things out."

"The Poltergeist *was* you sorting things out," George said, and in a way he was quite right. "You left because you got so mad at her."

"No. I left because I lost control of my Talents," I said. "Because I roused ghosts and endangered you all, and I couldn't face doing it again." I lit some candles and stood back. "Anyway, I'm here tonight."

George's face was expressionless. "Oh, yes. So you are. See how grateful I am." He broke off and looked at me. "*Now* what?"

I'd raised a hand for silence. Slow, heavy footsteps were passing overhead. With each impact the ceiling vibrated and the hanging light (it was a single naked bulb) jerked from side to side. I heard the creak of a door. Then silence.

I looked at George. "Hear any of that? See the light?"

"I caught it swinging. No sounds. What was it?"

"Footsteps. In the back bedroom. Think Kipps would be strolling around in there?"

"Not a chance. He'll be safe in his circle."

"That's what I think, too. We should go upstairs and take a look."

George made a nervous adjustment to his glasses. "Yes . . . we should."

"So let's go."

We passed swiftly along the narrow hallway to the stairs, turned and went up, two steps at a time, until we came out onto the landing. Kipps, sitting with his rapier on his knees, raised his eyebrows as we passed him, but we didn't stop. The corridor was quiet and dark; the door at the end was open, revealing a sliver of the back bedroom, softly contoured by the moonlight. We moved swiftly, silently toward it. Halfway along, I heard the clicking sound again. *Click-click-click*—three clicks, a pause, and then the same sound repeated. It was a crisp, pearly little noise, intimate and oddly familiar. It was impossible to tell where it came from.

I shone my flashlight into the bathroom as we passed. As the light moved across the wooden floor, I thought I saw someone lying in the bathtub. I jerked my hand up; the swell of shadow fell away, dropping in sync with the rising beam. No, it was empty, just a hollow space of dust and cobwebs. A trick of the mind and light.

George had moved past me, making for the bedroom. Suddenly he drew up short, grimacing in pain. "Ow! Ah!"

My rapier was in my hand; I was right by him. "What is it?"

"Stepped into a cold spot—just cut straight through me." He scrabbled at his belt, stared at the thermometer. "Came and went in a flash . . . Ah, it *really* hurt. . . . Now it's gone."

"Are you okay?"

"Fine. Just shocked me. Temp's normal now."

The bedroom was quiet, too, though one cupboard door seemed to have opened of its own accord since we'd last been in. Also, the clicking noise had stopped. Neither of us could detect anything out of the ordinary.

"Lockwood was right," George said. "This thing's playing tricks, most of them with sounds." He looked back along the corridor, gave the watching Kipps a wave. "Don't you have that foul skull with you? What's it got to say for itself? It never used to be short of an opinion."

"Hard to get anything out of it tonight," I said. "It's in a grump. It can't believe I'm working with Lockwood and Co. again."

"Jealous," George said. "Acting like a jilted lover. It probably thought it had you all to itself. You're the only thing that ties it to the living world. Well, we've all got our problems. Right, I'm going to put another PEWS in the lounge. You might want to encourage the skull to talk. This place gives me the creeps, and I haven't the first clue what the Source could be."

Nor did I. Nor did any of us, and the pressure of that ignorance weighed most heavily on me. Our vigil wore on; and steadily the repertoire of noises I experienced in that house began to multiply. I heard the footsteps several times more, always when I was downstairs, always echoing from the floor above. It was a peculiar, shuffling, slapping step, both abrupt and dragging, the kind that might be made by loose-fitting carpet slippers on a pair of swollen feet. Twice, once when I was in the basement and once in the living room, I heard a snatch of heavy, labored breathing, as if a very large person was struggling to move around. And once, when standing in the hallway, I heard behind me a soft, continuous rasping, as might have been caused by cloth, pressed against misshapen flesh, brushing along the wall. Any one of those would have been enough to unsettle me; taken together, and with none of the others hearing anything, they began to prey on my mind.

As haunted houses went, it was a *noisy* one. I understood why Penelope Fittes had wanted me there.

Penelope Fittes. Not Lockwood. Whenever I thought of that,

annoyance speared through me. But these last few months I'd become good at damping down my annoyance in perilous places. And nowhere in this house was as perilous, it seemed to me, as the dowdy wood-and-mustard-colored kitchen. I wanted to survey it properly; connect with what had happened there. It wouldn't be pleasant, but it was the fastest way to get to the heart of the haunting. I would clear my mind, do the job, and go home.

Eleven thirty came; we rendezvoused in the living room again. For everyone else, it had been a quiet couple of hours, with nothing but low-level malaise and creeping fear to disturb their vigil. I recounted my experiences, and Lockwood again questioned me closely, probing to see if I was still calm. Again I reassured him. After that, people swapped roles: George went to the basement, Holly to the first floor. Lockwood would be the roving anchor, connecting everyone during the midnight hour. I returned to the kitchen.

As I entered, I thought I heard the briefest snatch of whistling, followed by the three rapid clicks. Then nothing.

"Skull?" I said. "Did you hear that?"

No answer. I'd had enough of this. The skull had been silent ever since our arrival. I took the jar out of the backpack. The ghost's face floated in the green ichor. It still wore its haughty expression; as I watched, it slowly but studiedly rotated away from me. I set the jar on the floor beside the chains and walked around it to catch up with the face. "Didn't you hear?" I demanded. "The phenomena are increasing. What's your take on them?"

The ghost stopped rotating. It looked blankly left and right, as if suddenly aware of me. *"Oh, you're talking to me now?"*

"Yes, I am. There's something building here, and I sense mortal danger. I'm wondering if you have any perspective on it."

The ghost adopted an expression of enormous unconcern. Its nostrils dilated; I heard a dismissive sniff. *"Like you care a bean what I think."*

I looked around the moonlit kitchen, silent, seemingly innocuous, but drenched in evil. "Dear old skull. I do care, and I'm asking you as a . . . as a . . ."

"I detect hesitation," the skull said. *"As a friend?"*

I scowled. "Well, no. Obviously not."

"As a respected colleague, then?"

"Even that would be stretching it. No, I'm asking you as someone who genuinely values your opinion, despite your wicked nature, your vicious temperament, and my better judgment."

The face regarded me. *"Ooh, okay . . . I see you're going for the virtues of simple honesty here, rather than the honeyed words of flattery. Correct?"*

"Yes."

"Well, go boil your backside in a bucket. It's not good enough. You're not getting a word of wisdom out of me."

I gave a cry of rage. "You are *so* huffy! George said you were jealous, and I'm beginning to think he was right." I bent down and twisted the dial closed.

At that moment I heard a soft bubbling noise. A rattle and a popping. I turned around.

An old black-and-white stove sat in one corner of the kitchen. It was dark; no gas flames had been lit in it for thirty years. Nevertheless, there was something moving on top of it now, something rattling on a dusty burner.

It was a saucepan, a big one. I took a slow step toward it. The pan jerked and shook vigorously; whatever was inside was coming to a boil. Water fizzed and spat; a ring of small bubbles stacked themselves against the greasy rim.

I didn't want to look, but I *had* to see. I had to see what was cooking in the pan.

I started toward it. Slowly, slowly I crept across the kitchen. The side of the pan shone silver in the moonlight, but the interior was black. Something roundish sat there; the bubbles crowned and cradled it. There was a rich, gamey scent, carried on hot, wet air.

Closer, closer. *Rattle, rattle* went the pan. I unclipped my flashlight from my belt, and lifted it toward the burner. . . .

"Lucy!"

"Ah!" Next thing—me spinning around, flashlight turning on in Lockwood's face. He gasped and held up his arm, blocking the light with his cuff.

"What are you doing, Luce? Put out that light."

"What am *I* doing? Don't you see the—" I turned, raised the flashlight, shone the beam hard across the space. But the stovetop was empty. The pan was gone, and the air was clear and quiet. Moonlight shone through the window. I switched off the flashlight, stowed it away.

Lockwood had moved between me and the stove. "What did you see?"

"Something cooking," I said. "Something cooking on the stove. It's gone now," I added, needlessly.

He pushed his hair back and frowned at me. "I saw your face—you were mesmerized by it. It had snared you. It was drawing you in."

"I wasn't snared at all. I just wanted to see—"

"Exactly. I've seen you look like that before. All the phenomena are concentrated on you, Lucy. No one else is getting anything. I'm worried. Maybe we should call this off."

I stared at him, feeling a surge of irritation. "That's why I'm here, Lockwood," I said. "I sense things; I draw them out. You have to trust me, that's all."

"Of course I trust you." He held my gaze. "It still concerns me."

"Well, it needn't." I looked away. There on the butcher-block table was George's bell, sparkling in the moonlight. It was a useless object. We'd had a visitation a few feet away, and it hadn't done a thing. "I can cope with all that," I said. "As you should know. *If* you actually want me here."

There was a pause. "Of course I do," Lockwood said. "I asked you, didn't I?"

"Yes, *you* asked me. But it was Penelope Fittes who asked *for* me, and that's the difference."

"Lucy, what on earth are you—?" Lockwood said, and in the next instant he whirled around: the door to the hall had crashed open.

"George!"

He careered forward, glasses crooked, eyes wild. "Lucy, Lockwood, quick, come and look! Here, the basement."

We pushed past him, into the hall, where the entrance to the basement gaped wide. Lockwood shone his flashlight down the steep flight. The light made a yellow oval on the concrete floor. "What is it? Where?"

"Bones! Bones and—and bits and pieces. All lying in a muddle at the bottom of the stairs!"

We stared down at the concrete, rough and bare and blank. "Where?"

George gestured wildly. "Well, of course they're gone *now*, aren't they? Too much to hope that they'd stay put while I was getting you!"

"Maybe they're not gone," I said. "Lockwood, your Sight's best of all. If you go down—"

A shrill cry echoed through the house. That was Holly. Lockwood, George, and I took one look at each other and ran back through the kitchen into the little dining room. There stood Holly, elegantly distraught, staring at a blank space in front of the window.

We had our rapiers ready. "Solomon Guppy?"

She shook her head, face pale in the moonlight. "No."

"Well, what did you see?"

"Nothing, just a table. But on it—"

"Yes?"

"It was too dark to make out. Plates, cutlery." She shuddered. "Some kind of *roast*."

"Oh, yuck," George said. "And I think I just saw the off-cuts in the basement."

"You want to know the worst of it?" Holly's voice was faint; she cleared her throat and spoke more calmly. "There was this little white napkin, neatly folded beside the plate. I don't know why, but that detail . . . it really got to me. The whole thing was just a snapshot. Lasted a fraction of a second, then it was gone."

"The problem with all these snapshots," George said fiercely, "is there's nothing to stick a sword into. There's no clue to where the Source could— Lucy?" I'd gone rigid. "Luce? What is it? You hear him again?"

They stood beside me, the three of them in the darkness of the dining room, waiting for my word. "Not exactly *him*," I said slowly, "but . . . yes. Yes, I do."

From the shadows had come the creak of settling wood. Someone heavy easing their weight into a chair.

"Is he *in* here?" George whispered.

I shook my head. "It's just sounds, echoes from the past. . . ." All the same, my heart was beating fast; my head felt light and my limbs heavy. Fear pressed in on us. Now I could hear a familiar sound, very polite and delicate. The sound of knife and fork on china. "I think I hear him eating."

Someone coughed in the dark. Someone smacked their lips.

"Can we go out for a minute?" I said. "I need to get some air."

"Agreed," Lockwood said. "It's hot in here, isn't it?

No one was eager to stay. We hurried to the door, all four of us. As we did so, an appalling scream echoed through the house, filled with both pain and terror. It was the scream of a murdered man, or someone terrified to death. Somebody clutched my arm; I don't know if it was George or Holly.

"Oh no . . ." I said. "Kipps . . ."

Lockwood was out of the room in a flash, long coat swirling behind him. "Holly—you wait here. Lucy—"

"Stuff that. I'm coming with you."

Through the kitchen we ran, Lockwood, George, and I. Along the hall, past the basement door, around to the foot of the stairs.

The house was deathly still. Up the steps, three at a time, and onto the landing—

Where Kipps was still sitting placidly in his iron circle, reading a novel by the light of his ring of candles. He had a packet of biscuits open by one knee, and a flask of coffee by the other. His head was resting on one hand; he wore a look of boredom, which changed to puzzlement as we careered to a halt above him.

"What do you idiots want now?"

He hadn't heard a thing.

Chapter 10

It was cold out on the front porch, and there was a thin rain falling in the London night. You could hear it pattering on the hedges and on the concrete drive, and dripping from a broken gutter. Otherwise the city was quiet; we were in the dead hours, and nothing living was abroad. Cold, rain, and silence: that was a combo that suited us all right then. We needed to calm down.

One of the dangers of spending too much time in a haunted house is that you begin to follow its patterns and its rules. Since the rules inside the building are invariably warped and twisted, you find yourself slowly losing contact with the principles that keep you safe. We'd fallen into this trap in the Guppy house, separating too easily, becoming prey to individual psychic attacks. Holly, George, and I had all been affected; our nerves were on edge, and we huddled in silence by the porch lantern, munching chocolate and staring out into the dark. Lockwood and Kipps had so far not been directly targeted, Kipps either because he had rarely strayed from his iron circle, or because he no longer had the sensitivity to pick up on subtle manifestations. As for Lockwood, perhaps he was less vulnerable, and the entity had sensed his strength—it was hard to say.

Certainly he seemed relaxed enough now. "There you go, Luce," he said, catching my eye. "Aren't you pleased you came out with us tonight? No one can say that Lockwood and Company doesn't show you a good time."

I took a swig from my thermos. The night air was doing its job. My head felt clearer now. "Best evening out I've had in ages," I said. "Random body parts and mortal fear? That's better than Indian food."

He grinned. "You're doing great. If it was just Holly, George, and me, we'd have had a couple of visuals, maybe, but nothing more. Thanks to you, we've got almost too much information."

I couldn't help but smile at him. Compliments from Lockwood were always nice to hear. "Too much and not enough," I said. "I've *heard* Guppy in half the rooms of the house. I've heard him walking around, eating, whistling, even chopping in the kitchen. Holly and George and I have all seen secondary flashbacks—again in different rooms. Just about the only thing we haven't seen is the apparition itself. And we're no closer to finding the Source."

Lockwood shook his head. "I think we are. The table, the bones, that pot on the stove—they're *all* aspects of the apparition. Guppy isn't in one portion of the house, he *is* the house. He's not locked in one small area; he's everywhere. George—you told us Guppy almost never left the property if he could help it. Clearly he was obsessed with the place. He may be long dead, but that still holds. I think he's still here."

"Couldn't it be the spirit of the victim, though?" Kipps said. "Thanks to George we know how his remains ended up in every room. Feet in the lounge, toenails in the pantry—"

"*Eyeballs* in the pantry," George said. "In a jar."

"Yes, thank you," Kipps growled. "I don't need the details again. The point is, he could just as easily be responsible for all this, couldn't he? And you reckoned you heard his scream. . . ."

"We did," I said, "but I still think it's Guppy. All the sounds relate to his horrible activities. He's re-creating it for his own pleasure, and to freak us out."

"Is the whole house the Source, then?" Holly asked in a small voice. She'd been subdued since the incident in the dining room. "Is that possible? If so, maybe we should just burn the place down." She gave a little gulping laugh. "I'm not *really* suggesting that, obviously."

George adjusted his glasses. "I don't know. . . . We've set fire to houses before."

"Deliberate arson is not likely to impress Fittes or Barnes," Quill Kipps said. "Besides, there *will* be a more localized Source somewhere—the psychic heart of the haunting. The problem is, no one's ever been able to find it. Right, I'm going to make a suggestion in my official capacity as observer for the Fittes Agency. In our company, when psychic danger has been experienced and you haven't got a clue what to do, the general rule is to retreat. Retreat and recalibrate. Live to fight another day."

"You mean give up?" Lockwood was incredulous; he patted Kipps fondly on the shoulder. "That's not the Lockwood and Company way."

Kipps shrugged. "Then it'll keep sapping your spirits with little attacks until you're too frazzled to notice you've been ghost-touched. Unless you can draw the ghost out and persuade it to reveal the Source, which is hardly likely, I don't see how you'll ever get anywhere."

Lockwood snapped his fingers so suddenly that we all jumped. "That's it! You're a genius, Quill! We'll draw it out! Guppy's been having his way for far too long. Luce, you've experienced most of his tricks. I'd say the kitchen was where most of the phenomena have been concentrated, wouldn't you?"

"No question about it," I said.

"Then let's assume that *that's* the room he cares about the most." Lockwood's eyes glittered. "I wonder whether we can upset him. Everyone drink up. It's time we fetched our crowbars."

Short, light crowbars, the kind favored by burglars in the days when ordinary criminals dared to go out at night, are a standard piece of agency equipment. They're used mostly for knocking through walls or prying up floorboards in search of bones and relics, but they're more versatile than that. Over the years I'd used mine for breaking open waterlogged chests, levering a coffin out of a sandpit, and—since the bar was helpfully made of iron—skewering a Tom O'Shadows to a door. I'd never gone as far as destroying a kitchen with it, but there was a first time for everything.

It was silent in the house as we went in and filed back up the hall. It was even quieter than when we'd first arrived: there was no psychic pressure at all. Even the *lack* of pressure was ominous: it suggested that something had drawn back and was watching us. We had our crowbars over our shoulders—except for Kipps, who'd found a rusty mallet in the garage, which he thought was even better. We passed the dark marks on the wallpaper, the handprints on the glass pane. Lockwood closed the kitchen door behind us. There was the drab little space, with its wooden cabinets, its notched butcher block, its old stained sink with ugly taps. The moon had moved in front of the house, and the kitchen was darker than before. George's silver bell was still on the counter. He moved it to the windowsill, out of harm's way.

We double-checked the iron chains in the center of the room and relit some candles that had blown out. Holly turned the lantern down low. Then we gathered by the butcher block. Lockwood inserted his crowbar into a narrow space between a countertop and the cupboard below.

"Kipps and I will start," he said. "The rest of you keep watch."

He heaved up the crowbar.

Lockwood said this was no real crime, given what had been done here. Even so, my nerves jangled as the old wood splintered. Maybe it was rotten; certainly it came apart easily, with a single great *crack* that echoed around the room. I imagined that sound reverberating through the rest of the house.

Maybe we *all* imagined that, because for a moment, no one moved. Even Lockwood paused with the crowbar still embedded in the countertop.

Nothing but silence.

So he went to work again, ripping into the brittle particleboard, forcing it back on itself so that it burst in a shower of splinters. After a bit he moved back and let Kipps take over with the mallet. Drawers fractured; shelves snapped like broken bones. Already a great hole had opened to the left of the metal sink, and the kitchen that had remained untouched for thirty years was altered irrevocably.

Kipps took a swig of water. We listened. The house was quiet. He began again.

While the mallet swung, I moved away across the room, out of Kipps's sight. I felt in my backpack, and twisted the lever of the ghost-jar.

"*Ooh, the tension,*" whispered the voice. "*Even I'm nervous, and I'm a ghost. Five fools trying their damnedest to rouse a monster. But what will you do if he comes?*"

"Skull," I whispered, "it's your last chance. You've been useless this evening. Swallow your pride and give me some help here, or I swear next time I'll leave you at home under the bed."

There was a faint, dry chuckle. "*Oh, next time? But there won't be a next time with Lockwood and Company, remember? It'll just be you and me, mucking along together as before. That's our future, clear as day!*"

"Yeah? Here's another future," I snarled. "See this crowbar? I'll smash you and your jar with that and bury the pieces in the garden if you don't help me out."

The chuckling stopped. "*Bit harsh.*" The voice grew thoughtful. "*One day, Lucy, I'll have you in my power, and we'll see who dances to whose tune. Well, what can I tell you that you don't already know? The creature infests the house; his essence was drawn into the walls by sweat and blood and hideous obsession. Years pass; his awareness comes and goes. I felt it when we entered, then it drew back. He is sluggish. He dozes; perhaps you have seen his dreams."*

"But now—" I said, then stopped as an immense effort from Kipps broke a mustard-colored panel and sent it flying across the room.

"Congratulations. You've woken him, and he's not happy."

Kipps was standing upright, wiping his forehead with his sleeve. Lockwood had pulled some fragments of particleboard clear. He lifted his crowbar, ready to resume. I held up my hand to pause them.

Far off in the house, I heard it.

Click-click-click.

And all at once I knew what it was.

It was sound of teeth being tapped together.

Click-click-click . . .

It was a habit he'd had. He did it as he shuffled slowly around the house, looking in his recipe books, watching his neighbors from his windows.

Click-click-click . . . Click-click-click . . .

Watching, watching . . . Eventually selecting one.

"Got company," I said.

For a moment, none of us moved. Four pale faces stared at me in the swirling candlelight of the ruined kitchen. Kipps and Lockwood stood ankle-deep in shattered wood. They were covered in sawdust, glistening with sweat; they were as pale and hideous as Bone Men. Holly looked like a particularly anxious Floating Bride. George, hair disarranged, glasses shining like headlights, might have passed for some unhinged spirit manifesting as an owl. We looked and listened.

I pointed upward. The lightbulb in the ceiling juddered as heavy, shuffling footsteps crossed the room upstairs.

"Excellent," Lockwood said. "If he's stirring, we're on the right track. That means he definitely doesn't like it when we do something like *this*!" He swung the crowbar level with his head and smashed in the side of a cupboard halfway up the wall.

Click-click-click . . .

Something was walking along the landing, heading for the stairs.

"Come on, Guppy. You can move faster than that." Lockwood wrenched at a spar of wood that jutted up from the floor. The units beside the sink had been completely destroyed, exposing bare brick and moldy floor. He struck the sink's metal support, snapping it in two. He was aflame with sudden defiant energy, swooping and darting like quicksilver, tugging and striking and kicking away the debris. Even Kipps moved back to give him space; the rest of us could do little but watch as he sought to summon a horror by the application of pure will.

George sidled close to me. "What does Lockwood plan to do when it . . . arrives?"

"I have no idea."

Heavy footsteps on the stairs; I heard steps creaking as immense pressure weighed them down.

"Lucy," George whispered, "can I share something personal with you?"

"Yes."

"If you'd rather I didn't, you being a free agent and all, you only have to say."

"It's still me, isn't it? Just spit it out."

"Okay . . ." He nodded, took a short breath. "I *really* don't want to see this one."

"Guppy?"

"Right. I mean, I've seen a lot of apparitions in my time," George said, "and some of them have been . . . pretty grisly, you know. You remember that wormy girl we saw near Hackney Gardens? I couldn't eat Swiss cheese for months after that. But there's something about this one—"

I nodded. "I know. You don't have to say it. Me, too."

As I spoke, I was staring at the glazed glass panels in the kitchen door. They were fairly opaque, but you could see the glow of the lantern on the distant porch and the snuff-lights on the stairs. This light was stirring violently, and dimming, and now a great dark shape moved slowly into view at the far end of the hall. Holly gave a little squeal.

"Apparition's in sight, Lockwood," George said. "What do we do?"

"Exactly what we're already doing." Lockwood was grinning, his hair flopping over his face. "We bring him to us, and we wipe him out. Stand firm. He's trying to break us all with fear."

And making a pretty good job of it, if my own ghost-lock was anything to go by. I could barely move, but I edged to the back corner of the room. The shape was growing. Teeth clicked, lips smacked together. I could hear feet in carpet slippers shuffling along the hall.

I stepped away, turning my back on Kipps again. "Skull," I hissed, "now would be a *terrific* opportunity to prove your worth. There'll be no more talk of crowbars from me if you can spot the Source."

"I see. . . . First it's threats, then sweet words. Have you no dignity?"

"Not right now. Can you sense where it is?"

"Well, from the efforts it's making to get to you, I'd say it thinks you're on to something."

"The Source is near!" I called. I sprang across to the mess of shattered wood. "What's behind those broken cabinets? Keep an eye out for anything!"

Crouching beside the ruined sink, I began to hurl aside pieces of wood. Kipps and Lockwood joined me at once, but Holly and George stood transfixed, staring at the door. In moments a small space was cleared. I peered under the sink. The floorboards were rotten at the back, and in places didn't reach the wall. Loops of pipework dangled in the shadows like exposed intestines. I shone my torch around the darkened recess.

I thought of Emma Marchment's ghost—her hidden treasure, her precious thing. Guppy had kept something, too; he'd secreted it somewhere here.

"Any luck, Luce?" Lockwood's voice was calm.

"We're close. How long have we got?"

"Oh, about thirty seconds."

I squinted over my shoulder; beyond the glass, the shadow had resolved into a definite shape. You could see the black outline of the vast wide head, the swell of stomach spreading out from wall to wall. There was the rustling of cloth against the wallpaper, there was the clicking and clacking of the great loose mouth. I heard a crack of tendons, a knee protesting under dreadful weight.

It was almost at the door.

I swore under my breath. "The only place I can see," I said, "is where that floorboard's broken away. There, in the corner, behind the pipework—do you see?"

In an instant Lockwood was lying on his front, peering at the remotest portion of the wall. His flashlight turned on. "I see the hole. There's something shining in it. It's quite far in—would be hard to reach . . ."

Holly screamed. She was gazing at the door. There, halfway up, pressed against the glass: a huge white hand.

Lockwood jumped up. "George, snap out of it! We'll need your strength for this. Take a look." He tossed the flashlight to George, and in the same motion took his rapier from his belt.

Fingers curled around the edge of the door. The nails were broken and fouled with dirt.

George sprang over the pile of wood and lowered himself down beside me. He squinted into the cavity. "I see it. . . . It's a jar of some kind. But the pipe's in the way."

Lockwood flicked his coat back; he was checking the equipment on his belt. "Break the pipe if necessary." He walked across the room. "The rest of you, get inside the circle."

I rose to my feet. "Lockwood," I said, "what are you—?"

"I'm going to buy George some time. Get in the circle, Lucy."

The door was opening; a vast black shadow spilled through it like a lolling tongue. Lockwood threw a salt-bomb into the crack; there was a horrible high-pitched scream. Then he had slipped through the door and pulled it shut behind him.

Holly, Kipps, and I were transfixed, staring after him—

Ding-a-ding-a-ding!

All three of us cried out, all three of us turned. It was the silver bell, swinging wildly on its wires of zinc and spider-silk.

"Oh, it rings *now*?" I cried. "That thing is *so* useless, George!"

George was lying on his back, head out of sight. "Well, don't blame me! Blame the Rotwell Institute! They're selling any old junk!"

"Just get into that hole!"

"Got a tap wrench?"

"No! Why would I? I don't even know what it is!"

"It's this bloody pipe that's the problem—I can't pull the thing out."

I was staring at the door. Shapes moved beyond it; I heard thuds, slashes, and again and again that keening scream. None of us had gotten into the circle as Lockwood had ordered, and now we saw the chains sliding sideways on the linoleum floor. The chains had been folded over, but not tied. The outer one whipped away; the inner one held firm. A force blasted out across the kitchen, toppling the candles, making us stagger where we stood. For an instant I saw Lockwood's outline thrust back against the glass, then he was gone. The whole house seemed to shake.

"We have to go and help him, Kipps," I said.

Kipps didn't seem to have moved since Lockwood had left the room. His face was white. He gathered his wits. "Yes. We must. Come on."

"Lucy!" That was George, from below.

"What?"

"Got a spanner?"

"No! I'm not a plumber, George! I'm an agent! Agents don't carry spanners!" I was halfway to the door.

"It's all right! It's all right! I've broken through the floorboard . . . I've almost gotten it out . . ." Something grated against brick; George's legs thrashed from side to side. "There!" He sat up, holding a jam jar wreathed in cobwebs. It glinted an unpleasant white. "Get me a Seal!"

Holly was already standing by; she had a silver net in her hand.

Beyond the glass, a vast and swollen shape lurched toward the door.

The handle turned.

Holly dropped the net, swathing the jar in silver.

The door swung slowly open—

—revealing only Lockwood, leaning against the wall. His coat was dusty, his hair plastered over one eye. His right arm was slack, his right hand bleeding; from his left, his rapier hung loosely, trailing along the floor. We stared at him. He stood there, breathing hard and grinning, alone in that empty hall.

It turned out, once we'd inspected him, that a bruised arm and cut hand were the worst of what Lockwood had suffered, inflicted when he was blown back against the door. Perhaps he was a little quieter than normal; otherwise, physically, he was quite unharmed. While Kipps went to find a phone box to summon a Night Cab, he sat on the porch and let Holly fuss around him; meanwhile, George and I pulled our remaining equipment out onto the lawn.

When we were packed up, I went to stand beside Lockwood.

"Didn't we do brilliantly?" he said. "I think even Kipps is impressed, and that takes some doing. Thank you for agreeing to help us out tonight, Luce."

"It's fine," I said. "Not a problem."

"Did you take a peep at the Source? Did you see what it contained?" The jam jar, securely wrapped in silver and ready for its final journey to the furnaces, sat a little way off, shimmering under the stars.

"George told me. Lots of human teeth."

"A special collection of them. Must have been dear to Guppy's heart."

"How nice. Well, it's over now. I'm glad we did the job."

"It was good to team up with you again." Lockwood smiled at me, then looked away into the garden. I could sense he was about to speak. "Actually, Lucy . . ."

"Yes?"

"I was wondering something—"

"Yes?"

"Do you have any of that chocolate left? I saw you'd started a bar earlier."

"Oh. Yeah, of course. Here, take it all."

Lockwood wasn't normally one to overdose on sweet stuff; he left that more to George and me—or *used* to, when we worked together—but he tore the silver paper away and ate the whole bar, piece by piece, until it was all gone, staring sightlessly into the night. I thought he looked very tired.

When he'd finished, he gave a sigh of satisfaction. "Thank goodness for you, Lucy. Holly never carries chocolate, and George has always scarfed his before we're out of Portland Row. But I can always rely on you."

I cleared my throat. "I'm glad to be of service. And you're right," I went on, in a sudden rush. "It's great we got a chance to work together again. I'm really glad we could— Oh, and here's Kipps, back already. . . . He made good time."

A Night Cab had pulled up at the end of the drive, its horn blaring. Lockwood was slowly getting to his feet. The time for talking had passed.

Except for one last thing.

"Lockwood," I said, "when you went out into the hallway . . ."

The final smile was weary. "Lucy, you *really* don't want to know."

We ended up needing three taxis. Lockwood, Holly, and Kipps took the first one, carrying the Source off to Clerkenwell, while George and I waited behind with the bulk of the bags. When the other cabs came, I'd head to Tooting, he'd go to Portland Row. It was the parting of the ways. We sat on a garden wall opposite number 7.

"George," I said, after a while, "you'll know this kind of thing. Mummified heads. How common are they?"

George being George, the question didn't faze him. "As psychic artifacts? Rare. Has to be the right conditions for mummification: either very dry, or containing certain chemicals, like you get in peat bogs. Can't have much air, else the microbes get to work. Why?"

"No reason. Just I heard of two recently, and I was wondering how likely it was, that's all."

He grunted but said nothing. Silence enveloped us.

"George," I said again, "what Lockwood did back there—"

"I know."

"It was brilliant, yes, but also—"

"Crazy?"

"Yeah."

George took off his glasses and rubbed them on his sweater as he always did when considering something disagreeable. It was a different kind of rub than the one he used when he was excited, agitated, or simply being a know-it-all. I'd forgotten how clearly I could read him. If you'd hidden his face and simply showed me his glasses moving on his shirt, I could easily have told you his mood.

"Yes," he said, "and the really bad thing is that I wasn't at all surprised. This is typical behavior for him now. Lockwood's more reckless than ever. He throws himself into everything like he doesn't care. Most cases we go on, I don't have time to even do a quick background check, let alone research the haunting."

I stared into the dark. Lockwood's recklessness was part and parcel of who he was. I guessed he'd been that way since his sister died, when he was very young. It was also linked to the reasons why I'd stepped away from the agency, though it wasn't the full story by any means. "He's always been like that," I said. "That's just his way."

"But it's worse than before." George was staring down at his sweater. His eyes, exposed without his glasses, looked smaller, weak, and frail. "You know he was always brave, but not like *that*."

I knew what he meant. We were both thinking of the shape at the door.

"When did it start?" I said. "When did it get worse?"

George shrugged. "After you left."

"And you think . . ." I frowned, hesitated. "Why *do* you think that is?"

George put his glasses back on; his eyes sprang back into focus, sharp and questing. "Wrong emphasis, Luce. Why do *you* think that is?"

"Well, it's got nothing to do with me."

"Of course not. Your leaving the company had no effect on any of us. Why, a day after you left, we'd forgotten your name."

I glared at him. "You needn't be like that. That's hurtful."

George gave a sudden whoop of rage. "How d'you *want* me to put it? You waltzed off on a whim and left us to pick up the pieces. Now you suddenly swan back and expect us to carry on where we left off! You can't have it both ways—either we were affected by your departure or we weren't. Which do you prefer?"

"I didn't ask to come back!" I roared. "Penelope Fittes—"

"Has got nothing whatsoever to do with it, as you well know. It was *Lockwood* who came knocking on your door, and *that's* why you considered the proposal, and let's face it, *that's* why you said yes."

"Well, would you rather I hadn't?"

"It's none of my business what you decide. You cool freelancers walk your own path."

"Oh, for heaven's sake! Now you're just being childish."

"Am not."

"Are too."

Neither of us spoke after that. We sat in silence on the wall, waiting for our separate cabs.

III

Lost and Found

Chapter 11

Seven fifteen that same morning, I was awake again in bed.
At other times, in other years, I would have greeted the day in jaunty spirits. It had been an exhilarating night, and the artificial elation that you always get at the end of a dangerous hunt still coursed through my veins. I'd gotten back early enough to fall into a brief exhausted sleep, but had been woken not long after by trash collectors shouting in the street outside. And now that my eyes had opened, I couldn't close them again. My body was too tense. My mind was whirling.

So much of it was good, of course. The Ealing Cannibal had been a notable case, and news of its entrapment and destruction would spread widely; the reputation of all of us present in the house last night would definitely be enhanced. For me, the prospect of Penelope Fittes's approval was particularly gratifying. With her knowledge of her grandmother's Talent, *she* was unlikely to under-value me, as Rotwell's and other agencies had done. I could expect a slew of new cases as reward.

And Lockwood & Co. would do quite nicely, too; Ms. Fittes had made *that* clear enough. This pleased me. By helping them out, I'd maybe gone some small way toward paying off the debt I owed for having left so suddenly. Now that the case was successfully com-pleted, I could turn my attention to other things.

Yes, so much of it was good. Yet my room and bed seemed bleaker on that sunny spring morning than on any rain-lashed after-noon during the foul, dark winter. Lockwood had wanted me for one job, and I'd done that job, and now there would be no more, and the pleasure I'd felt while working alongside him—and George *and*, yes, even Holly—made that prospect bitter. But I could have coped with it, just as I'd coped these last four months, if I'd still felt secure in my original reasons for leaving. It was to protect Lockwood that I'd left the company, and even though it had been painful, I'd known that it was right. He was safer with me gone.

Or was he? If what George had said to me was true, I might actually have made things worse. He'd become even more reck-less without me there. And the varied implications of *that* kept me lying rigid in that bed, with the sun streaming over my rumpled bedspread.

Really, I should have tried to get back to sleep, but I was too keyed up—and keyed down; I was both hyped and befuddled at the same time. At last I got out of bed, only to stumble over the ghost-jar in the middle of the floor.

As I stood there cursing and rubbing my shin, an unsavory face manifested behind the glass. *"You look worse than me this morning,"* it observed. *"Well, when you recover, I await your groveling thanks. You know where I'll be."*

I went to put the kettle on. "Groveling thanks for what?"

"For my help last night in pinpointing the Source. You only found it after my tip. Quite clearly we make an excellent team, and I have an idea. I suggest we go into business together. 'Carlyle and Skull,' we'd call it, or possibly 'Skull and Co.' Yes, that's it, with a little picture of me over the door. I can see it now. . . ." Chuckling, it receded into the plasm.

I didn't respond. I wasn't in the mood. I picked up some of my scattered clothes, found my bathrobe, went across the landing to the bathroom. I came back and made coffee. I got out my casebook and tried to make a few notes about the evening, but found I didn't have the words. The other thing I needed to do was make out my invoice to the Lockwood & Co. agency. But I couldn't quite bring myself to do that, either. Not right then. So I took a shower, threw on some clothes, grabbed cash from my wallet, and went to get some takeout food. Obviously I should have cooked something, but I didn't have the energy. It was the same old story.

Or at least it was until I arrived back on my landing carrying the bag from the Thai place, the Styrofoam box inside already cradling me in lovely fragrant steam, and saw that the door to my room had been kicked in.

I stood there for five or six heartbeats, looking at the broken lock. The door had been re-closed, or nearly so, and I couldn't see inside. I glanced back across the landing at my neighbor's door. That seemed untouched. He would be at work now, as would most of the people on the floor below. It was very quiet in the apartment building, and there was no noise coming from my room.

I set my bag of food carefully by the wall. Then I moved slowly toward the door, my hand dropping automatically to my side, where my sword normally hung. But I was in sweatpants, and had no weapon now.

When I reached the door, I waited, straining for any sound that might indicate the intruder was still inside. But beneath the ongoing thrum of traffic from the Tooting High Street hung a profound silence. I took a slow and careful breath, then pushed the door open and stepped in.

Whoever had been there was gone. The place was a mess—as it always was—and as far as I could see, looked the same as it had when I'd left it a few minutes before. Except for one difference that I spotted right away.

The ghost-jar was gone.

I stayed where I was. I didn't move anything except for my eyes. For a long time I stood scanning the room. I surveyed it from the cluttered sink to the disordered bed, from the top of the open dresser to the stacks of equipment by the door. What else was different? What else had changed?

I looked at the table, where I'd slung my wallet the night before. The wallet was still there; it even had a couple of bills sticking out of it.

I looked at my rapier, propped against the back of the chair. A pricey Spanish blade that Lockwood had bought for me the previous summer. Still there.

I looked at my bags, stuffed with all the expensive paraphernalia of a freelance operative. All those salt-bombs and iron canisters, those cylinders of Greek Fire. You could get good money for those, if you knew the right people. But they remained precisely as I'd left them, completely untouched.

Nothing else had been taken. Just the skull.

Someone had come in, knowing the ghost-jar would be there, wanting it and nothing else. They'd taken it, and left. They'd done that during the (I made a rough calculation) ten or fifteen minutes I'd been out. So they'd been watching the building, waiting for me to leave. They'd known or guessed my movements. *That* bit wasn't difficult, since I did the same thing almost every morning after a case. The guy in the Thai place pretty much knew me by name. Half the street probably knew I'd potter out to get food at some time in the morning.

But whoever had been here had known about the ghost-jar, too.

They knew about the skull, which was something I took pains to keep hidden.

Who knew about it? Lockwood and George, of course. And Holly, too: I'd told her about it months ago. What about Quill Kipps, last night? No—I'd been very careful. In any case, stealing didn't seem Kipps's style. So who else?

Who else had seen it?

I stood a long time, thinking.

Then I went back out into the hall and brought in my breakfast, which was still hot. After all, there's no use wasting a good Thai.

After eating, I dried my hair properly, and changed into my work clothes. My coat smelled a bit of stale sweat and fear from the night before, but who was going to notice?

I put on my belt and made a cursory check of all its pockets. Not that I was expecting to use it against ghosts right then—I had a different quarry—but I needed it to hold my sword.

I picked up my rapier and strapped it on. Finally I glanced in the mirror, at my pale face and blazing eyes. Amazing what a theft does to you: all my previous weariness and befuddlement were gone.

With that, I left the room, pulling the door softly shut behind me.

A short walk south from the main compound of the Fittes furnaces in Clerkenwell was the paved, triangular space known as Clerkenwell Green, where tall lime trees sheltered a cluster of public benches, and a knot of sandwich bars and pubs serviced the needs of the furnace workers. Close by rose St. James's Church, with its empty, pretty grass churchyard, which had been depopulated of graves since an outbreak of Phantasms decades before. On pleasant days, as the early shift ended and the Klaxon sounded from the furnace chimneys, a stream of orange-clad men and women emerged from the gates and descended on the green to have their lunch and wash the taste of burning from their tongues. Furnace operators, oilers, stokers, storage clerks, and ash-boys: all of them thronged together to join the human tide.

As did the attendants working the booths of the vetting room. Or so I was prepared to bet that morning.

By taking the Tube and walking swiftly, I had arrived on the green just before the lunchtime rush. I selected a bench not far from the lime trees, where I had a good view of the cafés and an ornamental ghost-lamp kept me in shadow.

Far off, the sirens sounded; I sat and waited, and watched the sidewalks. In dribs and drabs, the flow began. Within a few minutes, the quiet green, like a stream in snow-melt, had become a surging mass of activity. People filled the square; lines wound from the sandwich bars; birds flew in panic from the rooftops; pigeons frenzied over pastry crusts; every inch of every seat was packed. I sat where I was, impervious, unmoving.

The lunch hour proceeded; the lines dwindled. Discarded sandwich wrappers drifted like baby ghosts across the green. I waited without impatience. The vetting room attendants began their work at dawn, and would do another shift that afternoon. It was a long day. Food was necessary. Sooner or later, he *would* come.

And so it was that, at approximately 12:36 p.m., I saw a familiar freckled young man tripping swiftly down from Sekforde Street. He wore a raincoat over his jumpsuit, and his cropped fair hair was obscured beneath a knit cap. His fists were driven deep into his coat pockets, and his narrow shoulders were raised high. It seemed that Harold Mailer felt the cold.

I peeled myself off the bench and watched him go past. He crossed the green and disappeared into a baked potato joint, from which he presently emerged carrying a bulky paper bag. Looking neither right nor left, but going slightly more slowly now, he started back the way he had come.

I did not wait for him but went on ahead, walking up Sekforde Street at a brisk pace, until I located a small alley on the correct side of the road. It was dark, evil-smelling, and mostly filled with trash cans, which suited me very well. I ducked inside and waited, and soon came footsteps on the sidewalk that told me Harold Mailer drew near.

There may be praying mantises that can strike with greater speed. If so, I haven't met them. One moment Mailer was meandering along in the bright spring sunlight, sniffing happily at the contents of his bag; the next he found himself pinned against the cold wet bricks of an alley with my knee in his groin and my elbow pressed against his neck.

"Hello, Harold," I said.

He made a curiously squeaky noise that might have meant anything. I shifted my elbow slightly. The strangulated cough that followed wasn't much better.

"Lucy! What are you . . . what are you doing?"

"Just wanted a word with you, Harold."

"Can't we do it at the booth? I'm late. Got to get back. My shift—"

"Couple of questions for you. Private ones. Best done quietly, down here."

"Is this a joke?"

"This morning," I said, "somebody stole something from me. They broke into my apartment and took a valuable ghost-jar, and the relic it contained. They didn't take my money or any of my other valuables. Just the jar. No one knew about that jar, Harold. No one but you."

Harold Mailer's eyes had a hooded quality that made them look both sleepy and evasive. They flicked from side to side, as if seeking help, then steadied. He grinned at me, his top lip clammy with perspiration. "I don't know what you're talking about. I haven't taken anything! Let go!"

"The last time I came to Clerkenwell you saw the skull in the jar, Harold. I know you did. Then you told somebody about it. Who?"

He struggled a bit then, so I increased the pressure on his windpipe. It was probably a mistake, since he coughed all over me, but I'd never beaten anyone up before.

"So what if I saw the jar?" he croaked when I relented. "Why would I care what weird stuff you had? Why would it mean anything to me?"

"Oh, but haunted relics mean a lot to you, don't they?" I said. "More than you let on. Let me ask you something else. Three nights ago I brought you a mummified head. You took it and gave me a receipt. What did you do with it then?"

"The head? I burned it! You saw me!"

"No, Harold. No, you didn't. You kept it. You sold it. And I know that, because it was bought up at a black market auction the very same day."

"What? You're mad!"

"Am I? I saw it there."

That was a bit of a lie, but what can you do? Harold Mailer would just have gone on denying it, which would have wasted my time. Besides, Flo had seen it, and she was reliable.

He moistened his lips. "What were you doing at a black market sale?"

"What are *you* doing selling forbidden artifacts, Harold? You know the penalties for black market trade. You know how seriously Barnes takes this—or you *will* very soon, when I go to see him."

"This is *so* mad, Lucy. You're insane."

"Who do you sell this stuff to, Harold? For the last time: Who did you tell about my skull?"

Close-up, I could see that his eyes were greenish, flecked with yellow-brown. Something changed in them then; defiance turned to fear, and I knew I had him.

"Can't tell you," he gasped. "I can't. Upon my life. The walls have ears."

"We're in an alley, Harold. No one's here. The only ears littering the place"—I brought my rapier slowly into view—"are going to be yours, if you don't start being helpful."

Since I'd collared him, one of his knobbly hands had been scrabbling at my wrist. For a moment, just for a moment, I felt the quality of the pressure change and knew he was considering fighting back. What would have happened then, I don't know; he was as tall as me, and not much weaker, and I wouldn't *really* have been able to cut off his ears or any other part of him. But he was a coward, physically as well as morally, and the moment passed.

"All right, all right, give me a little space." He blew out his lips as I moved back a step, holding my rapier at the ready. He flexed his shoulders, a small, scared teen in an oversized coat, trying to rustle up some courage. "I need time to think. I need time. . . . What's that rank smell, anyway? Is it your coat?"

"No, Harold, it's the alley."

"Smells like stale sweat."

"Are we going to argue about odors now? I want answers."

"Okay." He was looking up the alley, twitchy as a jackrabbit, and at first I thought he was thinking of making a bolt for it; but it was a different kind of twitchiness—he was frightened of who else might be near. A few yards away, in the sunlit street, furnace workers were strolling past in ones and twos, but none of them looked our way.

"Okay," Harold Mailer said again, "I'll tell you—not that I know that much. Some men made contact with me three months ago. Black marketeers, I guess—I don't know. They offered me money if I could slip them the best Sources that came in. Since the rules were tightened, the market for artifacts has gotten so hot; there are some people who'll do anything for them. I needed the cash, Lucy. You don't know what it's like, working here; you get paid peanuts, and the Fittes bosses treat you like scum. It's not like being an agent—"

"Yeah, yeah," I said. "Skip the sob story. So you pass them the Sources, and burn substitutes in their place."

"Only the best ones, the most powerful pieces. It's easy enough; no one ever looks closely at what we roll into the fire." He tried a weak grin. "I mean, where's the harm in it, really? Doesn't hurt no one."

I pressed the rapier against his belly. "Is that so? You forget, they stole *my* property. Because *you* told them about it. You gave them the tip. Why?"

"I'm sorry, I know that was wrong. It's just, they're getting impatient for good stuff, Lucy. It's like they can't get enough of it. Sometimes I don't have anything good, and they get angry. . . . But they like information, too, see? You have to keep them happy."

"So who *are* these men? What do they want the Sources *for*?"

"I don't know."

"Well, what are they like? Describe them."

"I don't know who they are."

I stepped away from him. "That's useless, Harold. You've given me nothing. I'm going to Barnes now. Get off my arm."

He lurched forward with a cry, and caught at my sleeve. "You don't understand. They're not nice people, Luce! You don't spend time staring at them. You transfer the stuff and leave. Everything's done after dark. Listen, I can help you. I'm giving them a package tonight. You could be there. You could watch—see them, follow them maybe, I don't know, as long as you keep me out of it. What do you think? I could do that for you. I could do that, Lucy, if you don't . . . What? Why are you laughing?"

"I know just what would happen. You'd hand me over to them and run off."

"No! I swear! I hate them! They're bad news, Lucy. I should never have gotten in with them. Only the money was *so* good. Listen, they're dropping off a message this afternoon, telling me the place. It's different each time. Always somewhere in Clerkenwell, but I never know where. I could meet you, once my shift ends. Here, or in the churchyard. I could tell you what's been arranged. Then you could wait tonight, maybe hide someplace. It'll be fine as long as they don't find out you're there."

Well, I could think of a thousand reasons why this was a bad idea, and all of them stemmed from Harold Mailer's complete untrustworthiness. It seemed quite likely that he would prefer to see me dead than ruin his lucrative little trade, and letting him go would give him ample time to set up such an outcome. Having said that, I clearly wasn't going to do much better here.

He was watching my face, sidelong. "I'll make it worth your while," he said.

"If anything happens to me tonight," I said, after a long pause, "if you betray me in some way, I have friends who will hunt you down and make you pay. You'll wish you'd thrown yourself into one of your furnaces instead of crossing me." It was the best threat I could think of, but it sounded pretty weak, not to mention clichéd. Harold Mailer didn't seem to care. He was nodding, white-faced, desperate to be gone.

"Dusk, then," he said, "at St. James's churchyard. There's a bench in the center, where the four paths meet. I'll be there. I'll have the information you need. But they can't know about you, Lucy. They can't. You've got to believe me. You don't know what they'll do. Promise you won't ever tell them that I spoke to you."

"If you keep your word with me," I said, "I'll do the same. Otherwise . . ."

"Oh, you agents always play fair, I know that." He was clutching for his lunch bag, lying abandoned on the ground. "Everyone loves the agencies." Then he was sidling away from me, his coat scuffing against the bricks, his face a queasy stew of duplicity, dislike, and fear. He got to the corner and rounded it like a rat, pressed close to the edge, gathering speed. "At dusk," he said again, and was gone.

Chapter 12

Strange how close the darkness is, even when things seem brightest. Even in the glare of a summer noon, when the sidewalk bakes and iron fences are hot to the touch, the shadows are still with us. They congregate in doorways and porches, and under bridges, and beneath the brims of gentlemen's hats so you cannot see their eyes. There is darkness in our mouths and ears; in our bags and wallets; within the swing of men's jackets and beneath the flare of women's skirts. We carry it around with us, the dark, and its influence stains us deep.

That afternoon I sat in the window of a café on Clerkenwell Green, watching the faces in the crowds. Because of my profession, I didn't get out much during the day, and my experience with ordinary people was mostly confined to the ghost-haunted and the dead. These folk passing me now—they represented everyone else, that terrified majority who kept their heads down, put their iron and silver in the windows, and tried to get on with their lives. The young, the old, busy enjoying the bright spring sunshine; they looked harmless enough to me.

Yet somewhere out there, perhaps even among the people passing outside my window, were those attracted by the dark. It found expression in different ways. Some joined the ghost-cults that had proliferated across London, loudly welcoming the returning dead and trying to hear the messages they brought. Others sought out forbidden artifacts for their danger and rarity; there were stories of rich collectors who had dozens of Sources, stolen from graveyards and secreted in iron vaults underground. And there were those who used the Sources for strange occult rituals. At Lockwood & Co., we'd seen odd markings in the catacombs beneath the Aickmere Brothers department store: evidence of an abandoned circle, surrounded by heaps of haunted bones. George had theories, but the exact purpose of the circle—and who was responsible for it—remained in shadow.

One way or another, despite DEPRAC's best efforts, the black market for artifacts remained strong. And it seemed that, with the wretched Harold Mailer, I'd stumbled upon one of its main supply lines.

What to *do* about it, though? Whoever Mailer's contacts were, it was likely the trail would lead to the criminal Winkman family. Flo had seen the mummified head in their possession, after all. If I could gain proof of the connection between the Winkmans and the theft of Sources from the furnaces, I would make a decent name for myself.

But that wasn't my main priority. If it had been, I probably would just have nipped along to Scotland Yard, seen Inspector Barnes, and gotten him to do the work.

No, what *I* wanted, most particularly, was to retrieve the whispering skull.

You heard me right. I wanted the skull back. *That* wasn't a statement I'd ever have expected to make.

In many ways, the ghost in the jar had been a thorn in my side for ages. When I'd first encountered it, upon joining Lockwood's company, I'd reacted with instant horror and distaste; and these feelings only intensified when it began to speak to me. It was thoroughly, defiantly, exultantly reprehensible; in fact, if you wrote down the ten most unsavory character traits you could imagine, the skull possessed the nine worst on the list, and it only lacked the tenth because that one wasn't quite bad enough. The ghost's name was unknown, and much of its past a mystery, though since what little we knew of its pre-death career involved grave-robbing, black magic, and cold-blooded murder, that wasn't altogether a shame. No one else could hear it speak, so the skull had formed a special bond with me. Since it had the language of a longshoreman and the morals of a weasel, I'd had to cope with constant psychic sarcasm and abuse, and also learned plenty of new words.

And yet, despite disliking it so much, I'd come to rely on that ghost.

At the basic level, it *did* help me, fairly often, when I was out at work. Its insights, no matter how fleeting, *had* saved me many times. It had pinpointed Emma Marchment's ghost, for instance, just a day or two before, and perhaps stopped me from blundering straight into her clutches. And last night it had dropped a hint—a pretty belated one, admittedly—about the location of the Source in the Ealing Cannibal affair. This was supernatural assistance that other operatives didn't have.

Which brought me to the wider point, the more profound reason why I hung around in Clerkenwell that day, hoping against hope that Harold Mailer wouldn't betray me. The skull was a Type Three ghost, one that could communicate fully with the living, and that made it incredibly rare. And *I* was rare, too; I alone had the ability to hear it. With such a powerful artifact at my side, I was uniquely successful; the first person since Marissa Fittes to *genuinely* talk with ghosts. All my confidence, such as it was, stemmed from this simple fact. Without it? I was an ordinary agent once again—skilled, but unspectacular.

Like it or not, the whispering skull helped define me. It was part of who I was. And now some grubby criminals were trying to take it from me.

But I wasn't going to lose it without a fight.

The Winkmans and their operation were formidable; I knew that from experience. But if I trailed them tonight and found their storehouse, they would discover I was formidable, too.

So I sat, drinking tea and dozing, while the sun went down beyond the houses. As dusk came, I put on my coat, tightened the straps of my rapier, and set off for St. James's churchyard.

Don't think I hadn't cased the place earlier, by the way. It had been the first thing I'd done after Mailer had scampered. I'd headed up toward the church, through the old iron gates, and into the square of open ground, where a few lunchtime picnickers lingered in the cool spring sunlight. It was almost entirely grass, that old yard, still undulating and irregular from where the graves had been removed in the great purge many years before, and it was surrounded on all sides by buildings. St. James's neoclassical facade loomed to the north; elsewhere were the backs of houses, high churchyard walls, and locked iron gates. One entrance opened onto Sekforde Street, and another onto Clerkenwell Green; these were connected by a simple concrete path. A second, smaller path ran from the church to a narrow alley in the south. Where the two paths crossed, roughly in the center of the churchyard, sat a single black wooden bench.

I'd walked past that bench a number of times, deep in thought. It was a curious choice for a meeting place, being both extremely exposed and actually—when you considered the churchyard overall—quite shut in. I didn't mind being out in the open, but I *did* dislike the ring of walls all around.

What had Lockwood once told me about making sure that you always had a way out? Before engaging with any psychic phenomena, it's vital to establish the terrain. Get a grip on the layout—particularly the exits and dead ends. Why? Because you've got to know how to vamoose if you lose control of the situation. I reckoned what applied to ghosts applied equally to crooked furnace workers.

I'd completed several circuits of that churchyard, making calculations, measuring distances, checking and rechecking till I was happy. When I'd finally headed for the café, I could have drawn the whole site from memory. Now, four hours later, I was ready to put my mental map to good use.

With the onset of dusk, the streets of Clerkenwell had emptied fast. The shops were closing, iron barriers were rattling down. Thanks to the sunny day, and the numerous ghost-lamps in the vicinity, a few pedestrians were still abroad, hastening to catch the final Tube trains. Some night-watch kids were already present. In St. James's Church, wardens tolled the curfew bell.

The churchyard was unlit. Lamps burned at three of its gates, with the black space between them suspended like a hammock. There were lit windows, too, high up in the buildings, which cast scattered squares of brightness across the lawns. I entered from the Sekforde Street gate, which was farthest from the central bench, and swiftly found a dark spot near the wall, where my eyes could adjust to the complex patterns of the half-light.

Was he here?

The path beside me curved faint and pale across the grass like a shining rib bone, and by following it, I saw where it crossed the other one. Close by, I could just see the low black bench and, by frowning, squinting—yes—make out someone sitting there.

So he *had* come. Good. But was he alone?

I took my time surveying the churchyard, letting my eyes roam the featureless ground. Everything was silent, everything fine. I could see no one else between the bench and the surrounding walls.

Keeping off the path, avoiding the illuminated squares of spot-lighted grass, I began walking slowly toward the bench. I kept my eyes fixed on the figure sitting there. It was Harold Mailer, all right; I recognized his raincoat and his narrow, spindly frame. He was sitting quietly, just waiting, staring at the ground.

My boots brushed through dark grass; soundlessly I moved toward him.

When still a ways off, I adjusted my approach so that I angled around behind him. Even from the back I could see how relaxed he was, his arms stretched out along the top of the bench, head slightly tilted, like a man taking a gentle doze.

My feet slowed. I came to a gradual halt.

He was as twitchy as they came, Harold. Nervy at the best of times, let alone at dusk, in a churchyard, on an illicit rendezvous, with his career—and life—hanging in the balance.

All at once his utter relaxation bothered me.

I stared at him. Why was he so chill?

Come to think of it, why was his head at such an angle?

Why didn't he move?

My hand stole to my sword. I was a statue planted in the grass.

My scalp prickled; I heard a cold voice drifting on the wind.

"*Lucy . . .*"

Out of the corner of my left eye, I sensed a shape forming in the air. It was soft, hesitant, knitted from yarns of shadow. It gathered blackness around it as if clumsily clothing itself. It hung in the dark beside me, close enough to touch. Cold radiated from it, sharp as knives. My lips drew back in fear; my teeth grinned in ghastly welcome. I kept hot eyes fixed straight ahead, still staring at the bench and its lifeless occupant with the twisted, broken neck. I did not dare look at the drab thing at my side, and particularly not at the half-formed face I sensed so close to mine.

My voice was barely a rasp. "Harold?"

"*Lucy . . .*"

"What have they done to you?"

A tiny cracking noise was the only answer; looking down, I saw flecks of ice spreading across the wrinkles in my sleeve, pincers of frost encircling my boot. The left side of my face burned with supernatural chill; my breath plumed white. The shape was very near.

"Who did this, Harold? Who killed you?"

A mumbled flood of words, splashing against my brain. So full of anguish and confusion . . . I could not make them out.

How thick my tongue felt, how dry and swollen. It was as if it were glued inside my mouth. "Tell me. If you tell me I can . . . I can help you. . . ." But I couldn't get the Lucy Carlyle Formula™ out. Not this time.

"You did this, Lucy. . . ."

Out of the corner of my eye, I saw a nebulous hand of cloud reach toward my face.

"No, Harold, no, that's not true. . . ."

"You did this." Its fingers stroked the air close to my skin. I flinched away. Ice blistered across my cheek. I could feel it building across the hollow of my eye. My mind hurt; my grip closed on the hilt of my rapier.

"No, Harold. Please don't—"

"It is at the place of blood."

"What?"

The shape was gone.

With a shudder, with bile rising in my throat, I lurched back and to the side, rubbing at my face, my boot tearing free of the frozen ground.

As I did so, three men rose up from the grass.

For a second I thought they were phantoms, too; the impossibility of their appearance numbed my brain. But I'd forgotten about the humps and ridges, the hollows left long ago, when the churchyard had been emptied of its graves. Some were deep enough to conceal a crouching man; they'd been hiding there while I'd merrily walked toward the body of Harold Mailer at the center of their trap. They were large men, dressed in black; large, but moving fast to encircle me. One was over to the left, back toward the gate where I'd come from; the others blocked the way to other exits. If I'd gotten as far as the bench, I would have had no chance of escape. They would have surrounded me with ease.

But I'd halted. The space behind me was clear.

I turned and ran.

Not toward one of the churchyard gates, where the lamps burned so faintly, but to the black mass of high wall midway between them. In the coffee-colored dusk, it seemed a solid and impenetrable slab. But I'd done my homework, and I knew otherwise.

Up a gentle slope, leaping over hollows, almost twisting my ankle on fragments of old stone, I reached the wall. Behind me, the three figures arrowed inward, converging on me where I stood.

There was an old door there: locked, but usefully designed, with protruding hardware and crossbeams that I could get a foothold on. I launched myself up, grabbed the top of the door, where it was loosely set in a crumbling arch, and began scrabbling higher. One toe on a beam, one on the lock; I straightened my legs, reached up—my fingers connected with the top of the wall. That was all I needed. A kick, an unbecoming wriggle, and I'd pulled myself up and over. I hung there for a moment before dropping lightly down into foliage on the other side. As I did so, something impacted hard against the door.

I was in the yard of an abandoned building, perhaps once the vicarage of the church. Stacks of bricks and piles of rusted scaffolding poles suggested that someone, at some stage, hoped to carry out renovations—but now it was deserted, as I'd noticed earlier that day. A first floor window gaped ahead of me, empty of glass, and I vaulted through it into a black space. I snatched a glance behind, saw figures hauling themselves over the wall, silhouetted for an instant against the stars.

The interior of the place was a mess, full of debris. I flicked on my flashlight; I jumped, dodged, went slaloming from room to room. To my dismay, the windows on the other side had been securely sealed and boarded. I could not get out that way.

Sounds behind me. They were already in the house.

A broad, dilapidated staircase opened before me. I sprang up it, three steps at a time.

There, at the top of the stairs, a window—glazed, but tempting. I pressed my face against it and saw a flat roof below, then a garden stretching away.

Was that window a nice modern one, easy to open? No, of course not. It was a sash affair, old and rotten and warped; it was all I could do to lift it high enough to admit my head and shoulders. It squeaked, juddered in the grooves, then froze altogether. I was going to have to wriggle through.

I looked behind me, and my heart nearly stopped. The three figures were halfway up the stairs. The leader had something silvery in his hand.

No time for wriggling. Stepping back from the window, I launched myself forward through the gap, shunting myself out into the moonlight. As I fell out and down, a hand caught my boot and gripped it tight. For an instant I hung there; then I thrashed upward with my other foot, connecting sharply with something very soft. The hand let go and I tumbled onto the flat roof below.

As soon as I landed, I flung myself violently to the side. Something struck the asphalt roof where I'd just been lying and stuck there quivering. I tore a canister of iron from my belt, turned, and lobbed it hard. It smashed into the window, just above a protruding head. Shards of glass dropped like dislodged icicles; someone screamed, the head whipped back into the house, and I was up and away along the low, flat roof, reaching the corner in five quick strides.

From that corner, I could see a high wall extending away between two gardens, with expanses of grass stretching left and right like black and frozen seas. I didn't relish being trapped in either garden, with no sure way out. The wall would do. It was three feet lower than the roof, and I had to turn and drop carefully onto the narrow crest of bricks. As I did so, I saw the first of my pursuers jumping from the ruined window.

Along the crest I ran, scampering as a cat would, looking straight ahead, ignoring the drop on either side. There were trees in the gardens; you could see silvery ghost-wards hanging from them, smell the lavender bushes out there in the dark. Behind I heard a shout; something flashed past my shoulder and was gone.

I got to a place where the wall split: it marked the end of the gardens of this street, and the beginnings of the ones on the next. To my right, a side wall sprouted off. To the left, a thick hedge stretched away. I looked back; one of the men had followed me along the wall, moving hesitantly, a small knife in his hand. Another had jumped down onto the lawn and was sprinting across the grass. *He* would have his work cut out for him, because the hedge would block his way. The third man was nowhere to be seen. Perhaps he had been injured by the broken window. I hoped so.

I continued straight, following the line I was on. I wanted to reach the road beyond. Ahead of me: the next row of houses. There, too, glinting coldly in the moonlight, an all-glass conservatory, where my wall came to an end. Beyond, I could make out the low roof of a garage, and perhaps a gap leading to the street.

The conservatory roof was higher than the wall. As I slowed to consider it, something struck my forearm. I felt a sharp lance of pain, and the shock of it made me stumble. I almost toppled from my perch; instead, I pitched forward against the side of the conservatory. My arm stung as I pulled myself up onto its roof; when I touched the place, my fingers came away wet.

Over the glass roof I ran, leaning inward, boots slipping and sliding on the tilted panes. Up off the glass, onto the roof of the garage. The street wasn't far away.

Another shout behind was answered by a second cry. I paused. Looking back, I saw the first pursuer had climbed onto the conservatory. He was bigger than I was, and considerably heavier; he couldn't bring himself to run across it as I had. Dropping to a sitting position, he began to shuffle across the apex of the roof like a chubby-thighed kid riding a ghost-horse at the fair.

I waited until he was halfway across, out of reach of either end. Then I took a magnesium flare from my pocket.

It wasn't a very nice thing to do, but I didn't much care right then.

When I chucked it, the flare hit the conservatory roof just in front of the shuffling man, exploding in a blaze of searing white light, and showering him in fragments of hot iron. He gave a cry and lurched back, trying to protect his face. Even as he did so, the glass under his knees cracked, then shattered completely. The roof collapsed; with a scream the man pitched forward into the silvery smoke and disappeared.

Something bounced against the brickwork at my back; a knife spun past across the asphalt roof. The pursuer in the garden had broken through the hedge and was running over the lawn toward me.

I gave him a rude gesture, then scrabbled away across the roof, dropped over the far side onto a car hood, and bounced down onto a cobbled driveway. As I hit the ground I was already running. It was a small mews, possibly quite pretty, but I couldn't hang around to admire the architecture. I was out of it in moments and sprinting full tilt through the silent streets of Clerkenwell.

It was only when I was a mile or so away, lost among the winding alleys near St. Pancras station, that I allowed myself to slow down a little. But I didn't stop moving even then. My sleeve was wet, and the side of my arm felt numb. It was a cold night; to rest would have made me prey to shock and exhaustion. Plus, it might have set my mind working. And I *really* didn't want to think about what had happened to me—and to Harold Mailer—right then.

One thing I *did* know, instinctively, without deliberation, was that I couldn't go back home. The men who'd tried to silence me knew full well where I lived. My little studio in Tooting wouldn't be a healthy place that night.

And so, by slow degrees, going by back roads, making a cautious loop through the northern districts of central London, I started on the long and painful journey toward the one refuge I could think of. The one place I *knew* I'd be safe.

I didn't need to think hard about this one, either.

I was making for 35 Portland Row.

Chapter 13

I t's only three miles as the crow flies from Clerkenwell to
Marylebone, but it took me several hours to cover the distance.
Weariness dragged at me, and I often lost my way. Also, I was
wary of pursuit, and so kept off the main roads, making lengthy
diversions to avoid encounters with the living. I saw a few vehicles
in the distance—mostly agency cars and DEPRAC vans—and in my
state of mind I trusted none of them. My paranoia kept me safe, and
no ghosts detected me, which was another plus, but I was a slow and
sorry figure by the time I reached the familiar street at last.

I trudged up the center of the road, past Arif's corner store, past
the rusty ghost-lamp, meandering listlessly between the silent chains
of parked cars. Everything was quiet, dark, locked down. Midnight
had come and gone. No one in their right mind was making house
calls now—except for agents out on cases. It was only then, as I
reached number 35 and saw its unlit windows, that I remembered

it was quite possible—quite likely—that Lockwood and the others would not be home. The realization made me sway; but it was too late now. I crossed over to the gate.

It was still crooked, and they hadn't changed the sign:

A. J. Lockwood & Co., Investigators.
After dark, ring bell and wait beyond the iron line.

I pushed it open, walked carefully up toward the house, over the uneven tiles. In the glow of the streetlight outside number 37, the iron barrier embedded halfway up the path glinted with a soft sheen. I could see the bell hanging from its post beside it. So many cases had begun with that bell clanging at odd hours of the night. Such different clients: the Slaine family's doctor, calling us out after finding all six of them vanished from their beds; the one surviving member of the Bromley Wick shooting party . . . In the Bayswater Stalker affair, wicked old Crawford's niece had pretty much swung from it in her desperation, with him floating behind her up the road.

One thing held true every time: it made a heck of a racket.

I reached for the clapper, looking back at the sleeping street— and for a moment a vestige of pride resurfaced. Perhaps I should wait until morning, for a more civilized hour. I could always find shelter somewhere, curl up on the step behind Arif's store, maybe, and—

Nope, *that* stupid idea didn't detain me long. I needed help, and I needed it *now*.

I grasped the clapper and swung it hard.

George once told me there was a theory that ghosts disliked

loud noises, particularly ones made with iron instruments. He said the ancient Greeks used to send evil spirits packing with metal rattles and tambourines. Well, if anything undead had been lurking in Portland Row that night, their ectoplasm would have dissolved the instant I began ringing. I nearly lost a few teeth myself. The appalling noise ripped a hole in the fabric of the night.

I gave it a good twenty seconds, and when I stopped, my heart's clapper kept pounding against my chest.

A short time passed. To my great relief, movements sounded in the house. A faint glow showed in the semicircle of petaled panes above the door. That would be the crystal skull lantern on the hall table being switched on. I heard the chain being removed, the bolt pulled back. I stepped away from the door, back across the iron line. Best not to come too close. Some people could be mighty jittery if they saw a dark figure when they opened a door at night, particularly if those people were George.

But it wasn't George. It was Lockwood. The door swung back, and there he was in his long bathrobe and his dark blue pajamas, with the spare rapier, the one we kept with the umbrellas in the hall, ready in his hand. His feet were bare, his hair rumpled. His lean face was wary but relaxed. He stared out into the dark.

I just stood there. I didn't know what to say to him.

"Lucy?"

I'd not slept at all that night, and for only a short while the night before. In the last few hours I'd fled from three killers, and come face-to-face with a newly murdered ghost. I'd been cut by a throwing knife; I'd sustained countless bumps and bruises during my escape, after which I'd walked halfway across London. I hadn't eaten since . . . When *had* I eaten? I couldn't remember. My leggings were torn. I was cold, stiff, and sore, and could barely stand. Oh, yeah, and my coat stank.

It was after midnight. I stood on his doorstep, looking just swell. "Lockwood—"

But he was already at my side, putting his arm around me, pulling me upright, ushering me up to the door and into the warmth and light. And talking, talking as he did so.

"Lucy, what's happened? You're shaking. Come on. Come on inside."

The familiar Portland Row smell enveloped me: that mix of iron and salt, and leather coats, and that curious dusty, musty tang that came from the masks and pots and Eastern curios on the shelves. For some reason, I suddenly felt close to tears. *That* wouldn't do. I blinked them away as the door clicked behind us, shutting out the night. Lockwood shot the bolt, pulled the chains across; he flipped the rapier into the old chipped plant pot we used as an umbrella stand. His arm was still around me; he led me up the hall.

"Sorry to disturb you so late," I said.

"Don't give it a thought! But you're exhausted, I can barely hear you. Let's get you to the kitchen."

Through to the kitchen we went; on came the light—bright and clean and hard enough to make me wince. I saw the cereals and salt bins, the cups and kettles. I saw George's moth-eaten cushion on his seat. And I saw the Thinking Cloth on the table: a fresh one, with unfamiliar doodles and designs. *That* made my eyes prickle, too. Lockwood didn't notice; he was saying something, pulling back a chair. As I sank into it, he caught sight of my sleeve, saw the congealed blood running from elbow to wrist. His face changed.

"What is this?"

"It's nothing. Just a cut."

He knelt at my side, pulled my sleeve back with his long, quick fingers, exposing the laceration on my arm. He gazed up at me with searching eyes. "A knife made this, Lucy. Who—?" He stood up. "No—explanations can wait. I'll get George; we can clean this, fix you up. You don't have to worry anymore; you're safe here."

"Thank you. I know. That's why I came."

"You want tea?"

"Yes, please. In a bit. But I can make it—"

"Not a chance. Just sit tight." He rose. "George wears earplugs these days, otherwise his own snores wake him up. Means I've got to venture into his room."

"If you don't come back," I said, "I'll come looking for you." I hesitated. "Actually . . . on second thought, maybe not."

He grinned, squeezed my shoulder. With a swish of his bathrobe he was gone. I sat there in the warm kitchen, and whether it was because I'd dropped off, or because Lockwood moved so fast, it seemed only a second later that the door burst open and in came George, pale-faced, pajamas flapping, bustling over with a first aid kit under his arm.

An unknown while later, I had a mug of tea in front of me and a mound of biscuits close at hand. The first aid kit lay open on the table, along with scattered scraps of cotton and antiseptic pads. George and Lockwood had cleaned and dressed my wound together, and though I thought they'd gone slightly overboard with the bandages—my arm looked like something you might see rising from a mummy's sarcophagus—I certainly felt a lot better. As they worked, as Lockwood boiled water and George poured cookies onto plates, I told them what had happened. They listened without interrupting. When I finished, we dunked biscuits in silence for a while.

"That little Harold Mailer," George said at last. "Incredible. Who'd have guessed?"

"Bad form to speak ill of the dead, of course," Lockwood said, "but I always thought he was a ratty little specimen. Laughed too much, too loudly. I never liked him."

"Doesn't mean he deserved to die," I said.

"No, of course not. . . . But why *did* he die? Why did they kill him? Two possibilities: either he was dumb enough to tell them about you, or they sussed out he was going to give you information. Whichever it was, they decided to eliminate the problem." He looked sharply over at me; I was staring at the table. "I hope you're not feeling guilty about this, Lucy. It's in no way your fault. You realize that, don't you? Mailer chose to get involved with those men. The fact that you challenged him doesn't make you responsible for his murder."

All of which was no doubt true. Still, I couldn't feel happy about it. "He could have ghost-touched me," I said quietly. "He was right there beside me, in the churchyard. But he didn't. He chose to hold back."

"Yes, that *was* good of him," Lockwood said, after a silence. "Fair enough."

"What was that thing he said to you?" George asked. "About the 'place of blood'? Any idea what that was about?"

I sighed. "Not a clue. Maybe I misheard. He was babbling a lot of stuff, and it was all pretty messed up. As it *would* be . . . under the circumstances." As it would be when you've just been *killed*, was what I meant. In my mind's eye I could see that lolling form, sitting abandoned on the bench. No doubt Harold's body was still there, alone in the dark and cold. . . .

I tried to concentrate on something else. "Lockwood," I said, "do you think some of the other attendants at the furnaces are in on this?"

He shrugged. "Wouldn't surprise me if they're all at it. It's a big deal, this scam, which is why those guys were so keen to shut you up, too, Luce. Obviously you can't go home now. They know where you live."

I stared at the table, cleared my throat. "I know. I was hoping, maybe, tonight I could crash here . . . ? Just till morning. Then tomorrow—"

"Oh, not just tonight." Lockwood got up, went to the fridge. "You can't go home, period. Not till we've found those men and put an end to this. She can stay here for a while, can't she, George?"

It was a testament to George that until that instant I'd completely forgotten about the recent difficulties between us. Tending to my injury, listening to my story, he'd displayed nothing but compassion and concern. Now, just for a second, as he looked at me and hesitated, I remembered his anger and the hurt I'd caused him. Then his face cleared. "Absolutely," he said. "'Course she can."

A warm feeling filled me: it was made of tea and biscuits and sudden gratitude. "Thank you."

"It'll make a nice change from Holly staying over," George said. "I always feel like I have to clean the bathtub after me when she's around, in case I've left hairs in it, or a ring of dirt or something. But it's different with old Luce. Old Luce doesn't mind."

Lockwood had produced a plastic jug and was taking out glasses. "You fret too much about Holly, George. She didn't complain last night, did she? You want some orange juice, Lucy? It's your favorite: the kind with pulp."

"Lucy doesn't *like* orange juice with pulp," George said. "Remember?"

"Oh, yes, that's right. It gets caught between your teeth, doesn't it?"

I was staring at him. My warm feeling had partially retreated. "I'll take the juice. So Holly stayed over last night?"

"Personally, I've always thought straining it through your teeth is part of the fun," Lockwood said. "You can pretend you're a blue whale." He caught my look. "What?"

"Holly. She's staying over now?"

"Oh, not always. Depends how the night turns out. Waffles, George?"

"Please. I *am* hungry."

"Luce?"

"Yes . . . okay, I'd like some waffles. How often is she staying over?"

Lockwood flicked the toaster on. "I don't know that it's really something for a freelancer like you to worry about. She's not using your old room, if that's what's bothering you." He whistled tunelessly as he poured himself some juice.

"She's not? So where—?"

"I keep most of my clothes up there now," George said. "My room's so full of books and experiments, it can't even hold my tightest shorts. Your attic does nicely. Otherwise we've left it just how it was when you went. You can sleep in it tonight, if you like."

"Thanks . . . that's kind of you."

"Sure. I'll try not to wake you when I nip up there to get dressed in the morning."

For a few minutes after that, food occupied center stage. Waffles were made, and orange juice drunk (strained or unstrained). I stared around at the kitchen. It was very spic-and-span. That was Holly's continuing influence; in my day, she'd run the house like a military operation. The only new thing I noticed was a bulletin board that had been hung on the cupboard next to the office stairs. On it was a map of southeast England, with London at the center, showing all the nearby counties. Colored pins radiated out in concentric ovals from a central point southeast of the city. I stared at it blankly. The precision and detail of the effort had the hallmarks of George.

At last Lockwood pushed his plate away. "So let's think about this," he said. "The implications of what you've told us, Luce, are huge. DEPRAC is assuming that all the Sources taken to the furnaces are being destroyed. Some of them—maybe the whole lot, for all we know—are instead being saved and funneled into the black market. Incredibly dangerous items are being dispersed that way. Take the jar of teeth from Guppy's house, for instance. We thought that it got safely burned that the other night—but did it? We just don't know."

I shuddered. The thought of the cannibal's spirit being unleashed again was frightful. "Who took it, at the furnaces?" I asked. "Was it Mailer?"

"No," Lockwood said. "Fellow named Christie. Seemed honest enough, but who can tell?"

"It would be a blow if that case started up again," George said. "You won't have heard, Luce, but Penelope Fittes was quite pleased about our efforts in Ealing. She wants to meet us again. I reckon she's got another job planned, but Lockwood thinks it might be a medal."

"Why not both?" Lockwood grinned at me. "Well, if she's pleased with that, just think how delighted she'll be when we crack this black market ring. It's our old friends the Winkmans, of course. They're at the heart of it, for sure."

"Hold it. When you say we 'crack' it," George said, "what exactly are you getting at? It's not our concern. The obvious thing is to tell Inspector Barnes."

"We could, I suppose." Lockwood spoke in an exaggeratedly bored voice. "*If* we want DEPRAC to mess it up. *Or* take credit. Or both."

That was my cue. I'd been hoping to say something for a while, but hadn't been sure how to begin. Lockwood's evident interest gave me my chance. "I met with Flo the other day," I said. "She said there's a new collector in town, someone who pays really well for the best Sources. The Winkmans are pulling out all the stops to fulfill this guy's needs. Flo said there are big night-markets, where transactions take place with the relic-men. And I *know* Mailer's stuff ended up at those markets, because that mummified head I told you about was there."

I paused, took in their reactions. Lockwood nodded, smiling just a little. I knew he was surfing the same thought. George, expressionless, watched me closely.

"So I was sort of wondering," I went on, casually, "whether I might drop in on the next meeting. See if I can find out how the operation works, who the collector is, you know."

Lockwood rubbed his chin; there was a faraway light in his eyes. "Flo's the contact," he said. "She might be able to wangle something for you, get you inside. Risky game, though, Luce."

"*I'll* say it's risky," George agreed. "Those gangsters have already tried to kill you. You'd be handing yourself to them on a platter."

I shrugged. "I guess that's true, yeah."

"Plus, relic-men hate outsiders. They're notoriously violent to anyone who pokes his nose into their business."

"I've heard that, too."

"And don't forget the Winkmans," George went on. "Leopold and Adelaide have personally vowed to tear us limb from limb. It would be a complete hornet's nest of danger."

"Yep, it's a dumb plan, Luce," Lockwood said. He stretched back in his chair. "Suicidal, even. *If* you did it on your own."

He smiled at me.

The warm feeling was back; when I surfaced from it, I noticed George had taken off his glasses and was rubbing them with a corner of his pajama top. It may have been a fairly agitated kind of rub, but I didn't look too closely, as in doing so he'd accidentally revealed a too-pink portion of his stomach. "There's no way, Lockwood," he was saying. "It can't be done."

Lockwood was staring at the ceiling, his hands behind his head. "Oh, there's *bound* to be a way. . . . We just haven't dreamed it up yet."

I spoke in a small voice. "We—I—don't mean for us to do anything stupid," I said. "It's just—" I hesitated. "The thing is, what I really want is—"

"I know exactly what you want," George said. "You want the skull."

I gazed at him.

"Go on, admit it. That's what's driving you. You want it back. You miss it. The Winkman thing is strictly secondary."

"Well, I don't exactly *miss* it." I gave a light laugh. "I mean, it's not like I need it to talk to, or anything. But yeah, I want it back. It's important to me."

"That foul old skull?"

"Yes."

"With all its horrid habits?" George scratched his belly button wonderingly with the frames of his glasses, then set them back on his nose. "Extraordinary."

"You know how unique that ghost is," I said. "Other spirits communicate, but only in fragments, snatches of words. The skull is different, and I—I don't want to lose that connection. If possible, I'd like to find a way. . . . I *could* try it on my own, of course, but if Lockwood and Company would be prepared to help me, I'd be very grateful. . . . As to that, it's up to you."

We sat there. For a minute or two, no one said anything.

"George," Lockwood said, "how many cases have we currently got?"

"A few. Hol will know how many. And there's a possible new client coming to see us this morning. You remember, the one from out of town. Which reminds me, we should really get some sleep."

Lockwood nodded slowly. "Well, Luce, we *could* look into this for you. Not just for the skull's sake, though I see that it's important. As far as I'm concerned, it would be because of what those men tried to do to you." He took a bite of waffle. "But, technically speaking, that would make you our client rather than our colleague. Would you be okay with that?"

He had that look that I knew so well: a kind of shining, as if the spark of adventure had been ignited within him. George was shaking his head and huffing mightily, but I saw the electricity in his eyes, too. It was strange: as a client, as someone firmly in their debt, things felt easier between us than they had since the day I'd left.

"I'm okay with that," I said, and I meant it. "Thank you, Lockwood. Thank you, George. And . . . and if we're talking about payment . . ."

Lockwood raised a hand. "We're not. Good. That's settled, then. Now, if you can remember your way upstairs, we all need to get to bed."

Chapter 14

My sleep that morning was as deep as death; and, on waking, I experienced complete disorientation. Surfacing like a free diver who had stayed below too long, I found myself staring at the sunlit beams of my sweet old attic bedroom. I sat up and looked around me, and for those few short moments I was still working at Lockwood & Co. and the events of the last months were nothing more than a twisted, fading dream. Then I noticed some of George's socks draped like weary snakes over the windowsill, and piles of his garments rising like sinister gravestones at the bottom of the bed, and the world tipped back again.

I took an awkward shower in the tiny bathroom wedged beneath the eaves, keeping my bandaged arm outside the curtain. Then I got dressed. The bright spot here was that I had fresh clothes. Upon opening my door, I'd found a neat arrangement of folded items waiting on the landing step. They were all mine, things I must have left behind in my rush to leave four months before. Someone—Holly, I supposed—had washed and ironed them in the meantime. I took them in and sorted through. In the end I had to wear the same skirt, but the rest was clean, which made me feel much more presentable.

My body seemed light, strange and bloodless, as if I were recovering from a fever. Moving slowly, I went down to the second floor landing. The walls were still decorated with odd items of bone, shell, and feather: the ghost-catchers and other Eastern curios brought back to England by Lockwood's vanished parents many years before. And there, closed as ever, was the door to Lockwood's sister's room, the place where she'd died. In short, everything was as it always had been—but it was as if I were seeing it for the first time. Forbidden rooms, unhappy memories . . . How close the past was in this house, how tightly it ringed poor Lockwood.

Voices were coming from the living room below. It was midmorning; the client meeting they'd mentioned must be in progress. I would not disturb them. I slipped downstairs and sneaked toward the kitchen.

There's a particular creaky floorboard near the foot of the stairs. A man had once died on that spot, and George claimed the noise (which he swore had only started after the death) was an example of an ultra-low-level haunting. Me, I thought it was just a creaky floorboard. Either way, I stepped on it as I went by.

The living room door was slightly ajar. At the sound, the voices stopped.

"Is that you, Lucy?" Lockwood called. "Come on in and join us! We've got cake."

Slightly reluctantly, I poked my head into the room. There they were, lit by diagonal shafts of sunlight—Lockwood and George, sitting by the coffee table, plus Holly, plus a kid I didn't know. There was a splendid checkerboard cake on the table, frosted with sugar, as pink and yellow as a cubist dawn. They were doing the client-welcome thing. Holly was in the process of pouring tea.

George glanced up. "Look, *another* of our clients! Got them coming out of our ears today. Check under the sofa! There's probably more hiding behind the curtains."

"Sorry," I said. "I didn't mean to interrupt you all. Hi, Holly."

Holly had quit pouring and was gazing at me with evident concern. In the old days I'd have bristled at her attention, suspecting it of being patronizing and insincere. Now it didn't really bother me; I was even glad of it, in a way. "Lucy," she said, "I'm *so* pleased you're all right." She frowned. "What have they done to your poor arm?"

"Oh, don't worry. It's just a graze."

"I'm talking about the bandages. That's simply the most incompetent bit of first aid I've ever seen. Lockwood, George—*how* much dressing did you use? I'm surprised Lucy could fit it through the door."

Lockwood looked hurt. "It was a pretty decent effort for two a.m. We thought it was better to be safe than sorry—we didn't want to find random bits of her lying about the house when we got up this morning. Maybe you can fix it later. Lucy, you're just in time. Come and sit down. This is Danny Skinner. He's come for our advice."

"Thanks," I said. "But listen, I'm good. I don't want to butt in. I'll see you when you're done."

"No, we could do with your wisdom." He grinned. "As long as you don't charge us for your time. Holly, more tea. George, another slice of cake. Then we can get started."

Well, what was I going to do otherwise? Sit in the kitchen by my lonesome, staring at George's map for an hour? And that cake *did* look good—better than a burger or Thai noodles, which is what I usually had for breakfast. So it was only with a minor hesitation that I drifted in, took up position in my old, familiar seat, and had my first real look at Lockwood & Co.'s second client that morning.

From the first there was one particular thing that made him stand out. It wasn't his disheveled appearance, his muddied, tattered clothes, or even the rat-a-tat trail of ectoplasm burns that ran across his coat like a frozen burst of gunfire. It wasn't the way he sat bolt upright, either, his eyes blank orbs filled with remembered horror, agitatedly rubbing the swollen knuckles of his left hand. We got stuff like that every day of the week. It wasn't even the lucid manner in which he spoke, spelling out the horrors inflicted on his community. No, it was none of those things that made us sit up and take notice.

So what did? His age. Or lack of it.

Danny Skinner wasn't an adult. Like I say, he was a kid. About ten years old.

That was unusual.

Children see ghosts. Adults complain about them. As George once pointed out, there are several almost immutable rules surrounding the Problem, and this (George's Third Law) is one of the most obvious. As psychic detection agents we get plenty of witness statements from children, but it's the grown-ups who actually come knocking on our door. They've got the financial firepower to hire us; plus, the kids are usually too busy out working (and dying) as Sensitives, members of the night watch, or even as agents themselves to ask someone else to help them out.

But here this kid was. Sitting on our sofa. Alone.

Or not exactly alone. He soon had Holly on one side, plying him with tea, and George on the other, offering him a hefty chunk of cake. If there'd been room, I probably would have been on him as well, plumping up his cushions or massaging his toes or something. There was a quality about him—fragile, but at the same time steely and undaunted—that managed to awaken your sense of pity without irritating you at the same time. In a world where no kid can really *afford* to be helpless, where most of us risk our lives as a matter of course, that was quite a hard balance to achieve.

He had the gaunt waif thing going on, that was the main reason for our sympathy: pale skin, unhealthily big eyes, and a pair of ears that would have carried him some distance in a strong wind. His light brown hair was untidily cropped. His Irish sweater looked several sizes too big for him; his head and neck protruded from it like a stork chick peering from a nest. It was all very disarming. Take it from me, if you had to choose between him and a basketful of supercute puppies to toss out of a sinking hot-air balloon, it would have been the pups sent spiraling down to earth.

George and Holly drew back; the kid, now heavily laden with tea and cake, blinked around at us.

Lockwood flourished a hand encouragingly. "Well . . . er, Mr. Skinner," he said. "I'm Anthony Lockwood; these are my friends. What can we do for you?"

Danny Skinner's voice was unexpectedly strong and deep. "You got my message, sir?"

"I did. Something about a"—Lockwood consulted a crumpled letter—"a cursed village, I understand?"

"That's right. Aldbury Castle. I was hoping you might come take a look at it."

"Aldbury Castle is the name of the village? I see. Where *is* Aldbury Castle?"

"Hampshire, sir. Hour's train ride south-west from Waterloo, and then a mile east along Aldbury Way. There's a Southampton train going at one thirty, so if you shift your backsides, we can just catch it." The boy made an adjustment to his dirty, tattered coat. "Don't worry, you won't have to sleep under a hedge. The Old Sun Inn still has a few habitable rooms."

Lockwood opened his mouth and shut it again. He cleared his throat. "Um, we don't want to get ahead of ourselves, Mr. Skinner. We haven't accepted the commission yet, or even discussed it."

"Oh, you're sure to want this case when you hear about it," the boy said. He took a loud sip of tea. "I'm just trying to save you time. I could always fill you in on the train."

"Tell you what," George said, "perhaps you can fill us in now. What's the nature of the curse?"

Danny Skinner set down his plates. "Ghosts, spirits, and what-not. We have a lot of them."

Lockwood leaned back in his chair and smiled. "Forgive me, but the whole country suffers from that affliction. What makes Aldbury Castle so special that we have to drop everything and come down now?"

"Our village has it worse than most." The kid's shoulders twitched in what might have been a shudder. "There've been killings."

Lockwood's smile faded. "That's bad. You've had cases of ghost-touch, then?"

"Sixteen this year."

Lockwood sat back; Holly looked up from her notepad. "What? *Sixteen?* Since January? You're not serious."

"Might be seventeen now. Molly Suter was sinking fast when I left this morning. Coming back from seeing her sick sister last night, she was surrounded. They caught her in the fields. The kids arrived with iron sticks, but it was too late. And when I set out first thing this morning"—the boy pointed ruefully at the plasm burns on his coat—"you can see that they nearly got me, too. Even though the sun was up, they were waiting in the woods for me. I only just made the train."

"They? You mean Visitors?"

"Of course."

"It certainly sounds bad. Tell me, why didn't an adult come to see us? Your father or your mother?" Lockwood hesitated in sudden doubt. "Or, forgive me, are they—?"

Danny Skinner sniffed; it was a short, sharp, angry sound. "If you're worried about payment, Pops has money. He's still above ground, just. He's not well, though—can't leave the inn. Mum's dead."

"I'm sorry," Lockwood said.

A shrug of bony shoulders. "The good news is, she hasn't risen again. So far."

There was a silence. "Try the cake," George said. "It's good."

"Actually, I'll pass," the kid replied. "I'm not a cakey person. But I'm serious about leaving, you know. You need to help us, and there's only one train we can take."

Was it just me, or did he seem marginally less cute than he had a few moments before? Stork chicks aren't usually quite so pushy.

A combination of discomfort and mounting irritation had made Lockwood's expression darken as well. He flicked an imaginary speck of dust off his knee. "Like I say," he said, "that's not going to happen until we've had many more details from you. Even then, we're unlikely to come down today. Tell us about these Visitors. What kind of ghosts does Aldbury Castle have?"

"Depends where you're looking," Danny Skinner said. He had a sulky expression; you could see he could barely contain his frustration that we weren't already out of the door. "There are Specters on the green, and Lurkers by the church. Got a Cold Maiden in the new estate, and that's just for starters. Where I live—the Old Sun Inn—there's a ghost that comes knocking on the door at night. I saw it once. Like a tiny glowing child. It's very small and puny and . . . it's evil, I think. Had a nasty, furtive look. Slunk across the flagstones and disappeared."

"Shining Boy," Holly said.

The kid shrugged. "Maybe. Best not to go downstairs in the inn after midnight, that's all I'm saying. The ghosts out in the woods are mostly Phantasms and Wraiths—as far as *I* can tell. I'm not an expert, like you *agents*. See how close they got to touching me? Old dead, *they* are, slain warriors most like. Quiet all these centuries, and now rising from the cornfields. And they're not the worst things walking in the dark at Aldbury Castle." He swigged his tea back with an almost violent flourish, and set the cup on its saucer with a *crack*. "Like I say, it's taking its toll. Half the village is gone. Mostly adults; the ones who can't see the Visitors coming. Those of us who are young enough to fight are doing our best, but we can't do it on our own, as I keep telling you." He glanced ostentatiously at his watch.

Lockwood ignored him. "Does DEPRAC know about this?"

"We've told them. They've done nothing."

"Other agencies?"

"Worse than useless." Danny Skinner looked around him in disgust. "Can I spit here?"

"We'd rather you didn't."

"Pity. Yeah, the Rotwell Agency has their institute just up the road. We've asked them to help; they even sent guys out to assess the situation. Said they couldn't help. Said it wasn't any worse than anywhere else these days—which is a *lie*." A vein stood out on the kid's neck; he seemed convulsed with an inner rage.

"You mentioned warriors, Mr. Skinner," George said. "You mean there was a battle once at Aldbury Castle?"

"Yeah, there was a battle," the kid said. "Vikings or some such. Long time ago."

"That might be part of it, then," Lockwood said. "Battle sites can be hot spots, can't they, George?"

"Sure . . ." George tapped his notebook absently. "But the country's pockmarked with sites of battles, plagues, and skirmishes, and they don't all flare up like this. And I don't know . . . Vikings? That's *so* ancient. You wouldn't expect *them* to stir up so much trouble."

"Are you doubting my word?" Danny Skinner asked. That vein throbbed. "Are you?"

"No, I'm doubting you're giving us all the necessary information. You're skirting around the central issue. All these ghosts you mentioned—it sounds grim, but you said there was something *worse* out there. What is it?"

Our guest looked down at his lap. "Yeah, there *is* something else. I didn't want to tell you straight off, in case you wet your collective pants and were too frightened to come down. I was going to tell you on the train."

At this, there was a certain amount of stretching of eyes. Lockwood spoke gently. "Well, since we aren't coming on the train, Mr. Skinner, certainly not today and perhaps never, maybe you'd be so good as to tell us about this very frightening thing. We'll try to contain ourselves as best we can."

The kid shook his head. "You know, I only came to Lockwood and Co. because you're young, like me. I thought you'd treat me right. . . . Well, the truth is, there *is* something else that walks by night in the village of Aldbury Castle." He shuddered, then drew his shoulders in and fiddled with his collar as if he suddenly felt cold. "No one knows what it is, or what its nature might be. But it has a local name." He took a deep breath, then spoke in a voice of guttural dread. "We call it . . . the Creeping Shadow."

He sat back and surveyed us with triumphant, hard-eyed finality, as if expecting us to utter groans and gasps of terror, throw ourselves off our seats, and roll on the floor in panic with our legs wiggling in the air. It didn't work out that way. Lockwood raised a polite eyebrow; Holly scribbled briefly in her notebook, then scratched a decorative knee. I took another bite of cake.

George stared at the boy from over his glasses. "Why?"

"Why what?"

"Why give it that name? Or *any* name, come to think of it? None of the other apparitions you've mentioned were called anything special. What makes *this* ghost so terrifying?"

"Creeping Shadows are a dime a dozen around here," Holly added as the boy frowned indignantly. "Almost every Shade or Lurker could be described like that."

"You need to give us more information," Lockwood said. "Prove it'll be worth our while."

"*Worth your while?!*" The boy gave a cry of rage. He banged his fist on the arm of his chair, making us all jump. "You agents think you've seen it all, with your precious certainties that make you turn up your noses at me! Those Rotwell agents were just the same. Well, I'll shake you up." He glared around at us, a hostile, white-nosed imp of fury. "The Creeping Shadow isn't like any other ghost you've seen. There's its size, for one thing."

"Well, how big is it?" Lockwood asked.

"It's a giant. Seven feet tall, or maybe taller, with a massive body, and bloated arms and legs. It wasn't a naturally sized man, whatever it was in life."

"The Limbless are often bloated," I said. "Might be a Limbless."

"I *said* it had legs and arms, didn't I?" Danny Skinner growled. "Are you deaf? How else could it creep? I saw it myself, in the pheasant woods below Gunner's Top. Came stealing through the trees, head lowered, creeping, creeping, with smoke or mist or whatnot pouring off it."

"Ghost-fog, you mean," Holly said.

"No." The boy shook his head. "I know what ghost-fog is. We get plenty of it on the green; the village is choked with it some nights. *This* is different. This stuff streams off the spirit as it moves. It trails behind it like a cloak, like a comet's tail. Almost like it's on fire. You never saw a Limbless like that."

George brushed some crumbs off his lap. "I admit you *do* interest me a little now. So there are flames on this shadow?"

"The edge flickers. If it's flames, it's the cold flames of hell."

"Describe the apparition. What details do you see when you look at it? Its face? Its clothes?"

"Nothing—just a black outline." The kid rolled his eyes. "Jeez. Why do you think we call it a shadow?"

"All right, all right," Lockwood said. "A bit of feistiness is all very well, but if you don't dial it down pronto, you'll find yourself booted out into the street. By Holly here, which will be super-embarrassing."

"What else can you tell us?" I said.

Danny Skinner looked at me. "I thought you were a client."

"Oh . . . yes. Yes, I am. I'm just watching. Don't mind me."

Whether it was inherent in him, or something built up by terrible experiences, anger pulsed through the kid in waves. You could see it flare up, then just as quickly subside. "The way it moves," he said; "the shape of the head, how it sort of rolls awkwardly along—I think it's deformed. Cold rolls off it, too; I near froze with fear."

"You saw it in the woods?"

"*I* did, but kids have seen it in other places. In Church Lane, skulking in the graveyard, and up on the barrows, other side of the green."

Lockwood frowned. "Sounds like it travels far and wide. That *is* unusual. Aside from general creeping about, do you get a sense of any purpose? What does it do?"

The boy shrugged. "I know what it does. It gathers people's souls."

This time the pause following his announcement was met with a more attentive silence. It wasn't that we were awed or scared. All of us were watching his face, trying to decide how to respond. With open incredulity? (My inclination.) With scathing disbelief? (George somehow turned a hog-like snort into a sort-of sneeze.) Or calmly, quizzically, as Holly and Lockwood did? "Can you expand on that?" Lockwood asked.

"There's a cross in the churchyard," Danny Skinner said. "It's very old. They think it dates from Viking times. There are carvings on it, very worn and weathered; most of them you can't make heads or tails of now—but one still has its shape. The old folk call it the Gatherer of Souls. It's a figure standing in a field of bones and skulls, and there are people arranged behind it, all pressed close together, like they've been collected up by it, you know. Well, I saw the Shadow. It's the same thing."

"You're saying that this Creeping Shadow is the same as the figure on the ancient cross?"

"Yes. They carved it like a giant, just like the shape I saw."

"When did the Shadow first appear?"

"Three months ago. Midwinter's Day."

"And there's no record of it turning up before then, not even in village legend?"

"Not as far as I know."

Lockwood shook his head. "Sorry, I don't see any link between the ghost and this old carving. They may both be big and bulky— but that's not enough to make a connection."

"Wrong. There *is* a connection."

"How? In what way?"

Danny Skinner spoke quietly. "It was three months ago that the curse on the village started. That's when the ghosts erupted. That's when the adults started dying of ghost-touch. Why? Because the Shadow stirs up the dead. They rise from their graves to follow him, like on the cross. You ain't seen anything like it, sir, till you've seen that. You *have* to come and witness it—and help us while you're there." The stork chick look was back, the big-eyed, big-eared waif, gazing beseechingly around at us. "You *have* to."

"Well, that was fun," Holly said as we sat in the kitchen later. "I thought he was going to physically assault you at the end there, Lockwood. I don't think I've ever seen anyone so mad."

Lockwood blew out his cheeks. "I know. It's not as if we even gave him an outright *no*. If we get a chance, we might run down sometime next week. There *were* actually points of interest in what he said. But I'm simply not dropping everything for the wild claims of some hysterical kid."

"He was certainly over-egging it," I said. "He really piled it on."

"And here's the clincher," George said darkly. "Note how he didn't eat his slice."

"We can hardly dis someone on the grounds they turned down cake, George."

"You bet we can. In my eyes, refusing cake is an immoral act. 'I'm not a cakey person'—those were his actual words. Brrr."

"And it was Holly's homemade one, too," Lockwood said. "Well, one way or another, we're in agreement that he seemed a bit nuts. I'm sure it's a bad cluster, but that Shadow business at the end was completely over the top. So, we'll worry about Danny Skinner another day—*if* we get the time. For now, there are far more urgent things on our agenda, namely Lucy's problem. And as to that"—he grinned at me—"I've just had a brilliant idea."

Chapter 15

Precisely what Lockwood's plan was, we didn't immediately hear. He refused to be drawn out and, not long afterward, went off somewhere on his own. Physically, I was still recovering from my exertions of the previous forty-eight hours, so I was happy enough to stay at Portland Row. I made myself useful as best I could, helping George with the dishes; after that, when he and Holly went down to the office to start on company business, I wandered into the garden.

The gnarled old apple tree was budding, and the unkempt grass sparkled in the sunshine. I sat on the patio, among the weeds, staring at the backs of houses across the gardens. Flowers whose names I didn't know were showing under the walls, and birds I didn't recognize swooped low between the trees, filling the air with sound. Last summer, once or twice, when we weren't out risking our lives, we'd sat here in the evenings. We'd always *said* we should do it more, but it never happened—we were just too busy. Besides, none of us really knew what to do with relaxation; it was so much more natural to just go out and stab something. So the garden was generally ignored.

It felt odd to have the time now to sit out there. I was in a kind of limbo, neither part of Lockwood & Co. nor entirely separated from it. And my emotions were similarly conflicted. Half of me still believed I should be somewhere else, holding fast to a solitary career that couldn't imperil Lockwood and the others. This side of me felt deeply uneasy about asking them to help find the skull. It would be a dangerous job, no question about it. And yet . . . I couldn't feel entirely guilty. Because right now I *needed* assistance. I *needed* some friends. And hadn't George told me outside the Guppy house that Lockwood had been continually throwing himself into danger these last few months? So what did it matter if I asked him to help me do something tricky? Why should I feel bad about that? What would it actually change?

It was hard to make sense of what I was feeling. The only thing I *did* know for certain as I sat in the garden was that it was nice to be back, even if only for a short while.

Shortly after lunch, Lockwood returned, smelling vaguely of rotten wood and seaweed, so I knew he'd been to see Flo Bones. The first part of his plan was apparently under way.

"I had to promise her a year's supply of licorice allsorts," he said, "but I talked her into it. The next relic-men's market is scheduled for tomorrow night. Flo's going, so she'll find out exactly when and where. She'll get us to the door. Once there, guys built like gorillas will vet us. If we pass muster, we'll be allowed into the meeting. If we don't, we'll be beaten senseless and our limp bodies will be tossed into the Thames. I think passing muster is the option to go for."

"I agree," I said. "So how are we going to do that?"

But Lockwood wouldn't say.

The next thing that happened was that Lockwood and Holly made a trip back to my apartment in Tooting to fetch my clothes. I wasn't allowed to come. In due course they returned, the visit having passed without incident, except that they'd bumped into my neighbor across the landing.

"He told us he'd heard noises last night," Lockwood said. "They were coming from your room. He peeped through the spy-hole in his door and saw two men with flashlights standing in your doorway. One of them had a gun. When they saw the place was empty, they left. I'd say it was a good thing you came to us, Luce, and didn't go back home."

Once again I couldn't disagree.

Holly handed me a couple of bags of my belongings. Her expression was somber. "I don't know how to tell you this, Lucy," she said, "but they . . . they messed up your place really badly."

I stared at her. "Oh no. What did they do?"

"Oh, it was *awful*. Your things were scattered all over the floor, the bedclothes strewn everywhere, your drawers open and the stuff all jumbled up. There was no rhyme or reason to it. It was like a bomb had gone off. I'm so, so sorry. You must feel dreadful."

I avoided Lockwood's eye. "Yes, I'm really distraught they made it look so messy," I said. "I'm glad I didn't see that."

Anyway, I had my clothes.

At the end of the afternoon I volunteered to make an early supper, and, under George's supervision, I put together a swift spaghetti Bolognese. Holly had provided sponge cake for dessert.

"How come she's suddenly baking now?" I asked. "She never touched cake before."

George was staring at his map of England on the kitchen wall. He spoke absently. "Oh, Hol's still fixated on salads, but don't worry. I'm corrupting her slowly. We'll have her scarfing junk food by and by. Have you added oregano to the sauce?"

"You already asked, and yes, I have. I think we're almost done. What *is* that map, anyway? Current hauntings?"

"Mmm?" George was somewhere far away. "No . . . exactly the opposite. These are historic ones, going back in time to the start of the Problem. Major outbreaks by decade." He pushed open the basement door and roared down the stairs. "*Grub's ready!* I got the info by trawling through old newspapers," he added. "You know me."

Lockwood and Holly emerged from below. I heated the plates under the hot tap, and served up the meal, staring at the poster through a pleasant cloud of hot steam. "I don't get it, George," I said. "There have been thousands of outbreaks over the years. You've got a lot of pins on there, but nowhere near enough to represent everything."

"That's because I'm only recording the first twenty clusters in each area," George said. "The colors represent different decades, and you can see from the rings how the Problem's gradually spread outward over the years. You remember the Chelsea case, Lucy, how I traced the original Source of that outbreak back to Aickmere's department store by looking at cases over time? Well, this is the same thing, on a much bigger scale. And it confirms what the history books tell us: the Problem began to the southeast of London, in the county of Kent."

"Where Marissa Fittes and Tom Rotwell were the first to fight it." Lockwood was doling out steaming clumps of spaghetti, slathered with sauce. "This looks great, by the way, Lucy. What are those shriveled black things?"

"Mushrooms, I think. Oh no, *those* are the mushrooms. Actually, I don't know what they are. . . . Enjoy your meal."

"The Fittes and Rotwell agencies have come a long way in fifty years," George said as we ate. "You know there's a statue in the town where it all began, where the two founders began investigating local ghosts? I've been down to see it. Frankly, it's not very good, but it shows the two of them as teenagers, as they were when they destroyed the Mud Lane Phantom—with Tom Rotwell holding his homemade sword, and Marissa beside him with her little lantern. The two objects that became the symbols of their separate agencies. It's funny to think of them actually being used, that first time."

"Isn't there a story about Marissa's lantern?" True to form, Holly had piled her plate with salad, but I was pleased to see a little mound of spaghetti, too. She twirled her fork with a delicate motion of her wrist. "Didn't she get it from a garden shed?"

George nodded. "From her parents' summer house. She used it when the ghost's psychic field began to mess around with the workings of her flashlight. They were good innovators, Tom and Marissa; they were the first to experiment with iron and silver. Tom also tried taking caged cats into haunted houses, to see if they worked as early warning systems. He gave it up, though. The cats went crazy."

"Doesn't sound like a very kind thing to do," Holly said. "Poor cats."

"Bet they were more effective than that bell thing you had, though, George," I said.

George sucked in a string of spaghetti. "The PEWS device? Maybe—but at least Rotwell's are still innovating. They're trying to come up with new ideas, like Tom did. The Fittes Agency doesn't bother with that so much. They just stick to rapiers and raw Talent, which was always Marissa's policy."

"Well, the founders were brilliant in different ways," Holly said. "We're all in their debt. They devoted their lives to keeping us safe."

"Took its toll on them, though," Lockwood said. "Both died young."

I thought of the photographs of Marissa I'd seen at Fittes House, the wrinkled woman dressed in black. "Not *that* young, surely. I've seen pictures. She was pretty old."

"Only in her forties. Prematurely aged."

"Anyway, it's interesting to see how the Problem has spread like any other epidemic," George added. "It behaves like a disease, rippling out from an original reservoir or core area: first Kent, then the southeast, then London, then the country."

"In spite of Fittes's and Rotwell's best efforts," I said.

"Yeah," George said, "in spite of them."

At the end of the meal, Lockwood made an announcement. "You all know that tomorrow is the relic-men's night-market," he said, "and we assume the Winkmans will be on hand to buy up all the best stuff. From what Lucy's told us, the whispering skull is likely to feature as one of the transactions, so we need to be there, too.

The aim is to get in, snatch the skull, hopefully find out a little more about this mysterious black market collector that the Winkmans are working for, and get out again—all without being spotted, cornered, and gutted with a fish knife. Nothing too hard. Flo's going to take us to the location, but to get inside, we'll need something that'll guarantee safe passage."

"A Source, you mean?" Holly asked.

"Exactly. I think two of us will go—probably Lucy and me—and that means we need two top-notch psychic Sources."

"Well, where would we get those?" George said. "The skull was one, but that's been pinched. We've got some bits and pieces knocking around the office, like that shriveled pirate's hand that Holly's always wanting to trash. We could use that, I suppose. Mind you, I *am* fond of it. I know it's black with tar, and one of its fingers is coming loose, but, well, it's got sentimental value. . . ."

"Relax. I'm not going to take the hand." Lockwood sat back. "No, we need something that no one's seen before—something so devilishly interesting, they won't look closely at who's bringing it. The good news is, I think I know where to find precisely that." He looked at his watch. "It's not yet dusk. We've got time. I'll show you now."

"Sorry," I said, "but where are we going?"

Lockwood smiled around at us. His face was calm and set.

"It's all right; you don't need your coats. It's in Jessica's room, upstairs."

Lockwood had never been very forthcoming about his past. Quite the opposite: since the day I first met him, mystery had clung to his vanished family and the circumstances of their departure from this world. Though the house he lived in—and its eclectic furniture and contents—were memorials to his parents, Lockwood rarely spoke about them, and he almost *never* mentioned his sister, Jessica, who had died in her bedroom so many years earlier. Despite this, a few details *had* gradually leaked out, and I knew enough to see how they affected him.

Jessica Lockwood, six years older than little Anthony, had looked after him in the years following his parents' unexpected deaths. Then, when he was nine years old, she had died, too—victim to a Visitor that had attacked her in her room. Since then, Lockwood had shut his grief away, clamped it deep inside, where it still burned fiercely, fueling his remorseless pursuit of ghosts of all kinds. And the room had been shut away, too, a dark, closed-off portion of the house. It was partly an unvisited shrine to Jessica, partly a storeroom for all the mementos Lockwood had of his parents and his sister. It was also a containment zone, for a powerful death-glow still blazed where his sister had fallen. Iron sheeting coated the door and silver wards hung in the room, but they had not yet been necessary. Jessica had never come back.

Lockwood led the way upstairs, Holly following, George and I lingering behind.

"But hold on, George," I whispered. "What about Holly? Does she know . . . ?"

"About Jessica? Yeah, she knows."

"He told her? Oh . . . okay."

Obviously it was good that Lockwood was loosening up about his past, sharing his secrets a little. It had taken ages for him to open up to me. It was healthier that he could do it more easily now. Obviously it was good that Holly knew. Obviously I was pleased.

The curtains were drawn, the room was dark. Lockwood led us in.

I hadn't been in the bedroom for months, but nothing had changed. Nothing *ever* changed in that cold square space. As ever, the death-glow, pale and oval, shone with piercing beauty above the bed. As before, the force of it rustled the roots of my hair and made my teeth ache. The boxes and crates that half filled the room in the perpetual dusk had their usual array of protective lavender pots, and the silver charms still hung, tinkling, from the ceiling.

Lockwood had put on his sunglasses to shield his eyes from the supernatural glow. He switched on the light. The glow vanished, but its power remained. He didn't open the curtains, but patted the nearest box. "I'm thinking that we should find something in one of these," he said, and his voice was soft. "You know that my parents were folkloric researchers, searching for an answer to the Problem. They traveled all over the place, studying the belief systems of other cultures. Wherever they went, they brought back junk. Their favorite pieces are on the walls downstairs, but there're things up here that have never been opened. Some of these crates only arrived here after they died. All we have to do is choose something that would fascinate a black marketeer. So . . . Lucy, why don't you pick a box?"

"Are you sure?" I kept my voice down, too. Somehow, none of us wanted to speak at full volume in Jessica's room. "But Lockwood— this is your parents' collection. . . ."

He shrugged. "Yeah, and it's gathering dust. Let's put it to good use. Pick a box."

Still I hesitated. I looked at the bed, at the white coverlet. Beneath that was the terrible black ectoplasm burn left in the mattress when Jessica died. It had happened while she was sorting through one of those very chests. "But isn't that"—I spoke with extra care—"a little bit dangerous?"

Lockwood's eyes were hidden, but I thought a flicker of impatience crossed his face. "No. It's not dark yet. And, don't forget, my mother and father packed these up originally. It was only because something was dropped—and its Seal broke—that the ghost got out at all."

None of us said anything. Yes, it had gotten out—and killed his sister. And Lockwood, still a little boy, had been the one who found her. Afterward, in his rage and grief, he had destroyed the ghost. I knew this because once, alone in this same room, my Talent had looped me back to the past, and I'd heard the echo of the tragedy. I couldn't erase the memory from my mind.

"Even so, Lockwood," George said, "we don't want to mess around in here. What do the boxes contain?"

"Search me. The same sort of things as on the walls downstairs, I guess. Curios from other cultures; devices linked to dealing with spirits. Bound to be a lot of junk, but I bet there's good stuff, too." Lockwood removed a vase of lavender from the top of a crate, his movements swift and brittle. You could sense the anger still contained in him. His fingers tapped the wood. "You could try this box, look—or this—or one of those. . . . Come on, Luce, it's your skull we're going after. You make a decision. Which would you like?"

"This one, then," I said.

"Good choice, Luce . . . good choice. I like the look of it, too."

He took his knife from his belt, eased it into the crack beneath the crate lid, and began to work it around. "Just like opening a tin of sardines," he said. "There we go. So then, let's have a little gander at what's in . . . *here*—"

A twist, a crack; Holly, George, and I all flinched. The lid came loose; Lockwood wrenched it back and let it drop behind the crate. A rich, resinous fragrance filled the air.

"That's frankincense," Holly murmured.

The crate was filled to the brim with yellow-brown wood shavings, acting as protective packing. Lockwood plunged his hand inside. "Aha . . ." He drew out a broad and bulky package, wrapped in something dry and papery that looked like straw. He held it gingerly, letting shavings fall onto the faded carpet at his feet.

"Careful," Holly said.

"Don't worry. We're not doing this after dark. That was the mistake my sister made."

I saw now that the wrapping was a kind of reed matting, very old and fragile, which disintegrated at Lockwood's touch. He brushed it away. Beneath it was something bright and colorful that showed like flowers coming out from under melting snow.

"What is it?" I asked. "They look like—"

"Feathers." Lockwood gave the object a shake. Like a tablecloth unfurling, it suddenly opened to an unexpected size: a cloth of blue and purple feathers that were small and neat and lovely, stitched so close together they appeared seamless. I didn't know which species of bird they came from, but I could tell that it lived far away in some warm and forested land. The dowdy, derelict room was lit by it; we stared at it in wonder.

"The other side's pretty nifty, too," Lockwood said. He turned it in his hands, and we saw the framework of minute silver links, tight as chain mail, that fused the feathers together. There was a silver clasp halfway along one edge, with a dangling hood beside it.

"You put it around your neck," George said. "It's a cape."

"A spirit-cape," Lockwood said. "Witch doctors or shamans used to wear them."

"It's beautiful," Holly murmured.

"More than that . . . it had a useful purpose." Lockwood laid it out over the top of the nearest packing case. "The shamans were wise men; they spoke to their dead ancestors. They did this in spirit houses, where—"

"Sorry, what?" I asked. "A spirit house? And how do you know all this, anyway?"

"My parents," Lockwood said. "They wrote articles about it. They thought the beliefs of other cultures might throw light on the Problem. Studied ideas about ghosts and spirits—saw what was different and what was the same. Whether it worked or not wasn't the point. They wanted to find out what people *believed*. They were after clues. I've got their papers somewhere. . . ." The edginess he had displayed since entering the room had left him, soothed, perhaps, by the loveliness of the cape.

"And did they?" George asked. "Did they come to any conclusions about the Problem?"

"No. Yes. I don't know." Lockwood took out another package wrapped in matting. "Looks like there might be another cape here. . . ." He delved deeper and, taking out a small wooden box, looked inside. He shut it hastily. "Ooh, I'm not sure I want to get *that* out. Never touch a mummified body part if you don't know where it's been. That's my motto."

"Holds true with un-mummified ones, too," George said. "That's the motto *I* live by."

"I don't want to know about either of your mottos," Holly said. "You were talking about spirit houses, Lockwood."

"Oh, yes. . . . Well, some of these cultures had more relaxed approaches to the dead. When an old person was near death, they were taken to one of these huts. They died there, and their bones were stored inside. In racks. The shaman would go there to talk to their spirits. When he did so, he wore a spirit-cape like this for protection. That's the story, anyway. Why don't we take the two capes tomorrow, Lucy? They're not Sources, exactly, but I bet the Winkmans would buy them as curios."

"Seems a shame to sacrifice them," I said. "They're so pretty. Why don't you have another look in the crate?"

"All right. . . ." Lockwood stuck his hand into the shavings again. "Okay . . . There's something here—feels like glass. Might be a . . . Ah, yes. . . ." He brought it out. His voice faded. "A photograph. Yes, it is."

The simple wooden frame was discolored, and the photo stained, either by water or weather. It was a black-and-white picture, probably taken with some heavy, old-fashioned camera on a stand. There was a formality to the shot, despite the mud in the foreground and the jungle trees that formed the backdrop. It showed a group of people standing in a forest clearing. Most were tribesmen and -women, scantily clad, some with astounding birds' feathers pluming from their hair like so much sculpted smoke. Everyone was grinning. In the center stood a man and a woman in European clothes: he with a crumpled jacket over a white shirt; she with a peasant blouse and long, sensible skirt. Both wore wide-brimmed hats that half hid their faces, but from the man's long, slim chin and fluted mouth, and the woman's gleaming smile, I knew full well who they were.

Lockwood didn't say anything for a long while. When he did, his voice had a forced jollity. "I think this is New Guinea," he said. "Soon after they got married. Must be the end of the trip. Look, my mother's holding the spirit-mask that the old witch doctor's just given her, the kind he wears when he's communing with the dead. He's the guy at the edge of the photo, the one with skin as wrinkled as a rhino's jockstrap, with my mother's binoculars hanging around his neck. She's given them to him in return for the spirit-mask."

The woman was holding up the mask and laughing; and you could tell the man beside her was looking at her, and her pleasure was making him smile, too. They were young, full of life and promise.

"I've still got the mask," Lockwood said. "It's the one on the shelf downstairs in the hall, next to the broken gourd. When I was very small I climbed up on the shelf and pulled it down and spent an hour looking through it, expecting to see ghosts all around. It didn't do anything. Just plain cut-out holes in a mask. Not that my mother would have cared. They came back from every expedition with stuff like this: spirit-masks, ghost-catchers, bottles of holy mountain water that, if you drank it, supposedly gave you mystic visions. They were a pair of unworldly academics. Silly fools, really." He set the photo facedown on the crate. "Luce, we'll use the capes tomorrow. They'll do nicely."

"And the bit about you both being recognized and horribly killed?" George asked.

Lockwood flashed a smile, but it was a token one; his mind was far away. "I haven't forgotten. All we need's a good disguise."

Chapter 16

It had to be said that, despite his unshakeable self-confidence, and a large wicker basket under his desk that contained the elements of many costumes, Lockwood's disguises weren't always super-successful. He had a weakness for big hats, and a tendency to try curious accents that attracted attention and, occasionally, outright hostility. His famous attempt at a winking East End chimney sweep, used to gain entry to Barleywick Hall in the Case of the Hovering Torso, had so outraged three Cockney footmen it ended with a breakneck chase into the nearest boating lake. As for the blond wig and wimple he'd resorted to while investigating a haunting near the Cobb Street Nunnery bathhouse, the resulting police search had made several papers, and it was probable two sisters and a mother superior would never be quite the same again.

Generally his disguises worked best when kept to a minimum, and that's the way our relic-men outfits ended up the next evening, after a long day of experimenting in the office, with a floor mirror propped against my old table, and George and Holly on hand to comment and make the tea. Relic-men being notoriously ill-favored, we'd tried all manner of humps, warts, and missing limbs, and clothes ranging from the holey to the ragged to the frankly indecent. In the end we scaled back to dirty black jeans, atrocious jerseys, and two stained leather jackets that George had scooped up in a charity store, while Holly used her extensive makeup kit to subtly worsen our complexions.

"I can blacken some of your teeth, Lockwood," she said. "Otherwise they're much too shiny. Some darkening around the eyes should make them look puffier, and a smear of pale paste on the cheekbones will give you a good unhealthy sheen. With a bit of work I can make you look sick, needy, and unattractive. Give me half an hour."

I was trying on a foul horsehair wig. "How about me?"

"In your case, I don't need to do too much. Five minutes should be fine."

The wigs capped things off. Mine was a jumble of dirty yellow strands, like a mop soaked in custard, while Lockwood's was a spiky black abomination.

He studied himself uncertainly. "I don't know. . . . It's like an evil hedgehog is squatting on my head."

"Think of Flo Bones," I said. "She looks like that on a *good* day. You'll fit in well."

Next we found two old satchels mildewing in the back of the basement storeroom, and George splashed tea over one and mud on the other. When they were dry, we took the spirit-capes that we'd found in Jessica's room and put them inside. We were almost ready to go.

"One last thing," Holly said. "Weapons. I don't like you going in defenseless."

Lockwood shrugged. "Can't take rapiers, for obvious reasons."

"Well, stuff a magnesium flare down your trousers. You'll need one if things get nasty."

"They might search us at the door."

"Holly's right," George put in. "You need something. All the other relic-men will be armed to the teeth. The water boys will have slime-flanges and cockle-hooks, while the housebreakers and tomb-sharks have their loops and grapplers and all manner of weird stuff."

I looked at him. "You seem very well-versed in relic-man business."

George did something with his glasses. "Maybe I chat with Flo from time to time. No law against that, is there?"

"No. . . . No, it's fine."

In the end Lockwood and I both took daggers, wearing them openly at our belts. They weren't great for combat, but would provide a final option. Plus, they suited the menacing aura we wanted to project as we entered the den of thieves.

All this took us till nightfall. Shortly after seven, two sinister, swaggering relic-men departed Portland Row and set off for their rendezvous with Flo Bones.

The district of Vauxhall, just south of the river, where the outflowing Thames curves north toward Westminster and the center of the city, was once the site of lovely pleasure gardens, where gentlemen and ladies used to promenade. Their bewigged ghosts still occasionally showed up incongruously among the automobile factories that now filled the area; the fortunes of these, too, had recently declined, and it was an area of deprivation, mostly abandoned after dark. As we crossed the bridge from Westminster, mists hung about the wharves and mudflats, and the lights of Vauxhall Station gleamed dully on the viaduct above like a row of taunting Wisps.

Flo was waiting for us in a deserted lock-up beneath one of the viaduct arches. She had her burlap bag wedged between her boots and sat slumped and pensive on a concrete barrier beside a lantern—like a squatting gargoyle, but with a stronger smell. As we entered, her hand darted to her belt; then she relaxed and spat welcomingly into the mud at her side.

Lockwood gave her a gap-toothed grin. "Aha! These disguises *must* be good. We had you fooled for a second there."

"The hair got me," Flo admitted. "But I recognize your walks. Your profile and her hips as well, but your walks mainly."

"That's great. The Winkmans should be fooled, then."

"Maybe. 'Specially at a distance. It's still the daftest thing you've ever done, Locky, and that's saying plenty. I can't take no responsibility for what happens. Licorice or no licorice, you understand the consequences are not on me."

"That's all right. We're fine with that, aren't we, Luce?"

"Yeah. We're fine."

"Hear the way Luce is talking, Flo? We've been practicing on the way down. She's got an estuary accent now."

Flo grunted. "Is that what she's got? I thought it was phlegm.

Okay, so listen. The boys on the door will want to see your artifacts. Don't give them any trouble. Once you're inside, it's a free-for-all, everyone trying to sell their Sources for the best price. If it's like last time, the Winkmans will be at one end, looking and buying, with their best stuff safely stored and guarded. How you're going to get away with this precious object you're after beats me." She took off her hat and scratched at her matted scalp. "Particularly the place we're going tonight."

"Which is?" This was a detail I was anxious to learn.

"No great distance. Vauxhall Station."

I glanced at the arch above us. "Doesn't seem very private."

"Not Vauxhall *Overground*, you silly mare. I'm talking about Vauxhall *Underground*—the station down below."

That rang a faintish bell with me, but I couldn't think why.

Lockwood knew. "But that's been shut off for years, hasn't it?" he said. "Wasn't there a rail accident there, some terrible disaster? And since then—too many ghosts. I thought DEPRAC gave the whole thing up, just concreted it all in."

Something was moving in Flo's bag. She gave it a nudge with her boot and the furtive motion stopped. "Yeah. There was a gas explosion down there. Forty-five years ago or more. It blew up a train that was just coming in to the station. Killed everyone on board. Wasn't long before the Visitors started appearing in the tunnels and Vauxhall Underground had to close. They diverted the line; whole area's bypassed now. And yeah, the entrances *were* sealed. But we found a way in."

"But why would you do that," I said, "if it's still so dangerous?"

I wasn't hugely excited to hear that, in addition to relic-men and gangsters, we had ghosts to deal with, too.

"It's good to go somewhere that's forbidden. Gives us a bit of peace and quiet. We keep to the main platform, put up barriers by the tunnels to keep the Specters at bay. I've seen them, hanging back, just beyond the light." Flo stooped, picked up her lantern; her teeth and eyes shone in its gleam. "They say the train's still down there, lost in the endless dark. And it's not just the original dead who sit on it now, but *newer* passengers, too—modern victims of the marauding ghosts."

Lockwood frowned. "You don't believe that."

"Not for me to say if it's true or not." Flo took up her bag, swung it over her shoulder. "I just make sure I don't go past the iron lines. Come on, enough chin-rattling. The market's started, and we need to get to it."

With that, she led us out into the night.

The original entrance to Vauxhall Underground Station was very close, its gates chained and boarded up, its steps choked with litter. On nearby walls, old DEPRAC warning signs were still barely visible beneath years of ghost-cult posters. Flo ignored it all; we walked half a block south down a narrow, unpromising lane between empty office buildings, until we reached a junction, where we stopped.

"This is where I leave you," Flo said. "I'm going on ahead. Give me five minutes, then you can follow. You take a left here, walk thirty yards, then left again down the lane. You'll see the sentries up ahead. Show them the stuff and they should let you in, you're that ugly. But here's the deal: once you're below, I won't recognize you, I won't help you. If you get caught and they beat you to death with sticks, I'll stand by and won't lift a finger." She gazed at me with her bright blue eyes. "Just so you know."

"Agreed and understood," Lockwood said. "Hope you get a good price for . . . what *is* in your sack, Flo?"

"That'd be telling. Five minutes. Try not to get yourselves killed."

After she'd gone, we took up positions against the wall— something midway between a loiter and a lurk—and waited. Five minutes ticked by; during this another relic-man—tall, ragged, and stooped like a grieving heron—slipped down the side road after Flo. We gave him an extra minute to get clear, then shuffled after him.

Down to the left. Thirty yards, then left again. It was more of an alley than a lane, dark as a cleft in the earth. Except at the end, where a naked bulb hung from a spindle above a metal door. In its cone of light, two very large gentlemen in long black coats stood like pillars, with a small ragged child between them.

The men were there to break your bones, but the child was the key—*she* was the Sensitive who vetted the objects being brought to the meeting. The ragged relic-man was in the process of showing her the contents of his bag. At either side, her henchmen waited for her decision. The bigger of the two held a stout black stick, which he patted occasionally into his cupped palm. He never spoke; he was the threat, the dealer of pain. The other was the talker who did all necessary interrogation. One spoke, one tapped his club. It was a fair bet that neither could manage both at the same time.

The relic-man passed muster. He closed his bag, pushed open the door, and disappeared inside. The men looked up at us. We approached casually down the alley.

Lockwood spoke through the side of his mouth. "Be calm. I'll handle this, Luce."

Something in the jaunty way he spoke alarmed me. Again I remembered what George had told me, how Lockwood's recklessness was escalating all the time. I felt a twinge of guilt. Tonight, for selfish reasons, I was depending on his willingness to take risks. Without me, he wouldn't have been here. I could feel the thrill of danger radiating from him now—intoxicating, but also scary. And we didn't have our swords. "Be careful," I said. "And also polite."

"Of course."

Lockwood's tall, but the top of his head didn't quite reach the shoulders of either sentry. He came to a halt before the child Sensitive, hands ready on his satchel.

The smaller henchman, the talker, pointed a meaty finger. "Show them."

We both opened our bags. The kid looked in. She was no older than eight, a fragile little thing, with blue veins on her forehead under translucent skin.

I held up my spirit-cape by a corner, so its iridescent beauty was clear.

Talker's frown deepened. Stick-Tapper stretched out his club and poked it against the feathers.

"Where'd you get these?" Talker said.

Lockwood pushed the club away. "Stole 'em, smelly. What's it to you?"

To be fair, Lockwood's accent *did* make him sound like an authentic relic-man. Trouble was, he was trying to be authentically insulting, too. At once Stick-Tapper swung the club around. It pressed hard against the underside of Lockwood's chin.

"You want Joe to flick that up?" Talker said. "He does, and it takes your head clean off. He does it *well*, your head lands back on your neck stump upside-down."

"Sounds like quite a show," Lockwood said. "But these here in our bags are foreign marvels. Adelaide Winkman will want to see them."

"We kill you, we take them to her ourselves," Talker said, and I couldn't help feeling there was a queasy logic to what he said. But the little child had put her hand on Stick-Tapper's wrist and was shaking her head.

"No, this is real good," she said. "She'd want it, like he says. Let them through."

Her word was law. At once the stick was withdrawn and the men moved back. With a cocksure flick of the arm, Lockwood pushed at the door.

"Hold it." Talker gestured at the daggers in our belts. "No weapons."

"Call these toothpicks weapons?" Lockwood gave a snort. "You must be joking."

Talker chuckled. "I'll show you whether I'm joking."

Thirty seconds later we'd been roughly frisked, relieved of our daggers, and kicked efficiently onward through the door.

"Do you *have* to be so rude?" I hissed, when we were alone. "You're drawing attention to us."

"Oh, relic-men are famously obnoxious. It'll make us fit right in."

"Yeah. Our broken corpses will fit in nicely, too."

Beyond the door was an empty room with rough, bare concrete walls. At the far end, a circular hole with a metal rim led straight down into the earth. The hole was dark, but the top of a ladder projected from it, and there was a grainy suggestion of a light far below.

"Old access shaft to the Underground," Lockwood said. "Guessed it would be something like that. It won't make getting out too easy, but what can we do? You first, Luce, or me?"

I went first; I didn't want him to get into an argument with a sewer rat or anything.

The ladder descended into the earth for a long distance, so much so that my hands went numb and I lost count of the number of rungs. It was very dark, and another unpleasant aspect of the experience was the sound that came rushing up the shaft: a roaring and a gusting of air, and what I thought were voices screaming. The noise seemed to come from far away, and (I guessed) from long ago; when I dropped down at last into a candlelit tunnel, all trace of it had died away. It was a different hubbub that surrounded me now, here on the forgotten platforms of Vauxhall Underground Station.

In layout, it was no different from countless other Tube stations still in daily use. Opposite the nook in which the ladder emerged, three rusting escalators rose into the shadows—silent, solid, their steps clogged with black dust. Lines of faded posters flanked them. That was the old way out, to the now sealed up ticket halls.

Down below was where the action was tonight. I was in a central space with three squared arches on either side. These led to the north/south platforms of the old Victoria Line. The curved walls still had their original white ceramic tiles, but in many places these had been levered off, and a shallow hole gouged out. Candles burned in these alcoves, their smoke weaving woozily against the ceilings, where old lamps hung like black, fat-bodied spiders. Everything shimmered with a soft and avaricious golden light: the tiles, the escalators, the black-garbed relic-men and women all around.

There were dozens of them, milling in little huddles by folding tables where food, drink, and various implements of their profession were on display. Some were young, like Flo; others, bent and weathered like windblown trees, showed evidence of age and long privation: all were dirty, calloused, and hard of jaw and eye. They conversed in low voices, guarding their words carefully; the atmosphere was heavy with distrust.

"Look at them." Lockwood had dropped down beside me. "It's like a medical textbook come to life."

"I know. I wonder if we gave ourselves quite enough warts."

Most of the relic-men seemed to be gravitating toward the arches on the right. A thrum of palpable excitement echoed from within, with many voices raised. And beneath *that* was a deeper psychic hum, like wasps buzzing in a buried pot. Muffled by silver-glass, maybe, but significant nevertheless.

And these weren't the only things I heard.

"*Lucy . . . Lucy, help me. . . .*"

I dug Lockwood in the ribs. "We need to go that way. Come on."

We passed through the arch into what had once been the northbound platform. Now it was an immensely long, low-curving room, lit along its length by candles and hanging lanterns. Nearby gaped one of the tunnel mouths, plugged in part by an enormous wall of sandbags. Some of the bags were filled with iron filings, some with salt; they'd been slashed open, and the gray-white powder lay across the surface of the wall, as dirty and crusted as month-old snow. Cold air drifted out of the tunnel and with it came strong psychic unease. Again I sensed the distant screaming.

At the base of the sandbags, the old tracks could still be seen, but along most of the room these had been concealed beneath rough wooden boards, built out from the edge of the platform. They had the effect of doubling the width of the space. A good many relic-men were congregating here, talking, arguing, making their slow, shuffling way toward a table halfway up the platform.

It was well-lit by black candlesticks, tall as a man, that had been arranged behind it; and even from a distance, I knew who sat there. I recognized their silhouettes: a woman, large-boned, with massive arms and shoulders; and a short, squat person wearing a broad-brimmed bowler hat.

Adelaide Winkman and her son, Leopold: the most powerful black marketeers in London.

One by one, the relic-men were arriving at the table, showing their psychic wares, being paid (or not), and moving on. I could hear the clink of coins. Beside the table stood three impassive, muscular men. My eyes narrowed. It was not too hard a stretch to imagine them being the murderers of Harold Mailer, the ones who had chased me across the gardens of Clerkenwell.

"Watch where the flunkies go, Luce." Lockwood was mouthing in my ear. "They're not storing the objects at the table, so they must be taking them somewhere. . . ."

It was hard to advance far along the platform. Most of the people there were hoping to reach the Winkmans' table, and they resented our efforts. Staying in character, we shrugged off their insults and shouldered our way on. Once I caught a glimpse of Flo, arguing with someone in the crowd. Her eyes met mine, but passed on without any sign of recognition.

And then, that voice again. *"Lucy . . . I'm here."*

My stomach twisted with exhilaration. We were close! I turned my face toward the wall so that no one would see me speak. "Skull? Skull—is that you?"

"Let me see . . . Ooh, no, it's another Type Three disembodied spirit who knows your name and your purpose and happens to be stored nearby."

That settled the matter. No other spirit could be that sarcastic. "It's you."

"Of course it's me! Get me out of this dungeon right now!"

"It's not that easy. And a bit of gratitude wouldn't go amiss, either. Where are you?"

"Some tiled room. Old cloakroom, maybe. Probably a former ladies' room, knowing my luck. Neon light flickering over the door."

I looked along the platform; a short way beyond where the Winkmans sat, I *did* notice a faintly flickering light. Its source was lost in the room's curve. "I think I see it. We're in line to get to you."

"What, are you queuing now? Just how British are you people? Don't just stand in line! Kill somebody!"

"Lucy . . ." Lockwood's dirty face loomed near. "You're mumbling to yourself."

"It's the skull. I can hear it. It's close by."

Lockwood glanced around at the shuffling, stinking relic-men. "I think we're all right. Half of these bozos talk to themselves all the time anyway. Still, keep it down."

"Lucy, you've got to get me out of here." The skull's voice broke in on my thoughts again. *"They're taking me to the place of blood."*

"The place of blood? What does that mean?"

"Well now, I should think it's quite a jolly spot where nice things happen and everyone's good chums together. . . . How do I know what it is? With a name like that, it's got to be bad news, even for me! There's some hideous stuff piled up here . . . Your friend Guppy's Source, for one."

"Guppy's Source?" I stared at Lockwood, who grimaced. "Not that jar of teeth?"

"Yeah. They were very pleased with that."

"Who's 'they'? The Winkmans?"

"Search me. A woman in a flowery dress that makes her look like last year's sofa, and some kid with a face like a slapped butt."

"That's them."

"It's their men who brought me here. They're not the bosses, though. There's a guy here, too. At the end of all this, they'll sell me to him."

"Ah! The collector! What's he look like?"

"Erm . . ." The voice grew vague. *"Just a bloke. About yay high, neither this nor that. . . . He's actually quite difficult to describe. Tell you what, you might see him yourself if you swing past and rescue me. Are you alone?"*

"No."

"Don't tell me. I know who it is. Stands to reason he'd help you."

Even at a distance, the appalling parody of Lockwood's voice was clear. *"What? A suicidal mission, you say, Lucy? Certain death, you say? Just what I enjoy. Sign me up!' Well, all the better if it is Lockwood. You can sacrifice him to rescue me. I call that a very decent swap."*

Fury filled me. "You foul skull! I swear I'm going to leave you right there."

There was a pause. The voice spoke again, more quietly. *"This isn't just about me, Lucy. This is big. Come and get me, and I'll tell you what they're doing. Death's in Life and Life's in Death, Lucy. This is the proof of it."*

I snorted. "Proof of what? What does that actually *mean?*" But the psychic connection had broken off, and Lockwood was shaking my arm. Taking a breath, I told him what I'd heard.

He scratched at his black wig; beneath the cheek paste and eyeliner, his face was genuinely pale. "It's not going to be easy, Luce," he said, "but I *can* get you access to that room. The catch is, you'll need to deal with whoever's in there on your own. Up for it?"

My anger at the skull still boiled inside me. The comments about Lockwood had made me feel queasy with guilt. But there would only be one answer. I nodded. "Yup."

"I've missed you so much, Lucy."

Okay, what with the wig and the makeup, and his blacked-out teeth, he didn't look too great right then; but behind his gappy grin shone the old Lockwood smile, and that smile and those words together swept everything else aside. All guilt and queasiness were gone, and I was conscious of nothing other than the thrill of being there with him.

"You, too," I began—but he didn't hear me. He was still talking, telling me the plan.

"So I'll cause a diversion," Lockwood said, "that'll distract everyone by the table. When they're busy, you just walk straight past and into the room. Then you'll have to be back out again with the skull in the blink of an eye."

Now if it had been *me* making that suggestion, and I'd been putting it to Ted Daley or Tina Lane or one of the other lame-duck agents I'd worked with in my freelance career, there'd have followed a long series of questions as they tried to weasel their way out of doing anything remotely dangerous. But it was *Lockwood* making the suggestion, and me listening, and though my veins fizzed at the danger *he* was putting himself in, I didn't waste time or effort. I only nodded. If Lockwood saw a way, I went with it. He trusted me. I trusted him. That's how we stayed alive.

"Great," he said. "Two minutes—and I'll meet you back here. Then we stroll to the ladder and get out. Ready? Okay. Three, two, one—go."

No sooner said than done. I set off, keeping to the curve of the wall. I slipped past the first few men in the line in front of me, ignoring their exclamations of annoyance. At every point I expected someone to pull me back. I drew nearer to the table, to where the Winkmans sat, surrounded by the men in black. And now I saw that there were two other men farther on, standing guard at a little arch, beneath the flashing neon light. At any moment I'd be spotted, and the enemy would descend on me. . . .

There was a sudden cry behind me, a heavy blow, a roar of rage. Everyone at the table looked up. I could hear the sounds of repeated punches, rude insults, the shouting of the crowd. It was an almighty clamor. All eyes were on it. The men beside the archway left their posts and ran past me without a glance. Lockwood's diversion was successfully under way.

Lockwood . . . My heart hammered against my chest. I was desperate to turn around, see what he was doing, but that wasn't part of the plan. Without a backward glance I walked quickly past the table to the arch, and stepped through it into a small room.

Chapter 17

W hatever the skull's complaints, I didn't think the chamber had ever been a ladies' room. It was far too spacious. It was a simple tiled recess, once probably used for railway supplies, and now a storeroom of a different kind. In its center, a long trestle table had been erected; on that table, and in neat piles on the floor to either side, sat silver-glass boxes and jars of varying size, and each one of those containers was full. I glimpsed bones, lumps of ragged cloth, pieces of jewelry, the usual bric-a-brac that makes up supernatural Sources. But there were powerful ones among them; I could feel the psychic buzzing even through the glass.

Very powerful, some of them. There, in a silver-glass box halfway up one pile, I spied the Ealing Cannibal's tooth collection.

And there, propped precariously at the end of the table, a certain familiar ghost-jar.

The ichor that surrounded the skull was thick and syrupy, but tiny pulses of green throbbed in its center, and the ghost's voice echoed in my mind.

"At last! Am I glad to see you! Right, stab this guy quickly, and let's be going."

I didn't answer. I needed to concentrate. I was not the only person in the room.

Behind the table, sitting on a plastic folding chair, was a man. A small man in a black suit with a dull blue tie. Those aspects I could instantly attest to. The rest was curiously vague; even as I looked at him, the details were slipping from my mind. He had nondescript brown hair, slicked back away from a bland, slightly shapeless face; he also had an expression of mild concentration; the tip of his tongue protruded from the side of his mouth. He had a cigarette in one hand, and with the other he was making notes on a piece of paper with a pen. But distinguishing features that would pick him out in a crowd? None.

Something about this overt and almost aggressive ordinariness made me assume that he was not the person I was looking for. He was a bookkeeper, an underling—certainly not the mysterious collector for whom the Winkmans toiled. But another part of my mind was jolted to sudden alertness. I felt as though I had seen him before.

Even as I made this connection, the skull's voice came again. *"Beware this man,"* it said. *"He doesn't look like much, but he's dangerous. Oh, great—I see you forgot your sword."*

The little man looked up and saw me standing in the doorway. "Who are you, please? You are not welcome here."

It was a precise, finicky, almost waspish sort of voice, and now I *knew* I was right. It was familiar to me. A voice that dealt in figures and paperwork and bureaucratic details, as well as the qualities of the strange, unpleasant psychic relics on the tabletop before him. A voice that kept tabs on things, that reported on them to others . . .

"Who are you?" the man asked again.

I'd met him. Not so long ago.

"Fiddler, sir," I said, giving a small salute. "Jane Fiddler. Mrs. Winkman sent me. There's been a mistake with one of the items. That manky skull in the jar. We should have brought you a different skull, sir. This one's a dud."

"Dud?" The little man frowned over at the jar, then down at his jottings. "It's in an official containment vessel. Old, too; it's the style of jar used by the Fittes Agency years ago. They didn't often make mistakes."

"Did with this one, sir. The thing's got almost no psychic force. Old bit of junk that needs burning, Mrs. Winkman says. She's sent for the good skull now; it'll be along in a minute. I'm to take the useless one away. She sends her apologies." I made a sort of tentative saunter toward the skull.

"Apologies? From Adelaide Winkman?" The man rested his cigarette carefully in an ashtray and folded his hands over his neat little belly. "That doesn't sound like her."

"The mix-up's caused all sorts of problems. Can you hear that racket?" I swiveled a thumb toward the door, where loud thumps and shouts could still be heard. Anxiety for Lockwood welled inside me, but I kept my voice calm. "Some of the boys out there are getting very worked up."

The man sniffed. "How tiresome. You people really are revolting." With an irritated gesture he picked up the piece of paper before him. It was attached to a plastic clipboard—and, with sudden startling clarity, I realized who he was.

Five nights ago, in the foyer of the insurance company. I'd looked down from the balcony, battered and bruised from my encounter with the ghost of Emma Marchment; I'd seen the Rotwell group, with Mr. Farnaby, my stupid supervisor, reclining in his chair. And at Farnaby's shoulder, supervising the supervisor, clipboard in his hand . . .

The man from the Rotwell Institute, the soft-spoken, anonymous Mr. Johnson.

I reached the table, stretched out casually for the ghost-jar. "I know. We *are* appalling, aren't we? Sorry. Well, Adelaide will be along in a minute to explain."

"My mother will be along to explain what?"

And with that, my outstretched hand curled up like a scalded spider and retreated from the jar. Slowly, stiffly, I looked back toward the arch.

It would be a lie to say the doorway was blocked by a menacing shadow. *Half* of it was, but only the lower portion, because while he was pretty broad (and broader still thanks to the ridiculous shoulder pads on his expensive fur coat) Leopold Winkman wasn't very tall. He had the bulky but diminished physique of a wrestler who'd been hit by a grand piano falling from a height, and the wide brim of his hat and loud checks on his designer suit only made him look more horizontal still. He was in his mid-teens, his face dumpling-soft and malleable, with a toad-like mouth strongly reminiscent of his father, the imprisoned Julius Winkman. Despite his soft and dandified appearance, his character was reminiscent of Julius, too. In the London underworld, Leopold had a reputation for precocious ruthlessness. His eyes were bullet-hard and blue.

I didn't say anything. We stood staring at each other.

Behind me, I heard Mr. Johnson's bland tones. "She wants the skull in the jar."

"That's right," I said. "Like your ma ordered. She *did* tell you, right? Go and ask her."

I didn't expect him to buy it; it was a hopeless situation. But while his brain worked, I ran my eyes over the tabletop next to me. I figured I had about five seconds.

"My ma?" Leopold Winkman said. "She wouldn't have asked a grubby little punk like you to—" His face changed; grew suddenly slack. Whether it was the limitations of my disguise, or because he remembered who had owned the skull, or simply because of the way I'd looked at him, clear-eyed and contemptuous, he finally got it. "Wait . . ." He took a slow step back. "Wait, *I* know who you are. Lucy Carlyle!"

"Don't worry." It was the skull's whisper. *"You can take him, big girl like you."*

Leopold flung back his coat, revealing a pistol at his belt.

"Or possibly not," the skull said.

But I was already diving for the table, seizing the skull's jar and tucking it under one arm, grabbing at another silver-glass box, and hurling it at Winkman. As I did so, I ducked. The gun went off. Glass shattered beside me; one of the boxes on the table exploded, fragments pattering against my back. The box I'd thrown cracked into Winkman's shins, bowling him over. He dropped the gun and rolled onto his back, squealing.

"*Shrimp down,*" the skull said. "*Nice.*"

There was a concussion of air beside me, strong enough to move the wig across my head. From the shattered box in the center of the table rose a blue-white shape. Winkman's bullet had freed its ghost. Mr. Johnson sensed it. He sprang off his chair, retreating to the back of the room.

I didn't stay to see how he fared. With the ghost-jar in my arms, I leaped over Leopold and made for the arch. . . .

Only to find it truly blocked this time—by a one-eyed relic-boy little older than me. He carried a curved knife with a serrated edge. Behind him, two of Winkman's men were also stepping bulkily into view.

"*My turn,*" the skull said. "*Lift up the jar and keep going.*"

I lifted the ghost-jar. It flared with sudden green other-light— casting a vile radiance on the men ahead of me. The youth with the knife stared deep into the glass—and gave an unholy scream. He staggered back, knocking into the men behind him, sending them all careering against the wall.

The skull chuckled. "*How was that? Gave him my best face there.*"

"Not bad." I made like an eel, twisting between the sprawling bodies, hurling myself through the arch and out onto the platform, where a full-scale brawl was under way. At its heart was a slim young relic-man with hair like an evil hedgehog; he stood near the Winkmans' table, swinging a long, black candlestick around his head and keeping the crowd at bay. Nearby, Adelaide Winkman was shouting orders and completely failing to bring the situation under control.

"*This is your plan?*" the skull said. "*Interestingly fluid. What happens now?*"

"I haven't a clue."

But Lockwood had been watching out for me. He danced forward, grasped the Winkmans' table, and overturned it, sending a sparkling waterfall of coins crashing to the floor. In the same movement he leaped over it and came racing toward me. Behind him, Adelaide and her helpers were engulfed as a frantic tide of relic-men made efforts to reach the coins.

"The arch beyond you, Luce!" Lockwood cried. "Cross to the other platform!"

I turned—but at that moment Leopold Winkman burst out of the side room. He ducked under Lockwood's viciously swinging candlestick, threw himself at me, and snatched at the ghost-jar under my arm. The impact knocked me over; Leopold and I tussled on the floor, kicking and punching. My wig fell off. I was conscious of Lockwood calling, of other people drawing near. All at once Leopold struck the side of my head. Lights burst in my eyes. My arm went loose; the ghost-jar was torn away.

"*Lucy! Save me—*"

"Skull!" My head rang with the blow. I raised it, blinking. Leopold and the jar were gone. I was lying on my back. Above me was a confusing blur of fighting forms—Lockwood, the Winkman flunkies, several relic-men. One man saw me move; he lifted a heavy stick to strike at me. Someone stuck out a dirty Wellington boot and tripped him. I glimpsed Flo's tatted straw hat as he fell away. Then Lockwood was wrenching me to my feet, hauling me onward up the platform.

"Lucy . . . !" A faint, despairing cry behind me in the crowd.

"The skull! Lockwood, I lost it—"

"I'm sorry. So sorry. But we *really* need to go."

Lockwood's face was bruised, his wig askew. His candlestick was gone. Together we ran toward the far end of the hall. The tunnel mouth was boarded up over here, but a connecting passage led to the southbound platform. We fled down it, pursued by a tide of noise.

"The ladder's a no-go now," Lockwood gasped. "It'll have to be a tunnel."

Fewer candles burned along the second platform, and there was no one on it. A few yards from us was the tunnel mouth, filled by another great pile of sandbags, salt, and iron. Lockwood and I jumped down onto the track, scrambled up to the top of the slope, and stared down into the blackness of the tunnel.

"It's unblocked," I said.

"Yes."

"It'll lead us out of here."

"I'm sure it would."

"So come on, let's go."

"No." He clasped my arm. "Ghost."

How had I not seen it? A gray form was standing in the tunnel, not so very far off. It was man-shaped, but two-dimensional and contorted, as if it had been cut from paper, then twisted. Its head was cocked toward us, as if drawn by our sound, our smell, our body heat—by whatever it was of life that the pale, thin shape had lost and still desired. As I stared at it, my foot slipped on a pebble; I jerked forward down the slope, just a little way; a few chunks of rock and sand fell onto the line. At once the ghost darted out of the tunnel, only to draw back when it got near the iron.

I wished quite a lot of things right at that moment.

I wished I hadn't followed the skull's voice.

I wished I hadn't encouraged Lockwood to bring me here.

Most of all, I *really* wished we had our rapiers.

The shape drifted nearer. Lockwood motioned with his head, and we stepped carefully back across the mess of iron and salt and rubble, down toward the old platform.

Where Adelaide Winkman was waiting for us in the light of the flickering lantern. She held a long, narrow-bladed knife in her right hand.

It wasn't *just* her, by the way. She was backed up by a host of relic-men, who in their ragged, shambling hideousness looked like a crowd of the agitated dead, plus the implacable flunkies with their knives.

But it was Adelaide your eyes were drawn to. It was that weird double adjustment that your brain had to make. First you saw what *looked* like a large blond housewife, pink of face and plucked of eyebrow, her motherly curves squeezed into a voluminous and flowery dress, yet standing among a crowd of criminals. Then, just when you were getting used to the strangeness of *that*, you realized she was the scariest of the lot. It was the blue-gray eyes, mostly; the pencil-thin slash of the lips, partly; plus bonus points for the swell of her forearms and her evident physical strength. She'd long sworn vengeance on us for having put her husband away. Perhaps this was why she was smiling.

"Mr. Lockwood," she said. "And Miss Carlyle. How surprising to see *you* at this market."

"Yes . . . I'm a great believer in late-night shopping," Lockwood said. He scratched at his lopsided wig and eyed the knife. "I see that you aren't."

"I'm a believer in giving intruders what they deserve," Adelaide Winkman said. "What did you want here?"

"We've been waiting to offer you some choice articles," Lockwood indicated his satchel. "I must admit, I'm not wildly impressed by your service. I've a good mind to complain."

The woman's eyes flickered toward the rubble, and the iron line. Down in the dark behind us, the shape moved. "Isn't there someone in the tunnel to take care of you?"

"Well, yes. Bit uncommunicative, I found. Doesn't say much."

"No, but very attentive, from what I understand." Adelaide Winkman gestured with the knife, and once again I found myself wishing ardently that we hadn't left our rapiers behind. "Why not run away into the tunnel? He'll see to you very quickly, I'm sure."

Lockwood nodded. "Or, possibly, we could stay here, talking with you."

Mrs. Winkman held up the knife and tilted it, so that its fine edges caught the light. "I wasn't always in the antiques business, you know."

"Weren't you?"

"No. I used to be a butcher. This is a slaughterman's filleting knife. I became quite proficient with it, a long time ago. Used it on all kinds of livestock—and other things."

"Fascinating." Lockwood took off his wig and ruffled his hair distractedly. "I had some other jobs, too, when I was younger. Delivered papers, washed cars . . . Sometimes I used to kick big women in the backside. That wasn't paid work; I did it just for laughs. I bet I haven't lost that knack, either. We could talk about this all night."

She moved closer. "It's the tunnel or the knife. I've a short fuse when it comes to snoops and interferers, as you'll soon find."

Lockwood smiled. "*Snoop? Interferer?* I protest at that description."

"You think it inaccurate?"

"Oh no; I'm both of those. But I'm an *agent,* most of all."

The woman shook her head. "An agent has his rapier. Tonight, you have nothing." She signaled to the men beside her. "Climb up and seize them."

"Agents have other weapons, too," Lockwood said. "Such as these." He rummaged around inside his wig and brought out two magnesium flares; they'd been concealed there ever since he'd left Portland Row. He threw the first one at Adelaide Winkman's feet. Even as it dropped, he was spinning, hurling the second into the tunnel, in the direction of the ghost. Then he pulled me to him.

For an instant we stood at the top of the mound, clutching at each other while the world exploded around us. Twin eruptions of fire on either side. Hot iron spattered against our clothes; we were buffeted first one way, then the other. Plumes of silver smoke billowed up at us, broke against our bodies, merged, and darkened into gray.

It all took three or four seconds, tops. Then we pulled apart, turned, and skidded down the mound into the tunnel. Screams sounded from the platform, but the silence up ahead was absolute.

The flare had done its work; the hovering shape was gone. Our boots rattled on dry gravel. The tunnel curled away. I scrabbled in my bag for a little flashlight. Every now and then I switched it on, watching the curve of the tracks, so we didn't run into the walls. Almost at once I noticed how cold it had become since crossing the iron line. The tracks were sparkling with ice now; the black gravel glittered with it. Our breath was frost. The sound of our panting echoed off the walls.

"Lockwood," I said, "the *chill*."

"I feel it, but we've got to keep moving."

Behind us, around the bend in the tunnel, we could hear the sounds of reluctant pursuit—heavy boots stumbling over rubble, Adelaide Winkman's voice urging them on.

"They'll have defenses against the ghosts," I gasped. "They'll drive us straight into—"

I didn't need to say it. We were getting close to the site of the train accident. You could feel the psychic pressure mounting, and sense presences very near.

"Maybe there'll be a side tunnel," Lockwood muttered. "They had them sometimes. If we could branch off, get away from this . . ." He gave a cry. "Switch that flashlight off!"

My light had picked out a cavity in the right-hand wall, a blank, flat recess where workers could shelter from the passing trains. But there was the suggestion too of white things jumbled among the dust and rubble. I switched off the flashlight. We kept on walking.

"Were those bones?" I whispered.

The answer hung in the dark ahead of us: a thin gray shape, a smear of shadow. Another Shade.

"It looks inert," I said. "Maybe it doesn't see us. Hold on, no— it's moving."

Lockwood cursed. "This isn't good. If only we had something we could use"—he clicked his fingers—"for *protection*. . . . Of course! Maybe we *do*." He stopped dead.

"What are you *doing*?" I hissed. "We need to move." I could hear boots some way behind us, slipping on gravel.

"Here. Stand close. Shine the flashlight on the ground." He had torn his bag open, pulled out his spirit-cape. With a shake of the hand, he let it unfold. Purple-blue feathers shimmered on their silver network. Like a conjurer completing a trick, he whirled it up and around so that it fell over me, soft and downy. Then he raised its hood to cover my head.

"When the medicine men went into the spirit houses to talk to their ancestors, they wrapped themselves in these," he said. He was looking in my bag now, getting out the second cape, wrapping it around himself. "We should do the same."

"But we're not going to talk to our ancestors!"

"We don't know *what* we're going to do, Luce. But it certainly won't do any harm. In fact—am I imagining it, or has the cold lessened already?"

"I suppose it has, a bit. What's the Shade doing?"

"Nothing now. It's just standing there. Don't know if it's the capes or not. But it's not attacking, which is good. Come on, we've got to run. They're coming."

Keeping our capes pulled tightly over us, we jogged down the tunnel, even as Winkman's party came into view. There were shouts of excitement as they saw us, then a shrill cry of alarm—someone had noticed the ghost. The clatter of boots abruptly stopped; their whispered discussions resounded behind us as we hastened on.

"Won't delay them long," Lockwood said. "But I can't believe those adults are going to want to go much farther. Oh . . . Oh no."

All at once we had emerged into a higher, wider space.

In some ways it resembled the areas of Vauxhall Station we had left behind. The rails curved around ahead of us beside the beginning of an open platform; steps led up to it from the trackside. Not far along, however, the platform was choked with dusty gray chunks of rubble, rising right up to the broken ceiling. There were no arches or doorways in the walls. The way was clearly blocked.

And the track was blocked, too. By a train.

Even in my flashlight beam, it was black. Whether it had been the gas explosion itself, or the fire that ran through the cars afterward, or even the corrosion from long years being buried underground, the surface of the metal was dark and pitted. From the angle where we stood, we could see the back of the first car, the door hanging open, the charred stubs of the first few seats.

"It's the one," Lockwood breathed. "The train from the disaster."

With the capes still draped over us, we edged out of the tunnel to the platform steps. From here the damage wrought on the train was even more evident. Halfway along, where it was embedded in the rubble, the entire central section of the train's roof had been crushed as if slammed by a giant fist. One wall had burst outward. Portions of metal curled up from the rubble on the platform like the ribs of some prehistoric beast. The train was silent, empty, its windows twisted in agonized contortions.

I saw nothing, but the roar of flames echoed in my ears. When I stuck my hand out from under the spirit-cape, I gasped at the sudden supernatural cold.

"Flashlight off, Luce," Lockwood said.

The recommendation when switching off a flashlight is always to keep your eyes closed for five full seconds—to give them a chance to get used to the dark. Just before I opened them, I heard Lockwood give a startled exclamation, and knew he was ahead of me. So I looked, too. There was a faint luminosity in the broken windows, and by this other-light it was possible to see that the seats of the ruined car *were* occupied after all.

Silhouetted heads showed in the darkness, bowed and still; long hair hung lankly above ragged collars and thin, thin necks. Skin as white as cave fish gleamed, and rows of coal-black eyes. Though their physical bodies had been removed long ago, the passengers of the train remained inside.

We stood there. Behind came sound of renewed pursuit, with Adelaide Winkman hallooing at the back.

"No choice, Luce," Lockwood said. "We'll have to go through."

"Through the train? But Lockwood—"

"It's either that or Winkman. We've got to trust in the capes."

"But there are so many of them. . . ."

"We've got to trust the capes."

And do so right away, because now a flashlight beam speared us each in turn, and then another, and the tunnel mouth became a brutal blaze of merging lights and running forms.

A shot rang out; a small hole appeared in the metalwork at the end of the car.

I don't remember how we climbed onto the train, who went first, or how we kept the capes around us as we scaled the rungs and squeezed through the narrow opening into the car. Fear blurred the experience—fear of what was behind and, mostly, fear of what sat in the seats around us now.

Fire *had* passed through the train, at considerable heat. The interior was stripped to its metal skeleton; the chair upholstery was gone, and some of the thinner metal struts were warped. Everything was black, the surfaces burned and thick with charcoal dust. Nevertheless, those sitting in the haze of other-light retained vestiges of old-style clothing, traces of suits, hats, and fancy dresses that weren't entirely scorched. They sat bolt upright on facing seats, on either side of the narrow central aisle. Close-up, you could see that their skin, like their clothes, persisted only in papery flakes and sections. How dry and dusty they were—except for their eyes. *Those* were as big and bright and moist as the eyes of toads, and all were fixed directly on us.

Another bullet whined overhead and struck something deep inside the train. I was grateful for it. Without the prompting, I believe we'd never have taken another step. Now we gathered the capes around us and started to shuffle forward—first me, Lockwood behind—past the glowing forms of men and women in their metal tomb, the rows of resentful dead.

An old woman, bones beneath her shawl. A man with a bowler hat blending with his face. Two young men, heads propped against each other, merged and fused. I shut my ears to the eager whispering that rose around us.

The floor was crispy where some synthetic layer had become a kind of toast. It felt crunchy underfoot. We moved very slowly, inching down the aisle. Eyes watched us. The occupants of the car didn't move.

As we progressed, we saw that not all the forms were burned and old. One or two had brighter auras and—I felt—jarringly modern clothes. A youth with an orange puffer jacket and dark blue jeans; a thin girl in a hoodie. They sat among the older ghosts like gold teeth in a rotting mouth. *Newer passengers, too,* Flo had said. She'd been right. It was not clear how they'd died.

We came to the center of the train, where the side had been blown away and the roof crushed low. We had to bend almost in half in order to progress, and there were ghosts here, too, squashed into appalling forms. I did my utmost not to take in the details. We passed into the second half of the train.

"Keep looking straight ahead," Lockwood whispered. "Don't meet their gaze."

I nodded. "They want us with them."

"And they'd *have* us, too, if it weren't for the cloaks."

As if in proof, an old man sitting by the aisle raised a withered hand as I passed by. His curled finger reached to touch me—but jerked away as the cape drew near.

At the far end of the train, there were fewer ghosts. We hastened on, made it to where the door hung open and the tunnel track stretched away. Legs watery with relief, we dropped through, stumbling on a few yards until we finally sank to our knees on the sharp gravel. Behind us was only silence.

"Hope the Winkmans try to come after us," Lockwood said,

once we could speak. "If they do, I reckon tomorrow night there might be a couple more passengers sitting in that train."

I shuddered. "Don't."

"Come on. If we follow the tunnel for long enough, we'll find a way out." He adjusted the hood of his cape. "Better keep these on until we're well away from here."

We got slowly, stiffly to our feet. "Who would have thought Portland Row had such treasures in it?" I said. "We owe your parents, Lockwood. They've kept us safe."

He didn't answer. It wasn't a place for conversation. With that, we set our backs to death and darkness. Walking side by side, we followed the train track slowly up toward the light.

IV
The Cursed Village

Chapter 18

Lockwood was satisfied with the result of our subterranean expedition, or at least as satisfied as it was possible to be given that we'd failed to retrieve the skull and had both nearly died. The fact that it had taken us nearly two hours to locate a safe way out of the Underground system and had almost been squashed by a moving train outside of Stockwell didn't bother him much either.

"Look at it this way," he said the following morning, when we were sitting with George and Holly in the basement office of Lockwood & Co. "The positives of last night massively outweigh the negatives. First, we went in search of an important psychic artifact and discovered that we actually *owned* two others." He glanced up at the suit of armor that stood beside his desk. The spirit-capes hung from it, glittering, resplendent, and slowly drying. They'd got a bit sooty in the Tube tunnels, and we'd had to dab them clean. "That's a major result," he went on. "Okay, maybe we won't want to wear them too much in public. People might think we were in some kind of novelty show. But those capes could really help us out in dangerous situations. Right, George?"

There was nothing George loved more than mysterious psychic artifacts; he'd hardly been able to keep his hands off the capes all morning. "Yep, they're amazing objects," he said. "Obviously the silver links in the lining help keep the ghosts at bay, but it's possible the feathers do something, too. Could be their natural oil, or some special coating the witch doctors used . . . I'll have to experiment. And, Lockwood"—his eyes gleamed—"we should really check to see what else is hidden away upstairs in that room."

"Maybe someday," Lockwood said. "When we've got time."

George grunted. "I know what *that* means. But you can't keep ignoring those boxes—can he, Luce?"

"I guess not." My reaction had been more muted than the others'. I was happy about the capes, of course, but that didn't resolve my disappointment about the whispering skull. I'd been *so* close to retrieving it. I'd actually had it in my hand. Once the adrenaline of our escape had faded, I'd been left feeling pretty empty inside.

Lockwood knew what I was thinking, of course. "You mustn't be too upset, Lucy," he said. "We don't know that the skull's lost for good. There's still hope—and that brings me to the *really* big result of the night . . . namely the sinister Mr. Johnson of the Rotwell Institute. You recognizing him there was *huge*. If you were still a member of Lockwood and Company, I'd give you a raise. As it is—"

"You'll give *me* one?" George suggested.

"No. But I will go so far as to say it's the most significant bit of work anyone's done since the Chelsea Outbreak. You're an amazing agent, Lucy."

Well, you can guess *that* made me feel a bit better. While I was digesting it, Lockwood got up and walked around the front of his desk; he leaned back against it, tall and slim and full of life and purpose. I had a sudden sense that everything was possible, that fortune and our assembled Talents would favor us. I could feel my despondency lifting. It was the Lockwood effect.

"The implications are incredible," he went on. "With one stroke, Luce, you made a connection between the black market and one of the most famous institutions in London. Holly—what can you tell us about the institute?"

Before coming to work at Lockwood's, Holly Munro had been an agent at Rotwell's—and then a personal assistant to Steve Rotwell, its chairman. She had not greatly enjoyed that particular job, Mr. Rotwell being a bullish, aggressive individual, but she had always spoken highly of the company in general. She certainly knew more than most about the way it was run.

"The institute is the agency's research wing," she said. "It keeps itself separate from the rest of the company. No ordinary operatives work for it. It's all adult scientists investigating the mechanics of the Problem."

"And making lots of lousy products in the process," I said. "Like George's silver bell thing we used at the Guppy house."

George gave a shrill cry. "Hey, that worked! Just a little too *late*, was all."

Holly nodded. "The institute's got a long history of inventing new defenses."

"And marketing them very successfully," Lockwood said. "Holly, when you were at Rotwell, did you know this Johnson?"

"Saul Johnson. Yes, I knew *of* him. He was one of the directors of the institute."

"And did he ever get involved with ordinary ghost hunts? Lucy first saw him when she was out on a case with Rotwell's."

"No. I never remember that happening before. The institute scientists kept to themselves. They were usually off at their labs somewhere."

"Right, so it looks to me," Lockwood said, "as if something new and special is going on. Johnson—and presumably the institute generally—is out collecting powerful Sources, despite DEPRAC's directives against doing precisely that. The mummified head you found last week, Lucy—Johnson will have seen that, clocked it, and given immediate orders to Harold Mailer to save it at the furnaces, ready for the marketeers to spirit away."

"Looks as if *everything* important is being kept back now," I said. "The Source from the Ealing Cannibal case was sitting on Johnson's table last night, too."

"Which raises the question," George said, "of *why*."

He said this in the kind of slow, deliberate way that made you feel a sudden thrill of excitement; you knew he had the answer and was about to reveal it in long words you only barely understood.

"Care to fill us in?" Lockwood said.

George paused. "Do I have to get up and come around to lean against the table in a cool, leaderish way like you?"

"That's entirely optional."

"Good, because my legs are too short to do it comfortably. My buttocks would keep sliding off. Think I'll stay sitting here, if it's all the same to you. Do you remember," George went on, "what we found in the tunnels beneath Aickmere's? Aside from a massive pile of human bones."

"I found Lucy," Lockwood said. His smile made me feel a little flushed. He'd had to climb down into the tunnels after the Poltergeist pulled me in.

"Aside from the bones and Lucy," George said, "we found evidence that someone had been conducting some kind of weird experiments down there. There was a cleared circle in the middle of the bones, and candles set up around the edge, and marks where something metal had been pulled across the floor. And there was a massive ectoplasm burn mark in the very center of the circle. The bones were all psychically active, and we reckoned someone was using them as a single massive Source. Now we know that ordinary Sources represent weak points, where Visitors can slip through from"—he hesitated—"from wherever it is they *ought* to be. Imagine them as holes worn in old fabric. Like when the seat of your jeans wears through, Lockwood, that sort of thing."

"I don't get worn patches on the seats of my trousers," Lockwood said. "And I don't *have* any jeans."

"Well, think of mine, then. I have plenty of old pairs. The fabric gets thin, then stringy, then widens to an actual hole. All of a sudden it's embarrassing when you bend over. It's the same here, except that it's not your underwear showing—something else comes through."

"This metaphor is disturbing in a number of ways," Lockwood said. "Right now I'm actually less worried about the ghosts than about the other images you're conjuring up. But go on. If you create a *giant* Source, therefore—"

"The weak point would be correspondingly bigger," George continued. "It would create a bigger hole, for want of a better word. We saw that with the bone glass, too." He was referring to an unpleasant artifact we'd once discovered—a mirror made of numerous haunted bones, designed by its maker to be a window to the Other Side. Whether it actually worked or not was unclear, since anyone who gazed into it invariably died, but the psychic frisson it gave off had certainly been strange and sinister. "I think whoever was behind the Aickmere's thing was trying to make a window like the bone glass," George said. "To do that, they needed a giant Source. Now Johnson seems to be out and about collecting powerful Sources—I reckon he's up to the same game."

"You think the Rotwell Institute was behind the Aickmere's incident, too?" I asked.

"Maybe. Remember how quickly their teams turned up to clear the site after we'd discovered it? But it's impossible to say. There was no clue as to who it was."

"We found a cigarette butt, didn't we?" Holly pointed out.

"Yep," George said. "A Persian Light. Quite a rare brand."

I sat up. "Hey, Johnson was smoking cigarettes."

George looked at me. "What? Were they Persian Lights?"

"I don't know."

He slapped the side of his forehead. "Oh, Luce. That was a missed opportunity. Didn't you sniff it? They've got a very distinctive aroma, like burned toast and caramel."

"No, as it happens I *didn't* take time out to taste his cigarette smoke, George. I was too busy trying to avoid being killed."

George slouched back in his seat. "You could have taken a quick whiff while running for your life, Luce. Where's your dedication?"

Lockwood had been thinking. He tapped his fingers on the desktop. "Did Steve Rotwell have much to do with the institute, Holly?"

She frowned. "I assumed that he was in charge of it. He was always heading off to see them."

"So he probably knows. Question is: What can we do about it?"

"Not a lot," George said. "Still can't really tell Barnes, can we? There's not a shred of proof."

"And Johnson will have spirited everything away somewhere," Lockwood said. "The Rotwell Institute is based in Westminster, isn't it, Hol?"

"That's its head office, but not much goes on there. All its research facilities are outside London. There are several. I can't remember them all offhand—sorry."

Lockwood nodded ruefully. "Several facilities . . . That's difficult. Do you think you could draw up a list for me? Might be useful, though to be honest I have no idea how we should proceed. . . ." He sighed. "In the meantime, we've got a more pleasant appointment to keep. Penelope Fittes's secretary rang first thing, Luce. You know she wants to thank us for the Ealing Cannibal case? Seems she's out and about this morning, visiting the Orpheus Society, of which she's patron, and wonders if we'd like to meet her there."

"The *Orpheus* Society? In St. James's?"

"The very same. Want to come along?"

He didn't need to ask me twice.

For some time we'd been intrigued by the secretive and exclusive Orpheus Society, an outfit in central London whose members included many of the country's most prominent industrialists. Officially, it was an upmarket London club devoted to discussion and research of the Problem, but we happened to know that it was engaged in more practical activities, too. George possessed a curious pair of crystal goggles marked with the society logo, an ancient Greek harp or lyre. Exactly what these goggles *did* had never been established; it was clear, though, that the Rotwell Institute was not the only organization developing equipment to use in the endless battle against the Problem. Unlike the institute, however, the society did not publicize its work, and the chance to learn more about it had never come up—until now. It was an opportunity not to be missed. Later that morning, leaving Holly to research the Rotwell Institute, Lockwood, George, and I set out later that morning for St. James's in a mood of eager anticipation.

We found the society at the end of an elegant cul-de-sac, a quiet street of stuccoed townhouses, where the brass plates on the pillars gleamed spotlessly and the flowers in the hanging baskets beneath the hotel windows bloomed with plush, complacent health. The plaque gave the name without pomp or fanfare; and at our knock the door was opened at once by a smiling old man, who bowed and gestured for us to enter.

"Come in, come in, and welcome. I am the secretary of the society."

The secretary was an amiable white-haired gentleman, stooped of shoulder but twinkling of eye. He wore a long frock coat and starched collar in an old-fashioned style, and his hair was swept back generously from an impressive forehead. We stood with him in a small, cool foyer. The floor was marble, the walls a deep maroon. Beyond him, an elderly man and woman were walking down a staircase. Somewhere nearby, a clock was ticking.

"We're here to see Ms. Penelope Fittes, sir," Lockwood said. "My name is Anthony Lockwood. These are my colleagues, George Cubbins and Lucy Carlyle."

The old man nodded. "I was told to expect you. Dear Penelope is in the reading room." He continued to gaze at Lockwood. "So you are Celia and Donald's boy? I believe I've read about you in the *Times*. Yes, yes, I think I see them both in you."

"Did you know them, sir?" Lockwood asked.

"Oh, indeed. They were candidates for membership in the society once. In fact, they gave a most interesting lecture in the very room I'll be taking you to now. 'Ghost Lore among the Tribes of New Guinea and West Sumatra,' or something of that nature. They were folklorists, of course, perhaps not *scientists* in the strictest sense of the word. . . . Still, their scholarship was impeccable. Their loss was a great one."

"Thank you, sir," Lockwood said. His face was impassive.

"Well, well, you didn't come to talk to *me*. It's just along here." The old man led the way down a softly carpeted corridor, past paintings of august gentlemen similar to himself. At the end of the passage, a stained glass window let in shafts of yellow and ruby light. Beneath it was a plinth with a stone carving of a simple three-stringed harp. The secretary indicated it. "Perhaps you've seen our little symbol?"

"Seen it around," I said casually. I thought of the pair of goggles back at Portland Row, which we'd stolen from a murderer some time before.

"Orpheus's lyre," George added. "That's what it represents, right?"

"Exactly so. You know about Orpheus, of course," the secretary said. "Greek fellow from the myths. He was the patron of musicians and of explorers into the unknown."

"He went down into the underworld, didn't he?" George said. "In search of his dead wife."

"Indeed, Mr. Cubbins." The Secretary turned left down a second corridor, where another aged club member, bald and smiling, stood aside to let us pass. "He sang and played his lyre so beautifully that he could charm the dead—and soothe the fearsome entities that guarded them. He even persuaded Hades, grim god of the underworld, to let his wife go. *That* is power indeed!"

"So the society takes Orpheus as its inspiration?" said Lockwood, who had been unusually quiet since arrival.

"We, too, seek to find ways of subduing ghosts. We are a motley band of inventors, industrialists, and philosophers—anyone, in fact, with an interesting perspective on the Problem. We discuss, we debate, we work on devices that might stem the ghostly invasion."

"A bit like the Rotwell Institute, in fact?" George said.

The old man clicked his tongue. His smile became rueful. "Not exactly. The institute is much too . . . *commercial* for our tastes. They seek profit above truth. Many of their products are frankly worse than useless. The society is for *idealists*, Mr. Cubbins. We hunt for real answers. There is a battle to be won—not simply against ghosts, but against death itself."

"What kinds of devices do you create, sir?" George asked. He had a spark in his eye. I knew he was thinking of the goggles.

"Many kinds! I will give you one example. Young people like you are fortunate—you hear and see supernatural things. But decrepit fellows such as me are powerless after dark. So we hunt for ways to help older folk defend themselves against the spectral foe. We have made progress, built prototypes . . . but they are not yet ready for public use."

George nodded slowly. "I *see*. You've built prototypes, have you? Fascinating. . . ."

"Indeed." The secretary stopped at a dark oak door. "Well, here we are—the reading room."

"What about Orpheus?" I said. "Did he bring his wife back in the end?"

The secretary chuckled. "No, my dear. No, he did not. He erred, and she remained on the Other Side. How I wish we could ensure the same for our dead friends today." He pushed the door open and stood back. "The assembled company of Lockwood and Co.!" With that he ushered us in and departed, closing the door behind him.

It wasn't a very big chamber, the Orpheus Society reading room; if Lockwood's parents had once given a lecture there, the audience must have been quite small. A band of dark bookshelves encircled a cozy, carpeted space of armchairs and reading tables, randomly arranged. Penelope Fittes sat in a chair by the hearth, staring into the flames. Her long black hair gleamed, her profile might have been carved from alabaster; she was so much younger than any of the other members of the society, her luster almost came as a physical shock. She turned and smiled at us.

"Hello, Anthony," she said. "Lucy, George. Come and sit down."

Above the mantel hung a painting in a golden frame: a woman in a low-cut black dress, holding a lantern. Her hair was worn high on top of her head; a fierce light burned in her eyes. It was a face familiar from books and stamps and the postcards they sold in the Strand. It did not have the worn, burned-out look of the photographs at Fittes House.

Penelope Fittes had noticed my appraisal. "Yes, my sweet grandmother," she said. "She set up this society, when she was still quite young. I continue to encourage them in their efforts. I have great regard for anyone who displays exceptional resourcefulness in combating the Problem. Which is why I have a proposition for you now."

"Another case, Penelope?" Lockwood asked.

"Greater than that. A far greater honor. I would like you to join your agency with mine."

Just like that; no mincing of words, no wasting time. She was smiling as she said it, but the impact of what she said was like a missile striking right between the eyes. I think I physically reeled; George made an incoherent sound. Lockwood's face was frozen. I don't think I'd ever seen him quite so taken aback. If the opening of Mrs. Barrett's coffin ranked as nine out of ten on the shock-o-meter, *this* was ten out of ten. Ten plus. He blinked at her; it was as if he didn't fully comprehend the words.

Ms. Fittes was too polite to acknowledge our stupefaction. "I was impressed with the way you tackled the very serious case in Ealing," she said. "Impressed, but unsurprised. I have watched you since that matter of the Screaming Staircase two years ago. Time and again I have seen your team achieve small miracles of detection, overcoming great odds, defeating Visitors of considerable power. Your psychic Sight, Anthony, is superb, but it is not your only Talent; you are a leader I would love to have on my side. And Lucy"—her dark gaze switched to me—"I'm *so* pleased to see that you took my words to heart and have chosen to remain with Lockwood and Company. Your gifts are formidable, and I could help you develop them even further. Dear George"—the gaze switched again; I felt like a fish out of water that had suddenly been thrown back in—"you have already worked for my company once. Perhaps we didn't fully appreciate *your* singular gifts. Come back to us and I will allow you full access to the Black Library at Fittes House—there are so many unread papers there, so much that is yet to be researched." She leaned back in her chair. "There it is: my offer. I don't make such proposals readily. But you have charmed me. Lockwood and Company is unique; with my help it could become immortal." She smiled at us. "If you wish to consult with one another, please do so."

A log crackled in the grate. A wall clock ticked. I couldn't look at the others.

"Thank you, Penelope, thank you, Ms. Fittes. . . ." When Lockwood spoke, his voice was thick; it lacked its usual fluency. "Thank you for the invitation. It is, as you say, an enormous honor." He cleared his throat. "But I do not think we need to consult on this. I'm sure I speak for the others—and I certainly speak for myself—when I say that our independence is something we value above all else. We like being our own little agency. I'm sorry, but I don't think we could happily become part of even such a tremendous organization as yours."

Ms. Fittes's smile remained, but she was as motionless as a stone. When she spoke, her voice was velvety. "No? Don't misunderstand me, Anthony. I would create a new division especially for you. You wouldn't need adult supervisors—you would operate exactly as you do now, except that the resources of the Fittes Agency would be at your disposal. I would trust you implicitly. You could even continue to work from your charming little home."

Another silence in the reading room—this one stretched out even longer.

"Thank you, ma'am," Lockwood said. "But again I must regretfully decline."

The smiled flickered. "Well, you know your own mind, of course. I will respect your decision."

"Please don't take my remarks the wrong way, ma'am," Lockwood said. "I mean no disrespect to you or your great organization. I hope there will be many more opportunities for collaboration between our agencies. We enjoyed working with Quill Kipps on the Guppy case," he added. "Perhaps we can do so again."

Now the smile was gone. "That will not be possible. Mr. Kipps is no longer employed by this agency."

"No longer employed?" This time Lockwood didn't bother hiding his astonishment; beside him, George and I were competing for whose jaw could drop the lowest. Kipps had made a seamless transition from agent to supervisor, and we'd assumed that he would go on to bore us for years with his rise through the ranks. "Did he—did he *leave?*" Lockwood asked. "Or was he—?"

"Oh no, he left of his own free will," Ms. Fittes said. "Soon after returning from the Guppy case. His reasons were . . . confused. I did not interrogate him. I have many agents. I cannot spend my time mollycoddling those misguided individuals who don't appreciate their own good luck. That being so, I had better get back to work. Thank you for coming in today. If you ring that bell, the secretary will be pleased to escort you out."

Our visit to the Orpheus Society had not been as straightforward as we had assumed, and an air of unease hung over us on the journey home, a feeling that an important moment had just passed. It was disconcerting; nothing had actually *changed*, yet somehow the ground had insensibly shifted underfoot. We didn't speak the entire way to Portland Row.

Holly was in the office. "How did it go? Did you get your medal?"

"Not exactly." Lockwood flung himself down in his chair. "All okay here?"

"Fine. I made that list of Rotwell Institute sites you wanted. There weren't that many of them in the end. Just five or six. It's on your desk."

"Thanks, Hol." Lockwood picked up Holly's list, glanced at it, put it down. He stared moodily out of the window.

George and I filled Holly in on the events of our visit. Her expression darkened. "Obviously you were quite right to say no, Lockwood," she said. "No question about it. It's flattering, I suppose, but you can't just give up your independence. This is Lockwood and Co."

"It was a strange offer," I said. "Ms. Fittes was very complimentary about us, but it was like she just assumed we'd cave in and do her bidding. I don't think she was very happy that we refused her, either."

"That's typical Fittes behavior." Holly normally maintained a facade of breezy good humor about everything, but now she was looking as cross as I'd ever seen her. "At Rotwell's we always used to talk about it. Penelope Fittes acts like she has a divine right to get whatever she wants, just because she's head of the oldest agency. Her grandmother was just the same."

"What about her mother?" I remembered the rather forlorn photograph I'd seen in Penelope Fittes's study. "Didn't she run the agency at one time?"

"Not for long," Holly said. "She was different, they say—a gentler character. But of course she died, and Penelope took over. When *was* that, Lockwood? You'll know."

But Lockwood was still staring out of the window. He didn't react even when the phone on his desk began ringing.

George looked at me. "*I* can't pick it up," I said. "I don't work here anymore."

"You never answered it even when you *did* work here."

George got up and answered the phone. Whoever was on the other end was talkative. For a long while George's side of the conversation was limited to grunts and sighs. Holly took up a feather duster and began doing unnecessary things to the suit of armor behind Lockwood's desk. Lockwood still didn't move.

At last George lowered the receiver and covered the mouthpiece with a hand. "Lockwood."

"Mmm?"

"It's that bloody Skinner kid again. He's still talking about ghosts in that stupid village. It's worse than ever, apparently. To hear him, you'd think they had Screaming Spirits jumping out of their breakfast cereal. Anyway, he's begging me to ask you again." George paused. "When I say 'begging,' it's the usual mix of verbal abuse and desperate fawning. But somehow that works on me, I don't know why. So I said I would." He looked at Lockwood, who hadn't moved. "You're obviously doing some very important staring into space. I'll just tell him to get lost. . . ."

"No!" With a jolt that made me spill my tea and Holly knock the codpiece clean off the suit of armor, Lockwood sprang upright in his chair. "Give me that phone! It's Danny Skinner, from Aldbury Castle?"

"Er, yes. Yes, it is. Why?"

Lockwood grabbed the receiver and put his feet up on his desk. "Look up the train schedule! Pack the bags! Cancel any appointments for tomorrow! Is that you, Danny? Lockwood here. We're going to accept your fascinating invitation after all."

Chapter 19

Lockwood's sudden enthusiasm for the Aldbury Castle case was startling, not to mention suspicious, but he was evasive when we interrogated him. "It's clearly a fascinating cluster," he said. "All sorts of interesting features. That weird Creeping Shadow story, for a start—didn't you think that was worth investigating?" He gave us one of his widest smiles. "At the very least, it'll get us away from London for a bit. We know the Winkmans were looking for Lucy a few days ago, and they're bound to be after us all now that we've raided their night-market. It'll get us out of harm's way until the heat dies down."

"I don't *feel* particularly threatened," I said.

"Ooh, anything could happen, Luce. Anything. Bit of safe country air will do us a world of good. . . ." He tapped his fingers on the desk. "Will there be anything else?"

"So the fact that there's an outpost of the Rotwell Institute a couple of miles up the road from the village doesn't have any bearing on it, then?" George said. That had been my thought, too.

"Oh, you remember that?" Lockwood wore his blandest expression. He scratched the side of his nose.

"Of course we do. Danny Skinner mentioned it, didn't he? He said they'd paid no attention to the problems of the village. Is it one of the research facilities on Holly's list?"

"Well, as a matter of fact it *is*," Lockwood said. "One of several, mind you, so there's no guarantee it's going to be relevant at all. . . ." He shrugged. "Okay, look, I wouldn't say the presence of that base has put me *off*, exactly. We might take a squint at it while we're down there, assuming all the ghosts tramping around the place give us any peace. But the village is our primary concern. That's what we're being hired to sort out, and if we're going to head down there tomorrow, we'd better get ready."

The rest of the day passed swiftly. Lockwood sent George off to the Archives to research anything to do with the village and its history; he sent Holly to Mullet's to order fresh salt and iron and arrange for them to be delivered to Waterloo Station. And he himself departed on a couple of errands, about which he was uncharacteristically silent. The results of one of these trips was dramatically revealed the following morning when we arrived at the station and saw a gaunt figure in black waiting on the platform beside the sacks of supplies.

"Hardly recognized you there, Kipps," George said, "without

your swanky jacket and sword. I thought if you took them off, you'd fall apart into separate wriggling pieces."

It was true that Kipps looked different. Perhaps more than any other operative, he had been defined by his connection to the Fittes Agency. His jeweled rapier, the unnecessary tightness of his trousers, the cocksure spring in his step—everything had always trumpeted his excessive pride in being a member of the organization. Today he wore black jeans, a turtleneck, and a black zip-up jacket. Perhaps his jeans were a trifle tight, his boots a trifle pointy, but it was fairly sensible attire, assembled almost without vanity. Fortunately he hadn't entirely changed. He still possessed his air of ineffable gloom.

"I just had a realization," he said when we were on the train and rocking slowly through the south London suburbs. "After the Guppy job. I mean, there we were—in a house possessed by a wicked and powerful entity, and you all were running around like madmen—fighting, screaming, being fools—but *dealing* with it . . . and I was just a fifth wheel. I couldn't see it, I couldn't hear it . . . I was too old to do anything useful. And that's what being a supervisor is: it's a life of sending others out to fight and die. I've known that for a while, but it took you to make me realize I couldn't bear to continue with it. I couldn't stay at the Fittes Agency. I'd rather do something else."

"Like what?" George said. "Art critic? Train buff? With that turtleneck, you could be almost anything."

"It was probably another dumb decision," Kipps said. "Like agreeing to come along with you today. Lockwood says he wants my expertise, but I'm not sure what I can contribute aside from standing around like a fence post. Maybe I can make the tea."

"Actually, I think it's admirable," I said. "Your decision. It's about being true to yourself."

He grunted. "You're good at that, certainly. That's why you've come back to Lockwood and Company, I suppose."

"As it happens, I'm only temporarily—" But the train was rattling over a particularly loud section of track, and then Lockwood and George were arguing over who would carry the salt bags, and Holly was handing biscuits around, and I couldn't get a word in edgewise. I sat in a corner of the compartment by the window, staring at the reflection of myself that ran like a ghost over the vista of gray roofs.

How had it come to this, tagging along with Lockwood once again? Was I truly like Kipps, rudderless and cast adrift from purposes of my own? A subtle shift had come over me in the last few days; a realization that I had allowed myself to change direction. After the loss of the skull, after Harold Mailer's murder and the pursuit through Clerkenwell, I'd needed help badly—and Lockwood had offered it. There'd been no one else to turn to. It had been a good decision. But after that—how one thing led to another!—it had seemed only natural to stay on at Portland Row, only natural to let Lockwood help me retrieve the skull, only natural to help him hunt for it in the night-market. . . . And now—was it natural to accompany him to Aldbury Castle, too? Sure, I could invent plenty of excuses to justify it. I was keeping myself safe from the Winkmans. I was (perhaps) pursuing the Rotwell Institute and the missing skull. I was giving Lockwood & Co. the support they deserved. . . . All that might well have been true. But it boiled down to the same thing in the end. I was simply happy to have the chance to be with them again.

It was with inconclusive thoughts like these that I occupied myself as the train left London and dawdled its way into the countryside. By ten o'clock, without danger or alarm, we had reached our destination.

For those wanting a detailed record of the horrors that subsequently unfolded, the village of Aldbury Castle occupied a pleasant rural location fifty miles southwest of London. It was set in chalk uplands, with wooded rolling hills on three sides, and a leisurely river winding on the other. The site was remote, reached only by a meandering road, and by a train stop (it would be a stretch to call it a station) on the main Southampton line, three quarters of a mile away to the west. There was no station office or building of any kind, just a white and winding path running off into the forest, to join the road on its way to the village.

If there ever *had* been a castle in the area, it had long vanished. The road crossed the river on a stone bridge, and then bisected the village green—a broad expanse of long dark grass, surrounded by cottages. Sheep grazed here. Three great horse chestnut trees dominated the center of the green, casting into shadow the fourteenth-century market cross and the trough rotting beside it.

On the other side of the green, the road forked outside the door of the one surviving pub—the Old Sun Inn, which our client, Danny Skinner, called home. All the other main buildings of Aldbury Castle were visible from here, too—the village stores, The Run (a row of terrace houses), and the church of St. Nestor, on a rise above the rest of the village. Outside the church, an ancient ghost-lamp, rusty and broken, stood on a low mound. A lane beyond the church led off through the woods to fields and hills.

Those hills were bathed in sunshine when we walked over the bridge and entered the village for the first time, but the green was wet and frosted with cobwebs. Shadows of the eastern woods stretched like fingers across the grass. There was a smell of smoke in the air. It was a beautiful spring day.

"Seems much too pretty to be a hot spot for ghosts," Holly said.

"You say that." I pointed to a great circle of blackened ground in a prominent spot by the road. "They've been busy setting fire to something."

"Or some*one*," Kipps said.

Holly wrinkled her nose. "Oh, yuck."

"Well, I don't see any charred legs sticking out of it," George said. "More likely to be objects that they think might be Sources. They're panic burning. But first things first. That cross is the one the kid mentioned. I want to have a look at its sinister carving."

He led the way through the long wet grass, which whispered and spattered against our legs. When we got near the trees, we flung down the bags of salt and iron; we were hot despite the cool air.

The base of the cross was stepped, and had been repaired, not very well, with modern bricks. The rest was ancient, weathered by the wind and frost of countless years. The stone had a grainy softness to it; pale green lichen extended over it in patches, like the map of an unknown world. You could see that the whole thing had once been intricately decorated—patterns of interlocking vines wound their way up the sides of the cross, with obscure objects cradled in their fronds.

George seemed to know precisely where to look. Halfway up one face, the lichen had been picked away, revealing the traces of an image. In its bottom left-hand corner, a set of tiny figures clustered. They were no more than stick people, lined up like bowling pins ready to be felled. To the right was a pile of skulls and bones. Towering over the lot, crammed into the center of the available space, rose a huge misshapen figure with sturdy legs and arms and a squat, almost squared body. The head was indistinct. Whatever the creature was, it dominated the scene.

"There he is," Lockwood said. "The dreaded Creeping Shadow. The kid told me on the phone that it had been seen again the other night."

George grunted skeptically; he was tracing its shape with a chubby finger.

"What do *you* think it is, George?" I asked.

He adjusted his glasses. "At the Archives yesterday," he said, "I found a mention of the cross in an old Hampshire guidebook. They describe this as a fairly common depiction of the Last Judgment, when the dead rise up from their graves at the end of time. Here are the bones, look; and here are the saved souls rising."

"And the chunky guy in the middle?" Lockwood said.

"An angel, presiding over it all." George pointed. "Yeah, see these marks here? I reckon he once had wings." He shook his head. "It's no graveyard ghoul, no matter what Danny Skinner says. Whatever's hanging around the village is something else."

"So maybe he *is* making most of it up . . ." I said. "Speak of the devil—there he is." A figure had come out of the Old Sun Inn and was waving to us across the road.

"He was right about the battle, though," George said, as we walked toward the inn. "There *was* a ninth-century dustup between the Saxons and the Vikings in the fields east of the modern village. At one time, before the Problem, it was a popular spot for antiquaries to go digging—a couple of centuries ago they turned up quite a few shields, swords, and skeletons. Farmers would find bones caught in their plows, that sort of thing. Must have been quite a skirmish. But like you said, Lockwood, it's not a massive battle by national standards—there are other, more recent sites that haven't caused nearly as much trouble as this one appears to be doing."

"Our job is to find out why," Lockwood said. "Assuming we don't end up strangling our client first, which is a distinct possibility."

The Old Sun Inn was a timber-framed building, half swaddled with marauding ivy. Much of it seemed to be in a state of disrepair. The main entrance, in what appeared to be the oldest part of the house, faced toward the church; another door led to the pub garden and the green. On a post hung a dilapidated painted sign showing a massive bloodred sun, hovering like a beating heart above a darkened landscape. Our client was swinging on the garden gate below this, waving as we approached. In broad daylight his protruding ears had a pinkly see-through quality. He was grinning at us with a kind of fierce pleasure that contained both delight and anger.

"At last! You took your sweet time. The Shadow was back last night, and the dead walked in Aldbury Castle, while the living cowered in our beds. And you all missed it again! You want lemonades? Pops will get you some."

"Lemonade sounds good," Lockwood said. "Maybe after we see our rooms."

The kid swung manically back and forth. "Oh, you want rooms? But you'll be out fighting Visitors all night, won't you?"

"Only some of the time." Lockwood put out a hand and stilled the movement of the gate. "And you *definitely* promised us somewhere to stay. Rooms *now*, please."

"Ooh, I don't know. . . . I'll ask Pops. Hold on." He slouched away into the bar.

"Is it just me," Kipps said, "or does that boy need punching?"

"It's not just you."

Presently our client re-emerged, as perky as a ferret up a trouser leg. "Okay, I got you rooms."

"Excellent . . . Why are there only two keys?"

"The inn has two guest rooms. One key for each."

We gazed at him, certain horrific permutations drifting through our minds. Lockwood spoke carefully. "Yes, but there are *five* of us, with a variety of needs, habits, and private regions that we don't want shared. There must be other rooms."

"There are. They're inhabited by me, my dad, and my mad old grandpa; I can tell you, *his* private needs and habits are well worth avoiding. There's also a storage closet in the kitchen, but that's damp, rat-infested, and haunted by the ghost. Cheer up—you've got five beds! Well, *four*, to be fair. One's a double. Here's the key for the double room; it's also got a cot. The other's a twin. I hope you have a lovely stay. I'll leave it to you to settle in, and see you in the bar later." With that, he departed.

There was a heavy silence. I scanned the others, taking in Holly's neat traveling bag, doubtless crammed with body lotions and skin cleansers; George's ominously light backpack, which lacked room for any conceivable change of clothes; Kipps's angular and palely ginger frame, the horrors of which were just hinted at beneath his turtleneck; and Lockwood. To share a room with any of them presented problems.

The others were making similar swift calculations.

"Lucy—?" Holly began.

"You beat me to it. Don't mind if I do."

"In that case," Holly said, plucking a key from Lockwood's hand, "we'll take the twin room and leave you boys to it. Good luck deciding who gets the cot."

We left them standing in the hall and went up to our room.

It was a small, neat space, surprisingly pleasant, with white lace coverlets on the beds, and a vase of fresh lavender on the windowsill. We put our bags down and stood at the window, looking out over the green. You could hear the jangling of the iron charms on the doors of the distant cottages and smell the lavender in the air.

"You know something?" Holly said. "I'm glad it's worked out like this. I'm pleased you're here."

"Well, if I wasn't, you'd have to share rooms with one of the boys," I said.

She gave a delicate little shudder and drew her coat elegantly around her. "True. . . . But I didn't just mean that. I've felt bad ever since you left. About you going, about the way it all ended back then. I felt responsible."

"Oh, don't *you* start!" I said. "*Everyone* thinks I left because of you. And I *really* didn't. If it was just about you, believe me, I would have stayed." I gave her a stern glare.

Holly lifted her hands in a peaceable gesture. "There you go with that look again! I just mean it was the arguments we had that brought it to a head—that made you lose control." She was referring to the Poltergeist I'd conjured up during our blazing fight at Aickmere's department store, and she was quite correct—but that didn't mean I enjoyed hearing her say it. My frown deepened. "Oh, you're getting angry with me again," Holly went on, "and I don't think I'm doing anything wrong. All I'm saying—"

"It's okay. I know what you're saying." I let my face relax. "Thanks for saying it."

"And I hope you find the skull one day," Holly added, after an unusually warm pause. "I know how important it is to you."

I could have denied it. I probably should have. "Yeah," I said. "I kind of miss having it around."

"I can't think why. It's a horrible thing, and I don't think it liked me."

I chuckled. "Well, no, it really didn't."

"It made unpleasant faces whenever I went by."

"That's nothing. It actively encouraged me to murder you once or twice. But don't worry, I'm not going to take up any of its suggestions, even the coat hanger one."

Holly looked anxiously around the room. "The coat hanger one?"

"It was a kind of garrote thing, using hangers like those ones over there. . . . Anyway, don't worry about that. Let's get settled in. Which bed do you want?"

"The one by the door."

Not long afterward we went downstairs again. At the foot of the stairs was a flagstoned hallway, dominated by its ancient entrance door. An arch beyond opened into the pub, a low-ceilinged chamber with a sweet, melancholy smell of stale beer. Here a broad-chested man with a pale, pained face and slate-gray hair was drying glasses behind the bar. From his protruding ears, I guessed him to be Danny Skinner's father, the owner of the inn. A wild-eyed old man sat in a corner by the fire. Otherwise, aside from the rest of our team, the place was empty. Lockwood, with Danny at his side, was ordering lemonades. Kipps and George stood glumly by, each with a subtly harried look.

I sat on a bar stool next to Lockwood. "I take it you took the cot," I said.

He nodded. "Leader's prerogative."

"I didn't sign up for this," Kipps said. "Horrific phantoms, yes. Waking up next to Cubbins, no."

"As soon as it gets dark we're going to have to deal with the inn's ghost." George, too, spoke with deep feeling. "Then Kipps or I will be able to sleep in the storage closet downstairs. All the other Visitors can wait."

Mr. Skinner, the innkeeper, nodded toward the arch. "Well, if you're interested in *our* ghost, that's where it happens, out in the hall. Glowing child, that's what they say it is. The big door there's where kids hear the knocking."

"They're making it up!" A shout made us turn. The old man by the fire was glaring at us madly. "It's nothing but the wind! Trees knocking on the window! Too much cheese at night! Claptrap and baloney!" He took a sip of beer.

"That's my grandpa," Danny whispered. "Used to be vicar at St.

Nestor's Church, until he got too crazy. He's too old to have ever seen a ghost, so he doesn't believe in them—*or* in ghost-hunters, naturally. If he insults you, just ignore him."

"Oh, we'll suffer in silence. You've given us plenty of practice at that." Lockwood was gazing out at the dark and quiet hallway. "Okay, we'll look into this midnight visitor for you. So there's no one else at the Old Sun Inn?"

"You're our only guests." The innkeeper shook his head sourly. "The Old Sun Inn . . . *there's* an inappropriate name for you. If there's a darker spot in all creation than Aldbury Castle, I wouldn't like to see it. Come outside with me a moment."

He flipped his dish towel over his shoulder, pushed the bar flap open, and limped out across the lobby, ignoring the cries of the old man for another glass of beer. In the garden the sun was drawing clear of the beech woods, and the sky was a cold, pale blue. Two children were playing far off, thrashing through the long grass on the green.

"Used to be kept mowed, this green did," Mr. Skinner said, as we trooped outside behind him. "Nice and neat, it was; we had picnics, bands playing, and whatnot. Course, no one bothers with any of that anymore. The only communal activity now is when we gather to burn the clothes of the recently deceased. Never does any good, mind. More ghosts than people, Aldbury Castle has, and more being added every day."

He pointed out across the grass. "There's a headless lady who walks under the chestnut trees," he said. "See where the shadows are darkest? That's supposed to be her grave. That bit of stained ground? That was where the gallows were. We destroyed them years ago, but the children say a shape still lingers there—the ghost of a peddler hung from one of the trees after selling pies with rotten meat."

"Bit severe," George said, "but you can understand their annoyance. Anything else?"

"The church has its ghost, of course. Fellow who fell from the tower while fixing the lightning rod, they say. And see along there? Half the cottages on that side of the green have been abandoned for years; an influenza epidemic one hundred years ago left too many unquiet souls in them. Then there's the duck pond. A teacher took her own life in it, twenty years ago. I remember that myself. Miss Bates, a sad and quiet woman, she was. Wouldn't say boo to a goose. Found her in the center of the pond on a bright spring morning, long hair floating out like river weeds. . . ."

"Oh, God, her spirit hasn't got lots of hair, has it?" George said. "Long, lank, black hair? I can't bear hairy ghosts. Or ones with tattoos."

"George."

"What?"

"Shush."

"There're dozens more. We've always been on the edge of things," Mr. Skinner said, "where the barrier between this world and the next wears thin. Not surprising, really, given our history."

"You mean the battlefield?" Lockwood asked. "Where *was* that, do you know?"

"Up Potter's Lane, there, beyond the church. Through the woods and between the hills. When I was a boy, the farmers used to still turn up the occasional bone in the fields there. Sometimes they'd be ground up in the combine blades. Mind you, the Rotwell place has tidied up most of that now. We used to go into the woods for dares; in the dawn light we'd see the warriors' ghosts standing in the mists, among the wheat. Passive things, they were; didn't cause any trouble, unlike the Visitors nowadays. Well, you'll have your work cut out for you here. You'll want food, will you, while you're alive? I can do you a tripe-and-turnip stew for supper."

"Oh . . . that sounds great. Is there anything else?"

"Just stew."

"Well," Lockwood said heartily as the innkeeper hobbled slowly back inside, "I think it's in all our interests to get this village taken care of as quickly as possible, don't you?" He smiled around at us. "And for Kipps's and George's sake, if there's a ghost in the Old Sun Inn, that's as good a place as any to start."

Chapter 20

That afternoon, spurred on by a tasty bar-snack lunch of stale cheese sandwiches, pork rinds, and more lemonade, we got speedily to work. Holly and I interviewed the inhabitants of the inn, and got some useful info from Danny Skinner and his dad. As well as the apparition that Danny had once seen near the old door, they both reported a permanent chill in one area of the hall-way, which lingered even when the radiators were on. Mr. Skinner had long ago stopped sitting in the armchairs in the hall, owing to feelings of faint depression and nausea. As for the kid, from his bed he regularly heard a loud hammering on the door as midnight came.

We got nothing worthwhile from old Reverend Skinner. As his grandson had predicted, he couldn't countenance the existence of ghosts. The cold spot was a draft; the spectral knocking was the drains; as for us, we were shameless hucksters pulling the wool over our clients' eyes. Despite his contempt, he seemed fascinated by our efforts and hung around like a headache as we carried out our daytime survey.

By and large, what we found backed up the Skinners' story. Even in the late afternoon, certain primary phenomena—mainly chill and creeping fear—could be detected in the hall of the inn, and also in the kitchen, which was reached through an interconnecting door. Both areas were laid with the original flagstones. Other first floor regions seemed unaffected.

The great front door was black with age. We unlatched it and inspected both sides. There were scratch marks on the external face, but they could have been made by anything. Beyond the dusty porch, a path led to an iron fence that barred the way to the churchyard.

The afternoon wore on. Suppertime came, and stew was served. We sat at the mullioned windows of the public bar looking out over the darkening green. The trees that ringed the village were black now, the old cross glowing with the last light of evening. The atmosphere was dark and sinister. Much the same could be said for the stew.

"I can see a couple of Visitors already," Lockwood said. "See out there, on the far side of the green? Two faint shapes hovering by the road."

No one else could see them, but we believed him. He had the best Sight among us—those of us who had any Sight at all.

"Well, this is where I become useless," Kipps said. He was stirring his stew around and around, as if by some alchemy it might become edible. "I don't know what I can do to help this evening, short of being tethered by the door like a goat to lure the ghost."

"That's actually not a bad idea," Lockwood said. "We just might do it. Alternatively, George has a suggestion. He's brought something along for you."

"Yep," George said. "You could try these." His backpack hung on his chair; he ferreted around inside it and, with a flourish, drew out a heavy pair of rubber goggles with thick crystal eyepieces. He handed them to Kipps, who took them wordlessly, turning them over in his pale hands.

"What are they?"

"Rare and expensive items," George said, "which I stole. Made by the Orpheus Society, used by John William Fairfax, late owner of Fairfax Iron. The lenses are crystal instead of glass. As to what they do—I have a theory. Try them."

Kipps was hesitant. "Have *you* put these on? What did you see?"

"I saw nothing. But they're not *for* me. I think they're for old fogies like you. Go on."

With any amount of grumbling and struggling with the strap, Kipps eased the goggles over his head. The thick rubber hid half his face, which was an immediate improvement.

"Does Penelope Fittes know you've got these?"

"Nope. And she's not going to, either. Quit moaning and look out the window."

Kipps did so. At once he stiffened; his fingers gripped the sides of the goggles. "I can see three dark figures out on the green. . . ."

"Are they there when you remove the specs?"

Kipps tore them away. "No . . . no, they're gone."

George nodded. "Excellent. That's because you can't see ghosts ordinarily. The crystals help your eyes—they refocus the light some-how. It bothered me for ages that I couldn't figure out what these goggles did—but I was being stupid. The Orpheus Society is full of old codgers who have been searching for ways to join the fight against Visitors. An invention like this gives them that ability. And it will allow you, Kipps, to see psychically again." He waved a hand. "It's all right, you don't have to thank me. At least not with words. Money will do fine."

Maybe it was the light, maybe it was the stew, but I almost thought Kipps's eyes had actually filled up. "I—I don't know what to say. . . ." he said. "This is . . ." He broke off, frowning. "But—hold on, if somebody's invented these, why doesn't everyone have a pair?"

That was what *I* wanted to know.

"The Orpheus guy implied it was a prototype," George said. "Maybe it hurts your eyes, maybe it's not actually that effective on most ghosts. We don't know. I was hoping you could test it for us, Kipps. We've brought a spare sword along, too."

"Even so," Holly said, as Kipps placed the goggles reverently beside his plate, "can it be right that people are dreaming up impor-tant things like this—and no one knows anything about it?"

Lockwood shook his head. "In truth," he said, "there's an awful lot about the Orpheus Society we just don't understand yet. We're going to have to look into it. But we've got other things to worry about tonight." He gestured at the darkened hall. "And the biggest of them is what's going to come knocking on that door."

After our meal, and bidding the Skinner family go to the safety of their rooms, we gathered our equipment and went into the hallway.

Night fell, the evening progressed. We made certain preparations.

As midnight drew near, the atmosphere in the room grew heavy, and our vigil more alert. Lockwood lit the gas lamps. We watched their green flames flicker and dance against the dark-striped wallpaper of the ancient hall.

"This is pretty scary," Kipps said, "but infinitely preferable to getting in a bed with Cubbins." He had the goggles on top of his head; every now and then he pulled them down over his eyes and squinted fiercely into every corner of the hall. "Think we're ready?"

"As ready as we'll ever be." Lockwood glanced up at the ceiling, from where the sound of slowly pacing footsteps could be heard. "All we need now is for the batty old fool to go to sleep."

Unusually for an adult in a haunted house, old Reverend Skinner had reappeared several times during the evening, asking questions and getting in the way. He had finally gone upstairs only after eleven, and was evidently not yet in bed.

"He doesn't trust us," Lockwood said. "Just like he didn't trust his own grandson. Wants to see things with his own eyes, which is ironic for a priest. Temperatures? I've got sixty degrees here."

George was over by the stairs. "Sixty-two."

"Fifty-three with me." Holly stood near the fireplace. Kipps, by the kitchen door, had fifty-three, too.

"Forty-two degrees here, and falling." I was sitting in a Queen Anne armchair to the left of the wide front door. A standard lamp with one of those mangy tasseled shades cast uncertain light on the flagstones. "It's got to be a focus. Woo! See that?" The light had flickered off, then on again. "Got electrical interference, too."

"Turn the light off," Lockwood ordered, "then everyone come

back into the circle." We'd set out a big one with nice thick iron chains in the middle of the hallway. The feeling we'd had since arriving was that the Visitor here was strong. All our equipment was safely within the circle. Lockwood lowered the shutters on the lanterns, as George, Holly, Kipps, and I rejoined him. Dim light shone around the bottom of the stairwell from some lamp upstairs. Otherwise the room was dark.

"I hear creaking," I said.

"That's just old Skinner, wandering about upstairs. I *wish* he'd go to bed."

Holly stirred. "Did you put the iron chain across the stairs, Lockwood?"

"Yeah. He's safe up there."

A little noise sounded on the front door of the Old Sun Inn. It was half knock, half scratch. We stiffened.

"Hear that?" I hissed. I always have to check.

"Yes."

"Do we answer it?"

"No."

The sound came again, a little louder. Cold air pulsed across the room.

"I'm guessing we don't answer that, either?" I said.

"Nope."

A sudden ferocious hammering on the old oak door. All five of us stepped back involuntarily. "Blimey, *someone* wants to get in," George said.

"Third time lucky," Lockwood said. "Lucy, if you could do the honors."

Don't think I was dumb enough to leave the circle at this point. No way. You get cases of Shining Boys (and, occasionally, Shining Girls), and by and large you don't mess with them. They've usually been wronged, and they're never too pleased about it. I was going to stay well away. So I picked up the cord that we'd tied to the door latch earlier and gave it a gentle tug.

The cord went tight. The door swung open.

Outside was that soft, deep darkness you get in the dead hours of the night. We could see the faint lines of the iron fence beyond the path. The stone doorstep was worn low in its center from centuries of feet on their way to or from the inn.

No feet on it now, though. There was no one there.

"Of course not," George said softly. "It's already inside."

As if in answer, a faint light flared near the armchair, just above the floor.

"I see it. . . ." Kipps had the goggles on. His whisper was stiff with joyous fear. "I *see* it!"

At first it seemed like a small fluorescent globe, no wider than my hand. It spun with other-light, slowly circling; as we watched, it swelled, took on the form of a tiny, radiant child with thin, thin legs and arms. The child wore a ragged coat and trousers; beneath the coat its chest was bare. It had a gaunt, malnourished face, and great round hungry eyes. All of us watching behind the iron chains suddenly found it hard to breathe; cold air stung our lungs, pressed on our skin like water fathoms deep. The shining child stood half in and half out of the armchair where I'd just been sitting, head bent, eyes lowered in a submissive attitude of shame or dejection.

It looked like a hapless little thing. My heart bled for it.

"I can hear faint sounds," I said. "Like someone shouting angrily. An adult, I think, but it's very far away."

"Very long ago, you mean," Lockwood said.

"It could never get past that iron fence outside," George whispered. "It's been in here all the time. The knocking on the door is some kind of re-enactment. It's replaying whatever happened in this room."

I'll tell you how it feels, hearing sounds from the distant past like that. It's like words written in chalk on a bumpy wall. They've been almost entirely rubbed away. A few edges remain, some scraps and fragments, but the rest is eroded and gone, and you haven't a hope of figuring out the message. I guess it's also like an untuned radio, emitting flecks of noise that you *know* mean something, but you can't tell what. It frustrated me as I stood there listening: I *wanted* to hear what the child had heard. The wan little shape kept flinching, so I guessed there'd been violence in the voice.

"I'm so sorry," I breathed. "I can't make out the words. . . ."

"Don't worry about it." Lockwood was busy loosening the canisters in his belt. Now and then he glanced back up to check that the Visitor hadn't moved. "The key thing now is we find out where it goes. If it leaves the room, we follow it. What do you think it is, George, a Shining Boy?"

"Reckon so." George had drawn his rapier; it gleamed coolly in the light streaming from the child. "It's a Type Two, so we'll have to spike it if it tries anything."

"I *see* it . . ." Kipps said again. "It's the first apparition I've seen in years!"

"Well, don't get carried away," Lockwood told him. "We don't know what it'll try."

From time to time I saw the child looking up, as if snatching fearful glances at whoever spoke to it. These glances were directed at the fireplace, and when I looked that way I noticed that, unlike the rest of the room, which was lit by the pale, trembling radiance of the ghost, this portion remained dark. My eyes were repeatedly drawn to the black and narrow space, wondering who had stood there; but, like the words spoken by the angry voice, that knowledge was forever lost and gone.

"It's moving," Lockwood said. "Stand by."

The child had drifted diffidently out across the room, veering toward us, head down, great eyes gazing at the floor. All at once its head jerked up; it raised its thin arms in a protective gesture above its face, and vanished. The room was black; we stood there, blinking. But it seemed to me that in the instant before the radiance went out, the stubbornly dark portion of the room had shifted, and borne down at speed upon the child.

"Think that's it?" Holly whispered.

I shook my head—a useless thing to do in a darkened room, but there you go. "No," I said. "Hold on. . . ." The atmosphere in the room hadn't altered. The presence remained. And, sure enough, now the glowing child was back in its original position beside (and in) the Queen Anne armchair, exactly as before.

"Replay," Lockwood said. He suppressed a yawn. "This could go on all night. Anyone got any chewing gum?"

"Lucy does," George said. "Well—one piece, anyway. I ate the others, Luce. Sorry."

I didn't answer. I was focusing my mind, trying to reach the child. It was a forlorn hope. To do so, I'd have to ignore the distant shouts, probe deeper into the hollows of the past, and also get beyond the psychic disruption caused by the iron chain. As always, *that* was part of the problem. The chain got in the way.

At that moment, a querulous voice—not loud, but by its unexpectedness intensely jarring—broke in upon us. "What's going on down here? Why is it so dark?"

Our heads snapped around; a thin form was silhouetted in the stairwell. The Reverend Skinner—old, confused, reaching for the light switch.

"Sir!" Lockwood shouted. "Get back, please! Don't come down into the hall!"

"Why is it so dark? What are you doing?"

"Oh, wouldn't you know it?" George said. "He's crossed the chain."

I looked back at the shining child, which had suddenly changed posture. Gone was its forlorn, abandoned look. The head had turned; it was looking toward the stairs with new intentness. The eyes were like deep wells. The child began to move across the room. . . .

Dazzling light burst upon us—harsh, electrical, and blinding.

"Aah! Turn off the light! Turn off the light!"

"We can't see. . . ."

"What are you playing at?" the old man said. "There's nothing there. . . ."

"Nothing that *you* can see, you mean." With a curse, Lockwood jumped over the chains, ran for the stairs. I stepped out and, still half-blinded, threw a speculative salt-bomb on the flagstones in the center of the hall. Holly and George had done the same: triple starbursts, triple scatterings like snow.

Lockwood was at the wall. He stabbed at the switch—darkness returned.

And the radiant boy was right beside him, reaching out with tiny fingers toward the old man's neck.

Lockwood fell on Skinner, protecting him with his body. He lashed out with his rapier. The ghost moved back, then tried to dart around the blade, its eyeless sockets staring. Lockwood and the old man collapsed back onto a nearby table, knocking into a tall and intricate model sailing ship made out of matchsticks. The ship spun to the edge of the table and hung there, teetering on the brink.

Lockwood's sword moved so fast it could scarcely be seen, blocking the feints and darts of the ghost's probing hands. George and I ran forward, blades patterning the air, seeking to create an iron wall above the table that the child couldn't cross. The ghost was pinned in a narrow space between our whirling blades.

Now here came Kipps, his goggles glinting. He had a salt-bomb in his hand. He threw it hard against the ceiling so that salt came down upon the ghost in a fiery rain. The iron and salt together was enough. The ghost trembled. It broke apart and fractured into plaintive strips that hung there, dancing.

The model ship tipped over. It smashed into a million pieces on the floor.

The fragments of the ghost grew faint. Its radiance drew together into a coiling wisp of light that fled across the hall and sank beneath a flagstone at the entrance to the kitchen.

There was darkness in the room.

"*Fantastic . . .*" That was Kipps's voice. "I've been wanting to do something like that for *years*."

Lockwood flicked at the switch. "Okay," he said cheerily. "*Now* we can have the light on."

As case finales go, it wasn't the most decorous we'd seen: a pop-eyed old ex-vicar, bewildered, bruised, and winded, sprawled over an ornamental table with Lockwood's elbow in his belly, a letter rack wedged in his pajamas, and the fragments of a matchstick tea-clipper ship made by (as we later learned) his favorite grandfather scattered all around him.

It might have been even worse if we could have understood his breathless moans.

I took a stab, though. He didn't sound happy to me.

"Oh, quit complaining," I snapped. "You're alive, aren't you?"

"Yes, you've lost a model," George said, "but you've gained an exciting three-D jigsaw. There's always a bright side, if you choose to look for it."

It's safe to say he didn't.

Chapter 21

We resolved the case the following morning. With old Reverend Skinner confined to his room, Kipps and Lockwood took their crowbars and pried up the flagstone beneath the kitchen door. After half an hour's digging they located a set of small bones, a child's, complete with tattered fragments of clothing. George estimated them to date from the eighteenth century. His theory was that the boy had been a beggar, who, after having knocked on the door, was taken in by whoever owned the house and then robbed, killed, and stowed under the floor. Personally I didn't think a beggar was a very likely candidate for robbery, but perhaps he'd been an unusually successful beggar. Up until then, anyhow. Whatever. It was impossible to know.

So that was the Old Sun Inn cleared; we'd rid Aldbury Castle of one of its ghosts, and we hadn't been there a day. It put us in a cheerful mood. Danny Skinner, though bug-eyed at the sight of the bones, was delighted, too. After a late breakfast, he volunteered to take us on a tour of the village, to point out the other supernatural highlights we had to look forward to.

Our first stop was the church next door. It was a neglected-looking building of flint and brick, with a stubby tower and a vestry roof covered with a tarp. Its churchyard was clearly very old, surrounded in parts by a stone wall, in parts by hedges on a raised embankment of earth. The gravestones were of the same material as the cross on the green, and many were worn away, their inscriptions gone. Some hung at extreme angles; one or two had fallen. It was a peaceful place, if shunned and overgrown.

"This is where the Creeping Shadow walks," Danny told us. "Little Hetty Flinders saw it here, with the dead rising from their tombs at its command. That's got to be high on your list, Mr. Lockwood, sir." Since our success with the Shining Boy, the kid's hostility had vanished; he was our jug-eared cheerleader, marching proudly at our side. "Reckon *you'd* fix it, no problem."

"You didn't see the Shadow here yourself?" Lockwood stared up at the stone tower, where crows circled against the pale sky.

"Not me. *I* saw it up in the eastern woods, on Gunner's Top. That's where that lane goes, see? Half a mile straight, you get to the place. Had spirits following it there, too—the dead from this church-yard, most like. Pale, shapeless things, caught up in the Shadow's burning cloak. Well, you'll see for yourself," he added, seeming not to hear George's skeptical sniff. "You'll fix it, you will."

"I wouldn't mind a word with Hetty Flinders," Lockwood said.

"Can't help you there. She's ghost-touched now. They caught

her outside her house, with her best blue frock on, poor thing. The other kids in the village'll back me up, though. Shall we head on?"

As we descended onto the lane, the peace of Aldbury Castle was broken by the sound of revving engines. Four vehicles—three cars, and a small canvas-topped truck—had driven out of the woods from the direction of the station. They slowed to cross the bridge, honking their horns at a gaggle of geese that had strayed into the road, then sped across the green. The cars were black; the truck's canvas side was stenciled with the Rotwell lion. Turning right at the Old Sun Inn, the convoy drove up the lane, past the church and into the eastern woods. Unsmiling men looked out at us as they went by. The noise faded. Clouds of dust slowly settled back onto the road.

"That Rotwell bunch again." Danny Skinner spat feelingly into the grass. "On their way up to the institute. They couldn't give a fig about us. *They're* not a proper agency. Not like Lockwood and Company. *They* don't get things done."

"Quite so . . ." Lockwood was gazing up toward the woods. "Danny, I want you to continue the tour with Holly, George, and Quill. Show them the rest of the village. Lucy and I will just take a quick walk up to Gunner's Top, where you saw the Shadow. I'd like to get a feel for the area. We'll catch up with you shortly."

Lockwood and I watched as the little party continued on without us.

"It's not *really* Gunner's Top you're interested in, is it?" I asked.

"The woods? That's just some trees. No, I want to see what lies beyond it, in the fields where this ancient battle happened. Come on."

We took the lane below the church and followed it out of the village and into the woods. The lane crossed a narrow stream on a rickety wooden bridge; after that, as Danny Skinner had said, it proceeded more or less straight through the oaks and beeches up steadily rising ground. The woods still had its winter colors, its cloak of grays and browns; but here and there the spring rebirth was beginning—bright fronds breaking through the earth, the faintest green haze showing on the trees.

It was no great hardship, walking with Lockwood through the countryside that spring morning. The air was clean and fresh, the birds were in business. It was a nice contrast to running or fighting for our lives. Lockwood didn't say much. He was distracted, deep in thought. I knew the signs; the thrill of the chase was on him. Me, I was just happy for us to stroll together, side by side.

After some minutes we came to a place where a narrow track, cut into the steep bank to our left, led away to an open quarry. A neat cairn of stones and cut flowers had been erected on the grassy verge. It was topped with a wooden cross and a photograph of a man, now faded by rain.

"Someone ghost-touched here, maybe," I said. "Or some accident in that quarry."

"Ghost-touch, most likely." Lockwood had a grim expression; he stared across at the exposed rock face. "That's what *everyone's* dying of around here."

We went on in silence until, half a mile through the forest, we saw ahead of us the brightness of open ground. Here Lockwood slowed.

"And now," he said, "I think we'll take to the trees ourselves. Just to be careful."

By leaving the lane and pushing up the slope among the trees, we soon breasted a wooded ridge—presumably Gunner's Top—from which we could look down on the land below. There were places where we could have stood out in the open, but Lockwood avoided these; he kept to the shadow of the trees, crouching as he advanced, remaining low, walking without a sound. I followed as best I could; at last we lay together, on the lip of the ridge, bedded by wet grasses, and looked down over the Rotwell Institute compound.

It was some ways off, in the center of a flat expanse of abandoned fields, ringed by low-lying hills. You could see it had been a good place for a battle, long ago; you could imagine the two armies massing in this natural basin. It would have been a spectacular sight—certainly a lot more spectacular than what we saw before us now.

I don't know what I'd been expecting: some giant, gleaming edifice, I suppose, like a cross between the furnaces at Clerkenwell and the swanky glass-fronted Rotwell building on Regent Street. A big warehouse complex, at the very least, spotlighted and shiny, with dozens of agents scurrying around. But that wasn't what I saw. The road curved away below us through the scrubby fields to terminate at an uninspiring collection of metal buildings. They were haphazardly arranged, clustered randomly together like a herd of resting cows. They looked like the sort of hangars that could be erected very cheaply and very fast: they had corrugated roofs and few windows. The ground between them had been leveled and laid with gravel.

There were a couple of tall floodlights to illuminate the place at night; their drooping wires had a shabby and neglected air. A fence surrounded it all. The vehicles that had passed through the village earlier were parked just inside the one visible gate. No one was in sight.

"It looks . . . dumpy," I said.

"Doesn't it?" Lockwood spoke softly, but I could hear the excitement in his voice. "Yet the Rotwell Institute is clearly very busy there. Large, temporary hangars, slap-bang in the middle of an old battlefield. I wonder . . ."

"You think it's the 'place of blood'?"

"Maybe. You can bet all that old carnage gives them a head start with whatever it is they're doing. Well, we can't try anything in broad daylight. That fence doesn't look like much, though. Bring a pair of wire cutters one night, and we'd be in. . . ." Lockwood looked at me. "Care to risk it?"

"I'd give it a go. The skull might be inside."

"I knew you'd say that, Luce." He smiled through the sunlit grass. "It's almost like the old days again."

How warm and comfy it was, lying there—the sun was far stronger than I'd anticipated. I could have coped with staying a little longer, but we had to see how the others were getting on.

We found them at the inn, sitting in a corner of the taproom, and looking somewhat dazed. Their tour of Aldbury Castle had ended with half the inhabitants of the village emerging from their cottages to regale them with desperate stories of ghosts and hauntings. Holly had done her best to calm everyone; she had invited them back to the inn to give their accounts in an organized manner. Kipps then jotted down the details, and George marked each manifestation on a map with a neat red dot. The final person had only just gone, leaving Kipps with a stack of scribblings before him, and George's map looking like it suffered from chicken pox. Three of the dots were ringed in black.

"Those are sightings of the Creeping Shadow," Holly said. "Here in the churchyard, here by the old barrows on the far side of the village, and here on the green, where two little girls told me they'd seen a 'big burning man' walking near the cross. But the Shadow's the least of our problems. There are so many ghosts here, Lockwood. I don't know how we'll ever tackle them all."

"That's what we have to decide," Lockwood said. "Great work, everybody. Brilliant data. Let's get some food, then we can try to analyze what we've learned."

By evening, we'd created a proper nerve center for our operation. We had our supply bags ready, and our evening meal prepared. Stew had been offered again, but mercifully George had made a trip to the village stores, and brought us backup in the form of fruit, sandwiches, and sausage rolls. We'd commandeered a corner of the bar, as far from the Reverend Skinner's fireside seat as possible, and shoved a few tables together to create a proper battle desk. In the center of this was spread George's map, with Kipps's notes alongside. We studied them. As Holly said, it was a sobering prospect.

"It's going to take us several nights," Lockwood said at last. "We'll have to work in teams, and systematically go from house to house." He looked up. "What was that?"

"Car pulled up outside," Kipps said. "Someone's coming in."

Lockwood frowned, looked to the window. Even as he did so, the door opened, bringing with it a swirl of cold night air and the smell of lavender from the braziers burning in the pub garden. A big man stepped inside; the door clattered shut behind him.

Silence in the bar. We gazed at the newcomer, who had stooped to get through the door; now he straightened, his tousled fair hair brushing against the ceiling. He was a well-built, handsome man in late middle age, a striking physical presence. His chin was strong, his cheekbones broad and high. He wore an expensive suit, with a heavy winter coat, woolen on the inside, and a pair of green driving gloves. His movements were deliberate and unhurried; a heavy air of entitlement hung about him. Bright green eyes surveyed the room; they alighted at once on us. He walked in our direction.

We knew who he was, of course. There were enough posters of him plastered all over London. In those pictures, he was invariably smiling, mouth grinning as wide as the keyboard of a grand piano, emerald eyes twinkling, holding out some clever artifact dreamed up by the clever people at his institute. He was often arm in arm with a cartoon lion, too. There was actually something cartoonish about Steve Rotwell in person, as well, for he was a large man, thickset around the arms and shoulders, but rapidly tapering through the legs to a pair of small, neat feet. He had much the same attributes as a cartoon bulldog. I didn't find him particularly comic, though, having once seen him skewer someone with a sword.

He pulled back a chair and sat opposite us. "Which of you is Anthony Lockwood?"

Lockwood had half stood in welcome. Now he sat, too. He nodded politely. "I am, sir. It's good to see you again. We met briefly at the carnival last year. You might remember Lucy, George, and Holly, also."

Steve Rotwell was the kind of man who sat with his legs wide, leaning back in the chair, in a casually dominant pose. He took off his gloves and tossed them on the table. "I remember Holly Munro. She used to work for me. And I remember the rest of you. You're Penelope Fittes's lackeys."

Lockwood raised an eyebrow. "Excuse me?"

"Always at her beck and call. Jump when she whistles. Fittes's lackeys. *I* know."

"That's an outrageous statement." Lockwood glanced around, caught sight of Kipps. "Well, *he* was until recently, to be fair. But the rest of us are fully independent. Would you like a drink?"

"I'll take a coffee," Steve Rotwell said. "It's been a long road."

"Could we have some coffee, Mr. Skinner?" Holly asked. The innkeeper, who had been watching wide-eyed from behind the bar, jumped like a jackrabbit and disappeared.

"If you're hungry," George said, "there's probably some stew."

Rotwell ignored him. He unbuttoned his coat, with no particular hurry, and sat back in his chair surveying Lockwood. "Mr. Lockwood," he said, "what are you doing here?"

"I'm drinking tea and studying a map. It's not very exciting."

"I mean here in Aldbury Castle."

Lockwood smiled. "It may have escaped your notice, sir—you, no doubt, having many other things to think about—but there is a dangerous cluster of ghosts active in this village. We've come to deal with it."

"Why should *you* come? You're a London agency."

"We were invited by the people of the village, who are in desperate need."

Mr. Rotwell was one of those men who, having been considered important or good-looking in his youth, had never seen much need to indulge in smiles in everyday life. As a result, his face was mostly immobile. He said, "You know that Aldbury Castle is very close to one of my Rotwell Institutes. It's on the doorstep, so to speak. We consider it our local patch."

Lockwood, smiling blandly, said nothing.

"It's considered common courtesy," Mr. Rotwell went on, "for an agency to respect another agency's territory. Their cases, their clients, their spheres of influence . . . There are unspoken rules we all adhere to. In such circumstances, I'm surprised to see you here. I assume that, now I've drawn your attention to the problem, you will be withdrawing from Aldbury Castle tomorrow."

"I was given to understand, sir," Lockwood said, "that your employees had been approached about the cluster of Visitors here, and had chosen not to respond. In such circumstances, I consider our actions eminently justified and reasonable."

"You won't be leaving?"

"Of course not."

In the silence, Mr. Skinner approached carrying a cup of black coffee, with a little jug of cream. He set them on the table.

"Thank you. Wait." Rotwell reached into his jacket, removed a wallet, and selected a crisp note, which he handed to the innkeeper without looking. He waited until Skinner had retreated, then curled a heavy finger into the handle of the china cup. He did not drink, but stared at the black liquid. "You have quite a reputation, Mr. Lockwood," he said.

"Thank you."

"A reputation for becoming involved in things that don't concern you."

"Really?" Lockwood smiled. "May I ask who says so? Have some of your employees or associates been complaining? What are their names? Perhaps I know them."

"No names. The fact is generally accepted. This means," Rotwell said, "that when I learn you've unexpectedly turned up near my institute, where important and delicate research is continually being done, I am concerned. I worry that you might be tempted to stray from the proper bounds of agency work and poke your nose into unauthorized matters." He lifted his hand, drained the coffee in a single gulp, and set the cup down.

There was a pause. Lockwood stirred. "Did you follow any of that, Luce?"

"Not a word."

"George?"

"Hopeless. Like a foreign language."

"Yes, you'll have to speak more plainly than that, Mr. Rotwell," Lockwood said. "George here often uses big words I can't understand, but even he's struggling to follow you. What is it that you don't want me to do?"

Steve Rotwell made a gesture of irritation. "You are here to deal with the cluster?"

"I am."

"That is your sole interest?"

"Why shouldn't it be?"

Rotwell grunted. "That is not an answer to my question."

"Well, it's all you're going to get," Lockwood said. "Mr. Rotwell, Aldbury Castle isn't your 'patch,' your 'territory,' your 'doorstep,' or anything else. If you object to me helping to clear this village of its ghosts, you will have to make an official complaint to DEPRAC and see where it gets you. Until you do so, I'm free to act here. In the meantime, do have another coffee and tell me about this 'important and delicate research' that's going on up at the institute. It sounds fascinating. Are we likely to see some new Rotwell products anytime soon?"

Instead of answering, Rotwell took up his gloves and got ponderously to his feet. He looked to the window, where dusk was advancing across the green, then started to leave. An afterthought halted him. Where he stood now, he blocked the light, casting Lockwood into shadow. "You're a precocious boy," he said. "I won't list your talents—you're evidently all too aware of them. What you lack, I suspect, is the ability to know when to stop. Because you, Mr. Lockwood, are an overreacher. I recognize that quality; in many ways I'm one, too. It means, I believe, that you will keep pushing the boundaries until one day you go too far. There are witnesses here, so I openly warn you now—don't cross me. If you do, you will regret it. I say that to you hoping in firm good faith that you will heed my warning. But I don't believe you will. You'll cross me, because that is what you wish to do. And I will deal with you then." He put on his gloves, buttoned up his coat. "In the meantime, good luck with your little ghost-chase. I'm sure it's a job you're well qualified for."

With that, Mr. Rotwell departed. The door clattered shut behind him.

We all stared at the door. Then we all turned to Lockwood.

He smiled at us. It was a long, lazy smile, but his eyes glittered.

"Well," he said, "the man's an accurate judge of character, if nothing else. I wasn't sure whether investigating what he's up to was worth the risk. I considered it a fifty-fifty shot at the very best. But he's settled the matter for me. We're *definitely* going to do it now."

Chapter 22

Night fell on Aldbury Castle, and we turned the lanterns low in the bar. Danny Skinner threw logs on the fire. The leaping flames danced on the rapiers laid out on the table; they danced in our eyes as we sat like robbers around a hoard, checking work belts, hefting bags of salt and iron into backpacks, drawing routes of attack on George's map. We had many hours of work ahead of us, and Visitors seldom come to full strength much before midnight, so with our preparations complete, we sat quietly for a time. Holly read a book; Lockwood stretched out on a bench and dozed. George challenged Danny to a game of chess and was soon, to his annoyance, in some difficulty. I sat by the fire, seeing figures in the flames.

Only Kipps found it impossible to relax. He paced, he stretched, he touched his toes and performed other extravagant warm-up exercises that cast distasteful shadows on the wall. His hair sprouted like gingery watercress behind the goggles perched on his forehead; he could scarcely wait to use them in the field. Finally, the urge overcame him. Pulling on his goggles, he swooped to the window and stared out toward the green.

"I just saw another!" he cried. "Faint as anything, but I definitely picked it out! The Phantasm of a man over by the bridge!"

I grunted. Lockwood lay with his arm over his eyes; he sighed heavily.

"And there!" Kipps rotated slightly, squinting through the goggles. "Two cloaked figures on the green. They're standing close together, hoods down, huddled like they're sheltering from the cold. Ghost-fog's rising from their capes. Now they're breaking into a run. . . . They're gone! Oh, this is *great*. There's so much to see!"

George looked up from the chessboard. "I'm pleased he's so happy, but did anyone else prefer the dourer, quieter Kipps? This could be a long night."

Kipps rotated again. "And oh, that's horrible. There by the fire! A gaunt, wizened thing with protruding teeth. . . ."

Danny Skinner spoke with dignity. "That would be my grandfather, remember? He's still alive."

"Oh, yes. Got a bit carried away there." Kipps pulled up the goggles, looked at his watch. "Come on, Lockwood, what's all this shirking? It's almost ten thirty. Time we were off."

Lockwood swung his legs around, pulled himself up off the bench. He yawned. "You're right. We need to get going. We'll do it as planned. Two teams, two hours in the field; then we rendezvous back here to see how things are going. Kipps and I will take the row of houses next door, where we've a couple of Specters to tackle. You others, start on the green. Come on, George; you're only two moves from being checkmated, anyway. The cursed village awaits us! Let's begin."

Out on the road, away from the meager lights of the inn, the immense dark of the countryside opened out above us. There was a moon up, but it was obscured by cloud. As Kipps had described, various patches of other-light drifted on the green. After swift farewells, he and Lockwood slipped silently away along the lane, while George, Holly, and I readied our packs. I moved away from the others for a moment. I had decided not to carry chains, feeling that the mass of iron suppressed my Talent too readily. Now, with a little psychic freedom, I detected a frisson in the air. It was just noticeable, like a battery's hum, a stirring of energies. . . . I looked up at the sky, at the dark ring of woods. Where did it come from? Impossible to say. This was where the skull might have come in handy. Once again I found myself wishing I had it at my side.

"All right," George said. "I'll read the map. That's my forte. Lucy or Holly—one of you had better be team leader. Give orders, make the snap decisions; you know the kind of thing. I'll leave that up to you."

There was a pause. "I don't mind," I began. "Holly, why don't you—?"

"Lucy, why don't you—?"

We fell silent. "Can't be me," George said. "I'm terrible at quick thinking." Humming gently, he scribbled something inconsequential on his map.

"Tell you what," Holly said, "why don't *you* take the first hour,

Lucy? Then, if you want, I can do the next. You're a more experienced agent than me anyway."

"Okay," I said. "Agreed. Thanks, Holly. Sounds like a good plan." I adjusted my belt. "So, then, George. What's first on our list?"

"That would be the malevolent black cloud hanging above the grass, just over there."

Our proposed route would zigzag between reported hauntings: it would be like a cross-country race, basically, with a ghost at every checkpoint. And first up was the entity lurking near the site of the old gallows. If it had once been a peddler, infamous for his rotten pies, it was now a weak Dark Specter, a shapeless, pulsing mass, sending out thin tendrils of darkness in every direction.

We approached with caution. "Well," I said, "they may have burned the gallows, but they clearly haven't sealed the place. I think this is a salt-and-iron job. Do you agree?"

Both George and Holly did, and since the site was small and well-defined, it was a relatively straightforward undertaking. Holly volunteered to draw the apparition out. First she stole close, goading it with careful jabs and flurries of her rapier, until, in a sudden rush, it sped for her. As she skipped away, parrying the tendrils with her blade, George and I nipped in with our bags of salt and iron filings, and sowed the burned ground thickly. Almost from the outset, the shape began to lose its inky density; it wore down like a stain being rubbed, writhing and diminishing until it became a shower of black sparks that fell into the grass and melted clean away.

I wiped my sleeve across my brow. "Well done, Holly. Think

we can cross *that* ghost off our list. They'll be having family picnics here by summer. What's next?"

Next was the Phantasm Kipps had seen on the bridge, and that proved equally easy to subdue. We followed it up with a Stone Knocker on the green, and a Lurker at a bus stop. Holly and I dealt with them all.

George chuckled. "This tour is turning out to be a piece of cake. Okey-doke, you've each had turns at combat. How about I take care of the next one?" He consulted his map and notes. "Looks like there was the Shade of an old woman seen in the backyard of a cottage in The Run. I reckon I could keep some old grandma at bay. Let's see if she's around, shall we?"

The Run was the row of cottages on the far side of the green. It didn't take long to get there. At the edge of the grass, a gate in the boundary fence provided access to a sunken lane, with the cottage lights glimmering up ahead.

It was dark in the lane; the hedges pressed close. Above us, tree branches carved black slices through the sky. We drew together as we walked; it wasn't a place to linger.

"The house is a bit farther along," George whispered. "We should see it in a—" He came to a halt. "Uh-oh. Who's this?"

In the darkness of the lane stood a figure, half-turned away from us, its back lit by the flickering other-light of a nonexistent candle. Long strands of hair curtained the face. Its arms hung limp, the head bowed, the shoulders slumped in an attitude of piteous sorrow, but the hand at its side was balled into a tight white fist.

We stood there. Neither we nor the apparition moved.

"It's got a nightgown on," Holly whispered. "That's never good."

"Is it a girl, do you think?" George breathed. "The legs don't seem like a grandma's legs. Not that I've looked at the legs of *that* many grandmas, obviously. I've got other hobbies."

Who knew what the thing had been? "Hang on," I said, "it's moving."

Bony feet shuffled on the dirt road. With miniscule jerky steps, and the flap of dirty cotton, the figure began to turn. The night's cold corkscrewed inward, twisting around us like a winding sheet. We pressed closer together.

"Visitors always rotate counterclockwise," George said in a tight, high voice. "Did you know that? They never turn clockwise. Fact."

"Fascinating, George," I said. "Now shut up a minute. Rapiers ready. I'll try to talk to it. Watch the arms, watch the feet. Watch for changes of expression."

"It would help if we could actually *see* the face," George muttered.

Holly flinched back. "There's blood on the front of the night-dress."

This was true: it was an apron of blood, a thick black staining, long and glossy and wet. Still the figure shuffled around, rocking gently from side to side; now it faced us fully, but the head hung low, so only its crown and its dangling lengths of lank black hair could be seen, shimmering in other-light. I heard a sound like the rustling of leaves.

"Who are you?" I said. "Tell us your name. What happened to you here?"

I waited. Just the rustling again, a little louder.

Now George flinched too. "I can't see the face yet. Can you see the face yet, Hol?"

"No. No, I can't. Lucy—"

"Steady," I said. I felt what they did, the swell of panic. It jangled down the nerve endings of my arms and sloshed in the liquid of my belly. "Steady, both of you. I'm getting something."

"Look at all that *blood*."

"Getting something . . ."

A voice like dry leaves, whispered through sandpaper lips. This time I heard it.

Oh.

"My eyes. Have you seen my eyes?"

The figure lifted its head. The hair fell back.

I don't know if it was George or Holly who screamed the loudest. Either way, they drowned out my own cry. Whether the Visitor actually lunged toward us, I don't remember. Certainly I slashed at it with my sword. Then we were back through the gate and away across the green. We ran as far as the market cross and halted, lungs raking air, gasping, cursing.

"Is it coming?" Holly asked. "Is it after us?"

I peeked back through the blackness of the night. "No."

"I'm so pleased."

"*Why* did it have to be its eyes?" George said. "Why couldn't it have been a less significant body part? Its thumb, say, or even an ear. That wouldn't have been so bad."

"Where did that ghost come from, Lucy? It wasn't on the map."

"Must be a new one. I don't know."

"Its toes! It might have lost its toes! You can't walk without toes. Then, if it went for us, it would just have fallen over."

"George," I said. "You're burbling."

"I am, yes. But, you know, I happen to think it's justified."

I made a decision. Everyone needed a rest. I led them back to the inn.

As it happened, Lockwood and Kipps were already there. Lockwood leaned against the bar, scribbling in his notebook. Kipps, with a Coke in his hand and the Fairfax goggles still enveloping his head, was striding exultantly around the taproom.

"Two Specters!" he called. "Two Specters and a Wisp! I saw them all! I saw them and I dealt with them, quick as anything! Ask Lockwood, he'll tell you."

"He's been yelping in my ear all night," Lockwood said. "I'm beginning to be sorry we gave those things to him. All the same, we've done okay so far. What about you all?"

We told him. "Lockwood," I said, when we were finished, "there's an odd atmosphere hanging over the village, some distant psychic disturbance. I can just about hear it—it's like a background hum. I've heard this sort of thing before, under Aickmere's—and the bone glass was similar, too."

Lockwood tapped his pen on the bar; he didn't speak for a moment. Then he said, "I'd like to swap things around a little. Holly, could you take Kipps and George and go back to deal with that eyeless girl? Then continue where you left off. Lucy, I want you to come with me. We'll see if we can't pinpoint this disturbance of yours."

———

Lockwood and I took a walk around the village. The moon gleamed over the eastern woods now. You could see the smooth tops of the hills shining just behind the trees, silver crescents suspended in the dark. There was beauty to it, but it was a still night and the silence was oppressive; I longed for an owl hoot, or the ring of a corpse-bell, a human cry—*something* other than the distant psychic hubbub buzzing in my mind.

Every hundred yards or so, we stopped and I tried to get a fix on it. No good; it never varied. Perhaps it was too far away.

"We'll try up by the woods," Lockwood said.

Our boots thumped on the hard dirt of the lane. We'd done a looping circuit and were coming level with the church now.

"Hope they manage to snare that Specter," I said. "Hope *George* copes with it."

Lockwood grinned. "He's got a hang-up about girls with parts missing. I have a feeling Kipps will fix it, though. He's champing at the bit, now that he's got those new specs. And Holly did okay, too, you say?"

"She was very good."

"I've been encouraging her to trust her Talents more. Her time with that oaf Rotwell didn't do her any favors. She sort of crumpled up inside, lost faith in her own abilities. It's nice to get her out in the field. You're a great role model for her, Luce."

"Well, I don't know about that. . . ." I drew to a sudden halt; for the first time I felt a change in the background disturbance. It had lessened, then flared. We had passed the rusty ghost-lamp on its little mound and were below the embankment by the churchyard.

The boundary thicket was above us. "Can we just nip up to the church a moment? I thought I felt something."

"Sure." Lockwood grabbed my arm, helped me up the steep slope. "Might be worth taking a look. If Danny Skinner's to be believed, the dead ought to be rising from their graves just about now."

But the churchyard was quite still, a mouthful of crooked stone teeth shining under the moon. From where we stood by the hedge, at the top of the earth bank, we could see its whole extent, from the stubby church itself to the lych-gate leading to the lane. I listened. Yes, the hum was pulsing. It had a different quality now.

"Quick question for you, Luce," Lockwood said. "It's about us. Are you still my client? Or should I be paying you for tonight? I'm confused."

"To be honest, I've lost track of that, too. . . ." But my heartbeat was getting faster, responding to the pulsing of the distant hum. My mouth was suddenly dry. Why? All across the graveyard nothing stirred.

"We'll have to come to some kind of arrangement," Lockwood went on. "Technically, we're each helping each other right now. I'm helping you with the skull and the whole Winkman thing; you're helping me here at the village. Two things are taking place at once. We're going to have to figure out a very complicated client-agent relationship. Or"—he looked at me—"we could always do something much simpler. . . ."

I wasn't listening. I shook my head, held up a hand.

The moon glinted on the black stones in the dumpy tower. The animal rustlings in the hedges had ceased, the wind had dropped utterly. A silence lay over the moonlit gravestones, and I suddenly knew that we were not alone. From the quality of Lockwood's silence, I realized he'd had the exact same feeling.

We looked down on the churchyard.

Something was coming toward us from between the stones.

Far off we saw it first, moving among the tilted crosses. So slowly did it approach that to begin with I thought it was the shadow of one of the twisted yew trees that fringed the churchyard wall. It was very faint, bent-backed and stooping, with massive rolling shoulders and a shapeless, questing head that swung from side to side. The arms were outstretched; great legs moved with furtive deliberation, one step, then another, plowing through the dark. Cold air swept over the wall like a salt wave, crashing against us, making us gasp.

"Look how *big* it is," Lockwood breathed.

The ghost of the Ealing Cannibal had been large. Even glimpsed through the kitchen door, its unnatural size and strength had been obvious. This thing was larger still: taller, reaching the top of the some of the tilted crosses; bulkier, with strange, stiff limbs grinding their way forward as if wading through treacle. The movement was awkward, and curiously mesmerizing. I've watched Raw-bones scrabble after me up concrete slopes; I've stood on high-rise apartment roofs while Screaming Spirits swirled around me like tattered hawks. I've seen stuff. But this giant figure in the churchyard—I'd never seen anything quite so alien and strange.

Unlike many apparitions, it conjured no other-light; it did not glow as the Shining Boy had, or radiate darkness like the ghost out on the green. It was not solid-seeming like a Specter, or grotesque like a Wraith. In many ways it was scarcely there at all. It was formed of a translucent gauzy grayness, and you could see right through its body to the jumble of stones and crosses in the yard beyond. Its extremities—the hands and feet, even the details of the head, were faint to the point of vanishing; you picked them out only by a twist or reflux in the air. But at its edges the shadow's substance seemed to dart and flicker, like quivering points of fire. It was as if the thing were continually, silently, coldly aflame. And from its back flowed a serpent of smoke that unwound across the graveyard like a magician's cloak, steadily dispersing, flexing ever outward across the stones.

"I've never seen anything like it," I whispered. "What *is* it?"

Lockwood didn't answer; he was staring at the spreading trail of mist that the Shadow left behind it. He motioned with his head; without looking at me, his fingers stole out and gripped mine.

I looked where he directed. My lips parted; my mouth was dry as sand. Because the shape that crossed the churchyard was no longer alone. Other figures stood there now, rising in its wake from grass and mound. They stood beside crosses and carved angels, they hovered over tilted slabs. You could see the grave-clothes hanging off their bony forms. At a glance you could make out Shades and Specters there, Wraiths and Wisps and Tom O'Shadows. There were dozens of them. It was a congregation of the dead. The inhabitants of the churchyard rose and stood and looked toward the Creeping Shadow as it moved away, entirely disregarding them, out through the lych-gate at the far end of the churchyard and up the lane in the direction of the woods.

Everything was still.

Then the ghosts moved. First one, and then another; now the whole pack was rushing toward the lane as if summoned by a voice we could not hear. Some came surging up the bank. We could see their hollow faces, their wild and empty eyes. I believe I heard the creaking of their bones. It happened too fast; we had no time to react. Another second, and they would have been on us. But all at once the hellish company veered away, out over the hedge and through the air, to swoop down into the road and away after the Shadow. The creaking and clattering faded. A tail of cold air sucked and pulled at us as it withdrew along the lane.

We stood there. The churchyard was quiet, empty, lit by nothing but the moon.

A blackbird in the tree behind us let out a sudden full-throated song, loud and sad and beautiful. It fell silent. Lockwood and I stood transfixed at the top of the bank.

Then I realized he was still holding my hand.

He realized it at the same instant. Our fingers kind of fell away, swinging back into vigilant positions at our work belts, ready to seize a salt-bomb or rapier at a moment's notice. Lockwood cleared his throat; I pushed my hair out of my eyes. Our boots did small, intricate shuffles on the frosty ground.

"What the heck was that?" I said.

"The Shadow?" Lockwood glanced at me from under his bangs. "Of course the Shadow . . ." He shook his head. "I have no idea. That was definitely the thing that Danny Skinner said would come. It had the size and shape, and it was burning—or seemed to be. But—but did you see *behind* it? The ghosts—?"

"Yeah, and Lockwood, it's *just* like he said. It's the thing from the carving on the cross—the Gatherer of Souls. It was gathering them up from their graves!"

"I don't believe that."

"What *was* it, then? You saw them rise up!"

He didn't answer me.

"You *saw* them, Lockwood."

"We need to get back to the others. This isn't the place to discuss it."

Over in the woods, a storm of birds rose shrieking into the night. They wheeled once and with a crack of wings flew off over the brow of Gunner's Top. We stumbled down the embankment and in silence hurried back to the inn.

V

The Iron Chain

Chapter 23

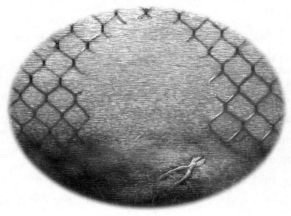

In the depths of the night the others returned, having had great success with the eyeless ghost and several other Visitors around the village. Their raised voices preceded them, echoing outside the taproom door; then they bustled in, George and Kipps bickering contentedly about some minor detail on the map, Holly Munro in the middle of wiping her sword clean with a pretty blade cloth. They found Lockwood and me sitting in near darkness, lit a dull, dark, glowing red by the dying embers of the fire.

"There's no doubt about it," Lockwood said, once we'd told them. "We saw the infamous Creeping Shadow. That's about the only thing we can tell you for certain."

"Other than it *definitely* stirs up the other ghosts," I said. "Don't forget that. Its cloak of mist was like a ladle stirring soup; they just came floating to the top as it passed by. Spirits came bursting out of the ground, before following it into the woods!"

"I *wish* I'd seen that," George said. "That's unique! That's *fascinating!*" His spectacles shone; he sat on a table, swinging his legs under him.

"*All* the bodies in the churchyard rose up?" Kipps asked. "A spirit for every grave? Or just some?"

"Lots," I said, "but not all. Maybe that's how it works, when souls are gathered. . . . Lockwood won't like me saying that," I added. We hadn't just been sitting by the dying fire. We'd been arguing.

"Because it's *not* gathering souls," Lockwood said irritably. "I don't know what the Shadow is, but it's not some demon or angel visiting on the Day of Judgment. It comes back every night of the week, for heaven's sake! I wish you'd get that stupid cross thing out of your mind."

"It draws the dead out of their graves, Lockwood!"

"Oh, give it a rest."

"Hot chocolate, anyone?" Holly said brightly. "Nice and soothing? Mr. Skinner's got a stash of packets behind the bar. Tell you what, I'll just go and put the kettle on."

"Must have been *something* seriously weird about it," Kipps said. He'd taken off his goggles and now tossed them stylishly across the room to hang from a coat peg. His swashbuckling finesse was only slightly undermined by the red rings they'd left around his eyes. "Must have been weird to have freaked *you* out, Lockwood. I never thought I'd see the day."

"I'm not freaked out!" Lockwood crossed his arms. "Do I look freaked out to you, George?"

"A triple helping of yes. I'm with Kipps on this one." George blinked and shook his head in unfeigned wonder. "This is a night of firsts."

"Well, maybe Lucy and I are right to be a little unsettled," Lockwood said after a grouchy pause. "Because its raising of the dead is only one of several strange things about this ghost. The kid was correct in everything he said. The Shadow *does* trail some kind of smoke, and there *do* seem to be weird flames licking around its form. It moves oddly, too." He sighed. "You ever read about anything like this, Kipps?"

"Never. It's not in any of the histories. Could be something about it in the Black Library at Fittes House. There's all sorts of stuff there. . . ." Kipps stretched back in his chair. "I must say I'm surprised that the Rotwell Institute hasn't caught on to this Shadow. They're missing a trick here."

Lockwood nodded. There was a grim light in his eyes. "They certainly are."

The kettle boiled. Holly made the hot chocolate. Kipps went to help her. George raided the cupboards behind the bar, locating potato chips and chocolate. A midnight snack was soon in progress at our operations desk in the corner of the room.

The distraction helped lift Lockwood's spirits; not just lift them, but switch them around entirely. He had the ability to flip moods like no one else; from being shocked and listless, he was suddenly galvanized, crackling with energy. Me? I ate and drank and felt a little better. I wasn't entirely calm, though. Nor, after my experience in the churchyard, was the Creeping Shadow the only thing on my mind.

Lockwood waited till all were seated, huddled around our mugs, and then sat forward in his chair. "Okay," he said, "I've got a proposal for you. It may sound crazy, but hear me out. Seeing that Shadow has changed things for me. It was *so* odd. It was *so* different. It's definitely a kind of ghost we've never seen before. And I think we need to respond by upping our game."

"How?" Kipps asked. "By laying a trap for it? By shepherding it into a ghost-pen? I've seen that done: you lay out a pen with iron chains, then drive it in with flares."

"Not quite." Lockwood glanced at his watch. "Actually, we're going to raid the Rotwell Institute in, let's say, an hour's time."

"What?" Kipps was less used to Lockwood than the rest of us were. We just sipped our hot chocolate in knowing silence. "*What?* Run that past me again."

"I've been planning to do it ever since we arrived," Lockwood said, "and that little visit by Steve Rotwell himself only reinforced my intention. But I was *going* to do it after we'd dealt with everything here at Aldbury Castle. But since seeing that Shadow? No. For a start, there's too much to deal with here. By the time we finish all the hauntings on our map, it'll be the middle of next week, and whatever's going on at the institute will long be over. Consider: Rotwell himself is part of it. He's not going to shack up in those sheds for long."

Kipps had taken a shrimp cocktail chip and was staring at it like it held the mysteries of time and space. "So what *is* going on in there?" he said. "At the institute?"

"That's what we have to find out. I've told you briefly, Quill, about Lucy's problems, and the theft of her rare and valuable haunted skull. I told you about this Mr. Johnson, and the Rotwell connection to the black market trade in artifacts. We know that all the stolen Sources will be at one of the institute centers—but the question was always *which one*. When young Skinner told us about Aldbury Castle's epidemic, that rang a bell with me. A sudden cluster in an obscure village in the middle of nowhere? With the institute operating nearby? Harold Mailer told Lucy that he'd been supplying Sources to the black marketeers for about three months. That's roughly how long Aldbury Castle's been suffering, too. Oh, and then there was this reference to the 'place of blood,' and the Rotwell facility set slap-bang in the middle of a battlefield. It's all too much of a coincidence for me."

"Another coincidence," George said, "is that all this started up not long after we put an end to whatever was going on in Chelsea. Are you going to eat that chip, Kipps? If not, I can give it a happy home."

"Chelsea's another reason I got you involved, Quill," Lockwood went on. "You were with us on that. If the Rotwell group stirred up that cluster, they've stirred this up, too. And among the things they've roused is this Shadow. A ghost that energizes other ghosts simply by strolling by! That's terrifying. We've *got* to get to the bottom of it."

"It could be part of the answer to the Problem as a whole," George said. "Remember my map back at Portland Row, showing how the epidemic has spread steadily across the country, like a disease? Diseases need carriers. This Creeping Shadow may be one of them. What if there are *lots* of Creeping Shadows? Maybe that's why the epidemic is spreading."

"I've got no love for Steve Rotwell," Kipps said slowly, "but I don't quite see how he can be blamed for all that."

"Nor do I—yet," Lockwood said. "But we're going to find out—tonight. No use waiting till tomorrow. Rotwell might be finished by then." He sat back. "What do you say?"

Kipps blew out a slow, heartfelt breath. "Raiding fellow agencies? Is this what you all usually do?"

I nodded. "Sometimes. We broke into the Black Library at Fittes House once."

"*What?*"

"Don't look so shocked," Lockwood said, grinning. "You're not with them any longer, are you? You're free to think for yourself for once. Which is a good point: you don't *have* to be part of this."

Kipps shrugged. "Oh, I'm part of it. I have nothing else to do. I might as well spend the next few years in prison. . . . Keep your paws off my chip, Cubbins. Go find your own."

"Good," Lockwood said. "Then we'll go. But before we do—Holly, you worked for Steve Rotwell, you must know him pretty well. What do you think drives him?"

It was a testament to how accepting I was of Holly now that all my attention had been taken up by Kipps's incredulity and discomfort. *He* was the newbie; she'd been sipping her chocolate just as calmly as George and me while Lockwood spoke of breaking-and-entering into a national institution. Okay, she still managed to be effortlessly, annoyingly elegant while doing so, but it now seemed to be just her personal variation on the Lockwood & Co. way. She'd even taken a couple of chips.

"What drives him?" she said. She tapped her shapely nails against her mug, her mouth drawn down in sharp distaste. "He likes his wealth and money. Beyond that . . ." She looked into the fire. "Beyond that I'd say it was his desire to keep up with the Fittes organization. He's always talking about them; always studying what they're up to, the successes they've had. He's always tallying the number of cases they've notched up each month, comparing them to the Rotwell figures. He's striving to be number one."

"Oh, Rotwell's has been like that forever," Kipps said. "You'll know this from the history books. Old Tom Rotwell and Marissa Fittes started out as partners in the fight against the Problem. Then they had a falling out, and it was Marissa who started the first official agency. Rotwell got his going a few months later, but it was never as popular—at least in the early days. The firm's been playing catch-up ever since. All this institute stuff, whatever pathetic commercial devices they may or may not be trying to create—that's just part of their desperate attempt to match the Fittes Agency." He sniffed. "It's all quite sad, really."

"Well, Penelope Fittes has her own little private thing going on, too, don't forget," Lockwood said. "The Orpheus Society seems to be under her influence, and *they* made your goggles, Kipps. But look, if we're going to do this, we'd better get a move on. There's only four hours till dawn."

We *did* get a move on. Turns out the equipment for burglary isn't that different from the equipment needed for ghost-hunting. For speed's sake, we jettisoned some of the heavier chains and a lot of the spare iron; George found wire cutters; otherwise we left our belts and bags as is. There were too many Visitors around to risk traveling any lighter. We were ready to go in ten.

It still felt funny going through my backpack and not seeing the ghost-jar there. A few bags of salt, an extra flare or two; even the spirit-cape—my new defense, carefully folded—none of them quite made up for its absence. After Vauxhall, I'd more or less given up hope of ever locating the whispering skull. Perhaps, if Lockwood was right, it would be out there now, just a mile away in the compound in the fields. I hoped so.

Before leaving, we made ourselves as dark and unobtrusive as possible. Being agents, we all more or less wore black anyway, and had gloves to cover our hands. But our faces weren't ideal for commando work; Kipps's in particular almost seemed to glow like a second, freckled moon. So Holly went to work with her makeup brush and soon we were all nicely dimmed.

Five silent shapes departed the Old Sun Inn. It was just after two a.m.

There were spirits wandering in the woods; we saw their other-light from afar, but none approached us, and we took care to give them a wide berth. We stayed away from the lane, too, hopping over the little stream a few yards down from the wooden bridge, circling around the quarry, and then following the course of the road through the trees. We kept going until the stars shone bright between the trunks ahead and we knew we were reaching the brow of the hill.

As Lockwood and I had done the day before, we covered the last bit in a crawl. There were no alarms. Soon the five of us lay in a row on the hillcrest, looking down on the Rotwell Institute. By night, curiously, it looked more impressive than by day, the floodlights masking its ugliness, giving the buildings a smooth metallic sheen.

It wasn't the *floodlights* that caught our attention as we lay there. They weren't the only lights around. Here and there across the black expanse, faint glowing figures stood like posts risen from the ground, like nails hammered into the winter field. Their light was tenuous, palely golden, shimmering and twitching, as if at any moment they might be pulled apart by the wind. What form they'd ever had was lost with countless years.

"*That's* why they aren't too worried about posting sentries," Lockwood breathed. "They've got Vikings to do the job for them."

"Must be some bones still left out there on the battlefield," George said.

"Not good." Kipps was scowling through the goggles. "What do we do now?"

"I think it's all right," I said. "We can just steer around them. There's plenty of space, and it doesn't look as if they've moved for centuries. It's not *them* we should worry about, anyway, if we're talking psychic threats."

"Still got that background hum, Luce?" Lockwood asked.

"Yeah. It's really loud. And it's coming from down there."

In fact, the sound had been building up all the way through the woods. It wasn't quite so heart-stoppingly immediate as when the Shadow was approaching the churchyard, but it was strong now, buzzing like insects in my brain. As with the bone glass months before, as in the hidden tunnels of Chelsea, it almost made me feel nauseous. There could be no doubt: it was coming from the site below.

Lockwood shifted where he lay; his hand touched my shoulder. "We'll follow your lead, Lucy, when we're in there. Anything you pick up, just tell us."

"First," Kipps said drily, "there's the small matter of *getting in.*"

A rough, stony escarpment led down to the level of the fields. We took this inch by inch, so as not to send pebbles tumbling, but once on the flat ground we picked up the pace again. The compound floated ahead of us in its island of light. No one was visible, which gave us heart, though in truth there was little chance of anyone under the floodlights seeing us as we drew near. Looking out into the dark, they'd have been almost blind.

I was right about the Visitors, too. We were able to curve between the softly glowing forms, keeping at a distance, and never once did any of them stir. They were scarcely more than pillars of creamy light, except for one, in which traces of a bearded face could still be seen. Then we were past them. Drawing near the darkest portion of the boundary fence, we flung ourselves down.

A minute went by, during which we allowed our heart rates to slow. The grass was cold; I was pressed between its blackness and the blackness of the sky. When I looked up, I could see the loops of wire a few inches from my face and, beyond, the backs of buildings. They were more substantial than they'd appeared from the woods; taller, larger in extent. The sides near us were very dark, but you could see that some of the structures were connected by passages. These were basically metal-ribbed tubes, with canvas sides that shuddered gently in the wind. It was silent; the place might have been abandoned.

"George," Lockwood ordered, "cut us in."

Snip, snip. George put the wire cutters into operation. With deft precision he cut five or six strands of wire, close to the ground, so that a stiff flap was formed. He pushed it experimentally with a hand. "We can squeeze through," he said. "Then it falls back. No one will see."

"Needs to be bigger," Lockwood whispered. "In case we have to exit in a hurry."

"*Psst!*" It was a sound like an elegant snake. That was Holly, giving the alarm. We flung ourselves flat again, covering our silver rapiers with our bodies. Boots crunched on gravel, coming around the side of the nearest building. We lay in the dark grass, faces pressed to the earth, while someone passed a few feet beyond the fence. The footsteps rounded a corner and faded.

Cautiously, I raised my head and pushed my curtain of hair aside. "All clear."

The others levered themselves up. "Not bad, Cubbins," Kipps breathed. "I never thought you could flatten yourself like that. At all, in fact."

"I never thought you could make witty comments," George said. "And I was right." He resumed snipping at the wire. Soon he had cut free a mailbox-shaped patch of mesh, shoulder-width, just high enough to squeeze through with a backpack on. He dragged it aside. No sooner had he done so than Lockwood was wriggling through the space. Even with his coat, his slim, spare form slipped through without difficulty. In a moment he was up and crouching, looking all around. He gave the signal. One after the other, with varying degrees of deftness, we followed him onto forbidden ground.

"Memorize this spot," Lockwood whispered. "The hole's

midway between those two black posts. Now—Lucy, any idea which way we should go?"

The psychic hum was louder than ever; I could feel it in the depths of my ears, in the soles of my feet, in everything in between. I took a few steps in one direction, then in the other, keeping my eyes closed, listening to the pattern of the sound.

"It's nearby," I said. "When I go to the left, it feels stronger."

With infinite stealth we inched toward the left-hand corner of the building, where light from the center of the compound spilled across the gravel. The wall rose above us like a corrugated metal cliff, black, featureless, and cold. By unspoken assent, I was at the head of the line. When I reached the corner, I peered slowly around—and almost cried out in pain at the thrum of psychic power that struck me in the face.

Away across an expanse of lit gravel stood a construction that I immediately knew to be the heart of the complex. In some ways it was no different from the other buildings—like a monstrous metal barn with a broad curved roof. But a ribbed passageway ran to it from the shed we stood by, and I could see another beyond. They were like spokes running to a hub. The central hangar had no windows, but a pair of double doors stood open at one end, facing the fence. Out of those doors streamed a soft and hazy light—and, with it, that blast of psychic power. Three or four men in white lab coats stood in the light. They held things in their hands, but I could not tell what these were. None of them moved. No one came in or out.

I leaned back in; let Lockwood take a look. "That's where it's all happening," I whispered. "Whatever *it* is."

He squinted out into the dark. "There's a gap in the boundary fence there—a missing panel—look, just beyond where the men are standing. What's *that* for?"

"So they can drive something in?"

"Why not use the gate by the road?"

I didn't have an answer to that. Craning my head around further, I noticed something else: a door in the building we stood by. It was made of smooth metal, with a tight rubber seal, and was just a few yards away. There was no clue as to what was behind it.

I showed Lockwood. "It's an option."

He hesitated. "I don't know. Risky. Might be half the Rotwell team in there."

"What, then? Can't just stroll out under the floodlights, can we?"

"No. . . ."

"Lockwood!" That was Holly, at the end of the line. She was indicating frantically behind her. Two men, dark-clothed, with equipment shining at their belts, had appeared around the far end of the building. Right now they were staring out into the night, where the pale lights of the Vikings flickered far out across the fields. They were talking, laughing, blissfully unaware of us—but the instant they looked our way, all that would change. We'd be silhouetted against the light.

"Quick, quick!" Lockwood was ushering us around the corner. We had the exact same problem here: the men by the open barn doors would see us if they chose to look up.

We collided against the door. Lockwood grasped the handle, turned it, pushed it open a crack.

"Quick! Quick! In, in, in!"

Ever seen a line of newly hatched ducklings jump one after the other into a stream? Not knowing what was coming, but with no choice but to follow the others, and to leap and hope? That was us, going through that door. Holly, Kipps, George—then Lockwood and me. We were through, fast as blinking, and the seal shut behind us.

It was the decisive action. Once through, we could never take it back.

Chapter 24

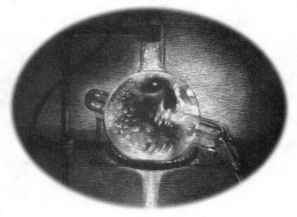

The good news first. Our arrival caused no outcry, no sudden alarm or attack. We were in a dimly lit chamber and, though it had plenty of horrors in it, no one from the Rotwell Institute was there. The corrugated sides of the building rose in a gentle arch high overhead. Soft lights hung on the walls, electric wires trailing between them. The floor was boarded with cheap wood. A partition wall at the far end of the room opened to another room, but this one would do for now. It was a laboratory.

Three long metal tables ran the length of the space, with chairs and shelved carts between them. On these, neatly separated by lengths of chain, sat an extraordinary variety of apparatuses: silverglass flasks, tubes and beakers, loops of iron piping, flaring Bunsen burners, crackling electromagnetic coils. Some of the flasks were small, others of colossal size, and all glowed with supernatural energy. You could see the Sources that powered them pressed against the dirty glass—yellowed jawbones, femurs, ribs, and craniums, and rusted lumps of metal that had once been helmets, sword hilts, or arm-rings. These were psychic artifacts of the battle that had taken place here, and the ghosts that clung to them were visible, too. Every container glowed with other-light, with eerie blues and yellows, with darkly sinister greens. The walls of the room swam with conflicting colors. And all the vessels were being experimented on—heated, compressed, electrocuted, frozen. . . . Plasm swirled against silver-glass: I caught a glimpse of twisted faces, impossibly contorted, pluming around and around. The vessels were sealed; I could not *hear* the imprisoned voices, but I certainly sensed their screams.

"*Look* at all this . . ." Kipps said.

George whistled. "It's like my bedroom."

Lockwood peered at a bulbous glass beaker in which a violet plasm boiled and bubbled above a flame. "Can you tell what they're doing here?"

"Ectoplasmic research, mainly," George said. "They're testing how it responds to stuff. To heat, to cold . . . This one's suspended in a vacuum, look. *That's* interesting: see how diffuse the plasm's become. . . . And they're trying to galvanize *this* spirit with a succession of electric shocks." He shook his head. "I could tell them that technique doesn't work. Tried that on our skull a year or more back. Didn't alter its plasm at all. Just made it grumpy."

I'd been listening out for the skull when I entered the room, but without success. Now I was staring at a rushing centrifuge, which whirled its imprisoned ghost on an endless loop. "It's not right," I said. "It's not . . . healthy."

George looked at me. "I've been doing this sort of stuff for years."

"I rest my case."

"It's all part of trying to understand the Problem, Luce," Lockwood said. "Finding out what makes ghosts tick. It's a bit extreme, but there's nothing exactly *wrong* here."

I didn't answer. Lockwood had no love for ghosts; neither he nor George ever spared much sympathy for them. Me? It wasn't quite that simple. I gazed at the busy work tables, with their pads and pens, their thermometers and stacked tubes. For some odd reason I remembered the vision I'd had of Emma Marchment's seventeenth-century workroom, filled with the pots and potions she'd used to help her in her witchcraft. This was more high-tech, but otherwise it didn't seem all that different.

"They're certainly hard at work in here," Lockwood said. "Everything mid-experiment. Which raises the question: Where are they?"

Kipps grunted. "Must be something better going on next door."

This was obviously true, and the laboratory, with all its cruel marvels, did not detain us long. We moved toward the partition at the far side of the shed. As we did so, George gave a cry. He swooped to the nearest table. "Yes! Yes! *That's* what I wanted to find!"

Holly stared at the container beside him. "A moldy pelvis?"

"No, you twit—these cigarette butts!" He picked up a jar that someone had been using as an ashtray, and gave it a quick sniff. "Yes, unmistakable—burned toast, a caramel tang! These are Persian Lights! The cigs we found at Aickmere's. No doubt now. We're dealing with our friends from Chelsea, for sure."

"You think *that's* good," Kipps said in a low voice, "you might want to take a look in here."

I could now see that the partition wall split the building neatly down the middle; the open arch led into a chamber that was almost the mirror image of the first, except with a tubelike passageway leading to another part of the complex.

The room had three long tables in its center. These, in contrast to the madly swirling glows of the tortured ghosts behind us, gleamed dully with more consistent light. They were stacked with boxes and neat piles of objects, laid out in ordered rows. There were canisters and cylinders and firearms. And other things, stranger still.

"Weapons room," Lockwood breathed. "Check out these flares! Ever seen any that big, Kipps?"

Kipps had pushed up his goggles and was gazing around the room in awe. "We used some pretty hefty ones in the East End once. These are bigger, though."

George whistled. "I'll say. They'd do some damage if you chucked them. They're as big as coconuts! Take the roof off a place, they would."

We walked along the aisles, opening boxes, peering into sacks. Professional fascination had overtaken us. This was ghost-hunting equipment designed for agents, but equipment we had never seen.

"Got guns here that fire capsules of iron and salt," Lockwood said. "They would have come in handy in Ealing. . . . But what's this?"

He stood before a metal rack, on which was sat a large weapon. It had a black stock, a long barrel, and, just in front of the trigger, a silver-glass orb strapped to the magazine with iron bands. You could see tiny bones lying in the orb. It glowed faintly.

"It's basically a traditional shotgun," Lockwood said, "but it's been adapted. I may be wrong, but I think that if you fire it, a ghost flies out. . . ." He shook his head. "It's weird. I'm not sure DEPRAC would approve of it."

"They wouldn't," I said in a small voice. I was staring at a tray of neat little wooden cylinders—batons, really—each with a glass bulb on the end. "They wouldn't approve of *any* of this." I picked up one of the batons and held it up to them. Supernatural light swirled in the bulb at the end. "Recognize these, anybody?"

No one spoke. They stared at the baton, openmouthed.

I took that as a yes.

The previous autumn, at a carnival in central London, two armed men had attacked a float on which Penelope Fittes and Steve Rotwell were riding. Guns had been used in an attempt on Ms. Fittes's life, but the attack had begun with a bombardment by ghost-bombs just like these. When broken, Specters had emerged from them, threatening many lives. Where the ghost-bombs had come from was unknown.

Until now.

"Well . . . *that's* interesting," Lockwood said.

"But—but surely," Holly said, "Mr. Rotwell can't be responsible. The assassins tried to kill him, too. . . ."

"*Did* they?" I said. "I don't remember them turning their guns on him. It was Penelope Fittes they actually shot at—"

"No! What are you saying? He fought against them! He killed one of the attackers!"

"Yes, that was good of him," Lockwood said quietly. "He came out of it quite the hero, didn't he? Even though *we* saved Ms. Fittes's life, and his primary purpose failed. It was always going to be a win-win for him."

"I knew the Rotwell organization hated Fittes," Kipps said, "but I never thought they'd go *that* far."

"I can't believe it," Holly said. She had tears in her eyes. "No, I can't. I *worked* for him."

Kipps frowned. "We've seen enough. We ought to get out of here. Go and find a phone, call DEPRAC, get Barnes over now."

"Not yet," Lockwood said.

"Are you insane? This is critical evidence, Lockwood."

"What would DEPRAC do? They wouldn't just barge into a Rotwell site, would they? Even if they believed us, which is a stretch, they'd delay things by getting search warrants, talking with lawyers— by the time anyone actually set foot in here, all this would be gone."

Kipps slapped the work table in frustration. "So what do you suggest? Keep strolling around in here until Rotwell finds us and stuffs one of these ghost-bombs up our nose?"

"The only place I want to stroll," Lockwood said, "is that central building. We've *got* to see the main event. That's where it is—through there." Eyes shining, he jerked his thumb toward the opening in the sidewall. You could see the ribbed interior of one of the makeshift canvas passageways stretching away, lit by dim lighting.

"Yeah, it's there," Kipps said, "and so are all the Rotwell crew. It's suicide to try it. We've done what we can." He looked around at us. "Am I *really* the only one who thinks so?"

No one answered. We were loyal enough to Lockwood not to

want to stand against him. Even so, the logic of Kipps's argument couldn't be denied.

"Let me make it even easier." Kipps plucked one of the batons from the pile. "We take one of these babies with us. We keep it as proof of what we've seen. We hold it under Barnes's mustache so even *he* can't deny the evidence of his eyes. That'll get the DEPRAC vans rolling out of London fast enough, I can tell you."

Lockwood shook his head. "No. We can't miss this opportunity. The stakes are too high. These batons are *nothing* compared to what's down that passage. You know it, and I know it. And we're wasting time—"

"What *I* know," Kipps interrupted, "is that you're putting your own curiosity over the safety of your team! Risk your own skin if you must, but—Holly's? Lucy's? Do you *want* any other deaths connected to your name?"

It seemed for a moment that Kipps had gone too far. Beneath the makeup, Lockwood's face was swept clean of expression. He took a step in Kipps's direction; then the emotional safety-switch went off inside him and he regained control.

"No, you're quite right," Lockwood said softly. "I won't deny it. I've not been thinking straight." He took a breath. "Okay, this is what we'll do. The rest of you are going to leave. Take the baton, go to DEPRAC, do what Kipps says. He's right; we've got to make sure word gets out. Me, I'm going to have a look in that central building. Shut up, George—don't argue. If they catch me, I'll provide enough of a distraction to ensure you get away. That's all. Get going now."

It would have been a significant test of his leadership, that moment, with Holly, George, and me all opening our mouths to challenge his decision. But as we did so, we heard a distant *clang*, and a burst of psychic energy wafted down the passage at our backs, strong enough to make the hairs rise on my arms. And with it came voices, footsteps hurrying toward us.

There's nothing like imminent disaster for putting an end to bickering. We scattered. Lockwood ran low, rolled across an aisle, came to a halt in a crouch at the far end of a table. Kipps and Holly vanished; George skidded past me in the opposite direction. I threw myself under the nearest table, wriggled between boxes, and kept on crawling as two sets of boots entered the room and went by. I looked back. Between the metal table legs I saw a man and a woman, both middle-aged, both with thick spectacles pushed up on their heads. They wore white lab coats, emblazoned with the rearing lion.

"How long now?" the woman said as they walked up the aisle.

"Ten minutes at the most. He's been away twenty. It's never more than half an hour."

"Better do this quick and get back, then."

Their footsteps continued to the partition door; they went through into the lab.

Something made me turn. There was Lockwood at the end of the table. He was crouching opposite me. His hair was tousled, his face smudged with makeup, but his eyes and smile were very bright. He met my gaze, waved a swift good-bye.

Then he was away, keeping low, ducking through the arch and up the passage.

I looked back into the room and caught sight of Holly, squeezed flat under the farthest table. Kipps was nearby, sandwiched between two racks of salt-spray guns. And, in the far corner, it was either the world's biggest salt-bomb or George's bottom poking out from behind a crate of magnesium flares. As I watched, his spectacled face rose up into view and blinked across at me.

They'd be all right.

You know what I'm about to say. It was another of *those* occasions. Those big/not thought-through/spur-of-the-moment/more-intuition-than-rational-analysis occasions.

The occasions that make us who we are.

I too got up and ran out of the room and into the passage.

The wind had picked up outside; the canvas walls were cracking and fluttering against the metal ribs of the tube. Weak bulbs hung from the roof. The passage was one long curve, smelling of salt and iron. It led me swiftly to the center of the site.

At its end was a swinging door, made of solid iron. A psychic barrier, like the one to Jessica's room at Portland Row. Lockwood was crouching there, rapier gleaming at his belt, clearly about to peep through. I fell into place beside him.

He started, cursed, rewarded me with a scowl. "What do you think you're doing? I told you to go."

"You forget," I said. "I'm not part of Lockwood and Co. I don't *have* to take your orders, do I? Anyway, you operate in a certain way, and so do I. You should know that by now." I flashed him a Carlyle grin.

"Oh, God. Yes, I suppose I should." He shrugged, then smiled; his excitement was too great to be sidelined any longer. He turned his attention to the door. "Well, I can't see what's in here, so we're going to have to chance it. Get your rapier ready."

But luck was with us, because when we pushed the door open a crack, gasping at the sudden psychic force, we saw no supernatural terrors or Rotwell agents; just the backs of many wooden crates, open, empty, stacked in piles. The floor was heaped with salt and iron filings, spilling out of the crates. Above soared a great high roof, glowing with pale light.

We'd arrived. The buzzing in my head that had bothered me since first stepping out of the inn that evening now reached its zenith. The din made me woozy; for a second I had to steady myself against the wall. Then Lockwood eased the door wider. Stepping through, we worked our way swiftly through the maze of crates until we came to the final stacks.

There was a narrow cleft between them. Beyond was brightness, movement, an enormous space.

We stood behind those crates, and looked.

"Oh my," was all I said.

From somewhere, Lockwood had produced the pair of black sunglasses that he only used for the brightest death-glows, the fiercest supernatural light. He flicked the frames open, one-two, in a hard, sharp action, like the double drawing of a knife blade. He was exultant; the remorseless drive and determination that Kipps had criticized, that Rotwell had understood, that had swept me up since I first met him, shone fulfilled in Lockwood's face that moment. It had led him to this.

"There it is," he said. "That's what we've been after, all along."

Laughing softly, he put the glasses on.

———

How to describe what we saw in that cavernous warehouse at the heart of the institute? It's hard, because even at the time the *exact* contents—what was and wasn't there—were oddly hard to fathom. For a start, the space was mostly empty; except for our end, where all the crates had been shoved, there was very little in it at all. Metal walls towered over us; soft lamps clung to the soaring roof. It was like being in the skeleton of a great church, looking down the abandoned center aisle. A passage similar to the one we'd come through opened off along the right-hand wall. At the far end, dimly, I saw the double doors we'd spotted from outside, open to the night. I say *dimly*, for despite the place's emptiness, something in the very center made them difficult to see.

Where *we* stood, the ground had been lined with a raised platform of wooden boards, but most of the building had no floor, just bare black earth. The grass that had grown there had long since died; the surface was hard soil, scattered with bones. This place had been the heart of the ancient battle; that was why it had been chosen. It gave the institute a head start with what they planned to do.

An immense circle of iron chains had been placed in the middle of the earth floor. It was wider than any circle I'd ever seen, maybe thirteen feet in diameter. And the chains themselves were vast; they were like the ones you saw at the London docks mooring ships to the harbor posts. They must have weighed a ton.

The *reason* for all this iron was instantly apparent. Inside the circle were Visitors.

Many of them.

Perhaps because of the restrictive power of the chains, they manifested only as pale gray shapes, superimposed upon each other and moving from side to side, like schools of fish in an undersized tank. Faint as they were, I could tell they weren't Shades or Lurkers or other feeble Type Ones. These were forceful spirits. It was their collective energies that I'd felt all the way back in Aldbury Castle.

Their Sources had been piled up inside the circle. You could just see them, lying on the ground below the restless, drifting forms. I knew at once that these were the objects looted from the furnaces, taken from the relic-men, purchased and stolen and gathered across London. They had been removed from their protective jars and cases and placed inside the chains, to create a single Source of monstrous power.

The skull had to be somewhere in there, but I couldn't spot it. Everything inside the circle was curiously hazy, as if light lost traction the moment it crossed the chains. The effect was almost like a thick column of mist blocking the center of the hangar, but that was too definite. It was more like a dullness of vision. You felt like you wanted to rub your eyes every time you looked at it. Mainly you just wanted to look away.

"What have those idiots *done?*" I murmured. "What's it all *for?*"

Lockwood nudged my arm. "Look at the chain, Luce. It's all about the iron chain."

Not far from the end of our wooden platform, a metal post had been hammered into the earth. Attached to it, at about (I guessed) the height of my shoulder, was a length of medium-weight iron chain. This chain stretched away from the post, maintaining the same height, passed across the boundary of the iron circle, and went between the piles of Sources. What happened to it after that was curiously hard to see, owing to the peculiar light in the center of the room. It must have been connected to something, but *what* that was, or *where* it was, I couldn't tell. The iron of this chain kept the Visitors in the circle at bay; the air around it, hazy as it was, was free of them.

The chain must have been of great significance, because the men and women of the Rotwell Institute who were present—I counted twelve in total—all stood near the metal post. Some had clipboards, and were dressed like the man and woman who had passed us in the weapons room; others wore thicker suits of protective gear, with plastic hats and oversized gloves. Among them was bland-faced Mr. Johnson (*his* clipboard much in evidence) fussing around, checking their data, looking repeatedly at a stopwatch in his hand. There, too, was Steve Rotwell, decked out like the rest with hat and coat, but recognizable by his bulk, his glittering rapier, and his shiny shoes. *He* stood apart, drinking from a silver flask.

All of them just standing, waiting for something.

Lockwood spoke in my ear. "Someone's in the circle."

"You see him?"

"No. The light's weird. But the chain provides a safe way in." He bit his lip. "Well, safe-*ish*. Well, not that safe at all, actually. Whoever it is must be wearing some kind of protective gear."

"What's he doing in there?"

"We'll find out. You heard what that pair said back there. It'll be any minute now."

As if in confirmation, the door from the weapons room clanged behind us; we saw the man and woman who had passed us hurrying back down to join their colleagues at the chain. The next moment,

Mr. Johnson's stopwatch had started ringing. The tinny sound made me jump. Johnson silenced it. Everyone watched the chain.

Nothing happened.

Steve Rotwell took another sip from his flask.

The iron chain gave a twitch.

As if jolted to life by an electric current, the Rotwell crew sprang into action. Men picked up spray guns, hoisted cylinders onto their backs; they stood in a broad semicircle around the metal post.

The chain was twitching furiously now. Within the circle the ghosts grew agitated, flitting chaotically to and fro. All at once they drew back, away from the chain.

Into the empty haze at the middle of the circle appeared a lurching shadow—faint at first, then darkening. It grew bigger and bigger. It had a creeping, rolling gait; a monstrous body; around its vast and shapeless head snapped leaping flames. Closer and closer it came, hand over hand, and the psychic hum from the circle suddenly cut out. In absolute silence the shape reached the barrier of iron. It did not hesitate.

Lockwood gasped; I cried out. One instant it was not there. Then the Creeping Shadow stepped straight over the chains with a sudden roar of noise and fire.

Chapter 25

In those first seconds, the figure could barely be seen. Pale fire ran across it, leaping from its smooth sides, darting and crackling above it like a living crown. Ice encrusted its surface, thick and veined with blue. To my horror, it seemed to have no face, just two narrow slits for eyes. Its size was huge; it was a head taller than the Rotwell attendants who now stepped near, spraying it with their salt guns, dousing it with jets of liquid that enveloped it in clouds of roaring steam. Joints screamed and ground together as, hand over hand, the figure moved slowly along the iron chain. Ice broke off of it and shattered on the ground. Flames died back, went out. And now I saw that the limbs beneath the ice were made of sheets of iron, hinged and riveted; the feet, the monstrous fingers—all were iron-clad. Concentric bands of iron encircled the lower torso, while vast oval plates sat atop the breast, with chain mail links showing between the cracks. The head was encased in a thick, ungainly helmet. Bolts attached this to the neck; it had no decoration. Like the rest of the armor, it was ugly, heavy, brutally functional.

The burning figure came to a stop, not far from the metal post. It stood there, swaying. A metal cart was wheeled close, and scientists in protective garb rushed forward. Hands in thick gloves snapped locks, twisted levers. A visor at the front of the helmet sprang up and a face, deathly pale, could be seen within.

Until that moment I had not been sure. Now there could be no doubt. This was the Creeping Shadow, the thing of flame and smoke glimpsed at the churchyard. And it was not a spirit, but a man. An ordinary, living man inside an iron suit.

A man at the end of his strength, who staggered and seemed about to fall. Attendants thronged around him like ants beside an ailing queen; his giant metal arms were held, his sides supported. In painful looking stages, he sank back onto the cart. Electric motors whirred; the cart was driven off, down the nearby passageway, with the Rotwell team hurrying behind.

Steve Rotwell had been standing a few feet away, impassively observing the whole procedure. He put the cap back on his flask, rubbed his nose, and strode after them.

The door clanged. The hall was empty.

All that time I'd been motionless. I felt I'd almost forgotten how to speak. "Lockwood," I croaked, "that man in armor . . . You really think—?"

He shook his head. "Not now. Got your spirit-cape?"

"Yes."

"Put it on."

I opened my bag, did as I was told. Lockwood was doing the

same with his cape, unfurling the iridescent feathers. "I'm not going near the circle without protection," he said. "This is our only chance to examine their setup. We *have* to take a closer look."

We came out from our place of safety, headed into the center of the room. Behind the chains, the gray shapes flowed back and forth in the column of milky air. The psychic noise beat against my head. It was very cold. We put on our gloves.

Even close-up, it was impossible to see the other end of the hanging chain. It was as if a fog hung over the circle; the chain went into it and disappeared from view.

"A man steps into the circle," Lockwood murmured. "He puts on the protective armor, and he goes inside this massive Source. Once there, what does he do? What does he find?"

"You remember George's trousers analogy?" I said. "How Sources are places where the fabric of the world has worn thin? Put enough Sources together, he said, and the hole becomes a window to the Other Side. If that's right, *this* window must be huge. They're trying to see through to . . ." The concept was so incomprehensible—and so dangerous—that I couldn't bring myself to finish.

Lockwood was staring calmly at the circle. "Yes. If a window is all it is."

He added something else, but I didn't hear him. Over and above the horrendous psychic roaring, something had called my name.

"*Lucy* . . ."

"The skull!" I said. "I hear it!"

I stepped closer to the chains, peering at the swirling silhouettes within. Which of the gray and rushing forms was it? Impossible to tell.

"Are you *sure* you hear it?" Even Lockwood, whose Listening abilities were practically nil, could sense the ferocious noise coming from the circle. To be honest, I was surprised, too. It *was* strange that I could pick out that one voice.

And yet there it was again. "*Lucy . . .*"

I shrugged. "I guess my psychic powers are getting stronger all the time. I must be tuned in to it on some special wavelength."

"*Well, that's one possibility,*" the voice said. "*The other is, I'm just over here.*"

I blinked around. To my left, piled against the wall, were stacks of empty silver-glass cases, open ghost-jars, and other discarded debris—plus one intact jar I recognized very well. It was on its side, as if hurled there; the hideous translucent face inside lay horizontal, too, nostrils flaring, bug-eyes glaring up at me.

"*I know, I know,*" it said. "*Every last stupid Source in the county got put into that circle, and they didn't bother with me. Bloodied hankies, socks, false teeth, bits of old rope; you name it, it all went in. I even saw them tossing in a couple of haunted buttons. But I'm not worthy.*"

"Skull!" I ran over to the jar, pulled it upright. The top of the lid showed scuffs and other signs of damage. "What have they done to you?" I cleared my throat and scowled. "Not that I care, obviously."

"*I admit I'm surprised to see you, too,*" the skull said. "*'Course, I knew you'd look for me. I just didn't think you'd have the brains to track me down.*"

"It's actually a complete coincidence. We're on another mission entirely. Still, since I'm here . . ." I swung my backpack down and made a space inside. "But I don't understand—why didn't they use you? You're a Type Three."

The ghost spoke in tones of cold outrage. *"They don't know that, do they? They're idiots. Plus, they couldn't get the top off my jar. It's corroded shut, or something. Tried to force it like I was a jar of pickled onions. In the end, they just lost patience. Ah, it's so embarrassing! Even that moldy, beardy mummified head we found—he went in. That witch's ghost is in there, too, shrieking around and around. But not me. What's that you're wearing, by the way? You look like a stuffed goose."*

"It's a spirit-cape. Shut up." I was busy shoving the jar into the backpack, looking over my shoulder as I did so. Lockwood was near the circle, studying the chain where it crossed into the column of haze. "Lockwood," I called, "the skull's here. We ought to go."

"In a minute, Luce . . ." He was staring into the swirling haze, fingering the feathers on his cape.

"I see you brought Lockwood along as cannon fodder," the skull. *"Good thinking. Look, now's your chance, while he's distracted. Let's slip away."*

I stood up with a start. I thought I'd heard a noise along the side passage where the Rotwell group had gone. "Lockwood . . ." I said. "It's really time we left."

"Just leave him be. You make too much of him. Always have. He is replaceable, you know. Hey, if you close your eyes or switch out the light, I might be Lockwood."

I didn't honor that comment with a reply. I was worried. Lockwood had an odd dreamy expression and was smiling faintly. I didn't like the look. He had the same bright light in his eyes that I'd noticed during the argument with Kipps. It was like he was looking at something far away. Certainly he was disconnected from what was around him, for now there was no doubt about it—sounds *were* coming from the passage. I left the backpack lying. Stepping over quickly, I grabbed at Lockwood's arm. "Wake up!" I said. "They're coming!"

He blinked. "What? Yes, of course. We'll go. Make for the lab—"

But we couldn't go back the way we had come. There were noises from behind the crates, too. The creak of an opening door.

And from the side passage came footsteps, voices, the hum of the electric cart.

I pulled at Lockwood again. "Quickly, then. The open doors at the end . . ."

But I'd forgotten the Rotwell agents we'd seen standing outside the double doors. When we started around the circle and got a clear view down the building, we saw they were still there.

We skidded backward. "Trapped," I said. "There's nowhere. Nowhere to go."

"*Nowhere. . . .*" That was the skull calling from my open rucksack by the wall. "*You're precisely right. Nowhere's your only option now.*"

"What does *that* mean?" And then the lightbulb went on. "Oh. No. No way."

"*Then say hello to Mr. Rotwell.*"

"Lockwood," I began, "these spirit-capes . . . how good do you think they are?"

But he'd had the same thought, and with a shock I realized

that it pleased him. He was already looking toward the iron chain. "Quick, Luce," he said, "follow me."

"I need to get my backpack! I don't have the skull!"

"Luce, there's no time! Hold on to the chain. Follow me, and don't let go."

"Oh, God. Oh no."

I'd followed Lockwood into many haunted rooms. I'd jumped off buildings with him, too. But taking those few steps toward the circle, with its icy supernatural cold beating against me, and the gray shapes swirling faster as if in welcome—*that* was the hardest leap of faith I'd ever had to make. I clasped the iron chain, pulled the spirit-cape tight around me. Behind came the voices of the Rotwell crew as they entered the hangar. The psychic roar of the ghosts screamed around me like a hurricane. The chain was freezing even through my gloves. Hand over hand . . . Nearer, nearer, up and over the heap of great black chains. Lockwood was first; he crossed the circle and disappeared from sight.

"*See you on the other side*," the skull's voice said.

One step, two steps . . . I closed my eyes tight.

"Lucy," Lockwood said.

"What?"

"You can open your eyes."

"Is it all right?"

"Er, I wouldn't *quite* say that. But we're okay now. We're okay. Just don't let go of the chain."

I opened my eyes. The first thing I saw was Lockwood. He was standing very close, facing me, the top of his hood almost meeting mine. He, like me, was gripping the iron links for dear life. Ice was forming on the outside of our gloves; the whole chain was crusted with it. Icicles hung beside us in the frigid air.

Ice was spreading over the outside of Lockwood's cape, too; crystals grew between the shining feathers, and I could hear it doing the same on mine. But the funny thing was, the underside of the cape was downy warm. It cocooned my body in a bulb of warmth and stillness, and kept the chaos all around at bay.

Chaos . . .

We stood together in the center of a vortex of whirling plasm. Shadows swirled past us, swimming close, darting back again. Clutching fingers reached out toward Lockwood, shriveled to powder, and were carried back into the maelstrom. At our feet were scattered many Sources, and only the power of the capes—and the iron chain—thrust the ravenous spirits away. The capes' effect extended to the sounds inside the circle, too. Close beside us, ghostly faces howled and gibbered, yet I scarcely heard them. If I had, I think I would have been driven mad.

"Well, this is jolly," Lockwood said. "I've got to hand it to those witch doctors—they knew what they were doing. That's how they went into those spirit huts and survived. These capes are only made of feathers and silver thread, but they're just as effective as the Creeping Shadow's suit of armor. More so—because they're *so* much lighter. Together with the chain, they'll keep us safe for as long as we hide in here."

A vast shape drifted out of the murk behind him; it was a silhouette only, buried behind other rushing forms, but I recognized it at once. It extended a colossal hand toward us, was caught up by the remorseless flow of energy, and swept sideways and away.

Lockwood caught my look of terror. "Seen old Guppy?" he said. "Yes, he's here. There are some other pretty horrific things, too. I wouldn't look at any of them, Luce, if you want to sleep tonight. Stay focused on me and the chain."

Just below shoulder height, the chain ran on past Lockwood and was lost in the mist beyond.

"Where's the other post?" I said. "Where's it tethered?"

"Looks like it goes straight through and out the other side of the circle. That's fine. We'll give Rotwell enough time to finish whatever he's doing, and then creep out again, one side or the other."

My attention was caught by a familiar face, red-eyed, jawless, spun about with smoke-like hair; it thrust forward from the vortex, glared at me, and retreated. So the skull had been right: the witch, Emma Marchment, was here, too.

"Lockwood," I said, "where do you think we are?"

His face was close to mine. He'd been staring out beyond me, narrowing his eyes as he always did when using his Talent. "Oh, we're still in the circle. Look, you can see the double doors over there, through the mist, and there's the outline of the crates where we first came in. And there's the pile of jars and boxes where you left the skull. It's some optical illusion that makes everything so faint and gray. . . ." His voice trailed off.

"An optical illusion?"

"Of course. That's all it is. Caused by all these Sources piled around us."

"I guess. . . ." It was true that you could sense the structure of the building, hovering beyond the swirling mist. The doors, the crates, the metal post, the platform at the end, were all just barely discernable in a faint and curiously flat way.

And yet . . .

It was the chain that really got me. The iron chain.

You know when you look at a drinking straw in a glass of lemonade? How it seems to bend at the point where it enters the liquid? That's refraction, according to George, and the weird thing was, the metal chain was doing precisely that. There was its line, right next to us, the links covered in ice. You could follow it, stretching out toward the metal post, to where the guy in the suit had collapsed. It was a straight line—I knew that because I'd walked along it—but it didn't *look* that way. At the point where it crossed over the ring of objects, it seemed to veer sideways, and also grow an awful lot fainter.

Why did it do that? It bothered me.

And where were the Rotwell people? We'd just heard them coming in. That's why we were standing there, by an icy chain, surrounded by a host of angry spirits, in the middle of that stupid building.

Try as I might, I couldn't see—or hear—them at all.

At least that meant they were unlikely to spot us, either.

"The armored man," I said. "You really think he was the Creeping Shadow we saw in the churchyard?"

Lockwood nodded. "Yes. Though I don't pretend to understand how, because when we saw him he was see-through, like a spirit. He wasn't solid, was he? He was hardly there at all. And how does that jibe with him standing in here? We're miles from Aldbury Castle. I don't get it."

I didn't either.

"Just a few minutes more," Lockwood said.

We stood there, surrounded by whirling horrors.

All of a sudden I needed to talk to him.

"Lockwood," I said. "Me leaving."

"What about it?"

"Really it was all your fault."

He glanced at me from under his icy hood. "What? How d'you figure that?"

"Because"—I took a deep breath—"because you always risk yourself for me. You always do, don't you? I realized I put you in danger by being part of the company. Then there was a ghost at Aickmere's. It showed me the future—it was a future in which you'd died for me. I knew you'd end up killing yourself, and I couldn't bear that, Lockwood. I just couldn't bear it. So . . ." I spoke in a small voice. "I left. *That's* why I did it. It's better this way."

"So it wasn't because of Holly, then?"

"Ah! Surprisingly, *no*. It was because of you."

"Okay . . ." He nodded slowly. "I see."

I waited. Out in the murk, pale fingers reached for us. Clenching, they jerked away. "Well, aren't you going to say anything?" I said.

He was looking at his icy gloves. "What is there to say? Maybe you're right. This way we don't see each other very often, and perhaps you extend my life. Although, let's face it"—he glanced out at the circling spirits—"I'm not likely to last long in any case, at the rate I'm going."

I touched his glove. "We'll get out of this," I said.

"Of course we will! But I don't just mean tonight. Kipps was right about me, and Rotwell was, too, for that matter. I don't hold back, do I? When I set out to do something, I never take the safest route. Sooner or later, I suppose my luck will run out." He shrugged. "I've always been that way."

I thought of the abandoned bedroom at Portland Row. "Why *is* that, do you think?"

He hesitated. His eyes met mine, then they slid away. "Don't look behind you!" he said. "I can see Solomon Guppy's spirit again. The other phantoms seem to want to avoid him, which shows even the dead have taste. . . . Okay, he's gone. Listen, thank you for telling me why you left. I should point out that, despite your excellent intentions, you've still ended up standing beside me surrounded by a tide of ghosts. . . ."

"Yeah," I said. "I don't quite know how that happened."

"I'm not complaining. Far from it. I'm glad you're here with me. I think you keep me safe, if anything."

Right then, the cape wasn't the only thing that kept me warm. I smiled at him.

"And I'd like to say something else," Lockwood said. "Back at Guppy's house, you mentioned something about it being Penelope Fittes's idea that I call on you. Don't deny it. You did. Well, she may *think* it was her idea, but I'd been looking for an excuse to get you back all winter. I just knew that, unless I had a really good reason, you'd tell me to get lost. And you would have, wouldn't you?"

"Yes." When I nodded, ice cracked on the back of my hood. "I would have."

"Fittes gave me the perfect opportunity," Lockwood continued.

"But we've moved on from all that. Anyway, I'd just like to add"—
he cleared his throat—"that if you ever *did* want to come back to
Lockwood and Company—I mean as a proper, permanent colleague, not just as a client, associate, or hanger-on, or whatever it
is you are right now—we'd at least have the pleasure of each other's
company for a bit before my untimely end. . . ." He looked at me.

I said nothing. Around us, ghosts screamed and unholy shapes
contorted. We gazed at each other.

"Wouldn't we?"

"I suppose."

"Think about it."

"I have. . . . All right."

"All right what?"

"I'm coming back. If you'll have me, I mean. If the others will
have me, too."

"Oh, I'm sure they can be persuaded. Though George will have
to find somewhere else to store his underwear. Great." His eyes sparkled. He grinned at me. "We should stand together in a haunted
circle more often. Get a few things ironed out. . . ." His head jerked
up. "Hold on. . . ."

I'd felt it, too, through the fabric of my gloves. A vibration in the
links. The chain jumped again.

We looked at one another. "The Shadow. It's coming back in,"
Lockwood said.

I peered along the chain, through the rushing ghosts. "I don't
see it."

Lockwood cursed. "I'm not meeting it in here. Heaven knows
what would happen. No choice, Luce. We're going to have to make

a dash for it. Let's nip out the other side, run for those doors. If we're fast enough, the men there will be caught off guard, and we'll go straight out into the fields. Happy?"

And you know what? Given the circumstances, I sort of was. "Go, then," I said. The chain bounced up and down; over my shoulder I saw a bulky shape swimming into view. It loomed beyond the ghosts. "Go!"

We ran along the chain as fast as we could, and again the capes had their effect—the Visitors parted for us, and we stepped over the circle and back out into the hangar.

"Run!" As Lockwood said it, he was gone, his spirit-cape flying out behind him. It looked as if he were about to take flight. He had his rapier in his hand. I let go of the icy chain—the other post was just ahead—and followed him down that long building, head down, arms pumping, and out through the open doors. No one tried to stop us; we plowed on, over gravel, through the gap left by the missing panel in the fence, and onto the black grass. We kept running, running across the field, but heard no signs of pursuit behind us. At last we slowed down and came to a breathless halt.

For the first time, we looked around us. The field had changed. It was covered with crystals of ice. All around us mists had formed, and the icy ground lay shimmering under a black sky.

Chapter 26

It was very silent. The wind that had blown across the fields earlier was gone, and the night was bitterly cold. Thick wires and horseshoes of frost lay in the dents and ripples of the hard black earth; the whole land was white with it. A flat brightness lay over the field and the escarpment beyond, and on the dark trees at its top. The source of this brightness was hard to make out. There were no stars in the black sky, and no moon showing. We stood alone in the field, looking back at where we'd been.

"Well, no one seems to be after us," Lockwood said. His voice sounded small; it didn't carry well in the freezing air. "That's good."

"Were there men at the doors?" I said. I found it hard to speak. "I didn't see any."

"No. They must have left. Lucky for us."

"Yeah. Lucky."

Looking back, I saw that the floodlights had been turned off.

You could see the poles hanging above the roofs like giant insects, bent and dead. The buildings showed like pieces of pale gray paper, stuck onto a dark-gray board. Even the lights in the hangar we'd just run from had been switched off. The institute was bathed in the same subdued, flat, gray glow that lit the field and trees.

"Power cut," Lockwood said. "Maybe that's what distracted them."

The outside of Lockwood's cape was thick with ice; I could feel the weight of mine hanging on me, too. The insulating qualities of the feathers still worked well, though—I sensed, rather than felt, the grueling cold all around. White threads swirled around us.

"Where'd all this mist come from?" I said. "All this frost? It wasn't here before."

"Some effect of their experiments?" Lockwood suggested. "I don't know."

"It's a strange light. Everything's so flat."

"Moonlight does odd things," Lockwood was looking toward the trees.

"Where *is* the moon?"

"Behind the clouds."

But there were no clouds.

"We'd better get going," Lockwood said. "The others should be halfway back to the village by now. They'll be getting help. We should join them, reassure them we're okay."

"I don't understand it." I was still looking up at the sky.

"We need to catch up with them, Luce."

Of course we did.

We started walking. Frost cracked underfoot, and our breath hung in the air so that we plunged through it with each step.

"It's so *cold*," I said.

"We were lucky they didn't come after us," Lockwood said again. He glanced over his shoulder. "Odd, though . . . I'd have thought *somebody* might come."

But we were the only moving things in that wide, wide field.

By unspoken agreement we took the lane through the forest. The light was different there, too. The gray haze seemed to penetrate everything. The lane was white as bone. Thin lariats of mist wound in and out of the trees.

"This is weird," I whispered. "There's nobody anywhere."

I'd thought we might see the others ahead of us, but the road was empty, and we could see a good distance in the soft, flat light. We hurried on, following the gradient downhill. We passed the side track to the open quarry, with its little memorial cairn of stones. The flowers that had decorated it were gone, and the photograph at its top was frosted with ice. There was no sound in the gray forest, and no wind. Shimmering crystal flecks fell from the surface of our capes, and our breaths came in brief and painful bursts. Soon we would reach the village. Our friends would be there.

"Maybe there *are* some people about," Lockwood said softly. Neither of us had spoken for a while. When we did, neither of us wanted to raise our voices; I don't know why. "I thought I saw someone walking down that side track from the quarry. You know, just beyond the cairn."

"You want to go back, see who it was?"

"No. No, I think we should just keep going."

We walked more quickly after that, our boots clicking on the frost-hard road. We crossed the silent forest and came to the wooden footbridge over the little stream.

The stream was gone. The bridge spanned a dark, dry channel of black earth that wound off among the trees. Lockwood shone his flashlight beam on it, the light frail and flickering.

"Lockwood," I said, "where's the water?"

He leaned against the railing, as if weary. He shook his head, said nothing.

I could hear my voice cracking with panic. "How can it have just . . . disappeared? I don't understand. Have they dammed it suddenly?"

"No. Look at the ground. Bone-dry. There's never been any water here."

"But that makes no—"

He pushed himself upright, his hand rasping as it pulled free of the rail. Ice particles glistered on the fingers of his glove. "We're almost at the village," he said. "Perhaps there'll be answers there. Come on."

But when we came down from the lane, the village had changed, too. Never exactly well-lit, the cottages around the green were now entirely dark. Their shapes merged in the half-light and could scarcely be seen. The green itself was filled with shifting coils of mist. Above us, the church tower blended with the pewter-black sky.

"Why are all the lights off here, too?" I said.

"Not just off," Lockwood whispered. He pointed. "Look by the church. The ghost-light's gone."

It was true. True, and it made no sense. On the little mound beside the church, there was an empty space. The rusty, disused ghost-lamp wasn't just gone—there was no trace of it ever having been there at all.

I didn't say anything. *Nothing* made any sense, not since we'd come out of the institute. A creeping, pervading wrongness hung over everything; in the cold, the silence, the soft, pale light, and the terrible, sapping solitude of it all. But it numbed you, too; it was hard to think.

"Where *is* everybody?" I murmured. "*Someone* should be around, surely."

"It's after dark—they're all at home. And George and the others will be safe inside the inn." Lockwood's voice didn't carry any conviction. "We know half the village is deserted, anyway. We shouldn't expect to see anyone."

"So we go to the inn?"

"We go to the inn."

But the inn, when we reached it, was as dark as all the rest. Its sign was blistered with frost. The door swung open to the touch, and a faint stale smell came from the black interior. Neither of us wanted to go inside.

We walked back out onto the green and stood there, wondering what to do. When I looked down, I saw that where my boots protruded beyond frozen drapes of the spirit-cape, the leather and steel caps were white with ice. Our capes were almost solid; they creaked whenever we moved. Then I noticed something else. A thin gray plume of smoke was rising from Lockwood's cape, drifting away into the dark air. The surface flickered, as if with heatless flames.

"Lockwood, your cape—"

"I know. Yours is doing it, too."

"It's like . . . like when we saw the Shadow. You remember how it left a trail of . . ."

"We need to think about this." Lockwood's face was drawn, but his eyes blazed defiantly. "What have we done that might have made things different? There's only one thing. Up at the institute, what did we do?"

"We went into the circle."

"Yes, and . . ."

"And we came out again." I looked at him, suddenly aware. "We left the circle on the other side. . . . We followed the iron chain and left on the other side."

"You're right. Maybe that's important. I don't know why it should be, but if it is . . ."

"All this . . ." I said.

"All this isn't what it looks like." Lockwood stared at me. "What if we haven't actually come out, Lucy? What if we're somehow still inside?"

How dark the green was, how thick the rising mists, how unyielding the silence.

"We have to get back to the circle," Lockwood said.

"No, look," I said, my voice rising in my relief. "We're talking nonsense. There they are."

I pointed across the green. On the far side, within the mist, three figures were limping slowly up the road toward us.

Lockwood frowned. "You think that's them?"

"Who else would it be?"

He squinted out from under his steaming hood. "It's *not* them. . . . No, look—they're adults. They're all too tall. Plus, I thought those cottages were abandoned. Didn't Skinner say—?"

"Well, anyway, maybe they can tell us what's going on," I said. "And look, here's somebody else coming."

It was a little girl, stepping out of a garden in front of a house. She opened the gate and shut it carefully behind her, before starting toward us. She had a pretty blue dress on.

"I don't recognize *her*," I said. "Do you?"

"No, Lucy . . ." Lockwood was turning on his heels, looking all around. The mists were pretty thick over by the duck pond, but we could just see someone walking along the opposite bank, between the barren willows—a lady with long pale hair. "Nor her . . ." Lockwood said, "Nor any of them. But we've *heard* about them all."

There were other movements in the mist, people coming out of their houses, latches lifting, gates being softly unlocked.

"Lucy," Lockwood said, "we *really* need to go."

"But look, that little girl—"

"Danny Skinner told us about her, Luce. Remember? Hetty Flinders, with her nice blue frock."

Hetty Flinders? Yes. . . .

She'd died.

With steady, unhurried steps, the girl in the blue dress and the other inhabitants of the dark village made their way toward us. You could see the details of their clothes—some modern, others less so. Their faces were as gray as the frosted ground.

For a few dreadful seconds it was as if some power pinned us where we stood; our blood was water, our limbs cold stones. But we had the warmth of the spirit-capes around us; and, deep inside, our willpower still burned strong. As one, we shrugged the death-clasp off. As one, we began to run.

We pressed close together, hoods low over our faces against the cold. We cut across the green, boots thrumming on the hollow, frozen earth. Smoke poured from our icy capes, extending behind us like a comet's tail.

The green was not a big space, but it seemed to expand as we went across it. It took a long time to get near the church. We passed beneath the tower at last. Looking up, I saw the shape of a person standing there; I felt him lock his gaze with mine.

We ran down the lane past the churchyard. From the other side of the hedged embankment came noises—the grinding of stone, the whisper of rustling cloth. Shapes appeared at the hedge. They began pushing their way through, framed against the sky.

Out of the village, up the cold road. It was hard to move fast; whether it was the chill, or something else, my limbs felt like lead. It was like walking through mud, like going the wrong way up an escalator. Lockwood, usually so fleet of foot, was having the same problem. Our breaths came in gasps. Over our shoulders, we could see the people of the graveyard and the people of the village congregating in the road, pooling toward us, following our trail.

We fled over the footbridge, over the dried-up stream, into the woods. We took the shortest way. At the turning to the quarry, a man stood waiting for us at the cairn. His face was the one we'd seen in the photograph atop the neat pile of stones; his features too were blurred as if by rain. He walked into the center of the lane and reached out for us. Lockwood and I veered away, off the road, up into the forest. The ground was thick with dead black brambles that burst into dust as we ran through them. The branches of the trees were sharp and snaring, snagging at our faces, catching on our clothes. We ran through light and dark, dodging, jumping, fighting against the cold, thick air.

I could see other people in the trees now, moving slowly, yet somehow effortlessly keeping pace. They were homing in on us from either side. Lockwood, just ahead of me, took a flare from his belt. He threw it at the nearest figure; it struck a tree root, bounced, broke open. The breaking made no noise; and nothing came out— no burst of light, no dazzling white fire. I'd instinctively squeezed my eyes tight shut; now I opened them, one after the other, to see our pursuers clambering over the roots, working their way implacably through brambles, still silent, patient, utterly unmoved.

We struggled up an icy slope, skidding, gasping; and all at once plunged down a steep hollow into a thicket. Black thorns stabbed my spirit-cape, intertwining with the silver, snaring it in several places. I was pulled back, trapped and twisting. As I struggled, the spirit-cape ripped. It tore in two. I screamed. A piercing cold like death stabbed me like a knife driven between the shoulders. I couldn't breathe. I fell to the ground. Feathers scattered on the frost beside me like smoking drops of blood.

I couldn't breathe. . . .

Then Lockwood was beside me, pulling me to him, dragging me beside him under his cape. Its softness enfolded me. The desperate cold lingered for a moment. It drew back painfully, like clawed fingers being withdrawn. I took a wrenching breath. I could feel Lockwood's warmth against me, and mine against him. We crouched together, side by side, his arm around me, my right knee pressed tight against his left. Our faces were very close, mine lower, his higher, leaning together as we peered out from under the burning hood at the swirling grayness all around.

Our descent into the thicket had been abrupt. Our pursuers were somewhere above us. Nothing was near.

"Are you all right, Lucy?"

I nodded, blinked ice out of my eyes. In that second in which my cape had fallen away, a coating of frost had adhered to my face.

"Am I pressing too close?"

"No."

"Say if I am."

"I will."

"We've got to go on, into the mist. But we have to stick together like glue. The cape's not very big. You'll have to stay really close to me, Luce. Can you do that?"

"I'll try."

"Quick, then. They're coming."

Up on our feet, out of the hollow and up a final rise. Dark shapes converged on us, bursting out from beneath the trees. We were almost at the brow of the hill. Gunner's Top was what it had been called; or something very like that. The name didn't seem appropriate here. Nothing under that flat black sky had a name.

The mists below now lay thicker on the fields than when we'd left them. The buildings of the institute were barely visible; their roofs rose above the murk, as dark and dead as standing stones.

We skittered and skidded down the slope, arms around each other, plowing up clouds of ice crystals at every step. Every movement was jerky, hard to take. We started out across the field. "No good," I gasped. "I've *got* to rest."

"Me, too." We stopped, turned stiffly together beneath our hood—just in time to see a tide of figures surging over the hillcrest, pouring down the slope behind us.

"Okay," Lockwood said. "Maybe a rest's not *such* a good idea."

Onward, in silence, through the mists; and now those mists parted, and we saw a tall bearded man, picking himself up off the ground, turning his head as we passed by. He carried a great sword. Both blade and skin were glimmering with frost.

Stumbling, almost falling, we ran on. The mists closed up again. Behind us we heard footsteps shuffling on hard ground.

"A Viking's all we need," I gasped.

"Like moths to a candle," Lockwood said. "Our warmth, our life—it draws them all. They followed the Shadow just the same. Last push, Lucy! We're almost there—"

We could see the fence of the institute, open, blank, and empty. Beyond, the doors of the central building hung wide and black.

"I'm never going to make it," I said.

"Keep going. We're there. We've done so well."

Through the fence, across the frosted gravel. We reached the double doors. The interior of the hangar was filled with mist. There was ice on the ground here, too. We paused, panting. We were almost worn out. Beneath the smoking spirit-cape, our gloves sparkled with ice. Our breath echoed like it was reverberating off our bones.

"How are we doing?" Lockwood said.

I looked back. "They're still coming. They're at the fence now."

"Better get on with it, then."

We stumbled through the open doors.

It was the same place—no doubt about that. The soaring roof, the metal walls. Far off through the mists, I saw the stacked crates. But the light was still odd, so that everything was layered, gray and grainy, as if with scales. That mist played tricks with my eyes. Nothing seemed quite straight, neither floor nor ceiling, hatch nor door. It looked as if everything was made of wax, and had been heated so that it swelled and softened, and was just about to melt. But everything was brittle with cold; thin cracks ran across the floor at my feet, and our boots rang out like iron.

The mist in the center of the hall was very thick. We couldn't see through it.

"The chain . . ." Lockwood gasped. "Where *is* it, Luce?"

"I don't know. . . ." Looking behind, I saw the shapes of our pursuers clustering at the doors.

"Oh, *God*. Where *is* it?"

"We're almost at the other end. We must have gone too far. . . ."

We circled in a panic, around and around. Lockwood wanted to go one way, I another; we almost tore his cape, tugging it between us.

We stopped, spent and despairing. I could hear many footsteps on the earth behind. All around us, just the swirling mists, the mist and melting wall. . . .

And there, slouching in a corner by the sidewall, a thin and rangy youth, hair spiked, hands in pockets, staring at me. He stood amid a pile of discarded jars and boxes. He was as gray as the inhabitants of the dark village, except for his grin, which gleamed sardonically even in the swirling dusk and was somehow most familiar. He stretched out an arm, pointed behind me. I turned, saw the post and chain.

"There it is!" I pulled Lockwood around. "Look!"

Lockwood cursed. "*Why* didn't we notice it before? Are we blind? Come on!" We circled toward the post. When I glanced back, the mists had closed in once more and the grinning youth was gone, and we were alone beside the post and its icy iron chain.

"Hold on to it," Lockwood said. "We go together. You first. Follow it right through. Don't stop for anything." He had drawn his sword, was staring all around us. The mists, swirling like stage curtains, grew darker with approaching forms. I caught a flash of Hetty Flinders's bright blue dress.

It probably wasn't *very* far we had to walk before stepping back into the circle. But it seemed to go on a bit, what with the awkwardness of being clasped together, so that we could only shuffle like penguins, and with the people of the village now erupting from the mist, and with us *both* swinging our rapiers to keep them at bay. When the vortex of Sources in the circle came into sight, it was a positive relief. I was almost ready to greet Solomon Guppy and Emma Marchment as old friends. Without regrets we threw ourselves over the chains, through the wall of whirling, shrieking spirits, and found ourselves again in the still heart of the iron circle.

The man in iron armor was nowhere to be seen. We inched our way along the chain toward the other side.

"If Rotwell's out there," Lockwood said, "we're just going to have to deal with it. I'd rather be killed by him than have something . . . *happen* to me back there."

I glanced behind us. "Think *they* could follow us through?"

"The iron will hold them up. But why not? It's a hole, and there *are* a lot of them. I only hope Steve Rotwell and his friends get to meet them, too. Got your sword ready, Luce?"

"Yep, and if I don't stab someone's backside with it in the next five minutes, I'm going to be sorely disappointed."

"Let's see if we can surprise them, then. Come on."

Again, just for an instant, the rushing ghosts were all around us. And then we were over the chains, and we stepped out together into the warmth, noise, and joyous, blinding light of the real world.

Where a battle was going on.

Chapter 27

E ven without the explosions, even without the blazing white magnesium fires, even without the shouts and screams and the whizzing flares, we'd have struggled to comprehend anything in those first few moments. The sensory contrast with the place we'd left was just too great. My brain was seared by savage brightness. The pain was numbing. I squeezed my eyes shut just as a wall of sound and heat hit me like a shovel to the head. I stumbled back, confused and helpless. Beside me, I could sense Lockwood doing the same.

All of a sudden I felt *wet*, too; the ice from the spirit-cape was melting. Freezing moisture ran down my neck, soaking my shoulders and arms. The shock jolted me into action. I peeled away from Lockwood, threw off the cape, took a mighty step—and promptly fell over something solid lying on the floor. I landed flat on my face in the soft, damp earth.

"*Have a nice trip?*"

I spat soil from my mouth. Then I opened my swollen eyes a crack, and through bleary but steadily improving vision saw the ghost-jar sitting in the open backpack, where I'd left it among the empty boxes. The reflection of white fires danced against the glass. The face behind it was watching me with unfeigned glee. I recognized the grin.

"*Hello again,*" it chuckled. "*You look so rough. It's really excellent. But you'd better wake up quickly and get involved, or they'll destroy the place without you.*"

"Who will?"

"*Your friends.*"

Shocking news delivered by a skull: that's about as good a recipe as I can think of for making you snap out of your pain, exhaustion, and psychic befuddlement. I didn't know whether to be thrilled or terrified—it was probably a combination of both. But I rolled over, forced my unwilling muscles to get me into a standing position; and by the time I'd managed *that*, I had more or less absorbed what was going on.

The old-time Viking/Saxon smackdown was no longer the most recent skirmish on that barren square of ground. A new one was in full swing. Everywhere I looked, magnesium flares were exploding, salt-bombs were bursting, pellets of iron filings were spattering viciously against the wall. Debris littered the floor; it was a piece of wood from the platform at the end that I'd stumbled over just now. The focus of the action appeared to be the corner of the building, between the piles of crates near the door to the weapons room and the side passage we'd seen the Rotwell crew leave through earlier that night. We'd heard them coming back in shortly before we'd gone into the circle, and sure enough they were still there, most of them. But they were no longer doing anything remotely scientific. No more clipboards for Mr. Johnson. No more flasks for Steve Rotwell. Instead, they and the rest of their team were scurrying around in panic as a rain of small explosions peppered them. A bright magnesium fire burned in the exit to the passage, preventing their escape. The electric cart was overturned, wheels gently spinning. It appeared to have been driven into the wall.

The origin of the ongoing attack was the pile of burning crates by the other door, and here three fast-moving figures could be glimpsed, popping out from cover at random intervals to hurl ghost-bombs and blast iron capsules down on the foe. Several of the Rotwell group were returning fire from behind the upturned cart, and the man in hulking iron armor, the erstwhile Creeping Shadow, was making strenuous efforts to climb up onto the crates, presumably to do battle. He wasn't having much luck. His armor was battered and his helmet slightly askew; and his progress was limited by his inability to raise his knee high enough to reach the wooden platform.

So intent was everyone on the fight that no one had noticed our arrival. There was a movement at my side. It was Lockwood, fearsomely disheveled, but calmly rolling up the wet and steaming spirit-cape and stuffing it in his backpack. "Everything okay, Lucy? Warming up a little?"

"Just a bit. *Look* at all this. What's going on?"

"It appears to be a rescue effort." He pointed in wonder at a slim shape half concealed between two crates. It had spikes of ashy, deranged hair, a ferocious, feral expression, and an enormous capsule-gun in its slender hands. "Is that . . . is that actually *Holly?*" he asked.

"You know, I think it is."

Kipps was visible, too, in a vantage point near the wall. Calm, steely, and implacable, he had a nice barrage of salt-bombs going. As we watched, he scored two successive hits on the armored man, knocking off his helmet and tipping him onto his back like a drunken, rolling tortoise.

But neither Kipps nor Holly was the most remarkable thing on view.

"Check out George," I said.

Lockwood whistled. "He's like a whirling dervish!"

George was, indeed, a thing to behold. Darting out from behind the crates to lob magnesium flares directly at Steve Rotwell, he repeatedly paraded himself in full view, as if daring the enemy to do its worst. His face still bore smears of makeup from our attempt at commando camouflage earlier in the evening. To this had now been added streaks of magnesium salt that slanted across his cheek and forehead like slashes of pale war paint. His teeth were bared, his hair stood up, his glasses blazed red in the flames flickering from the crates beside him. He had an enormous flare holster strapped diagonally across his chest, from which he pulled an endless stream of missiles. Occasionally he yelled shrill and incoherent cries.

"I could watch this all day," Lockwood said, "but I suppose we have to help them."

"You go, I'll follow. Just one thing I need to do first. . . ."

Twice since its theft I'd been close to retrieving the skull in the jar; twice I'd been forced to leave it behind. It wasn't going to happen again.

The ghost grinned as I hoisted the backpack over my shoulders. *"Ah, two firm friends, reunited at last! There should be sweet violin music playing for us, but I'll settle for the screams of the dying."*

My eyes scanned the carnage. "No one's actually dying, are they?"

"Maybe not, but it's not for want of trying. There's a few nasty magnesium burns on view. Some of those scientists are going to have trouble sitting down tomorrow morning."

"Good. Tell me what's happened, then." I stood, just in time to see Lockwood vaulting up onto the platform, using the chest of the armored man as an impromptu step. I had my backpack on, my sword out. I was ready to enter the fray.

"That's what I wanted to ask you," the skull said as I ran. *"I'm dying to hear about your adventures. I bet they're much more interesting than all this nasty violence."*

"Just give me a straight answer!" I ran up the front of the armored man, kicked out at a Rotwell scientist who was leveling a gun at me, and jumped onto the platform, where I ducked behind a crate. Something exploded right behind me, sending feathery plumes of fire fizzing over my head.

"It's a story quickly told. These fools were about to send another man through to the Other Side, only to be rudely interrupted by the arrival of your very angry friends. That's about it. The End. Now go and finish things."

"Okay," I said. "And . . . and when you say the 'Other Side' . . ."

"You know."

"But—"

"*You know perfectly well.*"

Maybe I did, but now, fortunately, was not the time to dwell on it. Keeping low, I slipped between the crates to join the others. Nearest was Holly. I tapped her on the shoulder, gave her a cheery grin.

"Aaah!"

"Hey, Holly! Holly, don't shoot me! It's me! It's *me*!"

"Aaah! But you're dead!"

"No—would a ghost tap you? Would a ghost talk to you . . . ?" I waited. "Would a ghost punch you in the face? You'll find out if you don't stop screaming."

"But you went in the circle . . ."

"I'm okay. And Lockwood, too—look, he's over there, with George. Well, don't start *crying* now." I gave her a swift hug. "See? Would a ghost do that? Come on. We're doing well. George is driving them from the field."

This was, in fact, mostly true. At Lockwood & Co., George was famous for not being able to throw or catch with any accuracy. Back in the kitchen at Portland Row, even the casual passing out of fruit or bags of chips became an exercise fraught with danger. Heads would be struck, glasses broken, peaches spattered on the wall above the sink. Curiously, that particular anti-talent boosted his effectiveness here. Whenever he ventured out from the crates and, with a savage cry, lobbed a flare or ghost-bomb toward the enemy, no one had a clue where it would land. Following the movement of his arm was no help; the item would as often as not shoot out implausibly in the opposite direction and send another Rotwell employee spiraling through the air. As a result, every time he popped into view, all the enemy agents ducked for cover. Many of them were already running down the length of the building, making for open air.

Sensing victory, Kipps emerged from his place of concealment, carrying a giant bag of ghost-bombs. Lockwood went to meet him; after brief greetings, he joined Kipps in lobbing missiles down the room.

"How long's this fighting been going on, Hol?"

Holly lifted her capsule-gun and wiped her face. Her hair and hands were dusted with a coating of gray ash. "Not long. Since we saw you enter the circle."

"You were here when we . . . ? How—?" Then another thought occurred to me. "But hold on, that's been . . . that was *ages* ago, wasn't it? Hours . . ."

"Don't think so, Lucy. About ten minutes."

"But—but it takes half an hour to walk to Aldbury Castle. Must be twenty minutes or more to run back. . . ." I spoke as if to myself. Yet it was certainly true that my whole experience on the other side of the circle now felt curiously insubstantial, weightless, almost dreamlike.

It wasn't the time to worry about it.

"What are you talking about?" Holly fired an exploding cap-sule down at the man in battered armor, who was fleeing awkwardly across the hangar. His breastplate had slipped off and was swinging like a pendulum. His boots, gloves, and other parts lay like scrap iron on the floor. She patted the side of the gun. "You know, this is a great weapon."

"It definitely suits you. Let's go and join the others. It looks like they're starting to mop things up."

The enemy ranks were thinning out. Many of the scientists had fled, and the rest seemed inclined to follow them, despite Steve Rotwell's ferociously shouted orders. Half-crouched behind the upturned cart, *he* had not retreated or resorted to firing any high-tech weapons. *He* had his rapier drawn.

George gave me a wave as I approached. Strapped to the back of his belt was one of the enormous flares we'd noticed in the weapons room, large as a coconut. "Hi, Luce."

"Hey, George. I see you're having fun. That's a mighty big one you've got there."

"Yes, that's my insurance policy. But I reckon these ghost-bombs will do the job for now."

Lockwood had just tossed one down at Steve Rotwell. It burst beside him. A gnarled female shape, translucent and shimmering pale blue, rose up at his back. Barely bothering to turn, Rotwell swung his rapier backward, snipping it neatly through the midriff. The ectoplasm fizzed and burst asunder.

"Ooh, see that?" George called. "He just sliced an old lady in two. That's low."

"Typical Rotwell behavior." Kipps threw another bomb, which bounced off a wall and came to an anticlimactic stop. "Hey, that one didn't even work!" He shook his fist at Mr. Rotwell. "What kind of a product d'you call this?"

"You've got to admit, Kipps," George said, "you didn't get a night like this when you were working for Fittes. Doesn't it make you feel better?"

"Feel better about what?"

"About being you. Watch out!" With a roar of fury, Steve Rotwell had thrown caution to the wind; he sprang across the cart in a single bound, took two great strides, and leaped up onto the platform, where he swung his sword at Kipps. Another blade swung to meet it; they collided directly above Kipps's head. Imagine an upside-down skull-and-crossbones flag and you'd have the moment perfectly.

It was Lockwood's rapier, of course, and for a few heartbeats he and Rotwell remained locked in that position, both straining, neither moving. Kipps had been frozen for an instant; now his neck slowly concertinaed down into his shoulders until his head was clear of the shivering blades. White-faced, he lurched away.

Steve Rotwell was taller than Lockwood, and considerably heavier. He exerted his weight on the sword; Lockwood, by careful twists and adjustments of his slim wrist, offset the force. Otherwise neither moved.

"I made a prediction earlier," Steve Rotwell said. "Do you recall it?"

"I do," Lockwood said. "You said I'd cross you." He gestured around at the burning building, at the screaming employees disappearing into the distance. "Does this count as crossing you? If so, congratulations—you were right."

"That wasn't all." Rotwell jumped back, swinging his sword away. He kicked a spar of burning wood at Lockwood, who jumped clear; it shattered against the crate behind him in a starburst of sparks. "I promised to deal with you when that happened. And so I shall."

He drove forward, twirling his rapier in a series of grandiose loops. Lockwood parried him once, twice, a third time, but was forced backward off the platform. He jumped lightly onto the earth, with Rotwell thudding down behind him.

"Years of work," Rotwell said. "Years of careful study, and you've ruined it in one evening."

"You brought it on yourself!" Lockwood was still on the defensive, straining to cope with the older man's savage attack. "Your experiments unleashed terror on Aldbury Castle! It's because of *you* that so many ghosts were raised! Dozens of people were killed! And all because *your* man in iron armor was out there, walking on the Other Side, stirring up the dead." He gave a deft shimmy and struck at Rotwell's wrist, but the blow glanced off the ornate hand-guard of the sword.

Steve Rotwell drew back. "You *do* know more than I expected . . . but I don't think you understand it all. If you did, you'd realize that the unfortunate deaths of the villagers was a small price to pay." With a twirling double stroke he knocked Lockwood back into the suspended iron chain. "And the same can certainly be said of *your* death, too."

He aimed an almighty blow downward; Lockwood ducked aside and the sword sliced straight through the iron chain. The portion of chain attached to the post fell to the floor. The rest was at once sucked inside the circle, like spaghetti being drawn into a giant mouth, and it disappeared.

Lockwood stumbled away, closer to the circle and its column of circling ghosts. He looked weary, and I thought I understood why. My own experience beyond the circle had left me weakened. My limbs were like water, my head still spun. If Lockwood felt anything like me, it was probably all he could do to hold the sword.

"He's beating him," Holly gasped.

Kipps nodded. "He's got Lockwood cold."

"Or so he thinks." George had a final standard flare in his shoulder belt. He took it out, winked at us, and hurled it straight at Rotwell's head. At least, that's what I assume he was aiming for. In actuality, the flare sailed clean past and landed by the edge of the circle of chains, where it exploded with great ferocity. When the smoke cleared, fires burned on the ground and the chains were blackened and twisted. Some of the links had almost split. At once the shapes inside the circle began to cluster at that spot.

"Ooh, that's not good," Kipps said. "Cubbins, where did you ever learn to throw?"

"He didn't, basically," I said. "That's the problem."

I ran past them and jumped off the platform.

Lockwood and Rotwell were clashing blades once more. Lockwood's sword was moving with desperate speed, but his face was pale. He was defending all the time, being edged back toward the circle. Rotwell sensed his chance. With two mighty swipes he knocked Lockwood backward, close to the weakened chains. The Visitors within sensed his proximity; they thronged at the boundary in ever greater numbers, pale hands reaching, mouths agape. The psychic roaring from the circle increased. I could see the broken chains stir slightly as a force pushed on them from inside.

Lockwood still had his rapier up. He parried, he dodged, but his normal energy and control had gone. The next moment, the sword was gone, too. Rotwell had contemptuously struck it away. Lockwood jumped back. He stood at bay in front of the iron circle, thin, pale, helpless—and still defiant. He stared at his enemy with blazing eyes.

"In a minute," Steve Rotwell said, "I'm going to kill your friends. But the first honor goes to you." He lifted his rapier.

And that was when *I* arrived.

Yes, Rotwell had his sword arm raised, but he was also stooping slightly, back bent, bottom out. In every respect, he presented an excellent target. I swung my boot in and around like a soccer player zeroing in on a goal.

It was a terrific kick, if I do say so myself. I connected well. Rotwell shot forward, straight at Lockwood, who flung himself to the side. Rotwell toppled right across the iron chains and lay sprawled on top of them, one arm lost in the haze beyond. He blinked; he grimaced. He gave a deep-throated cry of fear. He tried to rise. But ice was already crusting over his back; it grew out in thin fingers across the surface of his hair. With a mighty effort he got to his knees—you could see the sinews straining in his neck. But something prevented him from going farther. The gray shapes were congregating close. Something was tugging on the arm inside the circle. It jerked him inward, once, then twice. Both times, he succeeded in pulling himself away. But his strength was gone. Ice extended over his forehead, crested his cheekbones, ran down his chiseled jaw.

It was all over for Steve Rotwell. He made a last effort, cried out a final time . . .

And was sucked inside the circle. It happened so fast, so silently, so *weightlessly*, it was like he'd been inhaled. One moment he crouched there, a bulky man, encased in spreading ice; the next, the chains were completely empty. Steve Rotwell, chairman of the Rotwell Agency, was gone.

The gray shapes swirled in triumph. The chains shivered—the broken links moved across the ground. Something inside had struck against them with considerable force. They would not hold for long.

Lockwood got unsteadily to his feet; he picked up his sword. White-faced, he grabbed my hand, hurried us toward the others. "George."

"What?"

"We've got to destroy the circle. That monster flare of yours. Now might be just the time for it."

"What? Big Brenda?"

"You've given it a name?"

"I've grown kind of attached to her." George pulled the silver coconut from his belt and hefted it in his hand. "Oh, very well. Want me to throw it?"

"No! I mean—why not give it to Lucy? She's closer. No—just pass it to her. Don't throw."

George gave it to me. I was surprised by how heavy it was. "It's got a timer switch, here, Luce," he said. "What do you think? Set it to two minutes?"

I looked at the broken circle, at the mess of forms that pressed against the ruptured links of chain. There was Emma Marchment's ghost, hollow-eyed and red of mouth; there Solomon Guppy's swollen form. There too, I thought, half-hidden in the broiling mist, was something in a bright blue dress I recognized far too well. Very soon the links would break and the circle would open, and these spirits would spill out into the world.

I turned the dial and flicked the switch. "I think one minute would be about right," I said. "How fast can we all run?"

It turned out that the answer was "just fast enough." The primary explosion happened just about the time we reached the boundary fence and were heading out into the field. It was big enough to take the roof off the building behind us, and send us all tumbling, head over heels, across the grass. For an instant, night became day; you could see all the subtle greens and yellows of every weed and grass blade picked out in 3-D detail. Then the first bits of metal began raining down around us, and any interest in botany was over.

We kept on running. A few minutes later, we reached the comparative safety of the hillside. We collapsed at the top of the slope, beneath the birch trees, watching the institute facility burn.

When he'd gotten his breath back, Lockwood looked over at where George, Kipps, and Holly were sprawled in various attitudes of exhaustion. "Thank you for saving us," he said. "Lucy and I have never been so pleased to see anyone. We thought you'd all gone home."

"We nearly had," Holly said.

George nodded. "After you left us in the weapons room, we had an argument about what we should do. Kipps was all for leaving, like you ordered. But I couldn't do it. I wanted to go after you, and Holly backed me up. So then Kipps said that if he was going to jump off a cliff he'd do it with a gun in his hand, and he started loading us up with all the weapons we could carry. We were delayed by those two scientists coming through again, but we followed pretty quickly after that. You should have seen the three of us, marching down that corridor, armed to the teeth." He gave a chuckle. "Anyway, when we got to that big room, we slipped in behind the crates, and *then* things got really bad for us, because we were just in time to see you head into the circle."

"So it was *you* we heard?" My jaw dropped. "Lockwood and I thought you were more Rotwell agents on the way! That's why we ended up going inside!"

"Ah, well," George said, "sorry about that. But you can't blame us for coming back, can you? Anyway, seeing you disappearing in among the ghosts . . . That stunned us. Spirit-capes or no spirit-capes, we thought you were dead. And a moment later Rotwell and his gang all trooped back in, and that guy was there in his stupid armor, marching up the chain, ready to go inside."

"You were looking at the Creeping Shadow," I said. "No, don't ask. We've a lot to tell you, but we can do it later. So what happened next?"

"What happened," Kipps said from the grass, "was that George went mad."

George took off his glasses and rubbed his eyes. "I didn't know that bloke was the Shadow," he said, "but I knew full well what that circle was. And I thought you'd died there. So my numbness went away and I just felt . . . angry. Next thing I knew, I was setting fire to a perfectly good research facility." He gave a heavy sigh. "Hey, ho, that's how things go. It worked out all right in the end."

"I guess that's one way of putting it," Lockwood said. The

inferno had spread along the covered passageways and now reached the weapons room, with its stockpiles of flares and bombs.

"Well, we thought you were dead, didn't we?" George said. "We were upset."

Just then there was a colossal multi-plumed explosion. The remaining buildings of the Rotwell Institute facility vanished, to be replaced by successive pluming cauliflowers of white fire.

"Lucy," Lockwood said, "next time we're at home and George wants the last biscuit, remind me to let him have it."

"As far as I'm concerned," I said, "he can have the whole barrel."

We sat on the slope, the five of us, watching the destruction. Beyond the far hills, the first signs of dawn stained the eastern sky. Pretty soon, ash began glittering in the fields like frost.

VI

An Unexpected Visitor

Chapter 28

For more than a thousand years, probably ever since the last raven had finished picking at the skeletons left by the Vikings and the Saxons on their ancient battleground, Aldbury Castle had been a backwater, forgotten and ignored. Centuries of action and incident had passed it by. Even its recent epidemic of ghosts had earned it no attention. Yet the "Rotwell Incident" (which was how the newspapers subsequently named the disaster at the institute facility) changed all that overnight. At a stroke it became the most famous location in England.

The response started early. At eight thirty a.m., roughly three hours after explosions had lit up the sky behind the hills, and with the column of black smoke still funneling up above the trees, the first vehicles began rolling through the village. And they didn't stop coming. All that day a convoy of cars, trucks, and windowless vans, filled to the brim with DEPRAC personnel, Rotwell agents, and armed police, went racing grimly eastward through the woods. Before long, with word spreading and the first journalists arriving on the scene, DEPRAC cordoned off the village altogether. A barrier was erected at the bridge west of the green, and another on the lane, just inside the entrance to the eastern woods. Guards were posted, and no one was allowed in or out.

That suited us fine. We weren't in shape to go anywhere. We rose late and spent the day in the taproom of the Old Sun Inn, keeping out of sight.

From time to time, word came of activities out on the fields. Members of DEPRAC teams called in for sandwiches and refreshments, and from the tidbits of information they let slip to Danny Skinner and his father, we got a fair idea of what was going on.

Clean-up squads were wading through the wreckage of the Rotwell Institute site. Most of the facility had been destroyed, and what areas remained had been quickly sealed off from all but the most specialized operatives. The ruins of the central building in particular were out of bounds, but it was common knowledge that certain "unauthorized" weapons had been found in neighboring hangars, and that this was the probable cause of the explosion and the fire. Even more sensational was the news that Steve Rotwell himself was missing. He had been at the facility the previous day and had not been located. So far, he was the only presumed casualty. Several surviving scientists, found wandering in the surrounding countryside, had been taken in for questioning.

"And it won't be long before *we're* rounded up, too, I suppose." This was Kipps, speaking from his seat near the fire. His turtleneck was pulled high, and his face had a bruised and swollen look. All our faces did. We were like a selection of old fruit, dropped too often and left in the bowl to go soft.

Lockwood was playing cards with Holly. He shook his head, an action that made him wince and rub the back of his neck. "I think we'll be fine," he said. "What Rotwell was doing in that site counts as major criminal activity—all those secret weapons, for a start, not to mention the ghost-bombs that were used in the carnival assassination attempt last year. And then there's the iron circle. I'd be very surprised if Johnson and the others talk openly about what happened last night—at least at first. A lot depends on what the fires have actually left behind."

"I was wondering," Holly said. "Shouldn't we tell DEPRAC ourselves?" She had spent even longer than usual in our shared bathroom that morning, and by some magic was almost restored to her pristine self, despite flare burns on her brow and chin. But the gun-toting, wild-haired madwoman of the night before was in there somewhere, I knew. It made me look upon her with fond affection.

"Tell DEPRAC what?" George said. "They clearly have plenty of evidence about what's been going on."

"Well, no, I mean about the circle—about the man in armor going through. It's very important. We've got to, haven't we?"

Lockwood grunted. "Tell old Barnes? I don't know. . . . We have never been the flavor of the month with him at the best of times. Think he'll believe us?"

"Probably just clap us in prison," George said. "Arson, burglary, general assault . . . Let's face it, he'd have some tasty options."

"I think we *have* to tell him anyhow," I said. "Holly's right. It's just too big a thing to keep quiet about. When we stood in the graveyard that first night, we saw the way the Creeping Sha—that armored guy—stirred up the ghosts just by passing by. And then, last night . . ." My voice trailed off; I shivered, despite the fire. "We did exactly the same ourselves. There are so many implications. . . ."

"Implications that DEPRAC aren't likely to believe, I fear." Lockwood put down his hand of cards. "But maybe you're right. I guess we better *had* tell Barnes, if we get the opportunity."

Part of the problem about telling Inspector Barnes, or even talking about events among ourselves, was that what had happened to us was so overwhelming. Lockwood and I in particular found it difficult to talk about our time on the other side of the circle with any clarity. We knew what we *thought* had happened. We knew that we had crossed over to a place that seemed very like the world we understood, except that it was inhabited not by the living, but by the dead. In that place *we* were the interlopers, and our presence had roused the inhabitants to action, just like the Creeping Shadow's had. That much we sort of knew. But coming to terms with even *that* knowledge was like standing on the edge of a terrible precipice, and trying to take a step forward into space. The step could not easily be taken. The mind simply rebelled.

When, on our return to the inn, Lockwood and I described our experiences to the others, everyone had gone very quiet. Even George had not said much, though his glasses gleamed as he stared long into the fire. "Fascinating," he said, over and over. "That's *fascinating.* . . . This is going to need a lot of thought. . . ."

Holly's immediate focus had been quite different. "If this is true," she'd said, sitting alongside us and looking intently at our faces, "what I want to know is how *you're* feeling. Do you feel well? Are you both okay?"

"We're fine," Lockwood said, laughing. "Don't worry yourself. The capes did a great job of protecting us, didn't they, Luce?" And I'd smilingly agreed with him.

Glancing in the mirror later, however, I'd thought I looked more pale than usual. It was hard to be sure, just as I couldn't really tell if the weakness I felt was the normal end-of-case exhaustion. Probably it was. I didn't have the energy to care either way.

The one individual who certainly *did* have plenty of energy that first morning was the skull in the jar. Much to its chagrin, it had been locked up with our equipment in the inn's storage closet. Holly had refused to let it into our bedroom when we got back, and to be honest, I couldn't blame her.

"*What's the point of rescuing me,*" it grumbled when I popped my head around the door, "*if you lock me away in a damp cubbyhole like this? I haven't got a nose, but I can tell just by looking that it smells of onions and pee.*"

"It so doesn't." I stepped in, and took a hearty sniff. "Well, there's certainly no trace of onions. And it's a lot better than being incinerated like all those other Sources back at the facility, so you'd better be thankful."

"*Oh, I'm doing backflips of gratitude.*" The hollow eyes narrowed as it looked at me. "*And while we're on that subject . . . Is there anything you'd like to say to me?*"

I scratched my nose. "Should there be?"

"You're here for a reason."

"Actually, I'm here to get potatoes for lunch. George is cooking fries. . . . But I suppose, while I'm with you . . ."

"Come on. Spit it out."

I took a deep breath. "It was you, wasn't it?" I said. "On the Other Side. When we were lost and couldn't find the iron chain. You showed me where it was."

The face grinned. *"Saving your life? Now does that honestly sound like me?"*

"Well, whoever it was, I am grateful. And I think I understand something else. 'Death's in Life and Life's in Death,' you keep telling me. And now I know why. Because ghosts have entered the living world, while . . . while living humans have entered . . ."

I broke off. I couldn't quite bring myself to say it. Plus, the face in the jar was doing something off-putting with its tongue.

There was a short silence. *"Finally!"* the skull said. *"Finally we're getting somewhere! All these months, and you never figured it out. Yes, last night you were the walking proof of my words. And perhaps now you see why you and I get along so well. Because we both inhabit two worlds. You sense the other one all the time; you've always had glimpses of it all your days—and now you've actually been there, too. We're caught between life and death, Lucy, you and I. And that's what makes us the perfect team."* It gave me a companionable nod. *"Hey, remember my suggestion? Carlyle and Skull? The offer of a partnership still stands. I'll even let you put your name first."*

"You seem to be forgetting about Lockwood." I felt the conversation had gone far enough. I located the sack of potatoes and carried it to the door.

"Oh, Lockwood, Shmockwood. He's more drawn to death than either of us. You know that. He won't be lasting long. A partnership with me is a much better bet. . . . Wait, where are you going? Are you insane? We're on the verge of something special here, and all you're thinking about is fries?! Come back!"

But I was out the door. Sometimes fries are the only way to *keep* you sane.

The weather that day was unseasonably warm, so we ate our lunch under an awning in the pub garden. From time to time, DEPRAC vehicles sped by. Danny Skinner, roused to a crescendo of excitement by the events of the night, hovered near, asking questions that we couldn't or wouldn't answer. Eventually he left us to swing like an ape from the gate and stare at the cloud of smoke beyond the trees.

A big black car drove out of the woods and came to a halt outside the Old Sun Inn. Out stepped Inspector Montagu Barnes, looking wearier and more rumpled than ever. He pushed open the gate, with Danny Skinner still attached to it, and walked over the grass toward us. Here he stood for a while, appraising our bruised and battered faces.

"Morning, Inspector," Lockwood said.

George held out a bowl. "Want a fry?"

Barnes said nothing. He regarded us for a long time.

"Had a difficult night?" he said at last.

"They certainly have." That was Mr. Skinner, bustling out from the taproom. He, at least, was in good spirits; it had been the busiest day at the inn for many a year. "Mr. Lockwood and his friends have been hard at work ridding Aldbury Castle of its ghosts, sir. Only been at it two nights, and there's a noticeable improvement every-where. Cleared my house, and many others. Helping us all sleep soundly in our beds. Young heroes they are, sir, every one."

Barnes's mustache curled doubtfully downward. "Really? First I've heard of it." He said nothing further, but stood with his hands in his trench coat pockets until the innkeeper had returned inside.

"Glad to hear you're keeping busy," Barnes went on. "And out of trouble, too."

"Yes, Inspector," Lockwood said. I looked at him. He caught my eye.

We sat there quietly.

"Well, if there's nothing further, I'll be on my way." Barnes turned to go.

"Actually, Inspector," I said. "There *is* something."

"We urgently need to talk with you, Mr. Barnes," Lockwood said.

The inspector gazed at us. He lifted a hand as if something had just occurred to him. "That boy over there," he said idly. "The one swinging like a maniac on that gate."

"What about him?"

"Think he'd like to earn a little money?"

Almost before the last word had left his lips, Danny Skinner had crossed the garden and was standing to attention at Barnes's side. He performed an outlandish salute. "Anything I can do for you, mister? Just say the word."

"I need lunch for me and three of my officers. Think you could go in there and rustle up some sandwiches? There's five pounds in it for you if they're edible."

"Yes, sir. Certainly, sir. They'll be the best you ever tasted." He trotted into the house.

"Your five is safe, Mr. Barnes," George said. "The wrapper will be the only edible part, take it from me."

Barnes nodded grimly. "That's not the point. I *thought* he looked like a boy with excessively sharp hearing—leastways, his ears are big enough—and I was right. Tell you what, why don't you walk with me a minute, Mr. Lockwood, Miss Carlyle? Come out on the green and take some air."

Barnes left the garden, crossed the road. He led us across the green to a spot some distance from the inn. "Now," he said, "it's quieter here. No one around. What was it you wanted?"

"It's about what happened last night," I said. "About the institute."

"The institute?" Barnes rubbed his mustache and stared into the middle distance. "Well, investigations are currently under way at the facility. All I can tell you is there was some kind of accident there last night."

"Well, that's just it," Lockwood said. "It wasn't exactly an accident—"

"Some experiment that went tragically wrong," the inspector continued. "I hear there've even been casualties."

"Yes! And Steve Rotwell—"

"I wish I could tell you more," Barnes said, interrupting me, "I really wish I could. Thank you for your interest. Unfortunately, that's all I know."

We looked at him.

"And *you two*, of course, know nothing about it, either."

Lockwood frowned. "Well—"

"You weren't anywhere near that place," Barnes said.

"Erm, well, in fact we—"

"You were coincidentally dealing with some local ghosts in Aldbury Castle—in a case that was quite separate to whatever was going on out on those fields. You have no interest in Rotwell or his institute, or what they were doing in that building at the heart of it, and if you have any sense, you'll make that abundantly clear to anyone who asks you. And anyone who *doesn't*, for that matter. I'd spread that information loud and quickly, if I were you. Do you understand me? Mr. Lockwood? Miss Carlyle?" Barnes surveyed us with his tired, pouchy eyes. "One of DEPRAC's jobs, you see, is to prevent bad things from happening to agents, even irritating ones like you. I wouldn't want to wake up one morning and discover that there'd been four *more* accidents at Portland Row. It would really put me off my breakfast egg."

Lockwood looked at me. He took a deep breath. "Thank you, Inspector," he said loudly. "You've been very clear. I'm sorry you can't tell us more about what happened up at that institute. We'll just have to accept that we'll never know."

Barnes nodded peaceably. "Perfect. That's the idea."

We stayed at Aldbury Castle for two more nights, and made half-hearted forays on each to see what supernatural activity remained. But as Mr. Skinner had said, signs of the village ghosts had greatly diminished. With the destruction of the iron circle at the Rotwell facility, and the end of the Creeping Shadow's mysterious comings and goings, the cluster at once calmed down. Many of the Visitors did not appear at all, while those that *did* seemed weaker and less vicious. It was easy to claim (as we did) that this change was entirely due to our own zeal. We made lots of noise running about the place, and threw occasional salt-bombs around to make it look like we were doing something. Mostly we just stayed at the inn and played cards.

On our fifth morning in the country, things had quietened down over on the eastern fields. Many of the DEPRAC cars had left, and the cordons by the village had been lifted. By now our heroic status in the village was assured. There were still a few Type One ghosts kicking around, but nothing that needed to delay us. Kipps in particular was keen to head off—for two nights he'd been forced to choose between sleeping in the bed with George, or in the storage closet with the skull (he'd preferred the skull, for unnamed reasons)—but we were all eager to get home. A farewell committee from the village accompanied us to the station, Danny Skinner marching proudly at the head. We were given gifts of root vegetables. Lockwood took possession of an envelope stuffed with cash—our payment from the grateful villagers. The children threw garlands of flowers. When the train departed, handkerchiefs were waved until we disappeared from view.

On our way home, I sat opposite Lockwood. He seemed pale and tired. In the days since our visit to the institute, we hadn't spoken privately of what had happened to us. Occasionally, when our eyes met, we shared something that couldn't be expressed in words.

We smiled at each other, and gazed out at the woods and fields.

It was a beautiful spring scene. The column of smoke above the eastern hills had long since drifted away on the wind; nevertheless, a hint of it hung in the air. It had entered the train car with us at Aldbury Castle station, and through the opened windows, the smell of distant burning stayed with us all the way to London.

Chapter 29

TERRORIST LINK TO ROTWELL AGENCY!

FORBIDDEN WEAPONS FOUND AT RUINED INSTITUTE

STEVE ROTWELL STILL MISSING, PRESUMED DEAD

FIRST INTERVIEW WITH DEPRAC INVESTIGATOR

MONTAGU BARNES INSIDE

The sensational discoveries made in the rubble of the ruined Rotwell Institute facility in Hampshire continued yesterday, with confirmation that police had uncovered the remains of a large "weapons factory" in one of the outbuildings. Among the items recovered are said to be several unexploded "ghost-bombs" of the kind used in a terrorist attack on the London carnival last November, in which an attempt on Ms. Penelope Fittes's life was made. Several members of the institute staff, including facility chief Mr. Saul Johnson, have been arrested, amid claims that they and agency head Mr. Steve Rotwell were intimately involved in that attack. Mr. Rotwell's whereabouts remain unknown, but it is believed that he may have perished in the explosions that destroyed the facility.

In today's exclusive interview in the *Times*, DEPRAC chief investigator Mr. Montagu Barnes gives a detailed account of his team's dangerous exploration of the ruins. "It was an inferno when we arrived," he says. "But we managed to discover a store of illicit weapons, including deadly ectoplasm-guns. Ghost-bombs are just the tip of the iceberg, believe me." He refused to comment on the contents of the central building at the site, which was severely damaged in the incident. "Sadly, the purpose of that building is not yet clear. Rest assured that inquiries are continuing."

Police investigations widened yesterday, following reports of forbidden Sources found stored at the institute. Several arrests have been made among staff at the Greater London Metropolitan Furnaces in Clerkenwell, and more are expected in the coming days. However, such developments pale into insignificance next to the crisis surrounding the Rotwell Agency. With its leader missing, and other key executives also implicated in serious crimes, public confidence in the organization has plummeted, and its future hangs in the balance. Latest reports suggest that DEPRAC has invited Fittes Agency head Ms. Penelope Fittes to take temporary charge of the rudderless organization in an effort to stabilize its fortunes. She will run both companies from her offices in the Strand.

Full Barnes Interview: see page 3

"Ghost-bombs and Plasm-guns"—True Secrets of the Weapons Factory: see pages 6–7

"Maimed Lion": A Pull-out History of the Rotwell Agency: see pages 25–33

"Well," Lockwood said, "that's another investigation successfully swept under the rug." He tossed the paper onto the breakfast table and reached for the toast. "Old Barnes is a master at this sort of stuff. All that flimflam with the illegal weapons allows him to quietly gloss over the only important thing, which is the iron circle. Still, I suppose we should be happy that he's glossed over *our* part in the affair, too."

"I'm *very* happy about that," Holly said.

We all were. We were happy about many things that morning. And because of this, we'd decided to enjoy an official celebratory breakfast at 35 Portland Row.

It was the day after our return from Aldbury Castle, and the sun was shining bright. Holly had thrown open the kitchen door. Birds sang, new leaves sparkled; cool spring air flooded the room, almost driving out the smell of George's smoked kippers. Best of all, the team was there to share the occasion.

The *whole* team, that is. Including me.

Part of my happiness stemmed from the fact that I'd spent the previous night back in my old attic room. Back *for real*, I mean. In a symbolic gesture, George had even taken away most of his clothes. I still had to be careful what I stepped on—the floor was likely to remain a minefield of eerie socks and hankies for a while yet—but it was my place again now.

Well, mine . . . *and* the skull's. While I slept it had occupied its old position on the windowsill, from where it could (it claimed) enjoy looking out at the quiet night, and (more probably) try to scare the toddlers in the house opposite by glowing an unholy green. This morning it was down in the kitchen, too, since its retrieval was another thing we were celebrating that day. Within thirty seconds of arriving, however, it had disgraced itself by leering at Holly in such a knowing way that she'd dropped her plate of whole wheat waffles into her lap. It had then been removed from the table and placed in a dark corner by the sink, its jar half shrouded by a dishcloth.

The skull wasn't the only morally dubious guest that morning. Quill Kipps was there, too. While not himself a member of Lockwood & Co. (which would, in his words, be a fate worse "than being whipped naked across Wimbledon Common"), there was talk of him being a consultant who might be called in from time to time. He was with us that morning to discuss this, and also to celebrate our return to London. Eggs were being poached, bacon was fried, and even Holly's super-healthy waffles glistened temptingly under oodles of honey and fresh butter. We all ate contentedly and well.

Lockwood sat at the head of the table, passing laden plates, making sure everyone had their fill. I was relieved to see that he looked like his normal self. His color had returned, and he moved with his customary ease. Physically it was taking both of us a long time to recover from our walk through the iron circle. I still felt weary, and had been troubled by obscure nightmares—but these seemed to be lessening. On a morning such as this it was easy to imagine that the effects of our ordeal would soon fade.

At last Lockwood banged a fork against a milk jug. "Time for some toasts," he said. "I'd like to thank you all for your efforts in Aldbury Castle. George, Holly, and Quill—you did great things at the institute. Without you, Lucy and I wouldn't have survived."

Glasses were raised and orange juice drunk. Then Lockwood turned to me.

"Lucy," he said, "you deserve a special toast. First, for coming back to us. Lockwood and Company was incomplete without you. And second, for intervening when Rotwell had me beaten. You saved my life that night. Thank you."

His eyes fixed on mine. I did my best to look super-casual, but I could feel a bit of blushing going on. Then I realized that everyone was watching us.

"Ooh, awkward," George said.

Lockwood grinned and tossed a crust of bread at him. "The truth is, we all rely on each other. Take any one of us away, and we're all weakened. Together, there's nothing we can't do."

"Hear, hear," Holly said.

"And that brings me to my last toast," Lockwood finished. "To *new horizons*. Because after the Creeping Shadow and the iron circle and what Lucy and I found on the Other Side, I believe everything has changed. Between us, we've discovered things we never imagined. Barnes wants us to keep quiet about it, but we all know that's impossible. From now on, the scope of our inquiries will be wider. There are many new questions to answer, and our investigations have only just begun."

We drank and put our glasses down. For a short space everyone was silent; we listened to the birdsong through the open door.

"What *I* want to know," Holly said, "is what the Creeping Shadow guy was *doing* on the Other Side. Steve Rotwell alluded to some kind of purpose. He wasn't wandering around out there just for the fun of it. What was he after? Why would anyone take such risks? I can't imagine *anything* important enough to justify it."

"Doesn't *have* to be anything specific." That was George. Not content with his kippers, he was preparing a final bacon sandwich on an impressive scale. "Sometimes it's just about exploring the unknown. Give me a suit of iron armor and *I'd* happily travel to the Other Side."

"Might need to be an extra-large-size suit, particularly if you eat that massive sandwich," Lockwood said. "You can always borrow the spirit-cape, though."

"It's such a pity I lost the other one," I said. The memory made me feel bad.

Lockwood shrugged. "Can't be helped. Besides, who knows what's still packed away upstairs? But we were talking about the Shadow. He was definitely doing *something*. Rotwell said as much. We've got to find out what."

"First we have to get our heads around all of this," Kipps said. "I'm not sure I can."

"Nor me," Holly agreed. "I'm just amazed you've both come back in one piece."

I didn't say anything. Whenever I closed my eyes, I could still see the black sky stretching over the alternate, frosted world.

"Here's what I think," George said, chewing on a piece of bacon. "Lucy and Lockwood went to the place where ghosts come from. At least, it's where *some* of them are hanging around, ready to step through weak points to our world. Normally we don't have access to it, though those of us with psychic Sight get glimpses of it, I guess. But then the Shadow crossed over and started strolling around over there, and that got the spirits *very* excited. He had the effect of weakening the barrier between worlds. When you saw him in the churchyard, he was like a ghost, wasn't he? You were seeing him on the Other Side—the barrier had completely frayed."

"I wonder if any living person saw *us*," Lockwood said. "Never thought to ask."

"So what I'm interested in," George went on, "is whether anyone's stirred them up like that before. And if so"—he gestured with a mustard spoon at the map on the wall, the one showing the concentric spread of historic hauntings across the country—"what effect it's had on the Problem."

The doorbell rang. Holly was closest. She disappeared into the hall.

"Big mysteries," Kipps mused. "Going to be tough to solve."

"Have confidence, Quill," Lockwood said. "With the team we've got, I think we'll do just fine." He stretched back in his chair. "Who was at the door, Hol?"

Holly had reappeared, and in the instant before she spoke, we all noticed how pale she was, and how stiff her expression. "We have two visitors, Lockwood," she said. "I didn't . . . I couldn't . . . Well, I mean to say, they're here right now. I've had to let them in."

She stood aside. Behind her, smiling her glossy smile, was Penelope Fittes.

Ms. Fittes stepped into the kitchen. It was a small room, and there wasn't much space for her. She gazed around at the debris of our meal. She wore a green dress, mid-length, with a dark brown coat on top. As always, she might have been on her way to a dinner party. "Good morning, everyone," she said. "I hope I'm not intruding. May I come in?"

Well, she already *had*, of course. Lockwood jumped up. "Of course, of course. Please—"

"Just a little visit. No, don't get up. I wouldn't want to disturb you. I do have someone else with me, too." She gestured behind her at a slim young gentleman, with curly blond hair and a neatly groomed mustache, standing in the shadows of the hall. He wore an elegant tweed suit and had a sword-stick hanging at his side. "You know Sir Rupert Gale, I think? An old friend of the Fittes family."

"Yes, indeed . . . yes. I'm sorry about the mess here," Lockwood said. "Shall we go into the living room?"

Ms. Fittes gave a smile. "No, no. I'd like to see where you do your work in your little agency. What a busy breakfast you've been having! And this tablecloth, with all these sketches . . ." She leaned forward to inspect them. "So quaint! So charming . . . well, possibly not *those* doodles there."

Lockwood was hurrying over with a spare chair. "I'm sorry. I keep telling George to stick to ghosts. Please sit, ma'am. Sir Rupert, would you care to have mine?"

"No, no thank you. I'm good." Sir Rupert Gale took up position at the window. He leaned back against the sink and crossed one ankle over the other.

It was no great pleasure for us to have Sir Rupert in our house, since we knew him to be a rogue and a wealthy collector of illicit relics. His past encounters with us had been laced with the threat of violence. But in truth, having Penelope Fittes there was more disconcerting still.

This most illustrious person sat in our private space, smiling at us. The chair that she occupied was a fold-out wicker one, rather inexpensive, with a few ectoplasm burns along the back where it had played a part in one of George's experiments. Nevertheless, with her long limbs elegantly arranged upon it, and the sunlight shining on her emerald dress, the lady somehow made it look quite chic. She seemed at perfect ease. By contrast, we all sat (or stood) in nonplussed silence. Kipps in particular looked thoroughly morti-fied. He subtly insinuated himself behind the door, trying to keep out of sight.

Lockwood shook his confusion away. "Tea, ma'am? The pot's just brewed."

"Thank you, Anthony. I'll take a cup."

As the necessary formalities were completed, Ms. Fittes gazed around the kitchen, her eyes taking in every detail—the remains of breakfast, the salt and iron in the corner, the door to the garden, George's map of England on the wall. "I've come here to thank you," she said. "To thank you for your services. It's really been most kind of you."

"Services, ma'am?" Lockwood passed the tea over.

"I see you've been reading the papers." She indicated the front page of the *Times*. "You'll have gathered that there are many changes happening in London. In particular, you may have heard that the Rotwell and Fittes agencies are entering an association. Well, I can tell you unofficially that it will be more than that. It is a merger. Rotwell's is disgraced and in crisis; without swift action, it will fail.

So, from now on it will be fully assimilated into the Fittes Agency. That means it is *part* of Fittes, and its executives will report to me."

She looked around at us, this woman who now controlled the two largest and most powerful organizations in London. "Congratulations, ma'am," Lockwood said slowly. "That's . . . really quite something."

"Indeed. It *is* an outcome for the books. Much work lies ahead for me if I'm to knock Rotwell's into shape, but I am confident this can be done. At any rate, I am in charge of both agencies now. And I believe that I owe much of my good fortune to you."

It was one of those moments when everyone works so hard to look innocent and uncomprehending that the atmosphere at once becomes poisonous with knowingness and guilt. Over at the sink, Sir Rupert Gale smiled; he picked up one of George's favorite striped mugs and considered it idly.

"Pardon me, ma'am," Lockwood said. "I don't quite understand. We happened to be working in a village quite nearby, yes, but as to the events at the institute, and the cause of the disaster—if, if that's what you're referring to—we're in the dark, just like everyone else."

Ms. Fittes had an odd little laugh; I'd forgotten just how low and husky it was. "That's all right. I'm not that silly Inspector Barnes. You don't have to be careful with *me*. But there, I won't press you. Let us just imagine, for a moment, that you saw things you were not supposed to see. Perhaps they confused you. Perhaps they still prey on your minds."

It was obvious what she was talking about, but having denied it at the outset, we couldn't very well admit to anything now. Lockwood pretended to consider. "We did come upon some very frightening apparitions in the village. George in particular ran a mile from an eyeless girl—isn't that right, George?"

"I left her in the dust," George said.

The lady smiled at us. "You're very droll. Suffice it to say that some of the Rotwell scientists—I wonder, should I call them *Fittes* scientists now?—some of the workers at the institute have been talking to the police. There was mention of intruders."

"Five intruders," Sir Rupert Gale said. "Count them. Fingers of one hand."

"Now, I don't know precisely what it is you saw or heard," Ms. Fittes said, "but I would advise you to cast it from your minds. Poor Steve Rotwell was an eccentric, driven man who desired strange knowledge that is forbidden to us all. What dark experiments he may have chosen to attempt in his private facility are not for us to fathom. Certainly they should be of no consequence to any law-abiding agency."

We sat in silence, trying to gauge her words. Up by the sink the dishcloth hung dark and quiet, too. I could see a glimpse of the jar, but no stirrings within. At least the skull was keeping out of it. That was one blessing.

Lockwood spoke quietly. "I think I understand you. You're requesting that we 'forget' anything we may or may not have seen."

"'Requesting' isn't the word I would have chosen—but, yes, that's right."

"May I ask why?"

The lady sipped her tea. "For fifty years," she said, "we have been at war with supernatural forces. Tampering with them, or seeking to turn them to personal gain, as the foolish Rotwell did, is a recipe for spiritual disaster. The mysteries of death are sacrosanct, and must not be explored." Penelope Fittes regarded us. "I think you know that as well as I do. Some things are better left unknown."

George stirred. "Forgive me, ma'am. I don't think that's true. Surely knowledge of every kind is vital to us in our battle with the Problem."

"Dear George, you are so *very* young." That husky laugh again. "I can see that such concepts might be difficult for you to grasp."

"No, George is right," Lockwood said. "George is always right. We shouldn't fear uncovering things that are shrouded in darkness. We should shine light on them. Like the lantern in your agency's logo. That's what an agent *does*, after all."

Ms. Fittes looked at him levelly. "Don't tell me you're rejecting my suggestion again?"

"I'm afraid so. . . . Yes, we reject your 'request,' or order, or whatever it is." Lockwood's voice was suddenly crisp. "Forgive me, but we're not part of your organization. You can't waltz into our kitchen and tell us what to do."

"Oh, but actually, we can," the lady said. "Isn't that right, Rupert?"

"Certainly is, ma'am." Sir Rupert Gale stepped forward from the window, strolled in leisurely fashion behind our backs. "For some of us," he said, "actions will have consequences from now on." He reached down, plucked George's sandwich from his plate, and took an enormous bite out of it. "And for others, there will be no consequences at all. Like this. Mm, excellent bacon! And with mustard, too. Very nice."

"How dare you—" In an instant Lockwood was out of his chair

and halfway around the table. He stopped abruptly. There'd been a flash of silver, equally fast. Sir Rupert's sword was in his hand, the point hovering a short distance from Lockwood's midriff. He scarcely looked at Lockwood, but chewed placidly, inspecting the crusts of the sandwich.

"Threatening an unarmed man, are you, Sir Rupert?" George said. "Classy."

"You could pass me that butter knife, George," Lockwood murmured. "That would probably be enough for me to deal with him."

"You *are* a card," Sir Rupert Gale said.

Penelope Fittes raised her hand. "There will be no fighting at all. This is a civilized visit. Rupert, put your sword away. Anthony, please sit down."

Lockwood hesitated a long time, then slowly returned to his seat. Sir Rupert Gale sheathed his sword, still chewing.

"That's better," Ms. Fittes said. She gave her little laugh. "You boys! What *shall* I do with you? Well, the point I'm making is very simple, and I can't see why you should have any objection to it. You have a charming little agency, and you are more than welcome to keep on doing your charming little things. But from now on, you will stick to the investigations that suit you better—the small hauntings that so plague our society. There will be no more silliness like this"—she pointed to George's poster on the wall—"no more idle speculation, no more getting above your intellectual station. You, dear George, have always been full of foolish fancies. It would serve you better to forget them and spend a bit of time on useful matters. Your appearance, for instance. Tidy yourself up! Go out and meet a girl, make friends."

"Starting up an acquaintance with a stick of deodorant wouldn't go amiss, either," Sir Rupert Gale said. He patted George's shoulder.

George sat there, impassive.

"Don't look so serious, all of you!" Penelope Fittes smiled around at us. "You have all the makings of a perfect company, albeit in miniature. A stout and sturdy researcher—that's George. And Lockwood, of course—the resolute man of action. And you even have a perfect secretary and typist in sweet Ms. Munro here. Not perhaps the bravest agent, from what my new colleagues at Rotwell's tell me, but charming to look at—"

"That's enough!" It was my voice. My chair fell back; I was on my feet. "You know nothing about Holly—or any of us. Leave her alone!"

"Oh, Miss Carlyle." The lady turned to me, then, and for the first time I felt the full ferocity of her smile. "I can't tell you how sorry I am that you didn't take me up on my offer the other week. We could have done great things together. But there we are, there's no use crying over missed opportunities . . . which brings me to *you*, Mr. Kipps."

Thus for the first time Penelope Fittes acknowledged the existence of Quill Kipps, who stood behind the door, shrinking back against the trash can as if trying to compress himself out of existence. As she turned her smile on him, he flinched.

"I hear you've been busy, too, Quill," she said, "frolicking around with spectacles that don't belong to you. What fun. I hope you've enjoyed spending time with your new friends. But in all your excitement, don't forget the important thing, which is that by your own choice you are an outcast from my agency, and henceforth barred from all significant work and status. Backsliders like you will not be tolerated, and I shall make an example of you. Your pension will be confiscated; your reputation destroyed. I will see to it that you never work for any reputable psychic investigation company again."

"It's all right, Kipps," Lockwood said. "You can work for us, if you want. We're not reputable."

Kipps said nothing; he was very pale, his nose and lips a purplish blue. He looked almost dead from fear and mortification.

"Well, I'd better be going," Penelope Fittes said. "There's so much to be done. . . . You know, life is strange, isn't it, Anthony? You refused my earlier offer—yet now, inadvertently, you've done me more of a favor than I could ever have imagined. Thank you for the tea." She rose, looking around the kitchen a final time. "This is *such* a nice little house. So charming, so vulnerable. Have a lovely morning."

With that she went out. By the window, Sir Rupert Gale finished George's sandwich. Then he took a dish towel from the draining board, wiped the grease from his hands, and dropped the cloth into the sink. Smiling at us, he left the room. We heard the front door close, his footsteps fade on the path outside; shortly afterward, Ms. Fittes's car purred away into the bright spring day.

We all remained exactly where we were, sitting, standing, shrouded in silence—Lockwood in his chair, George and Holly on either side of the table, me at the far end, Kipps by the door. No one looked at anyone else, but we were all aware of how still the others were, how rigid. We stayed there, joined together by a little web of shock.

Then Lockwood laughed. The spell broke—we all stirred, as

though waking from a dream. We looked at him where he sat, smiling broadly, eyes glittering.

"Well," he said, "they've made their position pretty clear, haven't they? We're supposed to keep our noses out of this."

Kipps shifted his feet as if they pained him. George coughed slightly.

"So let's have a show of hands," Lockwood went on. "Who agrees that we *should* be obedient little agents, do what she says, and keep our noses clean?"

He looked around at us. None of us said a thing.

"Okay." Lockwood straightened the Thinking Cloth, making it nice and neat. "That's good to know. So, hands up, whoever thinks that in fact we ought to do the *opposite* of what she said. Whoever thinks that since Penelope has chosen to take the gloves off so completely, we are quite within our rights to make *her* the target of our subsequent investigations? No matter what threats she and that preening cad might make."

We all silently raised our hands. Even Kipps, though he made it look as if he was really intending to scratch the back of his head and only did it as an afterthought, with a tentative, half-bent arm. All of us raised them, there in that room where the spring sun shone brightly through the window.

"Excellent," Lockwood said. "Thank you. I'm glad, because that's what I think, too. Let's clear up breakfast. George, why don't you put the kettle on? It's time for Lockwood and Company to get to work."

—

Two minutes later I was standing at the sink, doing the dishes, staring out at nothing, when I noticed a green glow coming from behind the dishcloth. I flipped it away—to find the ghost in the jar watching me. For once, its face was only mildly repulsive. It looked very sober and serious. *"Nice speech from Lockwood, there,"* the skull said. *"Very prettily done. I could almost believe for a minute you weren't doomed. Which I suppose was his intention. So . . . fill me in. I caught a peek from under that cloth. Who was that who just came in?"*

"Penelope Fittes."

"Who's she?"

"Head of the Fittes Agency. And ruler of all London, it now appears—in *her* own mind, at least. Get with the beat. I thought you knew that."

"Oh, I'm just a poor old skull, I am. A bit slow on the uptake. So that's Penelope Fittes, is it? Head of Fittes House? Granddaughter of old Marissa who started it all?"

"Yes. And she suddenly isn't quite as friendly as we thought. . . . What's with you? Why are you laughing?"

"No reason. . . . How old would you say she was?"

"What, are you thinking of proposing marriage? How do I know?"

"I see she had a bodyguard with her," the skull said. *"That blond fellow with the peach fuzz mustache."*

I grunted. "Yeah. Sir Rupert Gale. A nasty piece of work."

"Yes, a smiling, blue-eyed killer. But it's no surprise. She always did have someone there to do her dirty work."

"Who did?"

"Marissa Fittes."

"We're talking about Penelope."

"Mmm . . . yes. Better rinse that plate again, Lucy. Still has ketchup on it."

I went on with the dishes, staring out into the garden. At my side, the skull continued to chuckle witlessly to itself.

"All right," I said finally. "Let me in on the joke."

"I met Marissa once," the skull said. "I spoke with her. I told you that, remember?"

"Yes. I know. She put you in that jar."

"It's pretty weird to see her standing there again."

"Does Penelope resemble her?" I thought of the wizened old woman in the photographs at Fittes House. But that was at the end of Marissa's life; perhaps earlier, she'd looked more like Penelope.

"You could say that. She's no different than she was fifty years ago. Eek, it freaks me out, and I'm a skull in a jar. Anyway, don't let me distract you. You've moved on to the silverware now. Ooh, jammy knives and eggy spoons. Exciting times."

"I'm sorry," I said. "You're losing me. Run that past me again."

"How has she managed to do that, I wonder? Because she really is no different. Eighty years old or more, and she almost looks younger, if anything."

I gazed at the ghost. It gazed at me. Then its eyes rolled in opposite directions.

"Let me put it in words of few syllables so you can understand, Lucy. Penelope Fittes isn't Marissa's granddaughter. She's her."

I stopped where I was, with my hands in the soapy water, and stared at the jar. Behind me, George was putting tea bags into cups.

The kettle was boiling. Lockwood and Kipps were arguing about something. Holly was in the garden, shaking crumbs off the Thinking Cloth. And all the time the ghost in the jar was watching me with its black and glittering eyes.

"She's *her*?" I repeated.

"*Exactly. Penelope Fittes is Marissa Fittes. They're one and the same person.*"

Glossary

Agency, Psychic Investigation—A business specializing in the containment and destruction of **ghosts**. There are more than a dozen agencies in London alone. The largest two (the Fittes Agency and the Rotwell Agency) have hundreds of employees; the smallest (Lockwood & Co.) has three. Most agencies are run by adult supervisors, but all rely heavily on children with strong psychic **Talent**.

Apparition—The shape formed by a **ghost** during a **manifestation**. Apparitions usually mimic the shape of the dead person, but animals and objects are also seen. Some can be quite unusual. The **Specter** in the recent Limehouse Docks case manifested as a greenly glowing king cobra, while the infamous Bell Street Horror took the guise of a patchwork doll. Powerful or weak, most ghosts do not (or cannot) alter their appearance. **Changers** are the exception to this rule.

Aura—The radiance surrounding many **apparitions**. Most auras are fairly faint, and are seen best out of the corner of the eye. Strong, bright auras are known as **other-light**. A few **ghosts**, such as **Dark Specters**, radiate black auras that are darker than the night around them.

Bone Man*—Name given to a particular variety of **Type One ghost**, probably a sub-type of **Shade**. Bone Men are hairless, emaciated forms, with skin clinging to their skulls and rib cages. They glow with a bright, pale **other-light**. Though superficially similar to some **Wraiths**, they are always passive and generally somewhat dismal.

Chain net—A net made of finely spun **silver** chains; a versatile variety of **Seal**.

Changer**—A rare and dangerous **Type Two ghost**, powerful enough to alter its appearance during a **manifestation**.

Chill—The sharp drop in temperature that occurs when a **ghost** is near. One of the four usual indicators of an imminent **manifestation**, the others being **malaise**, **miasma**, and **creeping fear**. Chill may extend over a wide area, or be concentrated in specific cold spots.

Cluster—A group of **ghosts** occupying a small area.

Cold Maiden*—A gray, misty female form, often wearing old-fashioned dress, seen indistinctly at a distance. Cold Maidens radiate powerful feelings of melancholy and **malaise**. As a rule, they rarely draw close to the living, but exceptions *have* been known.

Corpse-bell—A deep-toned bell rung in churches to announce funerals.

Creeping fear—A sense of inexplicable dread often experienced in the build-up to a **manifestation**. Often accompanied by **chill**, **miasma**, and **malaise**.

Curfew—In response to the **Problem**, the British Government enforces nightly curfews in many inhabited areas. During curfew, which begins shortly after dusk and finishes at dawn, ordinary people are encouraged to remain indoors, safe behind their home **defenses**. In many towns, the beginning and end of the night's curfew are marked by the sounding of a warning bell.

Dark Specter**—A frightening variety of **Type Two ghost** that manifests as a moving patch of darkness. Sometimes the **apparition** at the center of the darkness is dimly visible; at other times the black cloud is fluid and formless, perhaps shrinking to the size of a pulsing heart, or expanding at speed to engulf a room.

Death-glow—An energy trace left at the exact spot where a death took place. The more violent the death, the brighter the glow. Strong glows may persist for many years.

Defenses against ghosts—The three principal defenses, in order of effectiveness, are **silver**, **iron**, and **salt**. **Lavender** also affords some protection, as does bright light and running **water**.

DEPRAC—The Department of Psychic Research and Control. A government organization devoted to tackling the **Problem**. DEPRAC investigates the nature of **ghosts**, seeks to destroy the most dangerous ones, and monitors the activities of the many competing **agencies**.

Ectoplasm—A strange, variable substance from which **ghosts** are formed. In its concentrated state, ectoplasm is very harmful to the living.

Fittes furnaces—The popular name for the Greater London Metropolitan Furnaces for the Disposal of Psychic Artifacts, in Clerkenwell, where dangerous psychic **Sources** are destroyed by fire.

Fittes Manual—A famous book of instruction for ghost-hunters written by Marissa Fittes, the founder of Britain's first psychic investigation **agency**.

Floating Bride*—A female **Type One ghost**, a variety of **Cold Maiden**. Floating Brides are generally headless, or missing another part of their anatomy. Some search for their missing extremity; others cradle it or hold it mournfully aloft. Named after the ghosts of two royal brides, beheaded at Hampton Court Palace.

Ghost—The spirit of a dead person. Ghosts have existed throughout history, but—for unclear reasons—are now increasingly common. There are many varieties; broadly speaking, however, they can be organized into three main groups (*See* **Type One, Type Two, Type Three**). Ghosts always linger near a **Source**, which is often the place of their death. They are at their strongest after dark, and most particularly between the hours of midnight and two a.m. Most are unaware or uninterested in the living. A few are actively hostile.

Ghost-bomb—A weapon consisting of a **ghost** trapped in a **silver-glass** prison. When the glass breaks, the spirit emerges to spread fear and **ghost-touch** among the living.

Ghost-cult—A group of people who, for a variety of reasons, share an unhealthy interest in the returning dead.

Ghost-fog—A thin, greenish-white mist, occasionally produced during a **manifestation**. Possibly formed of **ectoplasm**, it is cold and unpleasant, but not itself dangerous to the touch.

Ghost-jar—A **silver-glass** receptacle used to constrain an active **Source**.

Ghost-lamp—An electrically powered streetlight that sends out beams of strong white light to discourage **ghosts**. Most ghost-lamps have shutters fixed over their glass lenses; these snap on and off at intervals throughout the night.

Ghost-lock—A dangerous power displayed by **Type Two ghosts**, possibly an extension of **malaise**. Victims are sapped of their willpower, and overcome by a feeling of terrible despair. Their muscles seem as heavy as lead, and they can no longer think or move freely. In most cases they end up transfixed, waiting helplessly as the hungry ghost glides closer and closer. . . .

Ghost-touch—The effect of bodily contact with an **apparition**, and the most deadly power of an aggressive **ghost**. Beginning with a sensation of sharp, overwhelming cold, ghost-touch swiftly spreads an icy numbness around the body. One after another, vital organs fail; soon the body turns bluish and starts to swell. Without swift medical intervention, often in the form of adrenaline injections to stimulate the heart, ghost-touch is usually fatal.

Glimmer*—The faintest perceptible **Type One ghost**. Glimmers manifest only as flecks of **other-light** flitting through the air. They can be touched or walked through without harm.

Greek Fire—Another name for **magnesium flares**. Early weapons of this kind were apparently used against **ghosts** during the days of the Eastern Roman Empire, a thousand years ago.

Haunting—*See* **Manifestation**.

Ichor—**Ectoplasm** in its thickest, most concentrated form. It burns many materials, and is safely constrained only by **silver-glass**.

Iron—An ancient and important protection against **ghosts** of all kinds. Ordinary people fortify their homes with iron decorations, and carry it on their persons in the form of **wards**. Agents carry iron **rapiers** and chains, and so rely on it for both attack and defense.

Lavender—The strong sweet smell of this plant is thought to discourage evil spirits. As a result, many people wear dried sprigs of lavender, or burn it to release the pungent smoke. Agents sometimes carry vials of lavender water or small explosive lavender grenades to use against weak **Type Ones**.

Limbless**—A swollen, misshapen variety of **Type Two ghost**, with a generally human head and torso, but lacking recognizable arms and legs. With **Wraiths** and **Raw-bones**, one of the least pleasing **apparitions**. Often accompanied by strong sensations of **miasma** and **creeping fear**.

Listening—One of the three main categories of psychic **Talent**. **Sensitives** with this ability are able to hear the voices of the dead, echoes of past events, and other unnatural sounds associated with **manifestations**.

Lurker*—A variety of **Type One ghost** that hangs back in the shadows, rarely moving, never approaching the living, but spreading strong feelings of anxiety and **creeping fear**.

Magnesium flare—A metal canister with a breakable glass seal, containing magnesium, iron, salt, gunpowder and an igniting device. An important **agency** weapon against aggressive **ghosts**.

Malaise—A feeling of despondent lethargy often experienced when a **ghost** is approaching. In extreme cases this can deepen into dangerous **ghost-lock**.

Manifestation—A ghostly occurrence. May involve all kinds of supernatural phenomena, including sounds, smells, odd sensations, moving objects, drops in temperature, and the glimpse of **apparitions**.

Miasma—An unpleasant atmosphere, often including disagreeable tastes and smells, experienced in the run-up to a **manifestation**. Regularly accompanied by **creeping fear**, **malaise**, and **chill**.

Night watch—Groups of children, usually working for large companies and local government councils, who guard factories, offices, and public areas after dark. Though not allowed to use **rapiers**, night-watch children have long **iron**-tipped spears to keep **apparitions** at bay.

Nimbus—A ring-shaped **aura**; a bright but grainy halo of **other-light** that may surround a **Source** or **apparition**.

Operative—Another name for a psychic investigation agent.

Other-light—An eerie, unnatural light radiating from some **apparitions**.

Phantasm**—Any **Type Two ghost** that maintains an airy, delicate, and see-through form. A Phantasm may be almost invisible, aside from its faint outline and a few wispy details of its face and features. Despite its insubstantial appearance, it is no less aggressive than the more solid-seeming **Specter**, and all the more dangerous for being harder to see.

Phantom—Another general name for a **ghost**.

Plasm—*See* **Ectoplasm**.

Poltergeist**—A powerful and destructive class of **Type Two ghost**. Poltergeists release strong bursts of supernatural energy that can lift even heavy objects into the air. They do not form **apparitions**.

Problem, the—The epidemic of hauntings currently affecting Britain.

Rapier—The official weapon of all psychic investigation agents. The tips of the **iron** blades are sometimes coated with **silver**.

Raw-bones**—A rare and unpleasant kind of **ghost**, which manifests as a bloody, skinless corpse with goggling eyes and grinning teeth. Not popular with agents. Many authorities regard it as a variety of **Wraith**.

Relic-man/relic-woman—Someone who locates **Sources** and other psychic artifacts and sells them on the black market.

Revenant**—A fortunately rare variety of **Type Two ghost** in which the **apparition** can temporarily animate its own corpse and cause it to break free of its grave. Though Revenants generate powerful **ghost-lock** and strong waves of **creeping fear**, they are easy to deal with because their body *is* their **Source**, thus giving an agent plenty of opportunity to encase them in **silver**. Also, if the corpse is old, it usually falls to pieces before doing too much damage.

Salt—A commonly used **defense** against **Type One ghosts**. Less effective than **iron** and **silver**, salt is cheaper than both, and used in many household deterrents.

Salt-bomb—A small plastic throwing-globe filled with **salt**. Shatters on impact, spreading salt in all directions. Used by agents to drive back weaker **ghosts**. Less effective against stronger entities.

Salt-gun—A device that projects a fine spray of salty water across a wide area. A useful weapon against **Type One ghosts**. Increasingly employed by larger **agencies**.

Screaming Spirit**—A feared **Type Two ghost**, which may or may not display any kind of visual **apparition**. Screaming Spirits emit terrifying psychic shrieks, the sound of which is sometimes enough to paralyze the listener with fright, and so bring on **ghost-lock**.

Seal—An object, usually of **silver** or **iron**, designed to enclose or cover a **Source**, and prevent the escape of its **ghost**.

Sensitive, a—Someone who is born with unusually good psychic **Talent**. Most Sensitives join **agencies** or the **night watch**; others provide psychic services without actually confronting **Visitors**.

Shade*—The standard **Type One ghost**, and possibly the most common kind of **Visitor**. Shades may appear quite solid, in the manner of **Specters**, or be insubstantial and wispy, like **Phantasms**; however, they entirely lack the dangerous intelligence of either. Shades seem unaware of the presence of the living, and are usually bound into a fixed pattern of behavior. They project feelings of grief and loss, but seldom display anger or any stronger emotion. They almost always appear in human form.

Shining Boy**—A deceptively beautiful variety of **Type Two ghost** that manifests as a young boy (or, more rarely, girl) walking in the center of cold, blazing **other-light**.

Sight—The psychic ability to see **apparitions** and other ghostly phenomena, such as **death-glows**. One of the three main varieties of psychic **Talent**.

Silver—An important and potent defense against **ghosts**. Worn by many people as **wards** in the form of jewelry. Agents use it to coat their **rapiers**, and as a crucial component of their **Seals**.

Silver-glass—A special "ghost-proof" glass used to encase **Sources**.

Snuff-light—A type of small candle used by psychic investigation **agencies** to indicate a supernatural presence. They flicker, tremble, and finally snuff out if a **ghost** draws near.

Source—The object or place through which a **ghost** enters the world.

Specter**—The most commonly encountered **Type Two ghost**. A Specter always forms a clear, detailed **apparition**, which may in some cases seem almost solid. It is usually an accurate visual echo of the deceased as they were when alive or newly dead. Specters are less nebulous than **Phantasms** and less hideous than **Wraiths**, equally varied in behavior. Many are neutral or benign in their dealings with the living—perhaps returning to reveal a secret, or make right an ancient wrong. Some, however, are actively hostile, and hungry for human contact. These ghosts should be avoided at all costs.

Stalker*—A **Type One ghost** that seems drawn to living people, following them at a distance, but never venturing close. Agents who are skilled at **Listening** often detect the slow shuffling of its bony feet, and its desolate sighs and groans.

Stone Knocker*—A desperately uninteresting **Type One ghost**, which does precious little apart from tap.

Talent—The ability to see, hear or otherwise detect **ghosts**. Many children, though not all, are born with a degree of psychic Talent. This skill tends to fade towards adulthood, though it still lingers in some grown-ups. Children with better-than-average Talent join the **night watch**. Exceptionally gifted children usually join the **agencies**. The three main categories of Talent are **Sight**, **Listening**, and **Touch**.

Tom O'Shadows*—A London term for a **Lurker** or **Shade** that lingers in doorways, arches, or alleyways. An everyday urban **ghost**.

Touch—The ability to detect psychic echoes from objects that have been closely associated with a death or **haunting**. Such echoes take the form of visual images, sounds and other sense impressions. One of the three main varieties of **Talent**.

Type One—The weakest, most common, and least dangerous grade of **ghost**. Type Ones are scarcely aware of their surroundings, and often locked into a single, repetitive pattern of behavior. Commonly encountered examples include: **Shades**, **Lurkers**, and **Stalkers**. *See also* **Bone**

Man, Cold Maiden, Floating Bride, Glimmer, Stone Knocker, Tom O'Shadows, and **Wisp**.

Type Two—The most dangerous commonly occurring grade of **ghost**. Type Twos are stronger than **Type Ones**, and possess some kind of residual intelligence. They are aware of the living, and may attempt to do them harm. The most common Type Twos, in order, are: **Specters, Phantasms** and **Wraiths**. *See also*: **Changer, Limbless, Poltergeist, Raw-bones, Revenant** and **Screaming Spirit**.

Type Three—A very rare grade of **ghost**, first reported by Marissa Fittes, and the subject of much controversy ever since. Allegedly able to communicate fully with the living.

Visitor—A ghost.

Ward—An object, usually of **iron** or **silver**, used to keep **ghosts** away. Small wards may be worn as jewelry on the person; larger ones, hung up around the house, are often equally decorative.

Water, running—It was observed in ancient times that **ghosts** dislike crossing running water. In modern Britain this knowledge is sometimes used against them. In central London a net of artificial channels, or runnels, protects the main shopping district. On a smaller scale, some homeowners build open channels outside their front doors and divert the rainwater along them.

Wisp*—Weak and generally unthreatening, a Wisp is a **Type One ghost** that manifests as a pale and flickering flame. Some scholars speculate that all ghosts, given time, degenerate into Wisps, then **Glimmers**, before finally vanishing altogether.

Wraith**—A dangerous **Type Two ghost**. Wraiths are similar to **Specters** in strength and patterns of behavior, but are far more horrible to look at. Their **apparitions** show the deceased in his or her dead state: gaunt and shrunken, horribly thin, sometimes rotten and wormy. Wraiths often appear as skeletons. They radiate a powerful **ghost-lock**. *See also* **Raw-bones**.

PRAISE FOR
THE LOCKWOOD & CO. SERIES

The Screaming Staircase

"Stroud (the Bartimaeus series) shows his customary flair for blending deadpan humor with thrilling action, and the fiery interplay among the three agents of Lockwood & Co. invigorates the story (along with no shortage of creepy moments). Stroud plays with ghost story conventions along the way, while laying intriguing groundwork that suggests that the Problem isn't the only problem these young agents will face in books to come—the living can be dangerous, too."

—*Publishers Weekly*

"Authentically spooky events occur in an engagingly crafted, believable world, populated by distinct, colorful personalities. The genuinely likable members of Lockwood & Co. persevere through the evil machinations of the living and the dead and manage to come out with their skins, and their senses of humor, intact. This smart, fast-paced ghostly adventure promises future chills."

—*School Library Journal*

"Three young ghost trappers take on deadly wraiths and solve an old murder case in the bargain to kick off Stroud's new post-Bartimaeus series . . . A heartily satisfying string of entertaining near-catastrophes, replete with narrow squeaks and spectral howls."

—*Kirkus Reviews*

"Stroud brings the seemingly disparate plot points together with his usual combination of thrilling adventure and snarky humor. . . . all members of this spirit-smashing trio get in their fair share of zingers, providing a comedic balance to the many narrow escapes, false leads, and shape-shifting specters that otherwise occupy Lockwood & Co."
—*Bulletin of the Center for Children's Books*

A 2013 *Los Angeles Times* Book Prize Finalist for Young Adult Literature

2013 Cybil Award for Speculative Fiction

CCBC Choices List

2014 Edgar Award Nominee

A Junior Library Guild Selection

The Whispering Skull

★"In fine form, Stroud sends Lockwood & Co. on a trail that leads from an upper-crust social event to the mucky margins of the Thames and into dust-ups with thugs, rival agents and carloads of ectoplasmic horrors that can kill with just a touch. For all their internecine squabbling, the three protagonists make a redoubtable team—and their supporting cast, led by the sneering titular skull in a jar, adds color and complications aplenty. Rousing adventures for young tomb robbers and delvers into realms better left to the dead."

—*Kirkus Reviews* (starred review)

★ "Stroud writes with a fine ear for dialog, a wry sense of humor, and a knack for describing haunted places. Creating tension that ebbs and flows, he slowly builds the dramatic narrative to a resounding crescendo, and he makes the quieter scenes that follow just as compelling. The second entry in the Lockwood & Company series, this imaginative adventure features one of the most hair-raising chase scenes in children's fiction. At the book's end, when the enigmatic Anthony Lockwood reveals a chilling secret, readers can only hope that more sequels are in the offing."

—*Booklist* (starred review)

★ "Lucy's growing abilities to communicate with the dead, especially the nasty spirit attached to a skull in Lockwood's home, add an additional layer of menace to an already creepy tale; Lockwood's secrets add intrigue and suspicion. The plot gallops along at a breakneck pace, giving little respite from the horrors within. For fans of scary fare, this page-turner is a dream (or nightmare) come true."

—*School Library Journal* (starred review)

PRAISE FOR THE BARTIMAEUS BOOKS
BY JONATHAN STROUD

THE AMULET OF SAMARKAND

★"A darkly tantalizing tale."
—*Publishers Weekly* (starred review)

★"One of the liveliest and most inventive
fantasies of recent years."
—*Booklist* (starred review)

THE GOLEM'S EYE

"Fast-paced excitement."
—*Kirkus Reviews*

"A must-purchase for all fantasy collections."
—*School Library Journal*

"The top of the class of the currently popular fantasy series."
—*The New York Times Book Review*

PTOLEMY'S GATE

★"[A] potent ending that is at once
unexpected and wholly earned."
—*Publishers Weekly* (starred review)

★"The trilogy wraps up with excitement, adventure
and an unexpected wallop of heart and soul."
—*Kirkus Reviews* (starred review)

★"[T]he best yet . . . a stunning ending to
a justly acclaimed trilogy."
—*The Horn Book* (starred review)

THE RING OF SOLOMON

★"A riveting adventure for Bartimaeus fans, old and new."
—*Booklist* (starred review)

★"So rarely do humor and plot come together in such equally
strong measures that we can only hope for more adventures."
—*The Horn Book* (starred review)

★". . . [T]his is a superior fantasy that should have fans
racing back to those [Bartimaeus] books."
—*Publishers Weekly* (starred review)

★"Definitely a must-purchase."
—*School Library Journal* (starred review)